"*The Greatest of Ease* takes you on a circus thrill ride. You'll fly through the air, face down tigers, and spend unforgettable nights with exotic men and women. Like the circus itself, this book fills you with wonder and joy."

—Ross Brown
Program Director, MFA in Writing & Contemporary Media
Antioch University

"A wonderfully realized and masterfully executed tale of high-flying literacy."

—Gary Phillips
author of *One-Shot Harry*

"Most writers wish they'd lived lives big enough to tell. Teri Bayus has lived many lives and then some, including running away to join the circus. I suggested she share this one. You're welcome."

—Doug Richardson
author of the *Lucky Dey Thriller Series*

"This story is like a rock and roll roadshow except the party animals are . . . actual animals! All aboard for one wild-ass ride!"

—Mark Parsons
author of *The 9:09 Project* and *Road Rash*

"Hup! Ready to run away to the circus without leaving home? If so, this page-turning book is for you. You'll love this high-flying adventure story of a young woman who's got the grit to follow her dreams—no matter what. Read it and reap."

—Sam Horn
author of *POP!* and *Someday is Not a Day of The Week*

"A life lived outside the norm is a refreshing and delightful new memoir by Teri Bayus. When young, who of us didn't want to run away to the circus? Well, Bayus did and joined her new husband's trapeze act on the road during the 1980s, learning that happiness doesn't wrinkle."

—Catherine Ann Jones
Author of *The Way of Story* and *Heal Your Self with Writing*

"Ever the girl on the flying trapeze, Teri Bayus writes the way she has lived her life— without a net. This is a love story under the Big Top. 'Having a fling' has been given new meaning in Teri Bayus' circus. Hold on."

—Peter Dunne
author of *Emotional Structure: A Guide for Screenwriters*

"Teri Bayus' novel, *The Greatest of Ease*, soars like the daring young trapeze artist immortalized in the wildly popular nineteenth-century song that inspired her book title. Her colorful and irreverent story about running away to join the circus is at alternately peripatetic, poetic, bitter, and surprising. This is a literary high-wire act that reveals her life in the proverbial spotlight but also the shadows lurking behind the spectacle. By pulling back the tent flaps of the Big Top, she provides us with a peek into the mysteries of her world and shows how the circus is far more than entertainment; it is an exhilarating source of reassurance. Anything seems possible for the rest of us if performers like her can fly through the air or dance on the back of lumbering elephants. With her winged words and contrarian humor, Bayus reveals hard-won wisdom that is worth the price of admission to the greatest show on earth."

—Phil Cousineau
author of *The Art of Pilgrimage* and *The Lost Notebooks of Sisyphus*

"As promised, Teri Bayus delivers an impossible universe that defies gravity on every page. It is tempting to react to her stories with, 'she's making that up!' But her hilarity explodes too spontaneously, and her heartbreaks ring too true. She proves to us that circus wisdom does not come without experience. No wonder that the hair on parents' heads sticks straight up at the idea of their child running off to join the circus."

—K. F. Makeyev, Ph.D.
author of *In the Green Room*

THE GREATEST OF EASE

A CIRCUS STORY

TERI BAYUS

Siafu

This is a work of fiction. Unless otherwise indicated, all the names, characters, businesses, places, events, and incidents in this book are either the product of the author's imagination or used in a fictitious manner. Any resemblance to actual persons, living or dead, or actual events is purely coincidental.

Siafu Productions
Pismo Beach, California

The Man on the Flying Trapeze

She floats through the air with the greatest of ease
You'd think her a man on the flying trapeze
She does all the work while he takes his ease
And that's what's become of my love.

Lyrics by George Leybourne

This book is dedicated to the Cooters: Doug Richardson,
Karen Richardson, Jeanne Veillette Bowerman,
Nadine Nettmann Semerau, Matt Semerau,
Becky Mosgofian, Isaac Mosgofian,
Tim Hoke, Zoe Quinton, and Gary Bayus.
My gratitude for your camaraderie, friendship, guidance,
and support is eternal.
Special props to my husband, my reason for living.
I love you all.

"If running away and joining the circus sounds romantic to you, think about sleeping nights in a parking lot and sharing your water with the elephants."

—*Lisa Hofsess*

"It's a semi-true story, believe it or not.
I made up a few things and there's some I forgot.
But the life and the telling are both real to me.
And they all run together and turn out to be a semi-true story."

—*Jimmy Buffett*

"I have always been a romantic, one of those people who believes that a woman in pink circus tights contains all the secrets of the universe."

—*Tom Robbins*

Prologue

The thunderous applause echoed off the arena's tin and cobweb-besotted ceiling, mixing with the smoke and dancing lights. An intense beam illuminated our plexiglass platform: the spotlight centering the audience's attention fifty feet above their heads. Our platform was eighteen inches wide and four feet long, approximately the size of an ironing board, with six of us standing on it. Most of us stood on one foot. All of us in a familiar relationship with each other. We were dressed like opulent sextuplets, covered in sequins and tights. Husband and wife, in-laws, and siblings. No secrets won or lost on this tight knit of traveling performers. The politics of the platform were on full display.

"Try not to mess us up this time," the teenager growled at me.

"Leave her alone!" my husband sneered through his full smile.

"Get on your toes and style!" my sister-in-law reminded me as she twirled around us.

Up on the second wrung, I arched my back and threw my hand outstretched in a ballet style. I put the riser on the platform for my brother-in-law to throw his triple.

The ringmaster's baritone voice boomed from below. "Ladies and gentlemen. Children of all ages! Please gaze your eyes above the center ring.

An impossible universe is about to explode. The world's best flying trapeze act will now present a triple somersault. A trick only they have accomplished. This act will leave you spellbound. The Córdobas will take flight in a brilliant display of aerial power."

On cue, we all styled as the music, "The Flying Young Man," rose to a crescendo and more lights flipped up to illuminate us. Phileap went first, grabbing the bar and leaving with such force that the rigging shook. He returned to the platform after doing a pirouette on the front end of the swing and catching the bar again. He landed with a thud, bending at the knees and then balancing on his toes to salute the audience with his athletic prowess.

Nicolás mounted the riser as I handed him the bar. He had one hand on the rigging and leaned out with the other to snatch the bar. Nicolás adjusted his grip, wrapping strong fingers and a torn palm on the trapeze bar for the perfect grasp. He nodded and shouted, *"Listo!"*

Sebastián took the cue and began his catcher's descent into an upside-down position, hands outstretched to catch Nicolás. Sebastián called him off with a "Hup!"

The drum roll started as the band hushed. At a flawless interval, Nicolás came off the platform, swinging so high his toes touched the ceiling. He returned with a midair seat, and Sebastián called him off the bar.

"Hup!" Echoed off the walls.

Nicolás swung up, let go of the bar, and rolled into a body-hugging ball rotating three times in the air. At the end of his tumble, Sebastián called, "Hup!"

Nicolás stretched out, and Sebastián grabbed him effortlessly with both hands. No jarring movement, just a magical connection from years of practice. They completed the swing, and Sebastián tossed Nicolás mid-flight as he half turned in the air to face the platform and catch the fly bar. One more swing up, and he mounted the board. The crowd reacted all at once. Their collective breaths—held for the whole trip—now exhaled, and they screamed with delight and relief. The music started again, and we all styled on the board as if we were also surprised it happened. Changing places with Nicolás, my husband took his turn to wow them. As he climbed the riser, Nicolás spat, "Good luck matching that, you fucking shit bag." Seeing only a smile on his face, the audience could not guess the vitriol going on up in the air. Despite their loathing for each other, this family produced impossible tricks. Phileap executed a perfect double layout. His form in the air was a flawless display of human splendor. He returned to the platform and kneeled with outstretched hands, begging for applause.

I was up next for the passing leap, as I was one of the daring young girls on the flying trapeze. This trick involved my husband and me producing seamless timing with his brother as he leaped over me and the bar, into Sebastián's hands. I had trained for over two years to make this part of the troupe. The family had thousands of hours of practice and a lifetime of resentment. A dynasty of seven generations of circus performers had been created for millions' entertainment. We did it seamlessly, and the applause floated up to us like a cloud of adoration.

We finished the performance by flying off the platform, doing a flip, and landing on the net. This dismount was an easier task than being caught by the catcher, but our body positions had to be pristine or else the net would break us. We would hit the net once, bounce again to correct our bodies in space, and then prance on the flexible net to the far side. We would lay on the net, our top half dangling, then flip down onto the ring, style, and point our arms up, signaling the next to tumble down. The crowd exploded at the last trick, and we twirled in unison, having donned our heavy satin and velvet cloaks in the center ring.

The spotlights whirled away and left us in the darkness as the tiger act began. We walked back to our dressing rooms in silence except for the malicious chatter of Papi, who was haranguing us for every little thing we did wrong during the act. This was my new reality. Adored and admired by strangers. Hated and berated by my family. This was my circus story.

1

They call me Gail or "Shit for Brains." I was born as a result of a whiskey hard-on in the backseat of a rusting Pontiac on prom night in 1961. I was never supposed to amount to anything, so I tried everything. At twenty, I left a four-year scholarship to Mills College, almost did a stint at the Nevada State Penitentiary, and joined the circus. I married a trapeze artist, learned to fly, and traveled the world (mostly the small towns of the world).

I've learned in sixty years on the planet that I am a unicorn. I'm a left-handed, redheaded, blue-eyed creature. My blood is O negative, I only had two wisdom teeth, and I have an IQ of 185. I love instantly and completely. I'm fearless and will try anything once. I read so much; I pronounce everything wrong. I have no sense of time and no regard for money, and I dance like I'm on fire. Mostly, I've learned that happiness doesn't wrinkle.

After the circus, I knew my life would become a dinner-party anecdote. My stories were now presented among matching plates for the pinkies-up crowd. At these parties, the soulless stick-figure crowd would swirl their Riedel wine glasses like they know the difference between swill and grape juice. Then they'd pick through appetizers of soggy crackers with organic sprouts, pretending to be attentive to the other guests' untruths.

My new husband consorted weekly with these humorless leviathans as an act of salesmanship for his political climbing. It was a requirement that I attend, but there were always caveats.

This time, it started with him opening my car door, forever the gentleman, and grabbing my hand. Once standing, he would swirl me the way our tango instructor had taught him and place his hands softly on each side of my head and look deep into my eyes.

"You know I love you, right? Since the minute you seduced me at the Men's Wearhouse."

"Yes. Your love encapsulates me."

He kissed me deep, then took my hand, guiding me through the extensive landscape to the sprawling front door. In the shadow of the arched entrance, he hissed in my ear, "Try not to be so you!" I laughed and tweaked his nipple.

He disapproved of my plunging neckline and feverish circus stories, but he accepted all my foibles. I'm his greatest appropriation and most compelling accomplishment. As he tells it, steady wins the race when you are dealing with me.

My flaming red hair and tremendous personality were an instant friend-maker to his male colleagues and a source of something hidden and unexplored to the women.

The candlelight leaked outside as the door opened. One last whisper, "Please, only pleasantly nod and smile? For God's sake, don't tell circus stories!" I took his hand, smiled, and made a grand entrance.

As we congregated around an enormous Italian marble table, they shared hilarious stories about their purse dog's groomer or what happened on the ninth tee. I try to melt into the Gucci wallpaper at these soirées, for I am not one of them. I'm made from S&H green stamps gumption and thrift store provisions. I will never have more than three matched glasses in my finger-smudged cupboards, and most of my cutlery has dug holes in my backyard.

Somewhere in the middle of passed raw tuna plates and uncorking the third bottle of French wine, a comment hit me in the back of the neck, a magical benign statement lobbed at me. I had managed to not mock their wild yet obtuse stories, but I was served. I must utter the phrase that silences entire rooms, leaves a lingering question on everyone's lips, and facilitates whispers at the water cooler, "When I was with the circus . . ."

I chose my stories to fit the crowd. If the crowd was tame, they received simple monkey and elephant stories, trapeze successes, and the casual mention of famous names. For the more than four bottles of wine and aperitif crowd, I spun dysfunctional tales while explaining how we made our G-strings. If they pressed on, I threw in a tale of drag queens and little people fucking.

This would all be met with my husband's subdued but exasperated admonishments on the ride home. He knew he was getting a colorful and well-traveled wife. I remained lost in my stories and usually went too far. I loved the spotlight. He loved me despite my need for an audience.

My narrative lives on in the imagination of my audience. They feel privileged to have encountered a real trapeze artist, a first for most. They can perpetuate my stories at dinner parties for the rest of their lives. I gave them the gift of a fantastical yarn, of a life lived outside the norms, of adventure and daring. When I ran away and joined the circus, it was heaven, but mostly hell. I earned those narratives and have the calluses on my hands and heart to prove it.

2

Summer, 1976, Reno, Nevada, USA

The circus renders a distinct smell. It's animal dander mixed with sawdust with a touch of greasepaint, popcorn, cotton candy, and the false smoke used as a distraction. That odor lives in my daydreams, my exotic reveries of a life filled with travel—and an audience.

I was acting as a helper at the circus for a charity by selling cotton candy. The circus came once a year, and teen volunteers would sell treats that could make up to $3,000 for our charities. We were saving balding children with sad smiles by slinging sugar. Plus, we got to watch the show over and over until the sequins and fishnets permeated our souls. This act of volunteerism started my wanderlust before I knew what it was to crave travel and new places.

We sold the cotton candy before the show and during the intermission, leaving us free to gaze open-mouthed as these super humans defied gravity, tamed wild beasts, and performed unthinkable feats of daring. I snuck backstage and into the makeshift dressing rooms trying to be noticed and, hopefully, swept away with the show. I dreamt every night of an acrobat swooping down from the ceiling, his legs the only thing holding him on the bar, wrapping his strong arms around my waist, and swinging me up to the shadows. Most of the performers acted as if I was a ghost they could not see. Being so young and full of myself, it became a self-imposed dare to become noticed.

One show, a young, pink-tighted man held me captivated. He was part of the "Moscow Circus," a troupe that toured internationally. The name was a generic term for the circus shows from the USSR that traveled abroad during the Soviet Era. Their act was called "Hoop Diving." It was a Chinese acrobatic specialty involving tumblers performing jumps through hoops stacked precariously above one another. It was mind-blowing to watch their calisthenics and manipulation of a simple steel ring.

They were wrapped in pink, skintight leotards that showed every bulging muscle. I wormed my way into the "tunnel" after their act, swinging my hips to catch the youngest performer. The tunnel is the main entrance for all acts; it is simply a load-in dock. But when the circus was in town, that tunnel became magical. Elephants lumbered, tigers roared while being pushed in their tiny steel cages, and graceful flyers donning heavy velvet capes pranced through to the center ring.

I hid in the shadows and then jumped out to offer my cornered Russian acrobat a free paper container of spiderwebs of sugar. Startled and delighted, he told me his name was Emile and he spoke no English. His form-defining sequined pants; long, flowing mane; and sapphire blue eyes drew me in to see if he would ignore me too. He did not. Using hand gestures and raging pheromones, I lured him into an afternoon of flirting and testing the hormonal ricochet we were both experiencing. We made out under the grandstands during the second act. Amongst the discarded popcorn tubes and Coke cups, no words were needed—only lips and secret touches. He would scurry out when he heard his music crescendo to cue the single trapeze with his sister. From my crawl space on the sticky floor, I could see the scorn on her face as she saw his swollen lips.

Two glorious days of being with an exotic boy were more intoxicating than stealing my mom's Blue Nun wine. My lips were bruised from so much kissing. It was my first heartache when he left, even though forty-eight hours prior, he did not exist. I cried myself to sleep, soaking my Cookie Monster pillowcases. I got a postcard from him in our barnwood mailbox that showed the Missouri Arch. He wrote "Hi! Emile" on the back. My heart miraculously healed, and I read every possible version of meaning into "Hi," including "He loves me and wants me to join the circus."

He stayed working in the States, and we became pen pals. His postcards came from every town in the United States and Canada and tiled my walls along with Michael Jackson and David Cassidy posters. My letters to him focused on my teenage angst, droning on about my friends, school, and horrible parents. Although I wrote weekly, they were sent to him in batches twice a year, as the main office of the circus only delivered mail at the beginning and end of the season. He learned to write in English, and I treasured his letters and vision of America through Soviet eyes.

3

Summer, 1977, Reno, Nevada, USA

The circus visiting became the most exotic part of my life. Yearly I volunteered to be the sugar-slinging *Candy Butcher*. Circus concessioners are so named because one of the first successful concessionaires of the American circus was a former butcher. This year, I met and instantly fell in eternal friendship with Ramon. Forgoing my yearly tongue-swapping conquest, I became best friends with him. With his witty humor and Mayan head, he won out over my teen surliness. This new boy could make me laugh until my stomach hurt, although I had no romantic thoughts for Ramon.

His act involved one acrobat, lying on his back, juggling another acrobat (in this case, his cousin) with his feet. They added chairs, boxes, and even a terrified house cat. It was hilarious and quite astounding. Ramon was the master at faking a fall or injury, making the audience gasp at his peril. Then he would pop up and do the trick flawlessly. He was also a juggler, magician, and wire-walker, all done with a finely tuned sense of humor. His skin was as black as a foggy night sky, his hair so dark it almost appeared purple and was cut like a floppy bowl on his head. When I first met him, he smiled wide, pulled six scarves out of my ear, and juggled them. He loved playing practical jokes on the circus performers, and I brought a new level of creativity to his pranks.

Our favorite caper was messing with the performers' robes. When they were not performing, the circus folk wore silken kimonos everywhere to cover their tights and sequins. When the routine is finished and the performers hit the ground, modesty kicks in, and they want to cover their scantily clad bodies with a slab of silk.

Before the act, the family appeared with robes on; each was a different color printed with ornate Japanese koi and flowers. While on stage, they set them on chairs outside of the ring and out of the spotlight. They appeared out of the darkness, dazzling the crowd with their precision and timing, juggling each other like balls of fairy dust, and when his family finished the performance, they charged to the chairs to put on the robes.

We had tied the kimonos' belts with four knots to the cold steel chairs, and they did not release when yanked on. We watched as they wrestled to untie them, desperate to cover up. After much struggling and flinging Spanish words at us, they stomped off as mad as the caged tiger. Ramon and I hid in the curtains howling like hyenas with laughter.

Ramon and I spent the "off-show" time together. I took him to his first movie, *Star Wars*, where he came out of his seat with joy. Being a master of illusion, he found the level of magic overwhelming. After, we munched on leftover popcorn and sat on the curb outside the multiplex.

"Gail, I don't understand dees Wookies?"

"Ramon, it's a costume."

"Si? Por que? Why?"

"Because it's on another planet."

"I don't understand *planet*."

"Not earth." I picked up a handful of sand from the ground and showed it to him. I pointed to the sky.

"No way!" I watched him try to noodle this new information through and saw for the first time that, although he was wicked smart in the ways of the circus and traveling, he had had no formal schooling.

Ramon hailed from Mexico City. He was touring and living with his brother's family, so his social life remained limited. He worked all day performing and then had to practice. Each year I took him on actual teenager activities like dragging Main (which baffled him to drive in a car going nowhere) and sneaking liquor.

At the beginning of each season, he prayed that a new family, with a young lass, would join the show, giving him access to a girlfriend. The new acts only contained more cousins. His English was not proficient, and his face carried dark secrets, making the town girls elusive. I introduced him to my friends. Although he consistently stole kisses from them, they all remained chaste. The language of laughter had turned many strangers into friends, but never sweethearts.

After the circus turned off the last spotlight, it packed up and rolled to the next town. Ramon and I stayed in touch, exchanging letters and postcards. I wrote him weekly rambling tomes about my solitary life on our little farm and my desire to see the world. When he was in town, I gave him stamps, so he could mail postcards to me. He had never been to a post office, but I knew he could find a letterbox. He did not write in English (or Spanish, honestly). The postcards contained only his signature and a hand-drawn picture of his act, and the front of the cards gave me clues as to where he wandered and worked. Exotic places like Kamloops and Lethbridge enticed me. My soul wanted to wander with intent and coddiwomple out of the Nevada desert.

4

December 19, 1980, Reno, Nevada, USA

As the song "My Sharona" blared over the stereo, I packed all my worldly goods into a ten-by-eight-foot storage locker. My life had fallen apart, and I had made the decision not to return to Mill's College. I needed to run away, to go into hiding. I was just not sure where I would run to. With the need to explain my sudden and immediate disappearance to my parents so they wouldn't alert the police, I met them at the Tabernacle Circus. My father had been a fez-wearer for years, and each year when the circus came to town, he was the bartender for the Tabernacles who sold tickets, paraded in clown cars, and terrorized elephants.

I went to the circus with the sole purpose of telling my parents I was going on an extended trip, but I ran straight into my old circus friend, Ramon.

The rest of the weekend dramatically changed the course of my ship.

"Gail! My roja friend! Como estas?" Ramon hugged like a grizzly bear squeezing the honey out of the tree. In his long embraces, time and stress all dropped away.

"Hey, Ramon! Good to see you! Tell me, who is new on the show? Any new chicas?"

"No, all cousins again. Do you have a girlfriend for me?"

He always made me bring girlfriends along, hoping to seduce one with his wit and exotic lifestyle.

"I can find one for you. But you need to find a distraction for me."

"Okay! I have eight distractions! Cousins and Chilean trapeze artists. Bring all your chicas bonitas!"

Ramon winked and turned to race toward the center ring, as the music for his act had started. As he ran to the ring, he tripped and fell into it. He started every routine with this gag, which made the audience gasp. As he progressed through his juggling and teeterboard act, he played the fool, much to the crowd's happiness. The teeterboard act was one of my favorite floor acts. It served as a warm-up for the aerialists. Picture an industrial nine-foot-long seesaw, with a steel reinforcement in the middle. Its sole purpose is to throw the acrobat clad in a sequined leotard into the air to perform a wild tumble. At each end of the board is a square padded area, where a performer stands on an incline before being catapulted into the air. The flyer performs various aerial somersaults, landing on padded mats, each other (a human pyramid), a specialized landing chair, or even stilts. Ramon's job was to miss these tricks, which was more challenging than sticking them. The master of playing the fool, he partook in the tears of a clown. The hot towner girls always went for the body-hardened star, not the jester. He was the clown that smiled through the tragedy and life's unfairness.

I watched the flying trapeze act next with awe. Traditionally, flyers mount a narrow board (usually by climbing a loose rope ladder) and take off from the platform on the fly bar. They must wait for a call from the catcher to make sure he leaves at the correct time. Otherwise, the catcher will not be close enough to make a successful catch. The flyer then performs one of many aerial tricks and is caught by the catcher, who is swinging from a separate bar. Once in their hands, the flyer continues to swing and is thrust back toward the fly bar in a maneuver called a return, which could consist of some kind of twist back to the bar. Once back to the fly bar, the flyer returns to the platform, and another takes a turn.

The net beneath the flying trapeze rig provides a measure of safety, but it is not called a "safety net." In fact, the net is often where the biggest risk of injury lies. Nobody gets injured in the air—the risk of injury is in the landing in the net.

The trapeze was invented in 1859 by a French performer named Jules Leotard. The word *trapeze* comes from the Latin word *trapezium*—a geometrical, four-sided figure is mimicked by the shape made by the ceiling, ropes, and bar in a trapeze bar. The flying trapeze is a specific form in which a performer jumps from a platform with the trapeze, and gravity makes it swing. The flyer goes to a catcher and back to the platform. The act of the flying trapeze always uses a net.

Considered the pinnacle of circus acts, flying trapeze troupe is the headline entertainment at every circus. All the troupes are family supported, and most stretch back ten generations.

I watched the act and borrowed three quarters from a volunteer dressed in complete clown garb—big shoes, white face, and all. Frank, the clown, patted my ass as I left to find a payphone where I promised my friends an evening filled with exotic performers and trapeze artists. The lure of the unknown is strong. Three girlfriends arrived as the second trapeze act started, a staple of the opening to the second part of the circus. The Flying Córdobas were a world-renowned troupe of brothers from Chile, and they dazzled the crowd with their feats of daring and the way they filled out their red leotards. The act was comprised of five brothers as the flyers. Two of their wives joined them on the small platform fifty feet in the air. The largest brother acted as the catcher. I observed that like baseball, the catcher called all the tricks and timing of the trapeze. It was clear these people had been flying together forever. The choreographed aerial dance seemed effortless. With their toes pointed and hands held in a perfect style, their mastery of the trapeze was breathtaking. Double layouts, impossible pirouettes, double forward somersaults, triple somersaults, and impossible double leaps were performed as if they were walking. It was their second nature; they were skilled and comfortable in the air. Their bodies rippled with muscles and dexterity. I watched with my mouth agape in admiration and raw lust. I had been mesmerized by the circus as a child, but year after year, as I met acrobats, learned where the magicians hid their secrets, and even made friends with a few elephants, the glimmer had faded. But even with my veteran circus understanding, these stunning tumblers with flawless bodies clad in shiny red leotards were beyond extraordinary.

Dizzy from the fantastic artistry, my friends and I watched the rest of the show. We waited until the audience cleared to go find Ramon and his now highly desired distractions.

It was a thrill to be in the same arena as twelve tigers, fourteen chimps, six polar bears, and the most majestic horses I had ever seen. But this flying act had already taken on a covetous type of awe.

As the spotlights dimmed to their neutral state and the house lights came up, the circus illusion shattered. The three rings became apparent. You could see for the first time that these circles that held charmed mastery were simply poorly painted round wooden railings with a ripped blue plastic tarp floor. Each ring carefully measured forty-two feet in diameter, maximizing the centripetal force that plants a performer upon the mount of horses, the original reason for the rings.

The guidelines and safety nets showed their spider-web pattern strewn from top to bottom. The cages of the animals were caked with food and feces. The tux-clad prop guys now were in blue coveralls, and their unshaven faces and toothless smiles showed their true essence. I could barely stand to see this version, so I ran outside.

During the show, the audience is distracted by the sparkle, the glimmering lights, the false smoke, the dramatic music, the humanoid-defying feats of acrobatic delight; no one saw the shadows of how the spectacle worked. It was all laid out to get the most performances into a two-hour period. The aerialists performed in the air as the animals were set up down below in the rings. The whole concept of three rings came to be so one ring could be set up while the other two were filled with spotlights and routines.

Standing in the well-lit unmelodiousness of wires and nets, a vision walked toward me. He was still in his tights and a cape, having spent the end of the show signing autographs. His black eyes, sharp features, and floppy brown hair added to his distinctiveness. Flanked by Ramon and his brothers, my laser beam focused on those red tights encasing, not hiding, every part of his exceptional body.

His physique was rippled and sculpted like a Venetian statue—his muscles taut and defined against the tight silk that encapsulated this beautiful man. I held a lungful of hot air. I exhaled when he turned to face me.

What is the atmosphere when two stars collide? I grew up watching *Star Trek*, in love with Captain Kirk, and understood the metaphors of the universe. But this was the first time I viscerally sensed the universe only contained two people. One I had to touch. Explore. Go where many had gone before.

"Gail, meet Phileap and his brothers Marco, Nicolás, and Alejandro."

Phileap came to me. I stretched out my hand and caressed his calloused one.

"I'm Gail."

Phileap looked into my eyes as he took my hand and kissed the back, never breaking eye contact. *"Mi corazón, ojos azules llamada mi."*

The connection was immediate, crackling with energy, a colliding of kindred spirits. Lightning bolts shot through my loins, and I experienced my brain discontinuing any rational consideration. The rare beauty of a shared passion that comes to people open to new experiences when their souls recognize each other instantaneously and they connect. It's ridiculously magical to the point of disbelief. When an authentic connection happens, it's not based on anything tangible or safe. It's a gut instinct, a recognized shadow in the well of your soul. The true essence of being human is to comprehend that bond. I would never be the same. I could hear icebergs crashing into the sea.

He tilted his head to one side, continuing to hold my hand. I stared into his sultry black eyes, imagining what I would do with him once he shed those tights. Time had stopped. Becky giggled, and I looked at Ramon as a balancing correction. Ramon chuckled like a hamster and blurted, "He doesn't speak any English."

Phileap glanced at Ramon, shook his head as only one of great beauty could do, and whispered, "Gail?"

"Yours," I whispered back.

Ramon broke the spell and yelled in Spanish for the acrobats to go get "town outfit," meaning dressed for a night out.

Phileap released my hand and smiled. His perfect white teeth encased in lips I now had to possess.

"Esperar?"

I purred, "I'll wait."

He twirled dramatically, brushing the hem of his cape against me, and headed to the dressing rooms. Even that tiny act of contact made me swoon. Later, Becky mused how quickly the "Ed Devotion" had dissipated.

Alone with Ramon, as they changed, I probed about this newfound creature of desire.

"He is Phileap—the most famous trapeze artist in the world."

"Does he have a girlfriend?"

It didn't matter. My plan was set whether it meant destroying a marriage or some poor girl's heart.

"He has a girl in every town. Maybe you'll be lucky enough to be his tonight."

The French have a saying that walking up to the door is the best part of sex. That the anticipation of what's unknown and about to be discovered is better than the actual act. This was true for my first soirée into Phileap's life. We flirted and touched all night, electricity flying between us like lightning bolts. He invited me to his "room," and I willingly followed him behind the animals' trailers and to the caravan trailer park. My anticipation turned a blind eye to the overstuffed trailer and the sounds of his family snoring.

5

December 20, 1980, Roseville, California, USA

I awoke with a start to the cacophony of tigers, lions, and monkeys. Thinking it a nightmare, I felt his strong arm draped over my back and comprehended the reality. I had spent the night in Phileap's bunk, in his family's trailer. This tiny space I now occupied with him was his home. It was no bigger than a twin-sized bed, a foam piece covered in an ancient quilt spreading wall-to-wall with cubbies on the side where he stored his clothes. His only interior designs were two Polaroid pictures of a Japanese girl, thumb-tacked to the wall. He had no window to let in the light. His worldly space an overhead compartment jetting over the bed of the truck. To ascend to his space, you needed to climb an aluminum ladder, and his only privacy was a black curtain on a rod. Phileap shared the twenty-eight-foot travel trailer with his mother, father, and brother Marco. This was the only home they knew. Although the trailer was built for families to spend a weekend camping, this group of acrobats lived there permanently.

I had to pee and wasn't sure if they had a bathroom in the trailer. Hearing Phileap's mama in the kitchen humming an ancient tune, and smelling the aroma of strong coffee, I climbed down the ladder. His mother turned and saw me, reacting violently. Yelling Spanish words I didn't recognize. Her intent was not misinterpreted. The matriarch was as mean as she was ugly, having lost her teeth to an errant priest who had his way with her and then knocked her out when she was twenty years old. She was born in a tent in Chile and spent sixty-five years in the circus and birthed seven kids on a sawdust floor. Her back was hunched from being tethered to a wicked man. Phileap jumped from the bunk and led me down the steel trailer steps. Saying nothing, he guided me to the women's dressing room inside the coliseum. On the way, I saw that their morning constitutions and all private moments were taken in the locker rooms of public buildings. Normally a locker room, now their privy, shower, and wardrobe. All the performers lived in travel trailers, and they lined up like straight teeth on the outside of the coliseum. The closest to the building were the animal trucks, huge 18-wheelers with custom-made cages. I could see and smell the chimpanzees, tigers, lions, horses, dogs, polar bears, and elephants. The elephants made me smile. The gentle giants were chained by the foot, all connected. They swayed to an unknown rhythm as they scooped up hay with their trunks.

Inside the makeshift dressing room, I brushed my hair and washed my face, reapplying the blue mascara. Surrounded by boas and sequins, I admired the lifeless glamor.

Emerging from the "Girls' Room," I found Phileap leaning on an ancient travel trunk. He grinned with the mouth of an expert lover. He inquired in Spanish if I wanted something to eat, using his hands to demonstrate the meaning. The memory of his mother's strong coffee begged me to say "yes," but the instantaneous hate she expressed made me rethink the idea.

Phileap took me to Ramon's trailer, where I found Becky. Ramon had a twenty-two-foot mobile palace all to himself. A total of 195 square feet of living space, but at least he had privacy. It was sparse but clean, with old feed bags for window coverings. The plates and silverware made of plastic, the glasses all jelly jars. He had one wall covered in circus pictures that he later told me were his cousins.

Needing to occupy my hands to not hurl myself on Phileap, I beseeched, "Will you let me make breakfast?"

Ramon took a dozen eggs and a pound of bacon from his Barbie-sized fridge. From under the table, he produced a bag of potatoes.

The boys sat on the bench seat, babbling in Spanish.

"Becky, come help me," I implored my friend, who seemed out of place.

"I'm not a scullery maid! That's your talent."

"Just come peel the potatoes."

Side-by-side, at the two-burner stove and the Easy-Bake Oven, we prepared breakfast.

Becky looked sleep deprived, her well-coiffed hair standing straight up and a bruised-looking layer of mascara under her eyes. As we assembled the food, we recapped our first circus night.

"Did you get to meet the package under those red tights?" Becky grinned as she saw me blush.

"Kind of, he lives in a trailer with his whole family. His bed is the size of your bathtub. There is no privacy for dirty deeds. I don't know how anyone in the circus ever has sex. I used braille to touch my way around, as did he. I like him."

"How do you know; you don't even speak the same language?"

Evading the obvious question, I turned on her. "How do you like Ramon?"

"He's hysterical. He makes me laugh nonstop. I had fun. Do you smell that smell?"

"It's the animals. Did you hear the lion roar?"

"Scared the shit out of me. This'll make for a good story, but I'm heading home tonight. This circus, tiny-home shit is not for me. What did you tell your parents about where you are?"

"I told them I got the scholarship to Mill's college and I'm there for a month or so."

"You're in between homes and stuck in lies."

I understood for the first time that I had no home. My only choice—to go back to my parent's house—not an option I would consider.

"Let's get through the day, have some adventures, and then we will decide."

Dining at the mini table made touching a necessity. Ramon translating for Phileap.

"He wants you to join the show today."

"But I know no tricks!"

"He says you do."

Ramon clarified we were invited to participate in the circus as showgirls. We'd be given costumes and join in the opening spec (short for "spectacular," a term coined by P. T. Barnum), the magic act, and the finale. It was a common practice for the circus to hire pretty local girls to fill in for the parade of performers.

Phileap's calloused hands stroked my thigh as we sat in the tiny dinette. I was picking up Spanish quickly, with Ramon translating and repeating words in his native tongue. Learning fast remained the best option because I barely trusted Ramon to dictate precisely what I was saying. He stayed a scoundrel.

I questioned Ramon about circus history. Acting like a reporter, I took notes.

The term "circus" describes the performance that has followed various formats through its 250-year modern history. Phillip Astley is credited as the father of the modern circus. In 1768, Astley, a skilled equestrian, began presenting exhibitions of trick horse riding in an open field called Ha'Penny Hatch on the south side of the Thames River. In 1770, he hired acrobats, tightrope walkers, jugglers, and a clown to fill in the pauses between the equestrian demonstrations. This format was later named "circus." Specialty acts were added over the next fifty years, along with large-scale theatrical battle reenactments. The current format, in which a ringmaster introduces a variety of choreographed acts set to music, was developed in the latter part of the 19th century.

The types of venues where these circuses have performed have changed dramatically. The earliest modern circuses were in open-air structures with limited covered seating. From the late 18th to late 19th centuries, custom circus buildings (often wooden) were built with various types of seating, a center ring, and sometimes a stage. The traditional large tents commonly known as "big tops" were introduced in the mid-19th century as touring circuses superseded static venues. These tents eventually became the most common venue. Many circus performances are still held in a ring, usually thirteen meters (forty-two feet) in diameter. This dimension was adopted by Astley as the minimum diameter that enabled an acrobatic horse rider to stand upright on a cantering horse to perform their tricks.

Circuses within North America have tended to favor a theatrical approach, combining character-driven acts with original music in a broad variety of styles to convey complex themes or stories.

The large cities had built an event center for sports, concerts, and traveling shows. The charitable fraternal organization, called the Tabernacle Club, saw the circus as a perfect fundraiser for the hospitals that they were building and sponsoring. Circus owners and promoters then gathered performers to create a traveling show and shared profit with the Tabernacle. Today, there are over fifty traveling shows, each having something specific for towns of all sizes. The performers change shows often to keep the audience entertained and in awe.

"Each year, you are with a different set of performers?" I asked.

"Sometimes, it is twice a year we change shows."

"That must get lonely."

"Especially if you have a face like mine," Ramon said.

Changing the subject, I suggested we play a simple card game. I told them Becky and I were psychic. A fad had just started about exploring the sixth sense, and Becky and I loved to try to read each other's minds, especially when we were on mushrooms. The mind tricks and giggles gave us a false sense of an attainable skill. We were seated at the small table, Phileap next to me and Ramon next to Becky. Becky picked a random card and looked at it secretly.

"Okay, I have my number. I am now telepathically transporting it to you." She closed her eyes and wrinkled her forehead in concentration.

My eyes bored into her mind. "Is it a five of hearts?"

"No."

"Damn. Concentrate harder. We do this all the time," she told Ramon with a touch of desperation. We had seen these men attempt and succeed at all kinds of magic; now she wanted to showcase ours.

"Is it a ten of spades?"

Giggling at the failure, "Sorry, not it."

At that point, the savvy Ramon understood Becky's need to make magic and held up three fingers behind her hair.

"Is it a three?"

She enthusiastically jumped up, exclaiming, "Yes! Yes! We got it! See, I told you we were psychically linked."

Vibrating with joy, she went again.

Ramon gave me the number, and I made it look like it took great deliberation to guess it. Each time, she screamed louder. As if we had tumbled into pure magic.

"Yes! Did you guys see that? We are clairvoyants!"

Each time, the three of us laughed harder. She never caught on. We cackled and stayed psychically linked until we were done with the meal, then we went to watch them perform.

6

December 21, 1980, Placerville, California, USA

The following day, Phileap had to practice before the show, and Becky and I followed to watch. This time, the leotards were deep purple. The whole family was there, warming up and getting ready. In the ring, Phileap wrapped his forearm with medical tape and attached hand protection. The pair of grips were made from leather coverings with holes going through his middle two fingers and coming down the palm of his hand and wrapping around his wrist. Ramon explained this helped his hands from ripping on the trapeze bar. They were called *bendts*. He took the resin bag and beat the dust all over his hands and arms.

Phileap climbed the rope and wooden ladder, followed by two other flyers I had not met yet but assumed were his siblings. The catcher, Santiago, towered at almost twice the size as my favorite flyer.

Mesmerized, I watched them take practice swings with all the lights on. During practice, it wasn't about showmanship, it was about the technique. Phileap remained beauty personified in the air. Toes pointed, legs straight, body in impeccable alignment for each trick, making it look easy. The only communication was the "*listo* call" (meaning "ready") as Phileap took the fly bar with his right hand and prepared to fly. The catcher would go down from his swing (the catch bar) into an upside-down position, hands outstretched. Climbing on the riser to get higher off the platform, when the timing was right, the catcher yelled, "Hup!" Phileap jumped up, grabbed the trapeze bar with his other hand, and begin to swing. At the precise stage, the catcher shouted "Hep," and Phileap started his trick. At the top of the swing was the force out, kicking the legs out at the peak of the flyer's swing to gain height. Then there was the hollow, basically a neutral position. Followed by a sweep, signifying kicking the legs back. Seven is the last part of a force out swing. The flyer brings their legs in front of them so they will not hit the board. It all is finished in the hands of the catcher. One swing with the catcher, Santiago twisted and threw Phileap, returning him to the bar. Swinging hard, he would arch his back and mount the platform. This ballet of flawless timing happened over and over. From the ground, Phileap's father yelled what I presumed were helpful comments. Ramon translated one of his declarations, and I found them mean-spirited venom. The flyers seemed unfazed and kept throwing tricks.

After practice, it was time to get ready for the show. There were three performances that day. Ramon took us to the women's dressing room where an effeminate clown named Billy was to be our guide through costumes and makeup. The room was a classic locker room: grey, dull lockers lining the walls; concrete floors; strobing, harsh lights flickering above, and long benches running down the middle. The women had moved in antiquated trunks and fashioned makeshift dressing tables using plywood placed between the benches. There were carpets on the floor and 1960s mirrored vanity sets with lights running up the sides inside open lockers so they could see their faces as they applied more than theatrical makeup. Makeshift rolling wardrobes held their tiny costumes and extravagant capes. Mile-high hats donned in feathers and sequins were placed by the door. One sink was the washbasin for soaking fishnets, and one was for rinsing, with a large trunk turned on its side for hanging things out to dry. The male smell of competition was not masked by the glamor of the ladies' wardrobes.

First, thick layers of greasepaint and wild colors were added to our faces, with false eyelashes glued to our eyelids. Looking outward, it appeared as though a spider were resting on my lids. Billy applied our makeup, and I found it creepy to be staring into his clown-goop-covered face for that long. While he applied our performance masks, Billy gossiped about everyone.

"Did you know that flyer is having an affair with the circus manager?"

My replies were muffled as he melded my face with a thick coat of magic.

"And that one is sleeping with her father-in-law."

"No!"

"Yup. There are all kinds of sexual shenanigans going on here."

Becky cut in, "Sounds like we'll fit right in."

"Oh no, you won't, you tart. These women are going to hate you. Interlopers are never welcome."

Our hair was pulled up in a bun to facilitate fastening the large, feathered hats that stood three feet over my temple. Filled with sequins and feathers, I was a tippy peacock. Becky's hat looked like a firework exploding from her brain. The costumes were long gowns covered in sequins and mirrors, pulled tight with curtain hooks to accentuate our curves. I wasn't sure I could walk, much less perform with this outrageous getup.

Talking fast out of the side of his mouth, Billy questioned and answered.

"Are you with Phileap? He has a new girl in every town. And you, you are with the tumbling clown? I guess a sense of humor can make you overlook his resemblance to the chimps."

Gesturing flamboyantly to the other women applying their masks, he continued, "See her? She hasn't bathed in weeks. This one is having an affair with the lion tamer."

Trying to stop his negative ranting, I proclaimed, "I'm excited to be doing this!"

Becky was not thrilled. "It's not our average Saturday night filled with slot machines and dragging fraternity boys home."

Billy brought Becky's costume over. "Let me guess, Becky. You're a size ten, right?"

"I'm an eight!" Becky yelled. The circus women looked our way, recognizing for the first time we were strangers among them. They went back to putting on what looked like nylons but ended up being fishnet stockings.

As we left the dressing rooms, I heard the audience filling the stadium. The familiar theme of performance anxiety was a welcome drug to me. I loved performing. In the tunnel, six elephants waited in line. One strong woman commanded them. She gave a sharp order when one stepped out of line, and the elephant returned to its proper place instantly. Billy escorted us to Dove and her elephants. "Good luck!" he snickered as he ran.

Dove looked us up and down. Disgust rained from her eyes.

"You the Towners?" Her voice betraying her gender but enforcing her strength.

"Hi! I am Gail, and this is Becky." I reached out my hand. She ignored it, and a command came from her lips. The elephant at the front of the line approached me and went down on one knee.

Pointing her hook at the elephant's knee, she scowled at me. "Get up there. We're about to start."

"I don't know how to ride an elephant!" My proclamation fell on deaf ears as she hiked me up on the mammoth knee and pushed my rear up.

Years of riding horses served my mount, but the wideness of the stead spread my pelvis into the splits. As I came to rest on the neck of the mighty beast, she stood. Now, residing nine feet in the air with my hat adding another three, the lumbering to the ring started as I rocked to the rhythm of my pachyderm wanting to look glamorous, but sure I looked like a monkey riding a bear. Dove yelled from below, "Put your arms out, style your fingers, and for God's sake, smile!"

Becky was run/walking beside me and laughing as I groaned with each reverberate forward movement. I watched the other girls aloft on the back of the giant beasts and tried to move like they did. The elephant parade moved quickly into the ring. In a circle, the animals twirled and pranced. With Dove in the middle commanding them, they rose up on their hind legs.

I was sure I would tumble off; I grabbed my mastodon's ears as she reared up. She responded by swatting me with her trunk. Not a punishing cuff, but one that reminded me she was the boss and I but a flea on her back. Our pack returned to the tunnel, and my steed bowed down on one knee. I unsaddled clumsily, almost tumbling off. That same trunk caught and righted me as I descended her. On the ground, she bowed her head to me, looking me square with her huge brown eyes. A sound like a helicopter landing emitted from her head. Compelled, I petted her forehead.

Dove attached the chain to her foot. "She likes you! Meet Zita. She's an eighteen-year-old girl who hates Tabernacles and most folk. But she's purring for you."

Astounded, "She's purring?"

"Yes, she only makes the sound when extremely happy."

"Can I come see her after the show?"

"Don't be ridiculous. This isn't a kitten. She is a six-ton elephant." And with a sharp command, the pack lumbered off behind Dove, chains clanking.

Becky came running up. "Are you okay? Are you split in two? Can we leave now?"

I was speechless and moved in a way a fresh love hits you. Breaking me out of my stupor was the high-pitched falsetto voice of Billy. In full terrifying clown garb, he grabbed me and pulled me to a man clad head to toe in gold lamé silk.

"Now, you are to be the magician's assistant. Gail, meet Osos."

I stuck out my hand, and he rolled his eyes, examining my costume and sky-high bonnet.

"She can't be wearing that tower on her head for my act!"

Billy swiped the hat off and pulled out my hairpins and ponytail. Running his fingers, he fluffed my hair.

"There, is this better?"

"Much. Too bad she's a redhead. It clashes with my gold."

"I don't know how to be a magician's assistant," I stuttered.

Billy smiled maniacally. "Two minutes ago, you didn't know how to ride an elephant. Welcome to showbiz."

Osos took my hand and led me back to the ring. It was dark as we stepped into it while prop guys were filling it with Osos' tools of the trade.

"Follow my lead, hand me what I ask for, smile, and style."

"What does 'style' mean?"

The lights came up, the music reached a crescendo, and the crowd applauded. I heard the ringmaster introduce Osos as the world's best illusionist. Osos took my hand and twirled me around. Arms outstretched and smiling like a pageant queen. Full of spectacle, this new experience was both terrifying and unknown. For the next few minutes, I tossed him rings, held coverlets, climbed into a box, disappeared, and was sawed in half. In absolute heaven, I reveled in the center ring. As the beaming spotlight blinked off, we were alone and invisible in the ring. In the other two rings, aerial acts had started, and I saw Phileap swirling on a single trapeze with his sister-in-law above ring number three.

"Good job for a Towner." Osos patted my back and pointed to the tunnel where Billy was waiting for me.

Back in the dressing room, I changed costumes for the second-act parade. This get-up was even more revealing than the first one. A one-piece bathing-suit style of sequined matter ran straight up my bottom and high on my thighs. My breasts pushed up and were accentuated with a rhinestone necklace. A feather boa wrapped around my shoulders. I looked like a deranged escapee from the Mustang Ranch. One of the circus women brushed by, eyeing me from top to bottom.

"Take off your underwear. It is showing." She expressed disdain for me through the tone of her words.

"But this is a borrowed costume. I have to wear underwear!"

"Then put on your thong."

"What is a thong?" She laughed at my naivety and slingshot a triangle of material no bigger than a small slice of pizza held together with white elastic.

I picked up the tiny G-string, trying to ascertain how it would function on my body.

Billy rushed into the dressing room and tugged me out of my stupor and into the ring. This post was the easiest yet; all I had to do was walk, smile, and style. I still had no idea what style meant. In a circle, I pranced with my arms extended and my smile wide, a pebble amongst all the stunning circus folk. The crowd applauded passionately. I drank it like an elixir for my soul. We pranced and twirled with the performers and animals. The crowd roared with approval, and I recognized Nirvana. We were all sparkly as we paraded in circles until the elephants led us back up the tunnel to the sound of applause.

"This is freaking cool! Are you having as much fun as I am?"

Becky growled at me as the train of tiger cages thundered by. Huge, beautiful cats were pacing and looking at us like we were nothing more than meat.

"The smell is going to kill me."

Back in the dressing room, we disrobed and dressed in the finale outfits. With time to spare, we donned silk kimonos to cover our costumes and went into the audience. The other spectators deemed us vile with our glammed-up faces and nightdresses. I heard a middle-aged, wide-waisted woman proclaim to her husband, "Whores at the circus! Is there no sacred place?!"

When the second act started, we moved to the top of the coliseum to watch the flying act.

The beauty of the aerial display again mesmerized me. The pageantry and grace Phileap exuded was palpable. People gasped at each magical trick. He gave an affirmation to the audience to tell them he existed solely for them.

We watched a few acts. I was enthralled. Becky complained.

"Can we please leave after the show? I need a full massage, steam room, and bottle of vodka to wash this away."

"I am in rapture. This is the best day of my life. I think I'm in love."

"With Phileap?"

"No, the circus."

"You're fucking crazy."

Back in the ring, we pranced again during the finale, the whole troupe there to leave one last indelible impression of magic on the audience. Tigers roared, elephants stood on end, acrobats twirled with silken robes, intoxicating the spectators' minds with a world exotic and unknown. I was so pleased with this new adventure; a permanent smile was plastered across my face.

As we were leaving the ring, the cage of chimpanzees came whizzing by me. The monkeys were dressed in little costumes and hanging from the faux tree branches in the wooden and plastic glass enclosure. I smiled at them as they frolicked. They went nuts. Rushing at me, fangs bared, fists tight and pounding on the Plexiglas. Their screams deafened me, pinning me to the wall in horror. Their trainer, who had been pulling the rolling cage, came around to see what the commotion was about. A hand signal stopped the pounding, but they were still poised for attack. She turned to me. "Did you smile at them?"

Stammering and pressed to the farthest corner, "Yes, they were adorable."

"You imbecile. They don't see it as a smile; they see a stranger baring their fangs and challenging them. Do you not have any common sense?"

Circus wisdom did not come without experience. I craved that wisdom as much as I did the fame.

7

December 22, 1980, Stockton, California, USA

To try and talk Becky into staying, I rented a motel room for the four of us. I figured if I got us out of the smelly circus, she might see romance in the traveling. I had no plan to run away and join the circus on my own. It was supposed to be something we would do together. Spend a month or so with the three rings, a true girl buddy movie moment, something to tell our kids about.

We checked in at the Stockton Inn. We lied to the clerk that we were all cousins, but he did not care and gave us a key to the small cabins that were separate from the main hotel. It was a rustic example of a room, one that late-night truckers spent an hour in with their special friends. The walls of the hotel were smokers-dingy with peeling wallpaper and suspicious stains on the carpet. The beds were covered in a scratchy polyester cover and the paintings were nailed to the wall. We could hear banging and moaning coming from the next room. This did not bother the boys, as public fornication was a staple in their lives. The room held double beds, with Magic Fingers boxes next to each base. The boys had no idea what this mystic machine was, so I produced a quarter and set the bed vibrating. Ramon giggled like a child as Magic Fingers made him feel all right.

Becky was accustomed to much better hotels, but this was the best they had in glorious Stockton.

We shared a six-pack of Bartles & Jaymes wine coolers and a couple of the all-new McRibs that had been recently introduced at McDonald's for a gourmet kind of evening. Ramon had gotten $10 worth of quarters so the bed would vibrate all night long. Each time the Magic Fingers stopped, he would yell, "More quarters! I need more coins!"

Phileap and I laid face-to-face on the pillow. We were exploring with our hands and getting to know each other's bodies, as physical intimacy was impossible with Ramon giggling and begging for more. Phileap looked divinely happy, lying on this bed in a strange hotel. I wondered, with hand signals, why he was so happy. Ramon had to interpret because Phileap's English was still extremely sparse. They chatted quickly in Spanish, Phileap not wanting to inject Ramon into our intimate experience.

"He's never slept on a real mattress before."

"What?" Both Becky and I sat up at this proclamation. Ramon inserted another quarter and told the story with a staccato voice as the Magic Fingers rattled.

"He sleeps on foam in the trailer or on a blanket on the ground. This is his first time with a real mattress."

"What about his home?" Becky asked with the same staccato from the Magic Fingers.

"He never had a home. He was born on the dressing room dirt floor in Chile. His parents lived in a wooden covered wagon; the kind you guys have in cowboy movies. Once the boys were two years old, they slept on the ground next to the wagon. He is seventh-generation circus. No one for hundreds of years in his family has owned a home. Coming to America was the first time they had hope for a proper home."

Phileap nodded in agreement with Ramon, although he did not understand a word—for all we knew, Ramon was making it all up.

"Tell me the truth!" I hollered at him.

"That is the truth! Quarter, please!"

Ramon ran out of quarters at 2 a.m. but went to the 7-Eleven and got more drinks, Better Cheddars, and another roll of coins. The rest of the night was spent with an exploration of bodies while my mind reeled with the stark truth of Phileap's past life. I was on the love roller coaster again, sure that I could fix him, give him a better life with the strength of my love. All he had to do was love me back.

With half-rotten curtains pulled aside, I saw that the moon was full, lighting up the sky like a lantern. The frogs chirped an ancient and temporary song. It was 70 degrees at 3 a.m. California, once almost dust from drought, was flooded from a recent rain. I was in bed next to Phileap with Led Zeppelin turned up to drown out the Magic Fingers.

I smelled the jasmine blooming and the bud bursts on the apple tree. It was sweet, like the sweat on his neck. My tongue discovered every scent his body made, now stored in my memory. My fingers mapped and drove him. His breath quickened. I wasn't sure if it was a request to stop or do more. I didn't care. It was my show. I would extract from him every essence, fluid, and pleasure I could. In a short time, I planned to imprint on him, so that the memory would last, tug at us, drive us to merge and repeat. It was the moon's fault. Like the surf, it drives me to pound and roar and reclaim my beach with waves of passion. My soul screamed for his recognition. My tainted heart wanted to run naked on the grass and fuck. My brain needed to be heard. My body wanted to be hurt, sexually damaged. The kind that would make us blush the next day over orange juice. But for now, the moon teased me with possibility.

No one slept that night, for the vibrating and my constant need for Ramon to translate what Phileap had just whispered in my ear. Some of the declarations were too sexy for translation, so Ramon would pretend he was asleep until the Magic Fingers timed out.

8

December 23, 1980, Napa, California, USA

On Sundays, there was a celebration for the circus performers, a coming together for a feast. Since they had gotten their weekly pay, it was a feast of barbecued meats. I was happy to whip up a fantastic pasta salad using Tajin spice and a ton of parboiled broccoli, carrots, onions, and cauliflower. Becky used her dad's credit card to buy Budweiser and Blue Nun.

We settled in, Becky and I laughing at how the boys called it "making a BBQ." The meat from the barbecue was not what Becky and I were accustomed to eating. No burgers, ribs, or hot dogs—it was all liver. Huge hunks of cow livers, the only thing masking their tin smell was the heap of onions on the foil next to them. I tried them both; Becky stuck with my pasta salad. I asked Ramon about the meat.

"Liver makes us strong. And it is cheap."

"You eat this every Sunday?"

"Most of us eat this every day. It is circus meal."

Afterward, we sat on the steam trucks filled with costumes and rigging, listening to the tigers roar and elephants call out into the night. Becky was set to leave and drive back to Reno. I didn't want to leave but had not been invited to stay. An impossible situation because Phileap had no room in his tin palace for me to sleep and having no discernible circus skills made me only a liability.

Common sense had never been my strong point. I schemed at ways I could stay, if only for a couple of weeks. I could brag that I ran away and joined the circus! Who wouldn't want that on their resume?

Talking with Bernice, one of Phileap's sisters-in-law from England, she told me the troupe had worked in London while she was a dancer on the show. She was shaped like an elegant ballerina with flowing movements. She was as graceful as she was beautiful and spoke with the soft, clipped tones of a posh British girl. She fell for Nicolás and followed him to the States.

"Córdobas have a way of getting under a girl's skin. They are dangerous men."

"I'm drawn to danger. And traveling."

"And you are fond of the men in red tights, no?"

I blushed at the truth of this statement.

"If you stay, you can take my place in the act. I am pregnant and will not be able to fly after six months or so."

I was thrilled that I now had my "in" to become a circus star. I could replace Bernice. Only I had never taken a gymnastic class, much less flown on a trapeze. "Can I mention it to Phileap?"

She smiled and waved away. "It's your life to throw away on a Córdoba. Go ahead."

I ran to Phileap with the fantastic news and had Ramon translate, who burst into laughter at each huge assumption I had come to in my fantasy world. He pointed out that Phileap had not requested me to stay. His family clearly did not want anything to do with me—a stout redhead flying with the greatest of ease. Impossible.

Ramon laughed as he explained my plan to Phileap. Not a word spilled from Phileap's lips as he took me into the dressing room. It stood dark and empty. I begged, looking at him, chattering like a monkey about how I could learn to fly. How hard could it be? He pushed me to my knees as he unzipped his jeans. I took his meaning. If I could give him a reason to keep me, teach me, I could stay. Well-skilled in the art of fellatio, I made him howl. I passed the test. I made a promise to start at 6 a.m. with 200 sit-ups.

We returned to the barbecue, and I told Becky I was staying.

"You're losing your mind. They don't want you here. You don't know how to be a trapeze artist? You don't even speak the same language as him. I am not leaving you!"

"Becky, I have nothing left in Reno except a pending arrest. I have no home, no boyfriend, I can't go back to my parents. I can't go back to college. The circus is, for all intents and purposes, a genuine choice. I get to travel, perform, and have sex with the magnificent flying creature."

"You are certifiably crazy. I'll be back for you. Call me, and I am there."

We hugged, and I experienced her sob. I was not empathetic. Why she feared for me, I was unclear. I remained sure I had made the best decision of my life.

As she drove away, I heard the angry squawks coming from Phileap's mother. Not understanding the words but knowing the intent, I listened as she screamed, displeased that Phileap had offered an interloper a place in her home, family, and business.

In the trailer, the brothers ascended upon Phileap, all with strong opinions about my joining them. Since everyone traveled and worked together, it was not an easy thing to take on another woman. Santiago was the oldest of the troupe, the catcher, and the kindest. Like a big, fictional bear, he was smiley and kind. He took the path of least resistance, avoiding family drama by laughing a lot.

"It seems like she could help with many things given she is American."

Nicolás scoffed, "I haven't even met her, and I hate her. No. Phileap cannot bring some strange girl into the family."

Santiago grabbed an empanada and clunked off in his wooden clogs.

Nicolás was the flyer who did the triple and was considered the star. He was twelve years older than Phileap, ancient for a flyer. His greatest asset was his gorgeous wife, for he had adopted his father's pervasive foul mood. He was handsome in a Picasso kind of way. Clearly on his last legs as the star, he was now creating the next generation of flyers by impregnating Bernice.

Marco was the youngest and spoke the most English. He was sixteen and already destined to be the catcher. Where Nicolás and Phileap were peanut-sized men, Marco was a zucchini. He had curly hair stacked upon his head and the grin of someone discovering sex for the first time, which he was doing in every town with a new girl. A trick he learned from his brothers.

"I think if Phileap wants a girl, he can have one."

"Like a puppy?" Nicolás sneered.

"I know that I won't get to have a wife until Phileap does, so I am all for it."

9

January, 1981, Las Vegas, Nevada, USA

Long ago the exclamation "the circus is coming to town" once signaled a fourth major holiday, equivalent to Thanksgiving, Christmas, and the Fourth of July. Shops, public offices, and schools closed, and an entire populace assembled to witness the parade of bands, clowns, exotic animals, and bejeweled performers marching from the rail yards to the circus grounds, paced by aromatic elephants and shrieking calliope music the whole way. But the circus did more than entertain; it reassured Americans that anything was possible.

They couldn't travel year-round with the top half of the country filled with impassable snow and sleet-covered roads. All the circus acts wintered in Florida, specifically in Sarasota. As with most things in the circus world, it all circles back to the Ringling Brothers. The five Ringling brothers worked together to start their own circus and then eventually merge it with the Barnum & Bailey Circus to create the Ringling Bros. and Barnum & Bailey Circus, which had a near monopoly on the traveling circus industry for decades. John Ringling, the last remaining of the brothers, moved the winter quarters of their circus empire to Sarasota in 1927. He helped develop the area into what it is today, making the entire city feel like a circus town, with little clown cars and all. It is currently home to more circus headquarters as well as retired and active performers than any other city in the world. The estate purchased by John and his wife, Mable, that once served as their winter home now serves as an art museum, housing pieces from the Ringling collection and a historical circus museum exhibit.

The Córdobas had decided that wintering in Las Vegas with the many new shows would be a better choice for them. Their agent told them that expensive topless shows were being added to every casino. This would give them the chance to work the act without having to travel. These new shows had seemingly unlimited budgets, for this was a way for casinos to attract more gamblers. *Jubilee!* was the show the Córdobas were first booked into as a trampoline act. It was a topless-centered spectacular revue. It opened with an initial cost of ten million dollars and was produced by Donn Arden, who set the standard for all the spectacular Las Vegas shows. It celebrated female beauty, in combination with a demand for only the best in costumes, set, and talent. The *Jubilee!* showgirls were an icon of the new Las Vegas; topless beauties wore costumes designed by Bob Mackie. The Córdobas worked every night from eight to midnight doing two shows, though their act only lasted five minutes. This was an easy work schedule and big pay. America was truly turning out to be the promised land.

10

February, 1981, Las Vegas, Nevada, USA

I moved to Las Vegas on a gloomy Tuesday. The two suitcases and two huge boxes were my dwindled-down collection of everything dear to me. The rest I left in my friend's garage to retrieve when I was done with my circus adventure. I told my parents I didn't like college, so I was going to try this as my gap. They did not know about the case against me or the police looking for me. My home team believed I would only last a month in Las Vegas, living in a 28-foot trailer with Phileap, his parents, and his little brother. I never even shared a room with my sister, and now I was to live in a Rustler Travelaire trailer with four other people. The tin can was my new domicile. It was smaller than I remembered.

Phileap's parents were pissed that I was there because he did not mention my arrival. My luggage and boxes were shoved under the trailer in the dust by Marco. I made a big meal the first night to try and smooth things, but the cacophony of strong Spanish slurs and yelling at the outside communal table said that I was not a welcome chef or bunkmate.

We made love on the net outside in the open air, a velvet cape over us. My lust had grown in the two weeks we had been apart. His lust had grown because he had taken ownership of me. He went into the trailer to get more blankets, and I put my face through the holes of the net and looked around.

We were on three acres of dust on the west side of Las Vegas with only pomegranate trees around us. There were five trailers, four full of Córdobas and one for the lion trainer's family. Parked in a horseshoe pattern with the big trapeze in the middle as well as many smaller apparatuses for practicing and working out, including a huge square trampoline that was next to a large wooden pyramid structure. I heard the cats roaring and protesting from the one freestanding garage. A huge ring of steel cages stood at least twenty feet high and were set in a solid circle except for one small door. I recognized it as an oversized tiger cage. There were twenty metal seats that looked like gigantic spools of thread lined on the wall and a huge cast-iron vat of water in the middle. I could smell cats and hay, then rotten beef and vegetables. There was a burn pile to the back of the property that was mostly animal feces and cockroaches. The sounds of the chirping insects lulled me to sleep. When the sun woke me up, I saw Phileap had never returned to me.

The rattling of the cages, bringing the cats out of the garage and into the ring, started the day. As the big cats bolted out of the tiny cages into the larger space, they stretched and roared. Their breakfast was administered via a six-foot pole with a slab of smelly meat on it thrust into the ring. I watched as the females ate first and then let the boys eat the scraps. The tigers' and lions' interactions were so like a house cat; I wanted to go pet them. I remembered I knew nothing of this world and stayed on my net. They lounged and slept on their individual perches after the meal. I could have lain there all day watching them, but dammit, I came to Vegas to be a trapeze artist, and it was time to get started. I dragged my bag into the garage, changed into a raglan pink cotton suit, and pulled my hair into a high pony, ready to practice. I'd have killed for a cup of coffee, but instead filled a dirty cup with water from the large metal sink. I was stretching by the small trapeze when Phileap emerged from the trailer with a steaming coffee mug. He only had one. He saw me and was confused at first, like he hadn't summoned me here. With little acknowledgment of me, he started to stretch. He was in a skin-tight leotard and wore clogs on his feet. He finally approached me and asked, "Why are you dressed like that?"

"I am ready for practice. I want to learn trapeze."

He laughed at my not-funny statement and stopped when he saw the hurt in my eyes.

"You have wrong clothes. Go see Bernice." He pointed to the farthest trailer. I slinked over, confused by his reaction to me, and wondered what could possibly be wrong with my fluffy bunny bedazzled suit.

Bernice leaned out and stared at me with disdain. "What?"

"Phileap says I'm dressed wrong for practice and to see you."

"What am I supposed to do with you?"

"Tell me what to wear? I don't know."

"Well, you can't fly in that." She waved her hand up and down the length of me like I was a hobo.

She went back inside, slamming the door. I heard yelling in Spanish coming from the slanted windows. I wanted to disappear back to Reno, but only jail waited for me there; this would have to do for now.

Bernice emerged with a ratty brown leotard. There were huge holes in the crotch and underarms. The tights were black with bleach spots on them.

"Here! You can pay me for these later."

I held them between two fingers, sure she was kidding. I slinked back to the garage and put on the ratty tights. Phileap ignored me, so I did a self-guided workout and planned to repair the holes in the ugly uniform after dinner. I sat on the old army trunk outside the garage and watched them practice. They flew until afternoon and took a break to eat. The first meal of the day, at 2 p.m., was only shredded carrots and lemon juice. Phileap, who barely acknowledged me all day, led me into the garage and banged me up against the rusty sink. I watched more practice, and I was told by Bernice that they were going to let me make the dinner meal for everyone. I was told to get the ingredients from inside Phileap's trailer fridge.

During dinner, there was another round of loud hostility. Afterward, Phileap joined me on the net.

"You can stay, but you must work hard and be quiet," he said in Spanish, but all I heard was *you can stay*.

"Papi is to teach you tomorrow. Three months on the ground and, if you make it, then you fly. Meanwhile, I want you." Again, I understood only the *Papi* and *teach* part. I was elated and blew him. We fell asleep after under the vast stars in the sky and the roars of the cats.

My first day learning was mostly asking Bernice questions and doing sit-ups— thousands of them—on a dusty wood plank.

"Why is their mother so wrathful?"

"She's worn out and disappointed. She gave birth to eleven children on a dressing room dirt floor in Chile."

"But Phileap told me that there were seven kids."

"Yes, but she was pregnant with eleven. Four of them did not live."

"Like, they died as infants?"

"No, like she couldn't afford to feed the first four, so the next four had to be sacrificed."

"I'm not sure what that means."

"Because you are privileged."

"I most certainly am not privileged!"

"You are American. And a towner. You couldn't fathom the poverty this family went through until the four eldest boys learned to do the trapeze. Then they were instant celebrities. Young, talented boys. Now they are old, and it's time for Phileap and Marco to carry the family."

"But Nicolás is only 30? That's old?"

"In the circus world, that is ancient."

I hung from the single trapeze bar on the ground and tried to swing. Every safe flying trapeze rig has a large net underneath the rig and an apron going up the back. I was afraid of falling off the big trapeze, so she explained the mechanic to me. Buckled around my waist was a belt made from seat-belt material that had steel rings on each side. These were attached to a rope that ran through the top of the trapeze rigging and down to where someone would hold it. This was the safety in flying. The belt, (mechanic) could increase your swing so you did not smack your back on the platform and slow your fall so you would not break your neck falling on the net. A trainer on the ground controls the lines and pulls them if the flyer is in a dangerous situation. Pulling on the lines will suspend the flyer in the air, and slowly letting go of the lines will bring the flyer to the ground safely. Once a flyer has mastered a particular trick, they will take off the mechanic safety harness (called flying out of the lines).

‿

That night, Phileap and everyone had gone to work at the new show on the strip. They left at 7 p.m. and were home long after midnight. The alone time was welcome for me; the solitude served me as I read and practiced on the trampoline. I insisted that better food was bought, so meals tasted better but always had the requisite liver and onions. Not that anyone said that or thanked me, but I took pride in them. I was a true scullery maid. My body hardened from the practice and the restricted diet. My mind was clear with no alcohol or drugs. I was only brought into town to buy groceries or get fabric for costumes, though I talked Bernice into letting me run into the library and grab a book weekly. I had gotten into a nice routine of practice, cooking, reading, and fucking. It suited me.

11

March, 1981, Las Vegas, Nevada, USA

We practiced all day on the dusty lot while Mama and Papi wasted the money their sons made on gambling at the grocery store slot machines. No one knew until the money was all gone that they were exploiting their children for an addiction that Las Vegas was based on enabling.

Of all Phileap's brothers, Payaso made me the most uneasy. He stayed to himself and only joined the act if a clown was needed. He slept in the back of a truck—no trailer or even tent. I never heard him speak. Only his father talked to him, and that was always in an angry tone. I would leave bowls of stew on the tailgate of the truck for him, but the next day it was always untouched. I often found him looking into the neighbors' properties. He spent way too much time watching the children.

My only communication to and about the family came from Bernice. She did not like talking to me, afraid a bit of my "Towner" would rub off on her.

"How did they get to the United States if they were so poor?"

"That is my favorite tale. Though I am not supposed to share it."

"Please, I'm dying for context."

"They were working with a famous Mexican circus. The owner loved the act and how talented the Córdoba boys were. He bought them a travel trailer to live in, as they had always lived in a wagon."

"Like the old west covered wagon?"

"Yes, so they moved in and loved having a tin roof and running water. Marta was married off to a fast-talking Mexican man who paid the family a dowry and then took Marta to the United States. The plan was for the family to join them. Marta's new husband, Sebastián, had promised to find them work and homes here. He had lied and made no effort to bring the family."

"Wow, is she still married to him?"

"Yes, and they have a child now."

"Phileap was cleaning out the bathroom of the new trailer when he found a sack of gold behind the toilet."

"A big bag of gold? Bars? Rings?"

"He found gold coins. Two hundred one-ounce gold pieces. He gave them to his parents, and they used the money to buy plane tickets for everyone. There was enough money left over to buy a fourplex in Las Vegas. But once they got here, all the money disappeared. Some believe Sebastián took it, as he bought Marta a big house, some say the parents gambled it away. There was only enough money to buy trailers."

"Wow. That is exasperating."

"Ya. Sebastián now runs all our lives. He gets or rejects the work and circuses. He acts as their agent but takes more than an agent's share. I'd stay clear of him—and Mama."

"Wise advice, thank you!"

"If you were wise, you would go back home."

Phileap and I were learning to communicate, but primarily we got to know what our bodies could do to and for each other. We would lay on the net after dinner, and he would point to something and say the word in Spanish. I would repeat in English. That was the extent of our language school.

I was an unwelcome guest in the tiny trailer, so I spent very little time there. At night, when Phileap was working, I read books gathered from the library with a flashlight held under my chin. I should have been miserable, but I was too dysfunctional to be anything but happy with this new life.

Most everyone ignored me, but Mama was out to kill me. She loosened the single trapeze when she knew I was going to be on it. She took springs out of the trampoline and left mousetraps in my suitcase (which was still in the cat garage). Those are the things I knew of; I am sure there were many other booby traps that I eluded. She spit in my dish when I left it unattended and crossed herself when I entered the trailer. The woman hated me, but I didn't care. She coddled the boys (Phileap and Marco) like they were both five, and I constantly heard her giving them directives that were answered with, "Pero Mama!" She served their meals and then cleaned up their messes. She washed their faces in the morning and made their beds. I was so glad when she went to work with them. For a few moments, the dysfunction was abated, but that only made me uncomfortable. I was used to and reveled in drama.

12

April, 1981, Las Vegas, Nevada, USA

We had settled into a routine. I finally met the lion and tiger act headed by Cupcake, Izic, and their eight-year-old daughter Brigit. They had just come off Ringling.

The Ringling Bros. and Barnum & Bailey Circus is an American traveling circus company billed as "The Greatest Show on Earth." Its first performance was in 1871. The five Ringling brothers purchased it following Bailey's death in 1906 but ran the circuses separately until they were merged in 1919.

After 1957, the circus no longer exhibited under its own portable "big top" tents, instead using permanent venues such as sports stadiums and arenas. In 1971, they sold the circus to Mattel.

At this time, there were two Ringling shows called North and South that ran on the trains still, but some of the performers started traveling and living in recreation vehicles because living with the circus animals in small train boxes was smelly. It was a yearlong commitment and considered the "Top of the American Circuses." But they paid less because of the long-term commitment.

Cupcake and Izic were happy to be off "The Greatest Show On Earth." They settled in Vegas with twelve tigers, five lions, one cougar, and one black panther that spent half the day in the dark garage in small cages, but cool mornings and evenings were spent inside the wire cage performing ring.

The huge wire cage, composed of two performing areas, took up almost half an acre. The cats had their stands inside, marking their territory, but were free to move about the cage. It was sometimes like a giant puddle of kittens as they groomed and played. Except for the big male lion, Alex. No one played with him, and I wondered why. They were loaded up before noon into their tiny transport carriers. These were six-foot by four-foot cages with giant casters on them that hooked together to transport the cats to and from the performance arena. The cats hated them, and a lot of human yelling, whip wielding, and raw-chicken throwing was used to get them inside. The garage was a two-car garage, so the twenty cats were stored like sardines in there with the air conditioner. This was also where the only phone on the property resided, so phoning home was an ordeal.

Cupcake, who stood five feet tall, was a formidable woman who wore six-inch-heeled go-go boots, a Dolly Parton wig, and false eyelashes to break-fast. Izic, bald as a cue ball, wore a curly dishwater brown wig that slid down his face in the 100-degree Vegas sun. Cupcake hailed from the south of France, Izic was Brazilian, and Brigit spoke both their languages along with tiger, lion, and English. I asked Brigit the first day about the cats as she was throwing frozen chicken carcasses into the ring for them to lick like lollipops.

"Are you afraid of them?"

She scoffed as only an eight-year-old can do. "Why would I be afraid?"

"Well, they can kill you."

"So can cars, and I get in one every day."

"Good point."

"If you follow the rules, it keeps them and us safe."

"What are the rules?"

She turned to me incredulous.

"You really are circus illiterate? I heard my parents talking about you. Are you really a Towner? I didn't believe it. Why are you here? Why would anyone choose to be with circus people?"

I laughed at her honesty and frankness. She had a good point. I decided not to share that I was on the lam, so in quick fashion, as children of alcoholics can do, I lied.

"I am here to write a book and learn the trapeze. I am also a teacher."

"Will you teach me? I have never opened a book before!"

"Yes!" I yelled, too excitedly, feeling like I now had an "in" to talk to her parents and something to do.

I talked with Phileap about it that night while lying on the net. He thought it was a good idea and then confessed he had never been to school.

"Not ever?"

"No."

"Do you read?"

"Read?"

"Like a book." I pantomimed a book. He shook his head in shame.

"It's okay. I will teach you too!"

He was less enthusiastic than Brigit but was open to the idea. I started by reading to him. I chose *The Old Man and the Sea* by Hemingway because I knew he would like the fishing aspect of the story and the ease of the telling. He became more proficient in English, and his mind began to open to possibilities that could help him become more than just another generation of trapeze artist.

❧

My training now included six hours of strength exercise for my torso and arms. The trapeze uses core muscles, and I had none. I did an hour of sit-ups. Not numbers, but a timed amount of torture with Phileap sitting on my feet, yelling and cajoling me to sit up one more time. Then we moved on to arms. Pull-ups were done on the low trapeze bar, then leg lifts on a slant board made from wooden crates, so my ass filled with splinters. Next, we did a push-up and squat combo, pushing up on the ground, leaping up on my feet, then finishing with a squat. We did it over and over until I was dizzy.

We used a small single trapeze that sat six feet off the ground. It was an upside-down "U" with a wire holding a trapeze bar. The trapeze bar was twenty pounds of steel that was five feet long and wrapped in wound tape (otherwise known as gauze). They bought the tape at the local drug store, so it was expensive and non-sustainable. The rig was held up with guidewires that came off the top and were hammered into the hard Vegas dirt. It was wobbly, which made it harder to swing and stay in a plank position, which was my current directive. Everything ached as I fell into bed each night. With this intense exercise, my stomach muscles were damaged and sore. I couldn't even laugh.

"My hands hurt so much." I had two palms filled with blisters and open sores.

"If you pee on them, they heal faster," Phileap barked at me like it was the most normal statement in the world. "Even better to get a child to pee on them. Ask Brigit."

"First, that's plain crazy and not true. Second, do not ever ask a child to pee on you, or you will go to jail."

"You Americans do not recognize the most basic things."

"Peeing on a hand will never be basic."

The next morning, I met with Brigit. Although she was only eight, she was my current best friend.

She worked out with me, giving me tips and tricks. All circus kids have an innate ability to do most of the circus acts because it was all they had in their world. It was their school, culture, and life. I went to the library on a grocery run and got Brigit homeschool supplies. I started teaching her every day after her parents approved that her chores were done. In return, she helped me learn what it was to be circus.

We laid on the ground as she practiced her letters, and I did sit-ups on the slant board.

"Why so many letters?"

"There are only twenty-six! And just think, every book and every movie are created out of those twenty-six letters. It's a miracle."

"What do you have to have to write a book? College degree, right?"

"Nope, just an understanding of those letters and words. More importantly, you only need a story."

"Anyone can write a book? There's not a requirement?"

"Nope, stitch some words together that entertain, inspire, sadden, or scare someone, and you have a book!"

"That seems crazy. You think there would be a book school."

"Writing is about imagination; anyone can do it."

"I believe you. A future that doesn't involve a shovel sounds incredible."

She heard her father bellow to come help prep the cat food. She ran off, and I went to watch the trapeze practice.

Phileap and the boys practiced for eight hours a day. They were trying to perfect impossible tricks to garner a higher price once the season started. Each time they climbed the rickety ladder, threw a trick, and then landed in the net, their father shrieked from the ground. Good or bad, his tone shamed them. He seemed more about humiliating his sons than helping them. I picked up the bad Spanish words first, and there was no mistaking his tone of disappointment. I thought the flyers were fabulous and often clapped with glee. Phileap had to tell me to stop doing that because it further enraged his father.

"What is he so pissed about? I think your double layout was fantastic!"

"He was born mad. He hates everything."

"But why?"

"He thinks he deserves better."

"Better?"

"Better wife, children, and life."

"That's not a healthy attitude!"

"What is *healthy* and *attitude*?"

"A way your head works?"

"Oh. Papi's head is bad."

The home-use video camera had come out, and the family bought one so that they could tape practices and watch them at night after dinner to tighten and perfect the tricks. Style was as important as function. If something looked too easy, they would add an element of failing to get the audience vested in the trick. I helped tape during the day and then hooked the huge camera to the TV via a tangle of wires to watch at night. It was helpful for them to watch themselves executing tricks, but it brought strife to the family to hear Papi's horrible diatribe of negativity. They had always soaked it in the minute of being in the air and pushed his ranting to the back when they tried new tricks, but to hear it ricocheting through the walls of the trailer was another matter. Nicolás and Santiago stormed out after the first run-through, refusing to watch, but more importantly hear, what their father had hurled at them. I learned after the first night to turn off the sound while filming, and it made the scrutinizing more serene and helpful.

Brigit started filming when they let me climb the ladder to the platform during practice. I was there to catch the fly bar, put in the risers, and help them with the mount. The trapeze fly bar must be actively "swung" by pushing it to keep it so flyers can catch it. Left to its own devices, it stops swinging. I would have to throw a long steel hook that was attached to a rope to catch it. It takes time and hand-eye coordination to do, something I had in short supply. I hung off the side of the three-foot platform, right hand hanging on for dear life as my left hand caught the bar on every swing, pulled it up, and slung it hard for one good swing back to me. As the flyers set up for a trick, I handed them the fly bar. Then I added a riser to the platform for them to stand on. The harder tricks, really anything more than a somersault, required the flyers to leave from higher than the platform for the vivacity of the trick to reach the catcher. After the flyer leaves the platform, I removed the riser, or it would hit them in the back on the return swing. This was all nerve-racking for me to be done at fifty feet in the air on a tiny platform, and I failed often. This gave Papi ammunition for why I should be sent home when he reviewed the films at night.

13

May, 1981, Las Vegas, Nevada, USA

I woke up to see we had new dirt lot companions. Dove and her elephants had arrived. Zita had a baby named Dumbo, and it was the cutest thing I had ever seen. Dove set up in the furthest corner from the cats, so the elephants would not be frightened. She had two huge eighteen-wheel trailers that were the inside homes. The elephant one had water and hay trays on the side. Dove's trailer was made into a three-bedroom home. It was opulent for circus living quarters, with wallpaper and doors with Thomasville couches and chairs. A real double bed was in the back with a full-size closet. Dove was proud of her home and had decorated it like something out of *Good House-keeping* magazine.

During the day, the elephants had their own large cage ring that they rocked and danced around in, with the whole pack focused on the baby.

In between practice, working out, and schooling Brigit, I spent all my time with the elephants. I loved getting to know their personalities and idiosyncratic behaviors. Dove reminded me of my best friend Kim, tough as nails but a pure soul. She let me feed, water, and groom the behemoths, and I treasured every minute. She prized the free labor. I picked up a book at the library to learn more about the Indian elephants, and I became determined to get them a watering hole. Dove said that I was crazy to try but didn't discourage my quest.

It is hot in Las Vegas, even in the spring, so I convinced a neighbor with a tractor to dig a vast pond. I thought I knew all about the neighbors as I watched them from sixty feet in the air. I could see them hanging on the fences and could tell everyone was curious. I know that I was fascinated with the elephants, so I was sure the neighbors would help if they could get a showing. I surmised that they stayed away due to Alex the lion's vocal concerts every morning and evening. He started with a loud roar, and all the cats joined along. The tigers, leopards, and elephants all did this ominous howling twice a day. It still startled. I was up close and personal with them all. They were highly trained and confined, so I learned not to be fearful.

I organized a potluck party and invited the neighbors, much to the dismay of the circus people. This concept of neighbors is foreign to them, and they do not grasp the value of having people around you who can make your life easier and more enjoyable. I made a paella, and everyone brought sodas. We did tours of the property, animals, and acts. The neighbors were enthralled.

"Do you all travel together all the time?" a blue-eyed teenage girl asked as she marveled at our costumes.

"We all travel, but rarely together. Each season, we are placed on a different circus circuit, and when it gets cold, we come back here."

"What do you do when you're not working?"

"We practice every day."

"So, no time off, like ever?"

"Nope. Circus life is full-time work."

Another boy stepped forward as we entered the lion's garage, which I teasingly call the Lion's Den. We stepped inside and let our eyes adjust to the dark room. There was silence as they treaded into a garage filled with killers. All the cats turned to look at us and, I swear, collectively licked their lips. The neighbors gasped. I approached Alex and he brought his neck to the cage, allowing me to pet his huge mane. He and I had become friends. I knew he was a big, noisy pussy cat. They gulped again.

Alex started his roar, and I recommended that everyone cover their ears. The boisterous discordance went on for a solid ten minutes, and we couldn't move. It was as if the loud noise had frozen us in place. We walked through the cages, and I explained each breed of cat and where it came from in the wild.

"Do they ever want to escape?"

"Why would they? They sleep all day, and someone brings them all their food."

The big male tiger turned his butt to us, and I knew he would spray us with pee, so I scooted everyone out back into the bright sunlight.

"Wanna meet the elephants?" A small girl let out a squeal.

We moved to the pasture where I wanted the watering hole. I had turned on the hoses, and the elephants were rolling in the mud playing with the water. As we watched, the elephants sprayed each other with mud and fussed over Dumbo. He was playful and curious. He heard me and came running up. With his big head on my tummy, he pushed me back while trying to get his trunk on my mouth. I fell backward, and everyone was laughing until Zita charged toward her baby.

"Okay, everyone, let's give them some space! Who wants to jump on the trampoline?"

The party was perfect, and each of the neighbors wanted to help us. The chicken guy would be giving us all his roosters for tiger food, the farmer would let us gleam his fields for the elephants, the watering hole was scheduled to be dug, and we even found out one of the neighbors was the head costume designer at MGM and said they would give us leftover costumes and sequins that the show rejected. They all wanted to help for the novelty. They were now part of the circus, and I was buoyed and delighted about the connections—the circus people, not so much.

They were furious with me.

"Why did you tell them all the secrets?" This was from Izic, who also does magic, and I had showed a couple of his props.

"I didn't tell them all the secrets; I showed them around."

Phileap sat by my side, reluctant like I was a snake he shouldn't touch.

"Apple Pie, you must never do this again. The circus and how we do things is our business only. Not for strangers."

"They aren't strangers, and they are now helping. That is what neighbors are for."

"Without our secrets, there is no magic. No need for them to ever buy a ticket to our show or any show."

Izic jumped in, "You never take people through the looking glass, you imbecile."

They all agreed and hurled admonitions my way. I honestly did not get it and skulked back to the elephant pond.

14

June, 1981, Las Vegas, Nevada, USA

Dove was there, feeding and hosing everyone off. It is sweet and so funny to see these giant pachyderms play like small puppies. I was delighted, but I also knew it was dangerous. To begin to believe these animals are pets is a precarious path.

"I hear you pissed everyone off, not only the Córdobas. Great job," Dove said.

"I was trying to help. We got some good support. And look at this pond! They love it, and you would not have been able to afford the tractor work or the water. Doesn't that count?"

"It does, but you're still acting like you're on vacation. Like this will all fade away, and the harsh realities of being in the circus are not going to catch up with you."

Her words exploded like land mines on my heart. I knew she was right. It has been my way to bend reality to my needs and not see the truth.

"Does it all have to be hard?"

"Unfortunately, yes. For example, we are out of money. Without it, we cannot get to the next job or make money. Without money, I can't afford to feed eight elephants. I have to sell Dumbo."

"What the fuck? You can't. He's still a baby. You can't separate him from his mother!"

My high-pitched hysterics caused the whole herd to look up from their frolicking to see what the problem was.

Dove growled at me. "Calm the fuck down. Do not upset them. They are free-range, you idiot."

I took a deep breath and let out a false chuckle. It was enough to calm them down, and they went back to rolling in the mud.

"If I don't sell Dumbo, he starves. You want him to go without food?"

"No."

I crept back to my trailer. My mind was going ten thousand miles an hour, trying to grasp and deny this ugly reality. As I rounded the corner, I saw a decrepit, old horse being led into the garage by the new neighbor. I heard one shotgun fired, and the ground shook as the beast hit the floor. The sound of chainsaws haunted my night.

15

July, 1981, Las Vegas, Nevada, USA

After three months of training on the ground and being "bar girl," I was granted that I was strong enough to fly on the big trapeze. My first lesson was to hit the net correctly. The net was the most dangerous part of the trapeze, and if you hit it wrong, it would break your spine, neck, leg, arm, or pelvis.

Climbing up the rope ladder was a nearly impossible chore for me until Brigit told me to get someone to hold it from the bottom rung to steady it.

The mechanic strap made from car safety belt material garnered from the junkyard. There were stainless steel hooks on the sides that were attached to ropes that threaded up through the rigging and were held by Papi on the ground.

Everyone starts new tricks using the mechanic. Even Phileap wore one for new tricks. My first task was to learn how to fall. I had to climb the rope ladder with eighty-five dowel rods as steps and mount to the platform. The platform was eighteen inches wide and four feet long with six of us standing on it. Once on the platform, you leaned out with one hand on the rigging and grabbed the bar. The fly bar is a twenty-pound steel pole attached to wires to the top of the rigging that is wrapped in gauze and constantly covered with resin. The flyer puts one hand on the bar, swings it up, grabs with the other hand, and jumps up and off the platform. The first time I did it, I felt the weight of my body through my shoulders; I believed I was going to split into two. On the top of the swing, the force out, you would kick your legs out. On the back of the swing, the hallow, you had to go into a sitting position. Otherwise, your back thumped the platform. I would be called out on the upswing and needed to release my hands and drop to the net in a prone position. Tight yet relaxed to absorb the bouncing off the net. I needed to be in a sitting position on the second bounce, then standing with knees loose on the third. Then walk the moonwalk across the pliable net and climb the ladder again.

The net is a rope hammock stretched under the entire trapeze with the apron coming up behind the platform. The holes, about two inches square, scratched and burned as your body made contact with it, as only rope can do. About the thirtieth time I climbed the ladder, my muscles had fatigued so much, I couldn't hold on to the platform.

I hit the net and left to go make dinner. The only reason I was still allowed to exist in those tin walls was because I could turn old slop into a delicious meal.

We started each day with scrambled eggs and café con leche. Then hours of physical exercise to warm up. Lunch was a yummy combination of shredded carrots with lemon juice, delectable liver and onions, and rice and beans. I made dinner from the half-off meat and vegetables. I turned them into stews and pan roasts. When you are tired, you will eat anything. Phileap's father thought this was the best diet to build strong flyers, and he was our trainer/tormentor.

Papi was a sixth-generation circus performer and a tenth-generation bully. His face was glued in a permanent scowl, and his body was stooped as if he were wearing an iron cape. He loathed everyone, especially his wife. As the patriarch of a family of seven, he was disappointed in all his offspring and felt it was Mama's fault. Papi was an iron-handed trainer, controlling our workouts, flying routines, and diets. He lived in the U.S.A. now but refused to learn or speak English because he thought the whole country should bend to his will.

My bloody hands and sore body became a way of life. I loved it, and I still loved the adventure of living on the dirt lot with this collection of misfits and animals. The circus people loathed me, but the animals loved me. After dinner, Phileap and I would lie on the net, looking at the stars and learning the language of each other.

"Why can't you fit in?"

"I am trying. I help and cook."

"Your attitude is bad."

"I'm going to stop teaching you new words if you use them against me."

"Ha! But I am right, no?"

"He's just so mean."

"He is the boss. To learn, to grow, we do what boss says. You eat the food. You do the practice."

"I will try. But liver and onions every day. I don't think I can."

"If you want to grow, if you want to stay. You will."

I stopped the argument with my lips on his lap.

In the absence of anything but practice, we explored what it was like to be lovers. No body part left uncharted. It was intense and the only real recreation to be had—we fucked daily. This translated into love for me, for I had never had a sustained relationship. He returned to my honey pot every day; it seemed a great gift. This intimate building of trust with each other's bodies was eternal. It was as if the world only existed for our pleasure and practice. Having no moral compass to find true love, this constant giving of my body felt like what love should be. I was convinced I was in love. I would do anything for this man.

I was learning things about myself sexually. It was like an awakening or a revelation. I had always struggled with genuinely letting go with my sex partner. I couldn't give up the last bit of control that would allow my complete release. I liked sex, was open to learning, and was good at reclamation. Loving Phileap manipulated my heart, and it stimulated me. I didn't crave sex now. Not like I craved the flying. I would never forego flying to have sex. It boiled down to desire. Maybe acknowledging desire meant I would have to relinquish some control over my life. I had moved to a dirt lot and left everything I knew. The illusion of control was a joke.

I did love the stimulating environment. With everything new and different, I felt complete. Phileap's undivided attention to my every need, in lovemaking, had relaxed me for possibly the first time in my life. I believed there was some predictability in this usually chaotic existence, even if it was here in this artificially constructed microcosm of society for a Towner.

As I awakened to the Vegas sun, I felt Phileap stir and rest his hand on my hip as he rolled toward me and pulled me on my side and against him. He wrapped his arm tightly around me, cupping my breast as he slid his hand between my legs. He spooned me, not sexually, but for warmth, not romanticism. I could feel almost every inch of his body in contact with mine. His feet on my feet, his knees touching the sensitive backs of my knees. His rarely soft penis nestled against my bottom, his stomach and chest pressed against my lower back and shoulder blades. It was like he was trying to mold himself to me. He nuzzled my hair with his face and found my neck. His lips gently grazing the soft contours and the ticklish place behind my ear. He nibbled at the lobe and pulled it gently with his teeth. I could count his slow, measured breathing as it brushed the side of my face.

We lay entwined for several long minutes. Eventually, I wiggled my butt and pressed back against him. I touched him as he began to stir. I prized the enraptured sex, my power to stimulate him and get a real and tangible response. We were late for practice and took a bunch of catcalls about our constant "snuggle time." We both flew with big smiles on our faces.

16

August, 1981, Las Vegas, Nevada, USA

My nana remained a tad worried about me leaving and joining the circus. I called her once a week to do a "proof of life" report. I didn't mind the call, because it meant I could interact with the cats unnoticed in the garage. I was fascinated with the felines, and Brigit was kind enough to teach me how to not become a meal when interacting with them. I had never been close to a black panther and was blown away to see he was spotted, but the coat is so dark, you could only see the spots up close. The male tigers would turn their backs to me and try to spray me with pee. Avoiding it took much bobbing and weaving. My favorite was Alex. While all the big cats acted much like their domesticated family, Alex had a ton of personality. Not the king of the jungle, but the low man on the pecking cat order, and he usually ate last. He would let me rub his ears, and when he tired of it, he would let me know by trying to eat my hand. I had learned that quick, loud verbal commands stopped them from bad behavior. I bellowed, "Cat off!" He would stop trying to chew on me and move on to pacing the cage.

When I would dial my grandmother and say hello, Alex always started a roar. This is not like the one seen before every MGM movie; this roar lasted for about five minutes. I would scream to my nana, "Hang on," as Alex huffed and bellowed. Then a tiger would try to spray me. By the time five minutes had gone by, Nana remained unraveled and sure I should come home immediately.

✌

One day, I was up on the trapeze practicing my turn-around. This is the act of moving your hands on the bar and switching body directions on the upswing. It was hard because the instinct to not let go overruled my training. At this point, Phileap's dad stayed on the platform with a bamboo stick to whack my legs if my toes weren't perfectly pointed or I bent a leg. It wasn't enough to learn how to do the trick. I had to learn to look good doing it all while needing to grab the bar with my right hand, jump up and add my left hand, swing straight, kick out in front, move my left hand behind and on the other side, twist my body so I faced the other way, legs straight, toes pointed, kick up to mount the platform, grab the brace bar, and let the trapeze go while the family shouted tips and callouts. It was maddening; I wasn't born knowing where I am in space like the flyers were. I had to learn the skill like a pilot does.

I mounted and sensed a whack on my upper thigh from the bamboo stick. I also heard all the dogs in the neighborhood going nuts. I looked way down the dirt road and saw Alex the lion taking himself for a walk. Casually strolling down the dirt road as every dog went bonkers. I laughed and tried to call Cupcake, which got me another whack. This time, I took the switch from the old man's hand and yelled *"suficiente"* in Spanish. I pointed at Alex.

Cupcake heard the commotion and ran down the road after Alex. No rope or restraining item in her hands, a small bundle of pissed-off chasing after a male lion. I watched from my bird's eye point of view as she caught up to him. She beat him on the head while yelling in French. Alex cowered and shook like the lion from *The Wizard of Oz*. She pulled him back by his ear, screaming like a crazed woman. Alex followed. The whole scene tickled my funny bone. I couldn't stop laughing. My next two flights were done with me heaving with laughter, which scored me two more wallops. Alex was safely secured in the ring when he started roaring. His small but loud act of defiance went on for the next hour.

The Vegas shows had not figured out how to add animals to the act, but Dove was there waiting and pitching to the bigger shows. Word hit the streets that a casino owner in Sparks, Nevada, had added an elephant to a show and was housing the animal and trainer on the property. We had finished our last contract with *Jubilee!* and did not get into the new show, *Folies Bergère*, at the Tropicana, so money was sparse.

The cats were only eating chicken and getting surly. But a new company called IBM had just made a commercial using Alex as their spokesperson, and if the commercial ran, Cupcake and Izic would get $5,000 per screening. This became Cupcake's new obsession, flipping through the three channels, trying to catch her cat, the star. When she would see the commercial, she would open her trailer door and scream, "$5,000!"

The money took six weeks to get to them, and they spent it like they were millionaires. Luckily, the company took off, and Izic's family and cats were set for life.

I knew about food banks, and after church on Sunday, I queried if they had one. We were attending a Catholic church because the Córdobas were devout Catholics even though several family members had fallen prey to bad priests while still working in South America. The kind father gave me the address of the food bank. I told Phileap we should drive by there. Our language barrier was still a slippery slope. He assumed we had been invited to dinner, like a barbecue, not to get charity food. The idea of getting free food enraged him, unearthing a sense of pride I did not fathom. It made no sense to me. We argued in front of the warehouse, making a spectacle of our Spanglish dialectal. I acquiesced, and the food was left behind. Dinner that night included a rousing fight, with many lethal insults slung at me, but my favorite was "*diablo de ojos azules*" (blue-eyed devil). His mother wanted to ask the priest to exorcise me out of existence. The other boys' wives still took a wide berth around me but loved translating the hate language. I was learning Spanish one insult at a time.

The following Sunday, I stayed home from church, loving the solitude of lounging on the compound and reading on the net while the family went to pray. I made a special Sunday dinner for everyone, trying desperately to get them to like me, if only for a moment. Cupcake gave me a raw roast meant for the cats because she wanted to help me fit in. Cupcake loved that I was teaching Brigit "book" learning, because they knew their daughter would be more than a lion tamer. She had smarts and panache.

After church, the family returned with another car following them, and I was glad I had food to offer guests. Out of the car stepped a priest, and the macaw-like chatter flowed from Mama's mouth. She considered me a curse on their house. When the priest stepped inside and saw me, he stopped dead in his tracks.

"You are real?" He stretched out to touch my arm.

"I believe so," I said, recoiling at his touch.

"She decreed a blue-eyed devil had possessed her son and was haunting her home. I was brought to exorcise you away."

Though I tried to appear unfazed outwardly, this stung inside. "I am not going anywhere. I am neither evil nor haunting. I happen to love her son. Would you like some pot roast?"

The priest sat at the table and ate while explaining to Mama that he had no power over me. This enraged her. Phileap remained embarrassed but never stood up to his mother for this behavior.

Despite his disloyalty to me and a clear siding with his crazy mother, I stayed. After everyone got a chuckle from the priest's attempted exorcism, we moved on to a daily grind of practicing.

17

September, 1981, Las Vegas, Nevada, USA

I continued hanging with the elephants as they can never be left alone. Dove loved the time away from the herd. On the road, she had many roadies to watch and enrich them. Here, she had me. The elephants ate every few hours and needed to be watched, or they would wander away and a swath of destruction would ensue. They loved to eat trees, tear them from their roots, and pick up items like doghouses and smash them to smithereens.

When I was with them, I sang to them and petted them. I also gave them puzzles to unravel, like ropes tied in knots and fruits stuck in glass jars. The dexterity of their trunks was impressive. Their devotion to each other was admirable. Except for Zita and Dumbo, none came from the same family, yet they now treated each other as such. I was fascinated with the family hierarchy and the devotion they shared. Zita and Dumbo were almost insep-arable, but the baby was beginning to venture out on his own. She stayed within eyeshot but was showing a bit of independence. It was a magical thing to watch each night.

I was getting stronger but spending more time with the animals than the Córdobas, which was fine by all. Dove and I were friends of convenience, mostly because I was a free hired hand. From her, I learned circus rules and traditions. Even with my short time on the road in the beginning, the circus culture eluded my brain. I was fascinated by the stories and was sure I could fit in once I was on a real show as a working flyer. Dove and I were sitting down to eat at the picnic table by the elephants one night, and she admired how I had got them to not destroy the table.

"You do have a touch with them."

"I think it comes from my youth on horses."

"I believe it is from your homesickness. They sense it in you."

"I'm not homesick. I did not like that place."

"Maybe, like them, you don't have a place."

I was struck by the truth of this just as Dumbo stretched out his trunk to see what I was eating.

Dove smacked his snout away.

"He can have my broccoli. I hate it."

"Don't spoil him. The new owners will not hand-feed him broccoli."

My voice and heart raised in a panic.

"You found new owners already? He's too little to leave his mother!"

Dove was enraged and spoke to me like I was a toddler.

"I told you we're in dire straits. Selling him makes sure we can get to the next season and everyone gets fed. I don't feel good about it either, but it's the circus reality."

I was close to tears and trying to control my emotions. "When does he leave?"

"We all leave tomorrow."

"All of you? For how long? What will I do?"

Panic gripped my stomach. I started to hyperventilate.

"Calm down. This is how it works. You will get used to the goodbyes."

"But when will I see you again?"

"Possibly never. Depends on which shows we move to. I mean, there is always a possibility we will end up on a show again for a season or even back here. It is all up in the air until we move. Welcome to the circus life."

I was distraught, and huge tears ran down my face as Dumbo stretched up with his adorable trunk and sucked the tears off.

18

Octover 1, 1981, Las Vegas, Nevada, USA

Along with time on the flying trapeze, I was practicing on the single trapeze daily. I understood that the focus was on the swing. When flying, you have gravity and a pendulum to work with. The single trapeze is a much simpler version of the flying trapeze. While I was secured with a safety line, I could still get hurt while swinging and losing my grip. The main difference between the two is that on the swinging trapeze, the flyer must manually produce the swing rather than generate the swing by stepping off a high plat-form and letting gravity do the work. I was learning momentum along with flying.

I grew stronger every day, as did my adoration for Phileap. In the secluded life with no friends, family, nor co-workers, and everyone in his family despising me, I fell hard for the one guy who behaved nicely. A Stockholm syndrome of love. With no outside influences, no money, and seemingly no way to escape, my heart propelled toward him. What, at first, was foreign and unacceptable became the status quo. I understood enough Spanish to get by. I knew the terrible things being preached about me as Mama tried to enlist the other boys' wives to her hate parade. She told them she had seen me looking at the husbands in a lewd way. The wives took a wide berth around me, only talking to me when on the platform. My flying became stronger, but my poise was weak. I didn't possess the panache of the girls born in the ring, no matter how much I practiced.

I continued to get prime cuts of beef borrowed from the cats and turned each into a gourmet communal meal, but even that plentiful and spendthrift act did not soften the hatred. My only saving grace was that I was now the only female part of the troupe that could fly; Mama was too old and everyone else was pregnant.

A business deal had been struck where the troupe would fly to Monte Carlo and take place in the Circus Olympics. Winning this would secure top-dollar pay for the next season's traveling circus. Practice time doubled, and everyone tried for much harder tricks. Hands bled and muscles throbbed, but no one gave up. They were to compete against the Flying Ramous, a family from Mexico who had perfected the quadruple somersault. Nicolás had nearly perfected the triple, but it took constant practice. If he missed one day of flying, he would lose the trick. Everyone was excited and nervous about the opportunity to fly into Monte Carlo and compete against such a strong family. Especially for me, a chance to travel to France and fly for the royal family of Monaco was a dream I did not want to miss.

Mama had other plans. She talked her only daughter, Marta, into coming out of housewife retirement to fly with her brothers. I was elated to have another woman on the platform, and Marta had always been kind to me. What I did not know was that Marta was my replacement. Marta, Phileap's sister, happily became a wife to a Vegas thug and lived in a tract home, a dream only imagined in her family. Marta was the first Córdoba to have a cement foundation under her feet. Everyone agreed I had poured my heart into perfecting tricks. The consensus in many secret meetings held by Mama was circus people only look out for their own, and I did not qualify.

The airline tickets arrived, and there wasn't one for me. Devastated, I stormed and bawled. Phileap did little to calm or console me; in his compliance, I recognized betrayal. I howled louder at the idea. The tigers and lions raged with me.

The fight lasted hours, both loud and public, with everyone in a ten-acre radius hearing my pleas and anguish. Finally, out of tears that only served to water the desert sand, I sat on the net with my chest heaving. Phileap stroked my hair and explained I had a much more critical role of staying on the compound and taking care of Nicolás' two blind dogs and Papi.

They left the next day for France. Packed in two large trunks were the new costumes I created and sewn. The dust rose on the road as they drove away, the blinding sting of tears newly replenished.

19

Nctober 2, 1981, Las Vegas, Nevada, USA

I missed the sound of the constant clanging of the rigging as they flew and released the bars from the platform. The constant "hup" and "Listo," the noise the body made like a wet bag of flour hitting the nets, even the sound of the constant belittling from the patriarch. It was all replaced with the sounds of the animals. Which was my kind of peaceful, but I was devastated about being left alone. My only job was to feed Bernice's two blind dogs and nourish Papi. I wanted to starve them, as both had bites that were lethal.

Cupcake was worried about me because I was despondent about being left behind. Trying to cheer me up and cure her wild curiosity about Towner life, she brought me into her tailer to ask how I got to where I was now: a dusty lot in Las Vegas all alone.

"You really want a story?"

She smiled as she placed a big mug of tea in front of me. "I want the whole story."

I reached my hand across her table and faux shook it.

20

1961, Winter, Reno, Nevada, USA

My parents were young and stupid and assumed my birth would end all the loneliness and uncertainty they were experiencing in their teen lives. What I did bring was sleepless nights, malodorous diapers, and a lack of sexual interest in each other. My mom had to give up her Miss America figure, and my dad had to give up his sovereignty to work 12-hour days at the phone company to keep a roof over our heads. The house was furnished with secondhand everything. The food came from a box. The mood resembled a gulag.

I was a flamboyant redheaded child with a flair for exaggeration and a need for an audience from the time I could toddle across the stained carpet. My parents quickly figured out that I wasn't the answer they were looking for and separated. Dad bugged off, and I began my lifelong penance of being a woman with a huge sense of abandonment.

Mom did remarry and gave me the best gift—my little sister, Sunrise. I was nine when she arrived. I carried and fussed over her like a living doll. Happy to just exist around her and play mommy until I hit puberty. Then, I heard my first David Bowie album and started reading grown-up novels while the red hair on my body blossomed. The quiet cow town and secondhand everything grew boring. Sunrise went to kindergarten, and I was no longer the center of anyone's universe. I wanted to find my own orbit.

My teen years were heavily influenced by the novels of Tom Robbins. *Even Cowgirls Get the Blues* offered me a life of traveling and a nontraditional existence. I mourned my not-fit-for-Nordstrom-store existence and dreamed of being on the road. Even Kermit the Frog went traveling in *The Muppet Movie*. If a green, felt frog could travel, I would find my way.

21

October 1, 1980, University of Nevada, Reno, USA

I ventured out into the world. My first house was an adorable bungalow on Taylor Street. The landlady had a full basement downstairs that she used as an office. She only worked nights, and by the sounds of the whips and moaning wafting up through the vents, I gathered she wasn't an Avon Lady. With a heavy German accent, two-inch-long pointed nails, and severely dyed red hair, she wore skintight leopard spots tube tops and leather pants. She was an early entrepreneur of the sex workers union. I needed a roommate to afford the rent, but what sealed the deal is that she gave me permission to get a cat. I had always wanted a feline companion, but my father was allergic. I picked the little tuxedo minx at the pound and named him Mercutio. I searched for a roommate to fill in as my friend and rent partaker.

I was slated to go to college in the Bay Area starting in January. Mills College had accepted me, and the fine old white guys at the Nevada State Assembly had gotten me a full scholarship. Mills was where politicians-in-training went, and they had big plans for me. I wasn't so sure this is what I wanted, but how could I turn down a full ride?

⁓

Living on my own now, I organized outrageous parties, inviting an eclectic bunch of friends. Retail, nametag-wearing lemmings mixed with wild actors who lived on speed and rich women's trust funds. I met Becky at one of my parties, and within an hour, we became fast friends.

Becky's smile was wide with perfect teeth, like a piano keyboard, and her vivid cerulean eyes reflected my soul and were easy to get lost in. She was dressed like a couture model with clothes I could never afford.

Sitting on my bed, we had our first chat. Becky was going to college to be a doctor.

"What's your favorite part of college?" I asked her, excited to learn everything about her.

"Drugs and sex are what win my heart."

"I can do both."

"Do you have mushrooms?"

"Yes, the best ones. We're heading up the mountain tomorrow. Join us! It'll be the best kind of drug day."

The same way a surfer looks forward to the perfect waves and wind conditions, I sought after the ideal climates for inducing wild psychedelic mind-walks. We had already figured out the drugs were not going to kill us. The generation before had been using drugs hard for about ten years, and people still died young of stupidity, not marijuana or mushrooms.

"We are a sophisticated group of druggies, operating under many rules to keep us safe." I winked at Becky as if in a spy movie.

"Rules? These I gotta hear!"

"Have fun, keep out of jail, be sure to get the most trip for the money, and stay alive. We only use drugs from true and tested sources."

"Where do you get them?"

I had this neighbor, Paul, who owned a record store, and that instantly made him cool. He would host these incredibly decadent parties where everything was available, and the only charge was a plate of nachos.

The next day, Becky returned to my abode. She had on expensive ski clothes and matching snow boots. She was excited to try the drugs, her attitude as happy as a clam. We went to Paul's house with our gourmet nachos: fried wontons covered with California rolls and tobiko. I learned that bringing decadent food was an instant way to make friends.

Paul had planned a mushroom field trip for us in the snow at the summit of Mt. Rose. We all assembled before hitting the road. His house was decorated with thousands of vinyl records hammered into the walls. The furniture was covered in tattered sheets. There were dusty cobwebs hanging from the ceiling that resembled small mummies. Paul had classic man cave decor with an old eraser board from a classroom leaned up against the fireplace, which was loaded with empty Olympia beer cans. The rules were written on the board in multicolored chalk.

RULES FOR PRACTICAL HIGH ON MAGICAL MUSHROOMS

1. Everyone is in a good mood, with no broken hearts or sullen faces.
2. Always have a "Tour Director," someone who is not taking this or any other drugs and has a driver's license.
3. Always do them outdoors.
4. Never mix with alcohol.
5. Everyone must have a buddy.
6. Clear your calendar for at least 13 hours.
7. Take them on an empty stomach.

We had learned that you were guaranteed a good trip and the maximum benefit of the drug if you followed the list. We hopped into four-wheel drives and headed up the mountain. At this point, I only knew Becky. There were twenty of us, and to get to know each other better, Paul gave each of us a different job. I oversaw the passing out of the shrooms from a paper shopping bag filled to the rim. I walked up to each person, but to Becky first.

"How much do you want? Do you prefer stems or caps?"

"Honestly, I've never tried them before. What do you suggest?"

"Try a little of both and take them with beef jerky."

"Why jerky?"

"They'll make you gag."

"You mean like swallowing?"

"Yeah, about the same aftertaste."

We giggled at the sexual innuendo and swallowed a handful of fetid enchantment.

"I don't know what to expect. Will I lose control?"

"Only in the best way."

Becky and I sat on the top of the snowy hillside. We were starting to trip and enjoyed getting to know each other. Being that close to the sky is always exhilarating, but add in the mushrooms, and it becomes euphoric. The evergreens and the snowdrifts loomed large and picturesque.

She was full of questions.

"Will we see snakes and monsters?"

"Only the best kind."

"How long does a mushroom trip last?"

"Forever. It will change the way you look at things. Mushrooms have been used by shamans and medicine men for thousands of years."

"How much is magic, and how much will be real?"

"It's all magic."

"How do you tell if you're high?"

"You do this." I waved my fingers in front of her face, the international sign for "Am I high?"

She ooohed at the tracers coming off my fingers. The sun glistened off the snow crunching under foot. We walked over to a clearing and saw eight bodies lying face down. At first, I was alarmed, but we heard muffled giggling coming from the bodies in the snowbank. I went over to shake one of the girls, and she popped up.

"Hey! I was talking to snow people. If you fall face-first with a straight body into the snow, after you hit, you bounce back, and there are about three inches between your face and the snow. Living in there are little snow people who will tell you the ways of their world."

Becky and I shared looks and launched into the snow face-first.

We stayed like that for a long time, and then I felt her tap me on the back.

"I need to pee."

"Me too."

"How are we going to get down?"

"I thought I might fly."

I jumped up and hurled myself down the mountain slope on my belly. I was giggling so hard, I peed in my snowsuit. Small amounts of pee spewed out from the legs and armholes of the snowsuit as I slid down the hill, leaving a yellow track behind. The more the pee squirted out, the harder I laughed and the more I peed. This sent the whole shroomed crowd into gales of laughter.

Becky took a slow sled down, met me at the bottom, and helped rid the liquid from inside the snowsuit. Nothing cements a friendship like peeing and drug trips. She moved in with me the following week.

My house was a combination of thrift store finds and trash-day come-across items until Becky moved in. She used her dad's credit card to buy us luxury items from Pier One. She bought new kitchen accoutrements that helped with my culinary exploration. Exotic spices from Africa and Brazil made my meals come alive. And I swore that eating on matching plates made everything taste better. Becky bought the ingredients, and I cooked every night. Each day started with egg burritos stuffed with chorizo, jalapeños, and an exotic cheese. I had only had Velveeta cheese up until then—Gouda and bleu made me cheesegasm. I felt fancy because a new culinary world opened. I was sure that this was as virtuous as life was going to get for me.

22

I was not able to hold a job longer than six months because of a tardiness habit as well as my opinionated ramblings. These judgments were never based on real-world fact. My need to control every situation made me unemployable. While a standard personality trait for adult children of alcoholics, my wild independence hurt my ability to sustain gainful employment. In a thirteen-month period, I worked as a collector at a collection agency, waitress, bartender, store clerk, jewelry store clerk, pharmaceutical clerk, law secretary, hotel desk attendant, and doctor's receptionist. I was stealing from every employer, supplementing my income and desire to cook. From the doctor's office, I took only the doctor's son's picture from the wall as I intended to bed him.

I kept this faux beau's pinched high school graduation picture over my dresser, believing that if I gazed into his two-tone eyes each day, I would draw him to me. I had only met Stuart briefly at his father's office while I answered the phone and typed death certificates. Pleasantries were exchanged and my heart skipped a beat. Luck would have it that around 3:00 a.m. at a local disco bar, where I had come to exchange stolen quaaludes for magic mushrooms from the bartender, Stuart bumped into me on the dance floor. We danced, pulling out my dirty disco moves. We screamed over the thumping base how surprised we were to meet in this wretched place.

"Hey, Miss Mills! What are you doing in a place like this?" (Miss Mills a reference to the college I had been accepted to.)

"Looking for love in all the wrong places."

"I thought you were a goody-goody."

"I'm good at some things. Want to give it a whirl?"

Retreating out back where the smokers hid and inhaled, I grabbed him hard by the shoulders and wrapped one leg around him, pinning his hardening body to mine. I French-kissed his quivering mouth like my life depended on it. Stuart was surprised and thrilled. He had thought of me as a mousy desk girl who always had a postage stamp in her purse.

I invited him back to the house, and he followed. I tossed him onto the couch and sucked his cock until he screamed in pleasure and agony for me to stop. He sensed my urgency and lack of self-worth in my sad blue eyes. Then he fucked me carefully as one would do to a sick lover, kissed my forehead, and bid me adieu.

I was torn, having never witnessed this tenderness. Confused by the night and having no way to get a hold of him, I began my stalking efforts to find this perplexing man and get him back into bed. I wiggled his number and address out of the nurse within a day. Not understanding boundaries, I showed up at his doorstep the next day, bearing fresh cherry pie.

Being a kind soul, he explained. "I am in the height of law school. I have no time to do anything except study."

"I can make you more relaxed with a blowjob."

"I have only one night a month that I could entertain anything besides studying."

"What night is that? I can put you in my Day-Timer."

"This won't be more than sex. I won't arrive until after midnight."

"That works for me!"

It became our relationship: the faux beau and the less-than-worthy girl. Each first Monday, he would celebrate with his comrades the passing or failing of the test, and then he would proceed to my house for much-needed sexual release. I adored this idea, for it gave me the rest of the month to find worthy boyfriends like mechanics to fix my 1976 Pinto, waiters to feed me, and 7-Eleven clerks for free cigarettes. Once a month at midnight, Stuart would tap on my window and sing Carly Simon songs until I would wake and let him climb inside. We would rejoice in the athletic prowess of his need and my dysfunction. Then we would drink cheap red wine, tell stories, and laugh. When the sun rose, he would leave by the front door.

23

October 16, 1980, Sparks, Nevada, USA

I had volunteered for a new theater group because my narcissistic need for acceptance had grown to the point where spotlights were required. Theater groups are an eccentric lot. Becky and I joined the off-campus dysfunctional cluster to find new adventures. The company was called Hadassah. They came to existence one night after a case of chardonnay was shared by several bored, pampered Jewish housewives who could not stand the fact that their most remarkable achievement in life had been raising spoiled children (especially since the nannies did most of the work). The group was formed with the sole theatrical purpose of performing *Fiddler on the Roof.*

The staff of actors, directors, and producers were chosen for their ability to take direction and entertain the jaded American princesses. The primary director, Ed, was a man of somewhere between 18 and 50. He was brutally handsome with Beethoven snow-white hair, a goatee, and crazed aquamarine eyes. His steady ingestion of illegal substances sustained him, making sure he never slept but was often in bed. I had good reason to believe he subsisted on sleeping with one or all the founding mothers of Hadassah. His ex-wife was the producer, also part of the company, and hated his guts. His girl-friend participated as the makeup artist and seemed forever in a state of para-noia. She was sure someone would steal this treasure of an unemployed, pill-popping, lying sex fiend.

Rehearsals were every night from 6 p.m. to 9 p.m. with Fridays off for Sabbath. The theater group had 50 thespians and support people, all dysfunc-tional showoffs.

I was to be the assistant director and Ed's secondary. For all his weak-nesses and idiosyncrasies, Ed remained brilliant. In my flawed erotic tastes, he became one that must be netted.

I believed if someone could harness his genius and guide him, miracles would occur. Becky loathed him and the maladjusted rabbit hole he was leading me down. I'd learned to gauge Ed's mood on what drug he was taking. His creative output was vast. He lived as a writer who would work for three solid days and then not be able to write his name. I was instantly sure I could fix him with my love.

Ed played fragile but strong, hanging on to life but always letting go. He created plays, poetry, and short stories but never finished them. He left each project abandoned when it stopped challenging him. He knew Hunter S. Thompson and drove a red convertible Mercedes SL450 on a suspended license. He volunteered in elementary school drama programs. He never wore long pants, yet he secreted a sexual power that remained unprecedented. Ed broadcasted to the back of the stage on our first meeting, "My goal is to capture you, fuck you senseless, and teach you to let go."

At nineteen, I lingered in a delusional fog of youth, unable to grasp that this man would be my undoing. I recognized his intellect and predicted I could learn everything I needed to make a creative existence for myself.

Ed's production crew was motley. Like him, sober times didn't come often. They dealt and used drugs for a living. Theater was a hobby. The production team met every night at the Mapes Hotel and Casino, a 60-year-old casino in the heart of downtown Reno. The beautiful old building was an architect's dream in the 1920s but now an eyesore in the neon-splashed 1980s. Red velvet walls, carnival confetti carpets, and decrypted slot machines greeted you with the smell of stale beer. The clanking of coins falling into steel trays from two cherries created a hope of wealth, and the windowless expanses of people throwing away hard-earned money told another story. We rehearsed on the top floor (twenty-two up from the casino) in the Grand Ballroom. This room was one of the premier performing spots in the 1940s. A magnificent, curved stage was created to carry a crooner's voice. Frank Sinatra, Dean Martin, and Elvis had performed there. The fold-down, velvet-textured chairs now had more gaping wounds than fabric. It was acoustically perfect, as the walls were covered in an ancient velvet paper. We stole lumber from the old props to create Tevia's village.

The ladies of Hadassah were in their glory. They had a purpose, teaching gentiles the art of bagel eating while everyone got Friday nights off for the Sabbath. They were consistently coaching the crew on the correct pronunciation of Jewish words. They had Ed to flirt and fiddle with as he made each woman believe she was the only one with a deranged sense of entitlement.

I auditioned the actors who would play the singing, abused Jews. An ancient holy man played the rabbi, and half of the cast was comprised of authentic Jews (per Hadassah's orders). The rabbi would leave practice about twenty minutes in to go downstairs to play Keno. The only normal person on the cast was Stuart, my late-night friend who was studying to be an attorney. His college instructor told him theater was a solid training environment for his courtroom work. He was as handsome as David Cassidy, with a long, flowing mullet that feathered back like Farrah Fawcett's hair. He was cast as a Russian soldier because of his strong physique and long legs. He was quick to laugh and seemed enchanted by me. I spent after-rehearsal hours teaching him how to Barynya. He became my faux beau, as everyone assumed that our afterwork was done completely horizontal. But we maintained the once-a-month rendezvous for it now suited my schedule.

Ed awoke each day around 5 a.m., popped six amphetamines, and ran off to the theater. He would sit on the half-constructed stage and absorb the energy of the wood and design. He would write, preach, and pontificate with one spotlight beamed on him. He would head out to service the Hadassah ladies for a couple of hours. He called it "errands." I believed it to be the first orgasms these women had in years, as they all began to smile and blush when he charged into a room.

When Ed discovered I was a budding chef, he came over every night, uninvited, for dinner and critiqued me while I cooked. I loved his company, trying to hang on to every word and gesture. He perched on the barstool, wide-armed, hanging on to the counter like it was moving. He spewed knowledge and creative ideas. He deemed me his scullery maid, and I found it to be a compliment. I believed there existed some unique magic in his eccentricity. He would smoke a joint to prepare for dinner, claiming it made the food taste better. After dinner, he would improv a one-man play. This nightly routine grew into an intimate situation, and soon he replayed the details of his daily sexual conquest. He professed to have an oral fixation that rendered him successful on the lonely housewives' couches. He loved to consume them until they screamed his name and promised any amount of money to continue his theater quests. He talked of the plays he had written. The poetry he knew he could write. The man he wanted to be. What got me, drew me in, was his talk of my potential. I was a diamond in the rough, and only he could add facets.

Ed would stare intensely into my eyes and promise, "I'll make you special. Hold on tight because it's going to be a bumpy ride. Can I please fuck you?"

I sensed that the act of fornicating would end the mentor program and make me one of the girls he ran from. The answer stayed, "Not yet."

Each night at rehearsal, we would squeak out as much talent as possible from the diminutive cast. I would take the actors aside and run lines, trying to pull out some depth. Some responded beautifully. Others remained like black and white TV screens, which I was sure was all their futures held. The actors would leave, and the production crew would work on the sets. They would hammer and laugh until midnight when Ed had to go to his only real job—night desk clerk at a rent-by-the-hour motel. This job was a gift from one of the Hadassah husbands. Out front was a dangling neon sign that blinked the words "Hourly Rates." When you checked in, you got a set of sheets and one facecloth with tattered edges. There was a dirty linen basket outside the front door to return them to when the excursion was done. It was situated in the heart of downtown Reno, so gamblers on a run and their companions visited daily. It was a busy place.

Ed worked from midnight until his girlfriend could stand it no more.

She drove her Pacer to the hotel to protect him. She would burst in, nerves raw and exposed, sure he'd be hiding "some bitch" under the desk. Her eyes would leak, and her mouth begged him to come home with the promise of a lengthy blowjob. He left the desk unattended and went home for his oral pleasure. After, he would pop sleeping pills and go to a dreamscape where demented minds trek.

When the drugs wore off around 5 a.m., he sprung to consciousness, manic and desperate. He picked up the pink princess phone to call me in this maniacal state, starting off both our days in disarray. I had become the voice of reason in his fevered brain. I soothed him, sharing stories that he later turned into prose. He simultaneously built me up and then would browbeat me. It was a relationship I was accustomed to.

24

November 1, 1980, Sparks, Nevada, USA

When the word got out to the theater group that I resided in a spacious house and loved to cook, cast and crew started camping on the couch. Coming over after rehearsal, they solicited to crash on my floor. I told them I would feed everyone, but they could only stay for one night. This was the first time I knew that food was my love language. It was also when my boundaries blurred. Not that I was ever good at confrontation. I wanted everyone to love me because my father hadn't. Not one trespasser helped pay rent or power or purchase groceries. Becky was amused with this cast of freeloaders, but I knew it would wear on her.

I was slotted to start Mills College in the fall. I had a full ride and was going to be the next governor of Nevada. Meanwhile, I worked to save for school and pay my rent. I happened to be the only legally working member of the cast. Becky still lived off her parents' credit cards. Ed reminded me I had an obligation to take in the homeless and hungry crew for the sake of the play. Not that I complained—I reveled in the instant party that coexisted with the theater bums. At night, our living room looked like a tray full of enchiladas: everyone bundled in their sleeping bags or Mexican blankets, all huddled together. Fascinated by the abundance of drugs they all had and shared, I tried new experiences. I wanted to replicate Ed's maniac genius using psyche-delics and surrounding myself with "his people." With each new drug, I was sure I could influence the isolated place where Ed's creativity flowed. I could analyze his gift and transmute it into my solid creative career.

25

November 30, 1980, Reno, Nevada, USA

The time of snow, freezing temperatures, holiday parties galore, family Christmas hell, and my birthday. I hated December, the curse of being born around the capitalist high holiday. I remained surly for the entire month. That year, I vowed it would be different. My hard work was going to pay off in a successful show, and I happened to be too busy to acknowledge a birthday. The *Fiddler on the Roof* run started December 10th and ran through the 29th, and I had decided to take Ed as a lover. Or he wore me down. Still trying to find the formula to get the brilliance out of Ed, I made up my mind on a mushroom trip. Through his stories, I discovered the only thing that would hold his attention for any amount of time was sex. This seemed a dangerous game with a regular theater man, but downright lethal with Ed's montage of ex-wives, girlfriends, and Hadassah clientele. I believed I could handle anything he threw my way if I kept the greater goal in mind.

I was in no way an innocent virgin, but my emotional center remained more damaged than I knew. My control was a façade. I had been hardcore regarding men and dating. To me, they were toys, an amusing way to pass the time and get a free dinner. Becky and I started to write a book called *Life in the Fast Lane as Seen By a Pedestrian*. It was a dating manual on how to get the most out of single existence. We considered our courting exuberance research for the book. We tried things like having three dates in one night without them knowing about each other. Common assumptions remained about only dating men who could serve a purpose—a mechanic to work on cars, a Pepsi delivery man for caffeine fixes, and many waiters for free food. Men were our commodities. We even had a manager from 7-Eleven for free cigarettes. Comfortable using and abusing men, I especially did not take them seriously. I saw no purpose for men in my life other than mild amusement and the off-chance to feel loved.

26

December 1, 1980, Reno, Nevada, USA

The cast of *Fiddler* had attended a Jewish temple ceremony after which I took Ed back to the house to feed him. The house was empty for a rare moment as the rest of the commune happened to be at Trader Nick's, drinking strong Polynesian drinks out of a dragon bowl with long straws. I lit the candles and turned on Cat Stevens. I brought out a bottle of Blue Nun wine. We sat on the couch, talking about the new play he had written. I listened, complimented him, and hung on every word. I went in for the kill.

"I had a dream about you last night."

The narcissistic genius loved that he was correct in the idea that he ruled my subconscious. He moved closer, began to stroke the inside of my forearm.

"Tell me about it?"

I botched a blush and continued, "I can't tell you, it's too embarrassing."

He moved closer, a gleam in his maniacal eyes.

"You can tell me anything."

"We were swimming together in Lake Tahoe. After, we lay in the warm sand, trying to bring our body temperatures back to normal after soaking in the freezing mountain water. You stroked and touched me with your silken hands until I shuddered from the warmth of it all."

He moved in closer and whispered, "Tell me more."

"I was taken aback by the beauty of your rippling muscles and the strength of your legs. I became frightened when I saw the length and size of your manhood and held my breath as you gently climbed on top of me."

Sucking air noisily out of his mouth, nostrils flared, Ed seemed captivated by the story and the promise of the forbidden land he would conquer. He moved closer, eyes heavy, wrapping his arms around my shoulder. "I'm going to consume you," he groaned into my ear.

"You made mystical love to me. I writhed and twisted my sheets. I woke up all wet." With the hook adequately set, he spun me and started to rub my back. I closed my eyes and moaned.

Moving around to the front, he whispered onto my lips, "That's it, what I've been waiting for, let me in, and let me show you the way."

We made love right there on the communal couch. Having sex with a madman was exceptionally different than the sane ones. Sane men take their partner's clues and desire to shape lovemaking. Insane Casanovas only think of themselves. Jumping from one debase act to the next, only reveling in their pleasure. This was the selfish indulgence control I was accustomed to because of my dysfunctional history. I had learned young that I didn't matter to the people who loved me. He jumped out of my bed at midnight to go to work. I pulled back the sheets to see if his form was seared into the sheets.

The next night after dinner, he started rubbing my thigh.

"Stop." But to no avail. He cocked his head and moved his hand up my thigh. "Please . . . I'm sorry," I squeaked in my little girl's voice. That stopped him. He stood still for a minute before he turned to face me.

He met my eyes but offered nothing.

"I'm scared," I panted.

"Scared of what? You are in your house. You own everything in the house and everybody around you! How could you fear anything?"

"I don't own you, and I never will . . . nor do I want to."

He didn't even know where to start. It was what he longed to hear from a woman but seldom did.

I moved closer to him and murmured in a soft voice, "I'm used to being in charge. I guess that's where I get my bravado. You scare me. You are an unknown, a wild card. I don't want to lose you. I'm willing to learn how to trust with you."

Not sure which head he was thinking with, he opened his arms, and I walked into them. We embraced until my body melded with his. I led him by the hand to my bedroom. We stood on the plush carpet and entrapped each other like jasmine vine. We fell on the bed and lay entwined for several long minutes. I felt him begin to stir and harden. I treasured the enraptured power I had over men. The ability to stimulate and get a real, tangible response. He moaned gently into my ear and moved his hand to pinch and pull my mammilla. He stroked my breast with the backs of his fingers, allowing his manicured fingernails to rake down the swell of my breast and shock my hardened nipple with the contrasting sharpness.

He lowered his hand and found my wetness. He barely grazed my pearl and stroked the wet folds of me, gently massaging my wetness around the outside of my sex. He marveled at how wet I got. He moved his hand to his own hardness and used it to guide himself into me. He pushed and manipulated the beautiful resistance and the welcoming clinch.

Later, the house was full of partying freeloaders, and the waves of laughter enticed Ed to them. He sauntered into the living room, wearing only my silk kimono. I moved from the wet spot to his side, which still burned with his essence.

27

December 3, 1980, Reno, Nevada, USA

I supposed I could entice Ed with sex for control, if only for a brief time. But this was no ordinary man. Off-kilter people live life on the fringes and do not hold up to the same pressure as the rest of the world. He had no worries, no preoccupations; he lived 100 percent in the moment. When a moment meant sex, he stayed Olympian in his technique. I was in a constant state of horny: panting, amazed, and tantalized by his gentleness and endless amount of energy. He made love with extreme confidence in trying anything new with pure joy and enthusiasm. After a four-hour romp, I had to call it quits, exhausted and overwhelmed. Ed was unaffected and hungry. Control wasn't going to be as easy as I had believed. A potential danger, I could see falling fast and hard for this man and his bedroom gymnastics.

I remained more affected by the lovemaking than I had planned. I became twitterpated. I understood why all these women were trying to hold on to Ed. He was a genius coital partner, and his oral skills were unprecedented. Sex was intense, pleasurable, and prolonged. After Ed, I vowed to always have a half-crazed lover.

My brain was beginning to melt. Instead of being focused and on task, my mind began to wander back to the sack with Ed. I was officially in trouble. Ed coexisted unaffected and went back to the business at hand as *Fiddler* was opening in one week.

He left our bed to go meet with one of the Hadassah Hags.

"Don't leave!" I whined from the soaked sheets.

"I have to get a check and do my obligatory serving."

"I will give you anything. Please stay!"

Ed looked at me and crooked his head the way a dog does when he hears a strange sound. "Are you trying to possess me?"

I shook my tresses to clear my mind and yelled a bit too loud to be convincing.

"No, no, no. Go, go. I will see you tonight."

After he left, I gathered my brain from the hazy fog of orgasm. I drank a huge glass of water and sat down to write a mission statement; more of a plan to net his genius. This writing to work out my feelings was becoming a compelling habit. I could script my way out of trouble—of that, I was sure.

I walked into rehearsal that night and saw Ed huddled over, romancing one of the young cast members. My mind liquefied. This behavior was nothing new for Ed. He chased everything from Yenta to Zidel. Suddenly, I wanted to smash the girl's skull. Jealousy had come for the first time, and I could not believe it. Here I was, snared in my own trap.

Furious and about to leave the play forever, I turned to go. He sensed my presence. Ed turned around, caught my eye, smiled, and winked like the mad hatter. I went weak in the knees.

Later, I paid him back. I was sitting with Ed's ex-wife (who he still fucked) and his pathetic girlfriend, discussing makeup and costumes. He entered, yelling at someone behind him. When he turned and looked, he saw three paramours happily sitting together and chatting. He froze. He couldn't move. In one flash, his life caught up with him, and he looked terrified. If anyone knew he had added me to his stable, a war would ensue, and the play would not go on. With a moment of clarity, I discerned the ball was back in my court.

Ed's schedule now included dinner and sex with me every evening before rehearsal. I was losing focus but occasionally would get a few moments of the genius I required. I became like a Brubaker Christmas Carousel, spinning faster as the candle gets hotter.

He burst into the door at 5 p.m., singing "If I Were a Rich Man." Arms thrust over his head and taking deep bows with his knees. "Hey, doll! What's cooking?"

He wrapped his arms around me at the stove and blew into my ear. "I'm hungry for everything, but first, let's eat!"

"I made homemade pasta with Calabrian chilies and baby broccoli. I scored a rib eye at the half-off sale."

"You aren't going to poison me with old meat, are you?"

"As long as you don't poison me with your old meat!"

He slapped my ass hard and crossed to the fridge to help himself to the Blue Nun.

We ate together while I gained self-esteem points as he inhaled the food and made yummy sounds.

Sex with Ed became an obsession and enhanced each time, as it does when you know someone's body and clandestine erogenous zones. Ed would throw me on the bed and talk in deep, silky tones about how beautiful I was and how he readied to taste every inch of my body. He kissed me with delicate lips, barely touching. He moved down to my neck and would attack it until I would tremble. He started soft on the nipples and bit down hard, a sensation that made me scream out loud. He moved down my stomach and buried his head between my legs, kissing my thighs gently and burning his fingertips into my skin. He touched and suckled me in ways I had never dreamed. I could sense his silver hair on my thighs, and his beard tickled my sex. He brought me to orgasm and started over. He insisted on multiple orgasms and continued to work, spelling out the alphabet with his tongue on my clit until I squealed in ecstasy. He slowly and gently raised himself up and entered. The whole time he fucked, he kept his eyes open, spewing heartfelt compliments and declarations of yearning. When he finally came, he roared like a lion and collapsed, panting on top of me, falling to sleep, purring like a kitten.

I became his beck-and-call girl. I was undone with lust, love, envy, and joy. All the good stuff.

28

December 8, 1980, Reno, Nevada, USA

After an extremely aerobic sex session, quietly making noise and basking in the glow of the eternal, he commenced my demise. Petting my side with the back of his hand, he hummed, "Gail, I need $1,000."

Still in an orgasm coma, I murmured, "Of course."

"I will pay you back, but I need it tomorrow. It's for the play."

Coming around, my hackles up, "I understood with those rich bitches backing us, we never needed money. Have you hit them up?"

"Okay, I will, but you know the toll I have to pay." Ed started to dress, leaving a cold spot on the sheets I wasn't ready to accept.

"Fine, I will write you a check tomorrow from work." Ed smiled and kissed me deep until my head began to swim again with desire.

I had a job as a bookkeeper for a moving company. I hated the job, the smelly moving guys and, especially, the owner. The steel desks were all scuffed on the sides, and secondhand desk chairs were stained with coffee and smelled of old milk. My office was in a double-wide trailer next to the garage filled with diesel-spouting moving vans. I had handled the finances for a year for this 500-pound momma's boy who pretended to run his parents' business. He hid in his office and subsisted on eating M&M's and watching soap operas. I had no respect for him or his rules. Some light adjusting of the ledger would handle this larceny. I was certain this Jabba the Hutt would never miss $1,000, and Ed had promised to pay it back. I justified the theft in my mind. Little to ask since Ed fucked me every night until my brain collapsed. This boss was an idiot, and Ed needed it.

The crime was easy. I wrote a check and forged the second signature, took it to the department store where my mother worked, where it was easily cashed. After handing the pile of money to Ed, he rewarded me by eating my pussy for two hours.

At this point in my frenzied sex-soaked life, I had five extra people crashing at my house. Becky had one room, and she was the only paying member of the fraternity. The rest slept on couches and floors and were all in the Fiddler play with their only paying gig being dealing drugs. They used the house as a dispensary and stored massive quantities of marijuana, cocaine, and magic mushrooms. There were substantial garbage bags of stinkweed stored in the hall closet, a pound of cocaine in the dishwasher, and two pounds of mushrooms on the sun porch. I did not know it, but the police had been watching the house and my freeloading friends.

29

December 18, 1980, Reno, Nevada, USA

I woke up on a chilly December morning and recognized it was my birthday. Having entered my twentieth year on the planet, I was optimistic that this day would not suck like the previous nineteen. Ed popped in for a pit stop at 6 a.m., done with his night job and on the way to his drama school position. He sang "Happy Birthday" loud enough to wake up the whole house as he fucked me from behind.

The house had a colossal celebration planned for that night. Less a recognition of my birthday, and more of a bacchanal because someone stole eight handles of hard liquor. There were new mushrooms to try as well as a new strain of pot. They planned to dance until they tore up the carpet. I left the party-planning to the couch surfers and went to work.

Sitting at my desk, smiling and still reeling from the birthday ditty, Jabba waddled into my office and grunted for me to follow him. I shadowed him to his office, where there were two plainclothes policemen—a fact derived from their bad-fitting suits, skinny ties, and mustaches. The color drained from my face. The officer flashed his badge and began a tale of a missing check they were investigating.

"Do you know anything about this $1,000 stolen check?"

"No, officer. I have no knowledge of any missing checks." Hands sweating little ponds of fear, I tried not to panic.

"Why is it made out to you and has your signature on the back?"

I shook my head, refusing to accept the pending doom.

"I have no idea."

I wasn't convincing. They handcuffed me and led me outside, his hand on my head as I entered the car.

As they drove me to the Reno Police Department, I struggled not to cry. I resisted the mindset to blame my birthday curse. I believed that Ed would bail me out. They set me in a stark room with a diligent detective who looked like a combination of Donny Osmond and Karl Malden.

"Gail, if you come clean, everything will be better."

Possessing skills that adult children of alcoholics acquire, I remained stoic and full of denial. I was never going to admit to the theft.

"We know there is a large number of narcotics in your house. We also know you don't sell them. Maybe use a bit, but the lease is in your name. You are looking at ten years in Nevada State Prison. Tell us who stole the check, and we may give you only five."

The detective's handsome nose grilled me for three hours. I kept my eyes glued to his Necco candy–sized wart. It held my attention and kept me calm. I never admitted to the forgery. Playing a part in a B-movie, I never cried. Outside, my composure stayed solid and sure. My insides were swirling with trepidation. After six hours, he released me. He advised me to find a new domicile and a good attorney as soon as possible.

Driving my Pinto over plowed, murky snow roads, I sobbed. I knew the police were not going to let me go. They knew about the drugs; they knew about the forgery. It was a matter of time before I would be locked away for a long time.

When I got home, the occupiers prepared for the party by wrapping joints and placing mushrooms in individual-sized helpings. They were also making their favorite party drink: "Get 'em Drunk and Fuck 'em Punch." This potent potion mixed in a fifty-gallon garbage can contained gallons of vodka, rum, gin, and Everclear mixed with slices of fruit and juice. They stirred the brew with a broom handle, and it ate the paint off.

Looking at what life had become, I comprehended with absolute clarity that I had to escape. With dysfunction ruling over survival, I indulged in one last hurrah.

Emerging from my room, I looked beautiful but contemplative, dressed in a blue satin camisole with blue eye shadow and ironed straight hair.

Becky recognized grumpy December birthday syndrome and attempted to cheer me up.

"Have some punch! Smoke a joint!"

I announced to the crowd, "This is the last shindig on Taylor Street; make it a good one, because in the morning, I'm moving out."

"Mushrooms are in order!" a Russian soldier ordered while performing a Prisyadka.

They doused me with three shares of mushrooms. I loved traveling down Alice's rabbit hole. We all ate handfuls of magic mushrooms served from a paper bag. Joints were rolled like burritos in a Pyrex dish with the garbage can full of hooch to wash it all down. I took a coffee mug of the punch and swallowed two servings of fungi. The winding mind trip came upon me quickly and occurred both magical and insightful. I retreated to my room. Sitting on the bed and looking in the mirror, my face looked like a deck of cards. I could smell the moonlight coming through the window. I could taste the pink color of the lace bedspread. My mind created astonishing works of art. I was having a magnificent psychedelic trip.

A sudden, loud knock upon the door triggered my paranoia. Even at twenty, I remained terrified of the closet at night. Childhood dramas played out in my wardrobe. When I heard noises coming from it, I was sure the monsters that had plagued my youth were finally going to succeed. The positive buzz that started this trip now turned to panic. Fear in a psychedelic state is magnified, and it can be dangerous. I was paralyzed, holding my cookie monster plush, too scared to move. I saw the terror of observation and could sense the essence of death. The screams of the black light deafened me.

Breaking the spell, Ed exploded into the room. He came to check on me, as he had heard declarations of an escape and wanted to prevent me from leaving at all costs.

"Hey, kid! How are you doing?"

"Check the closet."

"Your pupils are so dilated. How many shrooms did you ingest?"

"Check the closet."

When Ed opened the door, four people came tumbling out of the closet, all naked.

I screeched and pointed out the door. "Monsters dissipate!" I yelled. They ran from the room and entered the hall closet, slamming the door and shutting out the realm.

Attempting to calm me and regain his power, Ed began to kiss me. His kisses that just that morning filled me with desire now tasted of bile. His hands that had brought much pleasure now caressed like sandpaper. His mind that I rejoiced in exploring now seemed muddled. I fled to the backyard, stumbling past my friends that were dancing so hard, the carpet had been worn thin. They laid upon each other like milk-drunk puppies.

Now outside and leaving the proximity of Ed and the closet, I continued the pleasurable part of the mushrooms. Chasing dragons resembling silhouettes in the trees. Harnessing the power of the dragon's snuffle, I saw rainbows dancing. Reality splintered again with the arrival of Stuart, my faux beau, for his weekly romp. He sang to my window, but it went unanswered. He knocked at the front door. Seeing the advanced drug-induced state of everyone, he retreated to the back yard to find me. He'd always seemed to ground me, but I told him of my afternoon, and he was disturbed. As a budding new defense attorney, he told me wisely that I was fucked. Now the mushroom trip moved to paranoia. As his dire diagnosis progressed, the words came out backward and in slow motion. This psychedelic yo-yo arose to break me. Stuart knew I was in too deep to fuck, so he bid me adieu.

As I headed back to the house after depositing Stuart into his car, I saw Ed running down the street, wearing my senior ball gown, holding a pumpkin in one hand and his penis in the other. It was time to take flight.

The party went on until 6 a.m. I was torn up from the floor up. I had moved out by 8:00 with the help of Stuart, who also took in Mercutio the cat, for I didn't want him to be a pussy on the lam. I watched Ed sleep like the seraph he pretended to be and kissed him goodbye on his forehead. This may have been the first man to love me, accepting every sharp edge and curve. What I did not know was that this would be the last man to love me without constraints for a decade.

30

October 5, 1981, Las Vegas, Nevada, USA

"Whoa, girl! That was some dysfunctional storytelling."

Cupcake was now looking out at the tigers as they laid in the hot sun. She was shaking her head.

"That's how I got here, the long version."

"Well, it makes sense that you ran. I just don't see the sense in you running here. I get the romance but not the logic."

I heard her words and knew she was right. There was not a straight line that brought me to this circus compound. "The pink tights lured me?"

"Ha!" she snorted and opened the door to yell at Alex who was humping a ball.

31

October 9, 1981, Las Vegas, Nevada, USA

Papi had always lived in the twenty-eight-foot trailer with Phileap, Marco, and me. Now with only the two of us, it reduced in size and privacy. The first day, I arose early and stayed on the same practice regiment. I couldn't fly on the big trapeze because three people were needed on the platform, so I practiced on the single trapeze. I swung until I could not hold on and fell to the ground, defeated.

The first night, I fed the dogs and made dinner for Papi. I took my meal out by the lion cage, which seemed cruel, but I sensed I needed the big cat's power. My heart ached as much as my hands. Abandonment seemed to be my destiny.

After dark, I settled down in my bunk to read. Papi came back, shouting something about practice. Waving his hands widely, he approached me on the bunk. He placed one hand on my shoulder, pinning me to the bed. I could smell the whiskey as his face became entangled in my hair. I protested, and he touched my abdomen like he was trying to get me to flex my core. That was not what the old man was after.

He placed his forearm across my neck, stopping airflow as he grabbed my crotch. He positioned his body on mine. I screamed and tried to get out from under him as he drooled into my ear. The wet saliva gave me a power surge, and I exploded out from under him. I punched at him as he advanced, now looking like a version of the big bad wolf wanting to eat me. He launched and threw me on the ground, pulling his pants down as he restrained me. He humped my leg, and I felt a warm ooze drip down my thigh. My mind laser-focused as prey often does. One well-placed knee came up, and I connected with his balls. He screamed, groaned, and rolled off. I stumbled for the door and scampered down the steel steps, running for the garage full of tigers. Slamming the door, they all turned to look. They could smell my fear. The black panther licked his cage. The tiger slapped a powerful paw at the lock, and Alex roared.

32

ctober 10, 1981, Las Vegas, Nevada, USA

My first call for help went unanswered. Which was fine, as my parents had neither the funds nor charity of heart to rescue me. My second call was to Becky, who rescued me within an hour, sending her sister to take me from the compound to the airport. She met me at the Reno airport and took me to her house where I cried for hours in the bath trying to get the stain off me. She sat on the tub and filled a glass of wine for me.

"What the fuck is going on there?"

"It was okay until he left me."

"Here is an obvious question. Why did you stay when he left you?"

"I don't know. I was in shock. I assumed I was going, and then they left."

"That should have been the point when you ran to the bus. Jesus, Gail, this is bad even for you."

"I know. But the police are still looking for me. I have no money. I made the commitment to the troupe. I thought I was doing the right thing."

"You don't think too clearly when it comes to Phileap."

"I know. I can't believe his dad did this to me."

"You should call the police."

"I can't. He would never forgive me."

"You should never forgive him."

"I love him."

"You need your head examined."

She was right. I was still in a state of shock and had no idea what to do next. No one knew I was home except Becky.

❦

There was no way to get in touch with Phileap. He would not know I was gone until he arrived home from Monaco. A fitful night turned into an impossible day when Becky announced at breakfast that the Reno PD had been asking about me, and she was pretty sure I had a warrant for my arrest. I could not stay with her because I didn't want to involve her. I called my parents. They picked me up in my car and told me that I would have to pay to stay with them now that I was a famous circus adult.

"You aren't so smart now," my dad scolded as he drove me to Steamboat.

"I never alleged it was smart to join the circus. It was adventurous, exciting."

"This is stupid beyond even you, Gail. You left college to do this clown thing, and now you up and leave for no good reason."

"There was a moral motivation."

"You wouldn't know moral if it hit you in the face."

Beaten down and seeing what a farce I had turned my life into, I crawled into my old bed and stayed for a week.

33

October, 1981, Reno, Nevada, USA

The job market in Reno was easy to infiltrate, and I went to work at Gemco as the jewelry counter girl. My body was rock hard, and I hated to lose all the benefits of the training. I ran and climbed jungle gyms at the park every day after work. I continued my servitude as the culinary scullery maid for my parents but went out clubbing with Becky every night. It had been three weeks since Phileap had left, and he was due back in Las Vegas. I doubted he missed me. I wondered if he even cared I was gone. I had long conversations with Becky about how to handle the Papi situation. Becky assured me if Phileap truly loved me, he would stand up for me against his father. How wrong she was.

I did not assimilate back into life with my parents, working, or clubbing. It all was empty, like I was shimmering above them, waiting for my time to go back to the circus life. But the consideration scared me as much as remaining. I waited to hear from Phileap.

He finally called—collect from London. I accepted the charges even as my dad hissed in the background.

"Hello, Apple Pie!"

Drinking in the sound of his voice, "Hello, Phileap. How are you? Where are you?"

"We stuck in London. Visas not good. You help?"

Without hesitation, I told him I would help.

"You good, Apple Pie! We get you flying soon. I think about you often."

And the hook was set. I went about getting the Flying Córdobas back to the United States, forgetting all the ugliness.

Nevada is a small state, and it is easy to be connected to influential people. It turned out my faux beau Stuart was now a power broker attorney and was willing to help me again. He got the charges dropped and erased, so the fear of my arrest went away. All the theater drug dealers had fled to grow weed in the forests of Northern California. I ran into him at a club one night, and he held me tight, rocking to Seals and Croft. Stuart still housed Mercutio the cat and promised that I could visit and have a cuddle. We shared phone numbers and had been talking every night. He kept asking me out on proper dates, but I remained blindly loyal to Phileap. When I told him about the Córdobas' visa problems, he agreed to help. The favor cost me a lunch with Stuart, which I was happy to do as he always made me laugh. He pulled every string possible to get the Córdobas' visas approved, and within a few days, they boarded the next flight to the States. They landed in Las Vegas on a Saturday, and I did not hear from Phileap until Monday. My heart was baffled, hurt, scared. But even then, I was ready to leave Steamboat, no matter the cost. On the last night, Becky took me clubbing, and we did tequila shots as she dared strange men to touch my muscle-ripped stomach. She also entered me into an arm wrestling competition, making all the studs furious because I won every match. I was solid and disciplined in my body.

Becky and I had entirely too many Kamikazes. We danced and laughed all night. In a final attempt to get me from going back to Phileap, Becky took me to Stuart's house, left me on the front porch step, rang the bell, and ran. Stuart laughed and poured me into his bed.

When I awoke, the sheets were over my face. Still drunk, I did not recognize the pattern. Stuart rolled over and smiled. "Hello, Miss Circus!"

I sighed. "Thank God, it's you!"

He giggled. "You don't remember anything?"

"Did we fuck?"

"A gentleman never tells."

His home was a nice condo in the good part of town with heavy dark panels and crystal glassware for whiskey. His sheets were Egyptian cotton, and a massive cat condo looked out into a yard filled with birds. Mercutio hopped on my lap as I sipped bold French press coffee. I was struck that my cat was more adjusted than I. Stuart was doing so well having a conscience as an attorney in Nevada. He was being fast-tracked for the governor's office.

He made cinnamon pancakes topped with sour cream and brown sugar, and I told circus stories. He was captivated. The circus was now an anecdote for me, a way to seize any audience. Unsure if it was more, I probed about whether he wanted me to stay, to become his. He took his hands and cupped my face, staring lovingly with his two-tone eyes. "You need to be yours first."

34

November, 1981, Reno, Nevada, USA

I decided to go back to Las Vegas, even though I was neither invited nor welcome. I sold most of my belongings and packed what I could to take with me on this adventure back into the circus life. I left my parents my 1976 Ford Pinto that I had managed to pay off, because I knew I would need a car when I returned from life on the road. Phileap had a truck, so that would be my new transportation. I gave my clothes to my girlfriends. In my tiny new domicile, I would only have room for four outfits and a couple pairs of shoes. My biggest concern was what to do with my albums. Since I was eight, I had curated music, and each album represented so much more than a vinyl-pressed disc to me. It showed my growth, sadness, or enlightenment—my crossover from The Carpenters to ELO to Queen. I did not trust anyone to appreciate and save these for me, so I painstakingly copied them to cassette tapes. I decided not to do it one artist or album side at a time. I recorded a song and then a bit from one of my comedy albums between each track.

There was no way to do this job except to play them on the stereo and have my little yellow cassette player pressed against the speaker. I pushed record, started the record, and when the song was done, pushed stop. That's how I created twenty cassettes to take with me on the road. They became my lifeline for a long time. I played Queen, "Nothing's Gonna Stop Us Now," and a Monty Python clip from *Holy Grail* called "Bring out your Dead." I loved this combination of music and comedy and played the cassette on the long stretches of driving. David Bowie and *The Richard Pryor Show*. ELO and the Monty Python "Lumberjack Song" skit. Carpenters and a clip from Bill Cosby. Doobie Brothers to Rodney Dangerfield. Eagles to The Cars to Eddie Murphy.

This was the soundtrack that would follow me. In the middle of America, there is only country music playing on AM stations. There is only Pink Floyd and Kenny Rogers in Canada, and both can drive you mad on repeat. The front of the truck became my disco to program, and even Julio Iglesias snuck into my playlist.

Phileap let me know that they were back in Las Vegas, back at Cupcake's compound. Dove and the elephants were there too. That was the carrot to drag me over the edge.

I boarded the bus for Las Vegas at 11 p.m. The nine-hour trip was a welcome reprieve from everyone begging me not to go back.

The bus ride was sticky and hot, with a ton of sad-sack gamblers heading to a new city to lose more of their souls. I was so sure I was above them all, but I was gutting my pride. The smell of stale beer and cigarettes enveloped me. I sat next to an aspiring Elvis impersonator. He dreamed of playing the King on the new shows in Las Vegas. He knew every strange fact about Elvis and talked for nine hours about him. I shared my bottle of Blue Nun with him until it slipped out of my hand, rolling like a bowling ball to the back of the bus, clinking against the steel benches. He asked me why I was going to Vegas. I smiled and practiced affecting someone with my circus stories. I was instantly addicted to that feeling.

I knew I had to escape Reno. I knew I couldn't stay; there was nothing for me there except partying. Plus, I believed I was in love. Phileap would change and keep his father from me and, more importantly, take my side. I was destined to become a flyer and one of the famous Flying Córdobas. Delusional should have been my middle name. My fevered heart imagined this marvelous adventure filled with true love, travel, exotic animals, and a life worth living.

35

Spring, 1982, Phoenix, Arizona, USA

The lights came up, swirling and sweeping the audience. You could see the dust in the light beams and have a seizure watching the disco ball coat the audience in sparkles. The band played the "Daring Young Man on the Flying Trapeze" crescendo. I stood backstage next to Zita, the elephant, petting her sandpaper skin. I was nervous and thrilled. She purred to calm me.

I knew the six months of training had prepared my body and mind for the performance, but no one could have prepared me for the first time wearing a G-string during a show. The tiny strand of fabric riding up my crack made me dizzy.

The circus is all illusion. Every detail of the performance is made to give a sense of danger to the audience while keeping the acrobat safe. The whole costume was meant to look like we were half naked, but we were covered with nets and bendts because we needed to be caught in midair. We wore fishnet stockings so Santiago (the catcher) could keep a solid grip on our legs, like tiny jail cells on my thighs. The two-piece bikini-type outfit was filled in with flesh-colored mesh in the middle. Our arms were covered with fishnets, and around our wrists were bendts, or grips, a row of surgical tape covered with raw leather.

We had to make everything ourselves, the under as well as the outer parts of the costumes, because no one else wore this kind of getup outside of a Las Vegas showroom. Our costumes rode so far up our buttocks, accentuating our rumps, only a G-string would fit underneath.

Phileap had made me a couple of these daring panties with fabric that said "I love you" on the front patch. The top part of the costume had an underwire to increase our cleavage. We wore large rhinestones on our necks that attracted the light beams. On our faces, a thick layer of greasepaint, two pairs of false eyelashes, and a Maybelline pool of color was applied. A sequined feather boa sticking out of my hat completed the look. Some would say it was glamorous. I looked ridiculous.

"Are you ready?" Bernice, always the nice one, probed as I reapplied my right eyelash for the fourth time.

"I forgot about this part. I know I have seen you guys do it, but I never had to wear this mask. And how do you ever get used to this dental floss up your butt?"

Claudia sparkled next to me. She was from Mersea, France, and had been a flyer since she was three. She embodied grace and had abs of steel. She chimed in with her French accent, making each word sound insulting. "I love wearing a G-string. I wear them when I am not performing. It makes my rear look magnifique."

I adjusted my floss for the hundredth time, wishing it would make me feel sexy.

The first show was at 10 a.m., so we started makeup at 8. Bernice and I checked each other over and put on our capes of heavy velvet and satin fabrics worn by all six of us as we entered the ring. The music peaked, and the ringmaster announced, "The Flying Córdobas!"

My stomach triple somersaulted, and I was excited to touch a finish line of a six-month marathon filled with "You will never be a flyer." Arms outstretched, we twirled in unison and pranced about the ring. One by one, we approached the ladder, and the prop guy removed our capes from behind like an invisible butler. We stepped out of our high heels to climb barefoot.

As my turn approached, I prayed Papi was not again pissed at me. When mad, he would busy himself elsewhere and would not hold the ladder. This was a common punishment.

It was made of twelve-inch wooden dowels, two inches thick. They were threaded with a scratchy rope attached to the bottom of the platform and hung to the floor. If someone held the bottom rung with their foot, it was a bit easier to climb. If it was left loose, the effort to get fifty feet in the air as it whipped about was exhausting. Climbing the ladder was so hard that it served as the warm-up when we needed to fly. With one deep and dramatic bow, I dropped my cape off my shoulders and grabbed the ladder. Three rungs up, I felt it tighten. Thank God.

I climbed, pointing my toes between every step, and stopping to pose with a wave of my hand as I had been taught to do. My hands had to look pretty and relaxed—spaced right with the wrist arched back like a ballerina and jazz dancer combined. This was styling, and I still had trouble with it. Everyone else in the troupe seemed to come out of the womb doing styling and flying effortlessly. Only circus people style this way and, though the audience doesn't comprehend it, they perceive it when someone cannot do a proper pose. I was glad for the posing because it gave me a minute to catch my ragged breath and calm down. Although I had climbed this ladder thousands of times before, this was my first live performance.

When I got to the platform with everyone else, mixed emotions emanated, and I could sense it. There is little you don't know when sharing a six-foot by two-foot plastic podium fifty feet in the air with other acrobats and family members.

Phileap smiled. "You okay?"

Bernice winced as she naturally arched her back and styled perfectly. "Get up on your toes!"

"Oh. I forgot!"

Practice was about getting as much flying time as possible to make sure every trick stuck. The live performance's goal was slowing down and making it all seem dramatic and easy at the same time.

I was told to do the first practice swing so they would be sure I could pull off my trick. Nerves would not be my downfall. My hands were still blistered and torn to a bloody mess. I knew the only way to make them callused was to bear through the pain. (Yes, it worked. By getting a small child to pee on them.) I applied the chalk, tapping the bag hard on each hand, front and back. Nicolás called me to the middle, and I leaned out over the platform, staring at the net below. I grabbed the fly bar with my right hand and held the rigging bar with the left. It was about me getting a practice swing, so I wasn't reliant on Santiago to call me off the platform. The bar seemed heavier than its twenty pounds, and I adjusted my grip on the tape. Nicolás called me off again. The audience's heads were tilted up watching me. I resisted the temptation to pull the G-string out of my butt crack.

Phileap touched my hand on the bar. "You can do it. Turn around and come back." Nicolás glared at me as the crowd was now taking an interest in why I seemed frozen there.

Nicolás yelled, "Hup!" and I swung the bar up with my right hand, grabbed it with my left, and jumped up, setting my body in a sitting position. As I flew to the top of the force out, I experienced the familiar tug on my body as if my arms would come out of their sockets, but now I knew I was strong enough to not be drawn and quartered. I kicked at the top of my swing, keeping my legs straight. This was a taught position, not one that came naturally. They had hit me repeatedly during practice with a bamboo stick to keep my legs straight and toes pointed. As my swing became my sweep back to the platform, I sat airborne, legs out straight in front of me, the hollow. I learned that without this positioning of my body while in the air, my lower back would smack the platform edge.

I was on autopilot now and glad for my six months of training. At the front of the swing, with a bit of gravity letting up, I removed my right hand, placed it under my left, and let the swing turn my body. As I faced the platform, the trick was to get enough swing to overshoot the platform, let my legs down, and gracefully mount. Undershooting the platform or missing the mount was dreadful because the whole team would have to reach down and pull me up. If they missed, I had to drop to the net and climb the ladder again. Missing was not part of the show, and for any missed tricks, no matter how small, a portion of our pay was deducted. I had seen the show owner in the wings, watching me with his small yellow pad, waiting to save some money on my inexperience.

I pumped my legs and employed my stomach muscles and landed effortlessly on the platform. With no time for rejoicing, I moved to the side, arched my back, rose up on my toes, and styled. I was no longer cognizant of the audience, but I heard my own thunder of applause in my head.

My trick was the Passing Leap, and I performed it with Phileap. It was the last trick, so I began to calm down, only the sensation of the G-string resonating in my brain. For the trick, I flew out and, on the top of the swing, opened my legs. Santiago grabbed me by the thighs, and I let go of the bar. Hanging upside down as Santiago completed the swing, he called Phileap off the platform. Phileap pulled up, resting his belly on the fly bar. We came together in the air, and he leaped over the bar and me. Santiago liberated my legs; I grabbed the bar, then he caught Phileap. Phileap made this look even more daring by doing it blindfolded. He left Santiago's hands on my backswing, spun a pirouette in the air, and caught the bar next to me. In tandem, we kicked and mounted the platform together. I heard the audience this time because this was an extraordinary-looking trick, although not hard to complete for Phileap.

As an end to the act, we flew out on the trapeze and did some kind of trick landing in the net. Mine was to hook my knees on the front of the swing bar and release my hands. Hanging upside down (and styling), I would come off the bar and do a somersault. I had not consistently mastered this yet, but I decided the adrenaline of the night might get me through it.

A closed-mouthed, smiling-lips argument ensued on the platform.

"If she misses this, we get pay docked," Nicolás snarled.

"Let her try!" Phileap scowled.

Phileap looked me in the eyes to assess my fear state. "You got this, and you have done it hundreds of times. Remember, don't hit the net wrong."

We marveled when people would say, "You work with a net, that must not be so dangerous."

As the ringmaster announced my name mid-flight, I buoyed and pulled my knees to the bar, emancipated my hands, and thrust myself rearmost for the proper turn to land on the net on my back. The most challenging thing to learn was the concept of knowing where I was in space. I had captured the skill from grueling practice. Phileap called me out of my spin, and I hit the net. To do it, you must arch your back on the first bounce to stop the projectile. I saw in my mind that not only had I done it correctly, but my hands and fingers were also styled impeccably. Training makes perfection.

After hitting the net, you walk gracefully to the side, which is neither an easy feat nor easy on your feet. You then lie on your belly on the net with your head hanging off, grab the side of the net with your hands, and flip down to the ground. If the prop guy has done his job, you flipped right into your shoes. Mine wasn't the most graceful of dismounts, but I ended on the ground upright.

I remained animated, standing there and posing as the rest of the Córdobas hit the net and joined me in the ring. It occurred to me for the first time to look at the audience. They were clapping widely and exclaiming with glee. Their tension had built up while watching this dangerous act. This touched a part of my ego I had never caressed before.

I remember one lady in the front row. As I twirled around, I heard her yell to her friend, "Damn! That was a beautiful work of art. I think I had four heart attacks watching. Look how gorgeous they look!" The crowd loved me.

36

Summer, 1982, Las Vegas, Nevada, USA

I refused to move back to the trailer with Papi, so with my earnings from Reno, we were able to live in a small studio apartment in Las Vegas. It had a bed, bathroom, and kitchen¬—all that was needed for our love fest, living alone for the first time. We went to practice during the day at the compound and then returned to our love shack. I bought some old Vegas photos from the thrift store and framed them, covered the table lamp with a silk scarf, and used a batik sarong for window coverings. Pillows were thrown on the floor for our chairs, and we were happy.

Folies Bergère was newly launched and instantly successful, so every casino added circus acts to their shows. The smart circus people who settled in Las Vegas had been buying small houses as a retirement plan. The constant cash and the void of traveling rendered this new breed of circus performers reasonable. They saved, planned, and smiled. There were jobs aplenty in the land of big shows and bright lights. Each casino had a headliner show. We were filling in for the regular flyers who were on vacation. We got a hefty paycheck for performing twenty minutes per night with minor tweaks, better lighting, and music as well as bumped-up costuming. No set up or tear down. We would show up, get in costume, perform, and eat for free at the buffet. It was paradise, riding around in small cars and not trucks, having walls of drywall and full-size refrigerators.

We modified our trampoline routine into a comic relief act of jumping and falling. We would run up walls, tumble, and chase each other around. The perfect pirouettes and double layouts were now funny because we were dressed in bellboy outfits. Our act was to fill the time between big scenery changes for *Folies Bergère* at the Tropicana.

I was used to this "soft life," as Papi called it. He wanted to go back on the road. Nicolás was getting fat on endless prime rib, and Mama was gambling at the grocery store. Money was like a prolific garden, but no one was weeding it or watching over it. An attempt was made to buy a fourplex apartment complex so the family had a solid roof, but in the escrow, we discovered that Mama and Papi had spent every cent made in the last six months. This put me over the edge, as Phileap and I had made a deal that our money was separate. We had plans to buy a one-ton Chevy dually together for when we were on the road again and believed we had enough money to buy our own trailer.

We had to lend them our money to buy tickets to Japan where our next gig was scheduled. The money was from my savings, which I had put aside from the rest of the family, but Phileap gave his mother access because she insisted. We could only purchase a cab-over camper. This act of financial rebellion was the subject of many late-night scream fests between Phileap and me and his family and him. We were both haggard from the fighting, so we did nothing.

We had rested in Vegas, working only twice a day for six months, and were to head to Japan to perform for three months. This was a gig secured by Phileap's brother-in-law Sebastián who worked at the Tropicana as a bottom to a balancing act and wanted to become an agent.

Not naive anymore, I bought my own ticket. I did not trust the family to buy me a ticket after abandoning me on the Monaco trip.

A quiet had settled over Phileap and me, alone in our tiny room. For me, it was significant in space and exile. The family was pissed that we were on our own. They feared I would have more control over Phileap.

The day before we left for Japan, Sebastián told me I had to give him my ticket so he could get my visa details worked out. Because we would perform for money, a visa was needed for everyone. Sebastián was Marta's husband. He paid for her hand in marriage by getting the whole family into the United States. He radiated evil, and the family had whispered that he was also fucking his mother-in-law. I was not surprised nor shocked by this rumor, believing that both their souls were wrapped in an inky black stain, like a pissed-off squid.

At midnight, Sebastián came by (we had no phone) and told me he had sold my ticket and given the money to Mama, who now lived with him.

"You did what?" I screeched like a dog whose paw had been run over by a car.

"I gave her the money. She is mine now, and she wanted it."

"What? You pervert, you're married to her daughter."

"That is the bonus."

"Go get my money back. I am going on this trip."

"No go, she went to the casino and lost it all."

He stood there smiling, so proud that he had undone me. I slammed the door in his face, never letting him enter our studio apartment. With only five hours before the flight left, my screaming was futile and only affected the neighbor's sleep.

37

Fall, 1982, Las Vegas, Nevada, USA

They flew away without me. I had my own place, so it was not as devastating. Left again, I worked with the showgirls from the Tropicana. I dressed them and repaired their costumes. Backstage at a Vegas show is a swirl of lights, sequins, taping breasts, and running like you're on fire for two hours a night. The girls, the first of the somewhat mainstream topless performers in

America, were hardcore dancers. They worked all night and tanned topless by the pool by day. They loved to drink and gossip.

I was tiny next to their sculpted six-foot-tall bodies, but I told good stories, so they allowed me to be their mascot. Every weekend, some rich guy would take us out on Lake Mead in a houseboat. We would drink and giggle the length of the old lake. These Amazons could gulp gallons of chardonnay, and our hosts never tired of watching them glistening in the sun, laughing at the rainbows on the water.

I was beginning to enjoy life again. Drinking dulled the pain of betrayal and loneliness. I missed Phileap terribly but not his family. Word got out that I was partying with the showgirls, so Mama sent a priest over to our studio. I screamed a blue streak of blasphemous idioms and sent the monsignor packing, not feeling one ounce of regret or hellfire.

I had stopped practicing; I would not spend one minute alone with Papi at the trapeze site. Sebastián's partner Lou had taken pity on me and was keeping me sane by inviting me to the gym. He was the kindness to Sebastián's evil. He entertained me with stories of the old days of Vegas and the many stars he had worked with as a side act. He kept me motivated to stay in shape so when Phileap came back, I would be the preferred girl flyer.

I worked out in the gym that was open twenty-four hours, so I could go after the show at the Tropicana. I went out every night, mainly because it was free, and I liked being around the show people.

One night, I was backstage after the show, and Frank Sinatra sauntered in and sat down next to me on a fainting couch that had seen one too many G-strings. He introduced himself as Frank and kissed my hand.

"You are too short to be a dancer. What do you do?" His speaking voice melodic and sexy, even at 50 years old.

"I am a trapeze artist." A lie, for at the moment, I was only an abandoned girlfriend and a show girl dresser.

"Wow, are you bendy?"

I shook my head to clear the consideration of this icon tackily hitting on me. "Only in the air."

He laughed, head thrown back as if I was the first female to verbally spar with him.

"I like you. Are you married?"

"No, part of the Flying Córdobas, who are all in Japan performing."

"Did you get kicked out? Were you bad?"

I went on to tell him the whole story. Strangely, he was riveted by the family drama and the stories. He ordered a bottle of Cristal champagne from a passing waiter who was clearly on his way off work. Since the man obliged, he was tipped with three Benjamins. We drank and swapped stories. The showgirls ebbed and flowed around him, rubbing his shoulders, asking for Cristal.

He told me stories of the Rat Pack—the unbelievable, vulgar ones. Another bottle appeared, and we emptied it in our own little world of stories and laughter. When we realized that we were alone backstage, he tested if I wanted to go to his suite. Inebriated from sitting with this icon and drunk enough not to care how dangerous this act could be, I agreed.

His suite was the entire top floor, and it looked over the pool. I had never witnessed such opulence, and I walked around, running my hands on the cold custom marble, the Italian leather couch, and the serpentine curtains. He went into his room and came out in a plush white robe and a mirror with lines of cocaine. That was when I understood that I had made a stupid move. He took my hand and led me to the bed. I was planning my escape through foggy champagne brain. To buy time, I chatted.

"You know, my grandmother adores you. Can I get your autograph for her?"

He blinked uncomprehendingly at me.

"Excuse me?" he whispered a bit too loud.

"My nana has every one of your albums, knows the words to every song. She would be tickled pink to know I spent time with her idol."

He stood and crossed the room and, with quivering anger, pointed to the door. "Get out."

I took the opportunity and ran for the door. His ego burnt and temporarily bruised saved me.

As I left the hotel with the sun coming up, I was aware I was making poor choices again. I had left and joined the circus to get away from this lifestyle. I was unsure about anything anymore. With Phileap gone and without the performing and practicing, I was a prop—a thing of no value when the lights faded, a brainless girl who would follow a man to a hotel suite. I was nothing. Less than nothing because I was also stupid.

I went back to the studio and did not come out for a week. I did tell Nana that I had met her idol. I didn't go into details. My illusion was traumatized; I wasn't going to shatter hers.

38

Spring, 1982, Las Vegas, Nevada, USA

After three months of my lonely existence of working and sleeping, Phileap returned home. We had no communication the entire time he was gone. I heard about the successes and failures through Lou. The remaining stateside Córdobas ignored my presence. I was not aware of flight times, just a general day of arrival. I cleaned the apartment and made his favorite meal of meatloaf and apple pie. I paced a hole in the carpet waiting for him, like a tiger in a cage waiting for my next meal. When his shadow filled my doorway, I leapt into his arms and covered him with kisses. He was welcoming but a bit distant. He was proud of the accomplishments and accolades from the press and the circus owner in Japan. He was even more thrilled at the new tricks he had conquered, which would garner more money for the act. He had mastered the back, double layout dismount where he bounced off the net into a forward somersault, caught the bar, and flipped back down with another double layout. This trick had never been down before, so it was valuable in terms of future bookings. He started practicing the triple somersault because Nicolás had become less reliable with his. This thrilled everyone except Nicolás, whose loathing of Phileap intensified with the contemplation of losing his coveted place as the only one in the family who could throw a triple and catch it.

Phileap talked about the trapeze, but nothing was said about the exotic place he had visited. Never once did he ask me what my life was like for the past three months.

We settled into meal mode as he told me more of their successes and failures in Japan. He was wistful in his telling, and I wondered if it was the performing, being in Japan, or something else. My instinct told me it was something else.

Because it was a small studio apartment, Phileap had placed his bags in the bathroom. After dinner, I went in there to freshen up, yearning for a long night of passion. His bag was open; he had retrieved a present for me that I had not been offered yet in the excitement of his retelling three months of circus life. In the suitcase, I saw a leather-bound photo album that I picked up, excited to have Phileap walk me through his pictures and share stories of the land he visited. When I opened the book, my heart stopped. The gut-punch was visceral, the images an assault to my heart. The rage bubbled up as I flipped the pages, seeing an intimate portrait of a man and a woman in love.

The pictures were Polaroid, and she had written her name in Japanese characters along with the English translation. This lovefest with my boyfriend and a girl named Kazmi was evident in the twenty-two pages of photos. I was nauseous, enraged, and no longer a tiger pacing a cage, but one ready to pounce and kill.

The sound coming from my mouth was one of a hurt animal. The tears streamed down my face as I emerged with one Polaroid in my hand, spitting her name at him. He snatched the photo from me and cradled it to his heart. This act told me everything. He worshipped her, and he would never love me purely. The weight of this knowledge knocked the wind out of my furious sails, and I demanded that he explain.

"We met in England years ago. I never believed I would see her again."

"So, you didn't know she was going to be there?"

"No, but I was so happy when she was there. It made it all so special."

"Are you fucking kidding me? I sat here for three months, waiting for you. Why didn't you tell me to leave?"

"Because I knew she couldn't come back with me, and I couldn't stay. You were going to have to do as my life partner."

The frenzy came up again.

"'Going to have to do?' What the fuck does that mean? I'm the second choice, and now I know it?"

He was fearful of my anger and too self-absorbed to figure out the pain of what he was telling me. These excruciating words, these facts, would always be a black cloud over our life.

"I'm sorry, but I love her. I can't have her. I might as well have you."

The wrath emerged in a hurricane of throwing, ripping, and trying to excavate the suitcase for more proof of his infidelity, which was futile, but I had nowhere else to direct my wrath, and the suitcase became my victim.

The next few hours were a blur of a pointless war. I was angry and hurt. Yet, he was not remorseful, nor did he even think he had done anything wrong. He had loved this girl long before me and, in his mind, he was right in spending three months adoring her because he would never see her again. In the haze of violently unpacking his suitcase, I found a ring box. I opened it and found a single solitaire diamond on a gold band: an engagement ring. This renewed my fury as I berated him for asking her to marry him.

"The ring is not for Kazmi."

"Do not say her name in my house."

"Apple Pie, the ring is for you. She helped me pick it out for you."

The practicality of this shopping trip was an even bigger slap to my face and pride.

"What the fuck are you talking about?"

"I told her about you. What I have put you through, and she suggested I marry you. We picked out the ring together. I assumed you would be happy."

"You are fucking nuts? Why would I want a ring a woman you are in love with picked out? You know this is all insane?"

"She wants me to be happy without her."

The indignation started again with renewed energy. This was not my fairy-tale dream. My proposal of marriage was supposed to be a fairy tale. I had left my life to travel and wait for him, but I was in second place and always had been an acceptable substitute for the real thing. The first loser.

I slept in the bathtub, keeping the photo book with me and torturing myself by obsessing over every nuance and reverence-soaked picture. He stopped banging on the door and demanding the album back after the neighbors called the police. The officer told him to leave me alone until my storm lost strength.

The following day, I emerged puffy-eyed and out of tears. I was broken and ready to go home to Reno. I packed quietly and pled for him to take me to the airport. He protested, still so narcissistic he could not recognize my broken heart nor that I no longer wanted to be with him. He tried to give me the ring again, and I threw it at his face, taking out a small chunk of his eyebrow. This was the first time I broke a smile since the tornado of betrayal was unleashed. I loaded my suitcase in the truck and resolved to leave everything else behind, including my circus dreams and heart. He finally got into the truck after an hour and headed to McCarren Airport. He tried to explain again, and I lobbed him a glance soaked in murder, so we rode the next thirty minutes in silence.

As a survival mechanism, I focused my brain on what my future would be. How easy it would be without his fucked-up family and life. I saw Becky and me resuming our bars and shenanigans. I saw my theater life. I saw returning to Steamboat and living in my parents' house. I saw no job. I saw misery. Reno was not a place to run to, it was a place to run from. I started to sob. Fuck my life.

Phileap let me out of the truck in front of the terminal and handed me the suitcase.

"I don't want you to leave."

"I don't want to be the second choice."

"It's better than no choice."

The words stung, and I walked into the terminal. Like a zombie, I approached the ticket counter. I was not sure how much last-minute tickets cost or whether I even had enough money to buy one. In line, a family was in front of me. The woman cradled a baby with a toddler running circles around her legs. She had a look of pure bliss on her face as she watched her children. The father seemed uninterested in the family. He was scanning the crowd. When he caught me looking at them, he skimmed me up and down and smiled. He winked lecherously—it dripped of dirty hotels and things done never spoken of again. I looked at his wife, first with pity and then an understanding. She was the second choice. She made it work by loving the children and tolerating him. I hightailed it out of line and found Phileap still parked on the curb. I threw my suitcase in the back of the truck and climbed inside.

"I'll take your secondhand ring."

"Good choice," he said with a tad bit of sadness in his eyes.

39

Spring, 1982, Las Vegas, Nevada, USA

We were practicing the trapeze again with Dove, Izic, and Cupcake in the dirt lot in south Vegas. I was glad to have friends, both animal and human, in the compound because the family was even colder to me after Phileap kept me. They were enraged that I showed up with a shiny new bauble on my ring finger. They wanted to have Kazmi as a flyer; she was seventh-generation circus. She was an asset; I was a liability. They still had the bossy, redheaded American in their caravan.

I did not wear my engagement ring all the time because we were flying three times a day, and everyone understood that I was the second-string player more now than ever.

Bernice was pregnant and couldn't fly anymore, and Marta had been forced to back to Sebastián, even though his familial crimes were reprehensible. I was the only girl flyer choice. I practiced harder than ever, taking my inner rage out on the palms of my hands. Blisters covered my calluses. At night, I was so sore; all I could do was cook and fall into bed. We were back in the trailer with Marco after we had to give up the studio because I was not working anymore.

Phileap had listened to my story of what his dad had done to me and made no comment then or now. Lou had told me that Phileap would never choose me over his family, so I had to stand up for myself. I put my foot down about Phileap's dad living with us, so he was housed with Nicolás and Bernice. It became a rhythm during the hot Vegas summer to sleep during the day, start practice at 4:00 p.m., and fly until midnight. We did not have an air conditioner in the trailer, so some days we went to the casino to escape the extraordinary heat. The dollar oysters and beers in a cool casino dining room were a dream come true. The surface of Mars was preferable to the 120 degrees of a Vegas summer day.

Phileap and I practiced the flying leap. We were trying to get our rhythm back. It was all about timing with this trick. I would go legs across to Santiago, and Phileap would hop on the bar on his stomach and leap across me into Santiago's hands. I would swing back, and Phileap would get on the bar with me. If I lost any momentum, it took two swings to get back to the platform because I was heavier and less agile than Phileap. It happened often. It was hot, and I was tired on our tenth attempt of the trick. We were on the bar, arguing like two crazy people.

"Dammit, Gail! You need to fly stronger."

"I'm doing my best!"

"You must do better."

"Fuck you. I'm tired. It's hot!"

"You always have an excuse. I should have let you go."

"Don't be so fucking mean."

We were yelling and swinging. All the emotions took the power out of our swing, and we lost it. Santiago called for us to let go and drop down. My eyes were leaking as I hit the net. I went into the elephant barn and cried my tears in their outside shower.

When I returned to the trailer, he was tilting the pan and letting the omelet he had prepared slide onto my plate. I was wearing a short silk robe tied loosely around my waist. Having just showered with the elephant hose, trying to be as unspoiled as I could, the soft, clingy material revealed the outline of my softened nipples.

He stopped cooking and scanned me up and down. "You look radiant."

"I am as clean as I can get in this place, and I'm still mad at you."

"You need more practice. It can't take us two tries to get to the bar."

"That fucking bar. I'm doing the best I can. If you want me gone, I'll pack."

"No, I was frustrated. I cooked for you as an apology."

He placed the plate in front of me, and we sat down to eat. We spoke of the day's activities, practices, and the costumes that needed to be made.

As we finished, I placed my bare foot on his chair between his legs and massaged him to attention.

"Nice," the only word spoken.

I got up and came around the table and kneeled before him, pulling his shorts down to his thighs. I stroked him a couple of times, making a ring tightly around him with my thumb and forefinger. I took him fully into my mouth, lowering my mouth until he was down my throat. My nose rested against his pubic bone, and my lips touched his balls. I slowly pulled all the way off his cock and ran my tongue around the head. I gave the sensitive underside of the glans a couple flicks with my tongue, then stood and straddled him, lowering myself onto his cock. I loved the initial penetration. To me, it always felt like the first time. Once fully seated, I leaned into him, breasts resting against his chest, arms wrapped around his head, lips brushing his neck. No motion. Locked together in the human body's perfect example of form and function. Hard parts touching soft parts, sensitive parts touching sensitive parts. After a few minutes of tightly hugging each other, I rose and disconnected from him. Neither one attained completion. I leaned in and kissed him fully on the lips.

"That should keep me focused. We will finish this little session at our first opportunity after practice."

He looked down at his dick standing at attention and knew the tights would not fit easily today. I was edging him, trying to keep him aroused all day to make our next lovemaking session extremely hot and passionate. Also, to torture him for fighting with me in the air.

I was glad to be back with the large cats, but they were suffering in the heat too. Their "garage" had air, but it only cooled it to around 85 degrees. I took to buying bags of ice from the 7-Eleven to toss into their cage. They loved the cold treat and stopped spraying me with their pee.

We took jobs at casinos for acts on vacation and played in the big shows as a bumper while the set was being changed. Our trampoline act, The Super Locos, had gotten prodigious reviews. It consisted of a small trampoline that the brothers bounced off as well as a large wooden wall used as a vault to do tricks.

In The Super Loco act, Payaso, Phileap's brother, joined us dressed as a clown and wearing a whistle. He was different from the rest of the family. The features on his face listed to the right and were a bit droopy. He did not fly on the trapeze. He barely spoke at all; he had a predilection for the solitude of shadows and dark places to watch people. This act was musical and funny, something he seemed to enjoy. They would run for the trampoline, do a tumble before, use the trampoline to vault onto the wall, and tumble back down. This continued in a circle as they ran and tumbled. They added their epic tumbling stunts, which were a staple for the trapeze, so the act looked crazy hard but kept a comedic delivery. The audience loved it because it was spectacular and fast-paced. We worked consistently, with money flowing to the family. I sewed costumes and hung out backstage, reveling in the show-business aspect of my life.

Marco brought home a new showgirl every night. He chose soulless stick figures that were neither friendly nor even remotely human. They never ate and snorted cocaine for breakfast. Out of makeup, they were ugly as a pug. On stage, they stood on eight-inch platform shoes with boas wrapped elegantly down their outstretched arms and six-foot-high feather caps on their heads. They strutted sideways, crossing feet over, and walked upstairs. Their breasts were bare, and that was the novelty. This was a new wave of performers. They were not exactly dancers, just tall ladies who had no problems showing their breasts twice a night. Since Vegas started the topless shows, every night was sold out. The circus acts happened in front of the curtain as they changed the elaborate sets, and the girls donned another peacock outfit. Being a seamstress was a lucrative business when you had forty girls prancing on stage through eight costume changes. I had around twenty costumes a night to fix and had excessive sequins stuck under my fingernails.

We still flew when we got home at 1 a.m. because we were never sure when a new on-the-road job would surface, and we had to be ready.

Television was discovering circus life, and they started producing magician specials, *Circus of the Stars*, and hiring circus acts for the reality show called *That's Incredible*. We were engaged to do a special featuring Frankie Valli, B. J. Thomas, and a bunch of circus acts and showgirls. It was going to be taped in one day at the Tropicana in the *Folies Bergère* show room. Frankie did a melody of all his famous songs with showgirls draped across him and strutting across the stage. His wife and five kids were there to watch, but mostly to enjoy the opulent outdoor pool. B. J. Thomas sang his hit songs "Raindrops Keep Fallin' on My Head," "I'm So Lonesome I Could Cry," and "Hooked on a Feeling" accompanied by a monkey montage. It was especially hysterical with the monkeys dancing to the Ooga-Chaka part of the song.

Thrilled to be an audience member, I watched everything from the setup to the acts rehearsing and performing. The boys did The Super Locos act, and the producer went nuts for it and requested to book us on other shows. The traveling shows caught wind of our success and became interested in the trapeze and trampoline acts. Things were looking up on the job front, but no matter how much money I made, the family needed it more, and I was always begging for quarters to call my grandparents and Becky. I was becoming an indentured servant.

40

Summer, 1982, Salt Lake City, Utah, USA

With my bit of saved and stashed money, Phileap bought another nine-foot camper shell to go over our truck. Each season you had to buy a new trailer, as they fell apart after a year on the road. This meant we had to outfit the top of the camper with the trapeze rigging, but it was worth it for the privacy and removal from the hate-filled family tin can. The camper had no bathroom, but I didn't care. The call of nature and showers happened outside the home at fairgrounds or campsites. We did have a sawed-off gallon milk plastic jar that served as our pee bucket in the middle of the night or while driving.

Although it was minute, Phileap and I now had our own sleeping quarters. I was in heaven being alone together again and without his mother in my space every day, spewing hateful Spanish comments and asking Phileap repeatedly how he could do "this" to her.

"Oya Phileap! ¿Cómo puedes elegir a esta puta sobre mí?"

"Pero Mama."

That was all he ever answered. "But Mama." Not "fuck off, crazy lady"—"but Mama."

Although the camper was small, with a tiny table and one full-sized bunk over the cab, I did have a stove and a tiny fridge. Even better, we could fuck freely, a practice we excelled at and always craved more of. We rediscovered what our bodies could do for and to each other and were having a blast. Phileap's English was improving by me reading *Penthouse Forum* as we drove from gig to gig. This made for many pit-stops on the side of the road to try the new experience I had delivered, first in English, then in Spanish, and finally in body language. The family hated us stopping since they would have to pull over too because we traveled in a caravan, so no acrobat was ever left behind. If we took too long, Mama would come and pound on the door, asking for the devil to release her son.

Parked in the horse arena, we both slept in the nude, enjoying the sensual nature, feeling each other's body at will. Sometimes it was sex, sometimes adoration, sometimes both. If he woke first and still had his morning wood, we both knew it was good for about an hour of fun until we had to get up to pee. He rolled over against my back, pressing his hardening dick against me. I stirred and breathed out an "Mmmmmm." My way of saying, "Let's fuck."

He was hard and wet as I arched my back to him. I extended back with one hand and grabbed his cock and guided it toward my welcoming petals. Using his pre-cum to lubricate me, I pushed back until he overcame the initial resistance. I pushed again and then pulled. He picked up my rhythm and began his stroke. He reached around, cupping my breast, squeezing the nipple into hardness. Moving his fingers to my mouth, I sucked with the same passion I sucked his dick. I took pride in my work.

I kept the rocking going as he extended his hand to my clit and rubbed it from side to side at first. Using my natural moisture to wet his finger, he started rubbing it up and down. I couldn't take this long and pushed a final time against him and shuddered as I came. The involuntary contractions pushed him over the edge. After, he held me as we dozed for another thirty minutes. When we heard the banging on the door, we both jumped from the bed and giggled as we ran to our respective pee-pots.

We left for a four-week job in Texas. It was a great paying gig, and we were excited to be on the road. Movement suited us best.

41

Fall, 1982, Amarillo, Texas, USA

I awoke covered in humidity, as if a rain cloud had specifically searched me out and doused me with hot water. The sheets and pillow were soaked in the overhead compartment of our camper. I was sure the roof was leaking. I climbed down the ladder and opened the small slider window separating the truck's front seat from our tiny living quarters.

"Phileap, the roof is leaking. I am sopping wet!"

Not taking his eyes off the road, driving on a long, flat highway with no hills, trees, buildings, or anything in sight, Phileap yelled, "Not leaking, no rain in Texas whole year."

"Then why am I wet?"

"Humidity. Welcome to Texas."

I went back up to the bed and considered the unseen rain. Growing up in Nevada, I had never experienced moisture in the air. When I imagined it, I assumed it would be cooling, but this was stifling. I checked it off as another new adventure the circus life had presented me.

I hadn't been well for a couple of weeks—a mild flu had seized my stomach and made me consistently nauseated. Even sick, I was excited for these four weeks in Texas because it was a new show with the possibility of finally finding a friend on the road. I was not cleared to fly yet but could assist with other acts and teach the circus children. Plus, we were dead broke.

All the money we had left went to pay for the gas to get to Texas. We had to survive the week of performing without groceries. I looked at the bare fridge. Not a scrap of bread, milk, or butter. I deliberated how we would survive. The girls had pooled all the canned protein goods to come up with meals that would keep the flyers from passing out. I was the only girl not flying, but I still deserved a meal. The lack of food freaked me out. I had never been without food or the means to get subsistence. I wanted to ask people for help, but we were isolated on the road. I was told the new Texas troupe would be unimpressed if we rolled on to the lot and started begging. I was forbidden to tell anyone of our situation. It scared the hell out of me. I was weak and terrified.

We rolled into Austin at 1 a.m. with a 6 a.m. call to set up the trapeze in the morning. Luckily, I did not have to help set up, but I had a web rehearsal at 9. I warmed some rice and beans for Phileap and went back to lie in our minuscule bunk, the smell of the lingering food making me queasy. I dressed in a leotard and a sweatshirt because the humidity made me both hot and cold. My hair was an unruly mess of curls uncontrolled by a pink ribbon slapped on without a mirror or running water.

I wandered through the circus grounds. The smell of the animals lured me toward them. The horses were beautiful; they looked like unicorns, just standing in their pens. Long, luxurious manes and tails, and they tossed their heads expressively. My horse would just stand there, looking at me. These steeds were cleverer than the props guys scooping up their poop.

The cat act was in their small cages, snarling and snapping at each other. Six tigers and three lions along with one black panther. I got closer than I should have with my false expectations that all cat acts were to be befriended. One male tiger turned and lifted his tail to anoint me stupid. The elephants were one matriarch and two small ones. I had to wash off the tiger pee with a hose, so I was late for web practice. The head clown bellowed at me to come into the dressing room.

42

Fall, 1982, Dallas, Texas, USA

Billy, the head clown, shared a dressing room with the women as his yearning for the lads made the male acrobats not want him within sight—in or out of full clown face. Billy was wily of shape and fluid of sexuality. His face had seen the brunt of many homophobic fists, so the clown makeup hid the scars and misshaped fragments. He hadn't changed since I first met him in Stockton.

"So, you stayed. I'm shocked."

"Me too. It hasn't been easy or fair."

"You dumb girl, easy is only for people who work 9 to 5. Fair is nothing but a side show to the circus. Are you still delusional and in love with that flyer?"

"Yes, but the mirage collapsed."

"Then why would you choose to stay?"

"That is the question that everyone is asking. Including me."

"I too live life in a fantasy. It's not so depraved, until it is. Meanwhile, hiding on the road is a huge distraction."

"What makes you think I'm hiding?"

"Girl, that is the only reason that makes sense for you to continue this charade so far. Most of us are hiding in plain sight with the circus."

The year was 1982, and Billy had his nipples pierced with large rings. He wore a stainless-steel chain attached between them, which linked down his trunk and attached to a leather cock ring. Not a sight many people had seen, but a normal one in the makeshift dressing rooms of the circus. On the Texas tour, most of the venues were sports venues, filled with stinking lockers where sweaty-man-scent still lingered. With the cold, hard floors and the only warm running water available, it became the place where the magic was made.

The female performers brought in trunks of greasepaint, false eyelashes, and flamboyantly sequined costumes. We set up lighted mirrors with cushioned folding chairs and draped carpets on the floors. The shows were at 10 a.m., 3 p.m., and 7 p.m. every day. Between shows, we wore silk kimonos over G-strings and fishnet stockings with dense layers of makeup, looking like embattled prostitutes. The reality was that applying the fishnets and makeup was as hard of a task to complete as the double somersault. The girls and clowns stayed in makeup and costume for twelve hours each day.

Billy acted as an aide-de-camp to the glamor of the show. He had a flair for taking even the ugliest women and transforming them into bejeweled beauties, something the Texan girls wanted to be—and the men wanted to bed. A circus is an optimal place for misfits to not be found or punished for their misdeeds. We never spent enough time in one village to warrant a pitchfork brigade. But like finds like, and in each town, small or large, Billy had male company. This infuriated old circus folk because they did not like leaving a trace, especially of sin.

In the evening, the dressing rooms became the boudoir after the last show. Everyone existed and traveled in tiny travel trailers with their multigenerational family. The makeshift room was the only privacy offered to a horny wire-walker or prop guy. The muscular bodies in tights and strange accents lured the Towner girls in for a taste of the exotic, to kiss and have a story to tell their grandchildren. The debauched Towner boys came to see if their debase feelings were authentic.

After practice, the women and the married men would avoid the dressing rooms like a plague because that much fornicating could scare a person celibate.

Our flying trapeze act practiced every night along with the performances. We tried new tricks and perfected wobbly ones. I was still perfecting the passing leap with Phileap. I was strong and dedicated, but my lack of circus DNA slowed my learning. It had been a slow go, but my heart was there. I was as clunky as a toddler in high heels.

They flew as a family, five siblings and their partners, with Papi as the coach and terrorizer. I was a new artist and needed practice more than anyone. Payaso was with us and joined the clown act while also helping Phileap set up the trapeze. I would see the circus moms gather their children close when he was around. I wasn't sure if it was instinct or knowledge.

The youngest of the family, Marco, was now a part-time catcher. He passed puberty and became tall and wide of the shoulder. This was a curse to him, as the flying part of the lineage was a feisty fun-size. He was angry that life had dealt him a robust countenance. He preferred to be a tiny flyer. The act needed a catcher, so against his loud affirmations, he began to practice as a catcher as his pimples appeared.

I often wondered where this strong teen was looking as he caught my trick. Part of the act, a catch called "legs across" was coupled with the passing leap trick. Marco would call me off the platform after he started his swing, at the precise time, by yelling, "Hup." At the force out, I presented my legs open to him, and he latched on to my thighs, placing my feet behind his shoulders. I would release the bar, we would take one swing, and on the hollow, I twisted and grabbed the bar with my hands outstretched. He would release, and I would swing back to the podium. We did this every night after the arena cleared.

As a test, I used a coal pencil and drew an eyeball on the innermost point of my crotch and glued on a long set of eyelashes. When Marco caught me during the first practice, I could sense him chuckling as he held me in the air. The release back to the bar was rough with him throwing me back like flicking a booger off his finger, not the timed dance we usually produced. While the girls had the answer to where he was looking for three shows per day, my tomfooleries were admonished. Everyone in the troupe was furious at my prank because shenanigans had no place in the trapeze.

43

Fall, 1982, Fort Worth, Texas, USA

I had to pee and throw up, so I left to find the public bathrooms. We were parked on a fairground dirt lot. There was a carnival set up next to a steel building that usually housed basketball games and rodeos, but now it hosted a circus. The restrooms were cement boxes located outside: windowless, dirty, open-air environments with no doors. Open to anyone, anytime. It smelled of urine, cum, and shit. I peed and was glad my thighs were made of steel so I didn't have to make bodily contact with the gross place.

Hungry and wet, I walked into the center ring, looking for friendly faces. There were ten other women there, all stretching and readying their perfect bodies to climb the four-inch circumference web rope forty feet in the air. No one looked me in the eye.

The web was a required job that each of the acts had to lend at least one female to for the spectacular of the circus. This one had ladders at the top. We climbed up the rope in unison and did tricks using the rungs of the ladder dangling seventy-five feet in the air. For safety, we attached our wrists with a loop protruding off the top. Someone needed to hold the bottom of the web rope and swing it in a circular motion to the music as we styled and posed above, alternating from within the ladder rungs. The routine is the same from show to show, so we reviewed costumes and performance times more than choreography. Phileap was setting up the trapeze, a three-hour job every day, so a clown held my rope. I tried to strike up conversations with the other girls, but there was no idle time once a show was set up until after strike. Plus, they could tell I was not "circus bred" by the way I styled. Shaking with hunger and exhaustion, I made my way back to the trailer to see what combination of cans I could feed Phileap for lunch.

After eating, we had practice to check the rigging. The whole troupe looked hollow and hungry. To me, it was insane to starve. I was sure we were not the first or only ones to ever be in this predicament. I wanted to borrow money from the promoter against our wages, but the answer was a steadfast and loud "No!" every time I brought it up. They all flew weakly, more checking the rigging than throwing new tricks.

We set up our dressing rooms in a corrugated steel barn with no insulation or air. The dressing area had hard cement floors with pieces of metal plate pretending to be mirrors with no reflection. They had rented portable showers for us, but they only had cold water, and the showerhead buttons had to be hit every thirty seconds to keep the water flowing. We threw down carpets, erected wardrobe receptacles, and made it the workshop for our illusions of beauty.

"It is so cold in here, my eyelash glue won't stick."

The girl closest to me was on the liberty horses. They are majestic Spanish stallions that perform tricks such as wheeling, circling, and running in file in a group and without a rider. I had seen them practicing. I was enthralled with their skill and ability with these grandiose animals.

"Texas in the fall can be brutal. Even my horses are freezing and hungry."

It wasn't just us who had run out of food. I vowed to find some hay for the six mares. Liberty work was demanding for the horses.

"This is my first time in Texas."

"What? Aren't you part of the trapeze troupe?"

"Yes, but I'm new."

Now they were all listening. As if the word "new" was never spoken in a circus dressing room. I veered the conversation off me.

"What kind of horses do you have?"

"You *are* new," she said loudly to everyone in the room. "My horses are Spanish Lipizzans. The best for liberty work. Have you not seen a circus before? And you're with the world's most famous group?"

Conversations stopped cold. Every eye was on me. I felt like a goose in a swan pond.

"I have seen circuses and been practicing with the family for about six months."

"Wow, they must be desperate."

Another one in the corner laughed and looked at me. "I knew she was a Towner. Did you see her style?" They all laughed.

I took the slam with a grain of salt and was determined to make friends with these ladies.

The first performance went well. I knew I had to do better if I was ever going to fit in.

After three performances, I went back to practice the web. Phileap held it while he swirled me around. He called me in to my tricks and yelled about pointed toes and styling hands. I did all the ins and outs with the loop and felt good about the next morning's performance. Three times a day at this, and I knew I would fit in.

I had to fetch my costume in the makeshift dressing room after practice because it needed to be repaired. I listened outside the door before I entered, praying the fornicating had ceased for the evening. I opened the door slowly, and the lights were off. It was dead dark. I could hear a slurping and popping sound. Deciding it safer to see what base activity was causing this noise than to run into a dark room, I flipped the light switch. There in the corner was the familiar red Fez bobbing up and down on Billy's crotch. Those Tabernacle hats were distinct in many ways.

Back in the trailer, dinner was a can of spinach and garbanzo beans. I ran out of ideas, and the smells of the carnival's deep-fried meats made my stomach tumble. I skipped dinner, exhausted from the web, humidity, and hunger. I curled up to dream of mac and cheese.

At two in the morning, searing pain in my stomach woke me up. I was going to be sick, so I stumbled to the fairground bathrooms. On my way, I tried to wake Phileap, but he was out cold, a trick he learned from being born on the road. When they sleep, nothing wakes them.

With no flashlight in the pitch dark, I felt my way to the toilet, and a warm, sticky substance ran down my thigh. I sat down on the cold steel throne as the wave of pain took me again. I was sure I was dying, but instinctively, I knew what was happening—they were the worst period pains ever. I tried to get back to the camper. When I stood, I collapsed as a tsunami of pain ripped through me.

I screamed, and the sound echoed off the concrete walls. Terrified and alone, the waves of pain kept attacking me. I repeatedly screamed for help, but no one answered or came to my aid. An elephant trumpeted a call, the tigers roared, the chimpanzees beat against their cages, but no human acknowledged or approached to help. I knew that they could hear me.

With more ripping pain, I got back to sitting on the disgusting toilet seat and heard a plop in the water. The cool liquid splashed on my agonized nethermost region. I could tell I was bleeding. I passed out on the floor.

Sunbeams bending around the cement walls woke me. I was covered in blood below my waist and realized that I had miscarried a baby alone on a dirty Texas floor. Too weak to stand, I called for help again. A man with a neck tattoo peeked into the bathroom and asked in Spanish if I needed help.

"Si, por favor," I whispered.

He removed his filthy jacket, wrapped it around me, lifted me like a rag doll, and carried me to my camper. He knocked on the door, but Phileap didn't answer. I crawled up the stairs and opened the door. Phileap had already gone inside the arena to prepare for the three shows that day, showing no alarm that I was gone most of the night.

I missed the first day of the performance and was given a strict talking-to by Billy.

"Your empty web was a blight on my otherwise perfect spectacular."

Phileap never queried what happened or why there was so much blood on my clothes heaped in a pile by the door when he returned for lunch, which was not ready. I got up and opened a can of spinach, the only thing in the cupboard. He grabbed the can and a spoon and headed back to the ring, slamming the door behind him. I drank a gallon of water to fill my stomach and went to the arena to find a quarter and call my nana for advice or to cry my eyes out. I never found one, so I decided to watch the show, hoping that would salve my broken spirit.

There was an elephant act trained and performed by a small family. I looked down with delight to see Dumbo. They had bought Zita's baby, Dumbo. I was excited to see him perform. I was dying to see if he remembered me. Zita had been horrified and distraught as they took the baby away in a large trailer. An elephant calf gets the milk it needs to survive from its mother until it's about two years old. Once it hits that age, it can feed itself independently. However, it does not wean off its mother's milk entirely until five or ten years of age. Zita's baby was sold and sent away at two years old because Dove needed the money.

When elephants lose a child, they can die from a broken heart—they are the only animals that die because of heartbreak. Other elephants in their herd try to comfort them, will them back to life, but it rarely works. The offspring are even more traumatized. Just like humans, they have a sense of abandonment. I vowed to spend as much time with Dumbo as possible and try to ease his pain.

The family bought another baby, and the act featured their ten-year-old son, Henry. The small boy working with two baby elephants was a coveted act. The cuteness factor was through the roof. During that afternoon's performance, Dumbo got spooked by the crowd and took off running out of the ring, out the door, and on to the carnival promenade. I watched the baby elephant run toward me, terrified. He was running into the unknown, away from the life he knew.

I had a powerful need to help, so I ran toward him, calling his name. He stopped at the familiar sound and looked at me. He recognized the sound of my voice but not my face. He tentatively approached me while I kept talking and telling him that he was okay. When he got close, he wrapped his trunk around my waist, the tip resting on my empty womb, and purred. We ambled, swathed around each other, back to the ring.

Still desperately needing food, I was relieved when I saw an oyster bar across the pasture from the fairgrounds. Its neon lights beckoned me with a "$1 beer and oysters" to cross the ten-acre weed parcel. I scraped together $2.25 in change from under the seats of the truck and went to the restaurant. The bar was a vomitorium of old liquor signs and oyster shells and reeked of stale beer smell. In the middle of the day, I was the only patron. The bartender watched a roping competition on the eight TVs while I sat at the bar and devoured a whole basket of sourdough rolls and ordered a beer and a dozen oysters, each with the bargain happy-hour price of a buck. This meal stimulated and sated me. When I got the bill, I put down my $2.25 in dirty change.

"I'm sorry I don't have a tip today. I promise I'll pay you on Friday when we get paid."

The bartender looked like an ex-rodeo stud with his silver-tipped shirt collar and huge belt buckle. His whiskey-stained boots had seen better days. His hat covered down to his eyebrows, with bushy sideburns exploding out.

"Where do you work?"

"I'm with the circus."

"No way! That is so cool. What do you do?"

"I'm with the flying trapeze troupe, but I do several acts."

"Where you born into it?"

"Ha! No, I'm a unicorn. I ran away from Reno to join the circus."

"Were you an acrobat?"

"Nope, a shit-kicker."

"I want to hear more. I'll feed you every night in exchange for circus stories and tickets."

I had extra free tickets that Billy had given me because he knew I was the official "shopper" for the family, and he wanted me to leave them at the market counter.

I admitted we were dead broke, and I was unwell. It was astonishing that this stranger was so sympathetic when the people I now worked with could care less about me.

He gave me a big bowl of vegetable soup, which I inhaled, feeling a bit stronger. I returned and did my web act, not sharing the surprising bounty with anyone else. They had left me to die in a dirty bathroom. I was not in a mood to nourish them.

44

F all, 1982, Austin, Texas, USA

The next town was Austin, Texas, and as we rolled in, I was filled with foreboding. I still hadn't recovered from the blood loss or the fact no one came to me when I was screaming and losing a child on the dirty bathroom floor.

We finally received a paycheck, but instead of buying a ton of food, we were forced to get the brakes repaired on Nicolás's truck. The idea of being hungry again, combined with feeling so alone, haunted me. I saw for the first time that I had no safety net.

To remedy at least the food part, I went to social services, and they gave me $100 in emergency food stamps. I cooked a communal meal for the whole show because it seemed everyone was food insecure. My lips were sealed about where the money came from. Not even Phileap knew. My trust in him had eroded like the frayed lines on the net. They were too proud to take a "handout" from the Towners, but I knew how to survive.

Phileap went to scout the arena for how to set up the trapeze. Every building was different, and solving the puzzle of making it precisely the same for us while flying was a never-ending battle. The trapeze, when in pieces, was a series of steel poles, guide wires, ratchets, and rope. It had to be precisely the same when assembled for our tricks to fasten. One inch off, and we tumbled to the net instead of into the catcher's hands and were docked pay. Setup required removing seats in the stands, searching for ceiling catwalks, and unraveling the geometry that was the trapeze act. It never went smooth—there was always loud, foul language and pissed-off brothers—but when the music swelled and the lights came up, we were geometrically correct.

While the boys set up, the women assembled the home base, arranged the dressing rooms, and cooked. The best parking was closest to the electrical jump box. The animals got priority and were always the nearest. If you wanted to watch TV in your trailer, the scent of monkey shit was part of the deal. I parked and plugged in next to the elephants, a favorite spot of mine that Phileap and his parents loathed. But they left me in charge of parking, and I squatted where I wanted. Feeling as if my only friends were the animals, I longed to be near them. I had heard them wail for my unborn child as his life drained from me.

Parked next to the elephants, I talked with their boy trainer to learn as much as I could. Henry, the cheeky boy whose first performance had ended with his elephant in my lap, now led these giant animals and was excited that an adult took an interest in him and his pack. He was not allowed to talk to Towners, and the rest of the show had always been around pachyderms, so their inquiries were nonexistent.

"Tell me about them."

"Like what?"

"How about the ten most interesting facts about them?"

"I can do it. Want me to write them down? I can write, you know."

"I'd like to see it. A list would be magnificent."

Henry took his time assembling his list while I watched the herd and helped to feed them the leftover vegetables the local grocery stores had donated in exchange for tickets. I loved how they rocked and purred to each other. The way their trunks were more like an arm with fingers than a nose. The quiet and sweet looks in their eyes.

Henry gave me his list. Most of the letters were backward but still readable. I knew from what I saw that he was dyslexic, and he would need some help managing it—a goal was established.

Henry's list
Top 10 Facts About Elephants

They're the world's largest land animals.
There are two kinds of elephants, Indian and African
You can tell the two species apart by their ears.
Their trunks have super fine motor skills.
Their tusks are actually teeth.
They've got thick skin.
Elephants are constantly eating.
They communicate through vibrations.
Calves can stand within 20 minutes of birth.
Elephants NEVER forget.

I queried Henry about the list, and his answers were born from his ten years of life with elephants. He explained his elephants were Indian elephants found in Southeast Asia. While I watched them manipulate the apples with their trunks, Henry invited me to touch them. I scrubbed my hand over their thick skin, and little Dumbo purred. He did remember me and tried to place his trunk on my mouth. At first, I thought it was cute, but the suction almost pulled my lung out of my throat when he sucked in. I had a hard time prying his trunk from around my neck, but I was successful and admonished him. He puffed and made the sound of a helicopter and turned his back on me.

I spent an hour with Henry, and he asked about Towner life and school. He had never been in a traditional classroom or even read a book. I promised I would get him one and return the next day. I was the first Towner Henry did more than sell an elephant ride ticket to. I was a fascinating character to him.

When another paycheck came after a week's performance, Phileap's father distributed the funds. There was no rhyme or reason to how he did it, and no one dared question him. Since I had arrived, Phileap got the smallest amount, even though he threw and consistently caught the most complex tricks during the act. To my way of thinking, since we were both performing, we should both get paid. My way of thinking was flawed and logical, so it fell on deaf ears.

Phileap stepped into the trailer after the money meeting.

"How did it go? How much did you get?"

"The whole troupe was paid $5,000 for the week. Papi gave me $200."

"For the whole week? What the fuck? What about my web and the magician assistant?"

"Papi claims you owe us money. My brothers agreed."

"How do I owe them money?"

"Training and rent."

"Did you argue? This is complete bullshit."

"It doesn't help to argue with Papi. He makes the rules, we follow them."

"You are a grown man. I am helping."

"Papi gave me vida. I will not argue."

I threw a plate at his head, and he jumped out of the camper.

Back in my trailer, I unhitched the cupboards and turned the bed into our table. I prearranged to go out to do some provision shopping. I still had food stamps and had to shop alone to keep my secret. Learning to go to the market as we pulled into town was a survival technique because that was the only day my face wasn't painted like a fresco. I had missed my opportunity and went between shows. Going into a small-town store with my circus makeup and false eyelashes was a soul-shattering event. They did not see Daring Gail of the Flying Córdobas; they saw a painted lady, a whore, an interloper there to corrupt their boys and steal their husbands. I would smile and try to work something about being with the circus into the conversation, but the stares bore holes through my core.

❧

I braved going to the library to get Henry and the other kids some books, but my Nevada library card didn't work. I hatched a plan and appointed myself the teacher of the traveling show. After a bit of begging, the librarians let me check out two children's education books. I promised to have them back by the end of the week.

At the store, I encountered nothing but Mexican food provisions and many women crossing themselves after staring at me. Sometimes the red hair and blue eyes were enough to do me in. I kept my head down and bought my supplies.

Four young Hispanic men followed me out to the parking lot. When I reached the truck and put the key in the lock, one grabbed me, twirling my body around and pinning me against the door. The second took my groceries and flung them in the back of the truck. I heard glass breaking. The one who held me put his mouth to my cheek. His breath smelled of stale beer. He spewed hot air on my cheek and called me *puta*. My knee jammed into his crotch; he released my arm as he fell to the pavement. Another one came at me; I kicked him in the groin. Placing my keys between my fingers, I punched as the next one approached, ripping a bloody gash in his cheek. I was able to get the door open and jumped in, slammed the door, and locked it. They came at the truck, and I jumped into gear, tires squealing. I escaped the parking lot rattled but not hurt. When I returned to the compound, I went right to my sister-in-law's trailer. I thought that our language barrier would stifle my story, but she took one look at me, hugged me tight, and made hot chocolate.

The next day a bruise appeared around my wrist, and the family speculated that I had gone to market and had sex with a Towner. Phileap queried me about this fabricated story, and I defended my honor, horrified he believed such filth about me. Our fight was long, passionate, and witnessed. The three smiling observers who longed for me to exit their lives forever mumbled *puta* under their breath.

Later in the night, lying in our tiny bunk, I had the clarity that comes after a violent attack. My life was spent on shifting sands. Solid roots and footing were an illusion. My life was as temporary as a wave. I was uniquely alone. Lovers, family, friends, parents, even children could not help me. The only moments wrapped in warmth were those when we picked up the blanket to drape on our own shoulders.

I forgave myself because it was my nature to seek out adventure. Through it all, my 20-year-old optimism had believed in Phileap, and that the circus was my one chance for true love, a compassionate family, and an adventure to be proud of. Now, I believed we came into this world cold, naked, and hungry, and that is how we spend our time.

With my sad heart and empty womb, I turned over and made love to Phileap for the first time in weeks. I climbed in beside him, and we held each other, stroking each other's backs and sides. I inhaled in his scent fully and tasted his lips, his neck, and gave his ear a nibble. He was rock hard in minutes, and it was all I could do not to take him in my mouth. We touched, explored each other's bodies like a braille chart. He squeezed my sensitive nipples, and a bit of mother's milk came out. He tasted it and went below the sheets to explore me with his mouth.

Rising on his elbows, he entered me powerfully, and I cried at the beauty of it—slow and sweet, alternating with hot and hard. We continued to fuck until the next show bell rang. Off to the bright lights we went. I was temporarily sated and buoyant again.

45

F all, 1982, San Antonio, Texas, USA

I walked between the trailers, following the intoxicating aroma that lured me from sit-ups to culinary exploration. I had been saddled with feeding the entire family and needed a new repertoire of recipes. My nose led me to the wire-walker's trailer. Like most of the elderly in the circus, their Argentinean grandmother was held as an indentured servant in a 28-foot trailer. She cooked, cleaned, and sewed costumes, only leaving the trailer to market and buy sequins.

I knew she spoke no English from prior encounters.

Juanita was portly but carried herself with the grace of a retired wire-walker with her head held high, constantly searching the horizon for a balance point. Her hair was the color of a battleship, with jagged edges from trimming it with a kitchen knife. She made her own shampoo out of lavender weeds found on the coliseum grounds. She had shared some with me in Dallas where the bugs were as big as birds and tried to suck everyone dry. The lavender was a deterrent for both bugs and chimps.

The chimps were the most dangerous of all the animals I now cohabited with. They were smelly, vile creatures, and the scent of lavender on my hair turned their attention toward the equally smelly prop guys. One weed saved me from savage mosquitos and chimps. I instinctively knew the key to survival was friending the grandmas, those left behind by the bright lights.

I knocked at the door; the aluminum dented under even the gentlest of rapping. Juanita peeked from behind the pink handmade curtains to see how safe the visitor was. Living in tin cans in public parking lots made every member of the circus cautious, especially those left alone for hours at a time. Juanita opened the door a crack, and the smell of deliciousness enveloped me.

"Que?"

I attempted to explain I wanted her to teach me to cook. The language barrier in full force—I mimed putting food in my mouth. Juanita took it as hunger, and her kind heart led me inside.

The tiny stove had only two burners and an Easy-Bake–sized oven. The ingredients for the empanadas she was making were on the table, which at night folded down and became the youngest boy's bed. Juanita motioned me to sit and plucked a hot pocket of meat from the oven. From under the couch (which was also a turncoat bed), she pulled a blank bleach jug and spilled homemade wine into a jelly jar. She handed it to me, and I smelled it, nearly gasping at the strong fumes.

There was no way to refuse this kind of offer without offending the host from whom I desperately wanted cooking lessons, especially after taking the first bite. I knew I had found a kindred soul in this wine-producing matriarch.

The wine steadied my resolve and calmed both our fears. After eating, I joined Juanita at the stove, miming questions and not letting up. She finally understood why I was there and was pleased to help. The company was a rare gift Juanita was not afforded. She was a lost one of the circus, necessary but no longer a performer. In circus life, only performers mattered. Children performed by the time they were two years old. Everyone had to work for the act and family to survive. Although her support was necessary, the lights shown for her no more.

We didn't speak the same language, but cooking bonded us as we giggled and created through the afternoon. I left with empanadas for the whole troupe and shouted, "Mañana!"

After a week with Juanita and learning more than cooking tips, I branched out to the other grandmas. I called them the Scullery Maids, and they loved having a title, even if it was a bit insulting.

Each day, I went to a different trailer to get an authentic cooking lesson from a home chef. The languages were French, Spanish, Russian, Chinese, Portuguese, and German. They all played out with gestures, laughter, and tastes. The Scullery Maids loved the company and being needed. I loved the food techniques and flavors. More importantly, I was starting to belong. The women forced their young masters to treat me amicably; though they did not wield much power, what they did have reign over were politeness and civility.

In my own camp, I was struggling with the family. Phileap's mama had taken to inviting all the performers to call me "*Ojo del Diablo Azul*" (the blue-eyed devil). Phileap would shake his head at his mother. She would shriek, "*Oya Phileap! ¿Cómo puedes elegir a esta puta sobre mí?*" (How come you chose this whore over me?)

His only response was, "Pero Mama."

It was my turn to fight with him. "Can't you see how horrible she is?"

He didn't respond. He left me standing in the kitchen with my indignant mindset.

Phileap never defended or scolded his mother for her behavior, which included spitting out anything I cooked as if it was poison and stealing any cash I had in my purse. Phileap's father was abusive while training with both the physical bamboo hits and his demeaning tirades about what a waste of breath I was. The brothers still never spoke to me, addressing all questions through Phileap. It was a hostile environment, on the trapeze and off. My Spanish was getting better, so I understood the bad things the family was saying about me in their nightly gatherings for which I cooked and cleaned up.

The cooking lessons and teaching the children were a happy reprieve from the brutal training and rat-in-a-cage sentiment. Classes were held every day before the first show. Learning took place in the elephants' makeshift barn, which also hosted the large cats. The kids would throw a raw chicken into the lion's cage and watch him devour it in between math and history.

"Miss Gail, why do we have to do school?" The oldest boy was the wire-walker's son.

"So that you know things. With learning, you have options."

"What are options?"

"Like a choice of what you want to do for a living."

"But we are a circus. We wire-walk."

"But with schooling, you could have more options."

"I could do an animal act?"

"You could choose to go to college."

A young animal act girl piped in. "What is a college?"

"It is a larger school where you go to learn a career."

"What is a career?"

"What you do to make money as a grown-up."

The wire-walker boy gazed despondently and said, "This fact will never change. My grandpa says that we are what we are until they put us in a box in the ground. Even books can't change my life, Miss Gail."

"Then how about we do school to get out of chores?"

They all agreed it was a good idea, and I had their attention for about thirty more minutes.

46

Fall, 1982, El Paso, Texas, USA

The next Texas date was in the town of El Paso, which borders Mexico. Juarez is the city on the other side of the border. Juarez was the kidnapping and murder capital of Mexico; yet, for some reason, a bunch of circus ladies decided to go visit it for a day. It was mostly to get spices and foodstuffs not available anywhere in the U.S. I decided to join them, as did our female ringmaster, Jody. As one of the first lady ringmasters, Jody was a unique draw to the audience and a pain in the ass for the male performers. The circus is a regimented life with specific unwritten rules. A ringmaster introduces the various acts in a show and guides the audience through the experience, directing their attention to the various areas of the arena and helping link the acts together. At the same time, equipment is brought into and removed from the ring to make the show flow.

Jody was a genius at the job, with her graduation from ringmaster school combined with her incredible singing and oratory skills. Traditionally, part of the ringmaster's job is to use hyperbole whenever possible while introducing the acts to enhance the audience's expectations. Declarations of the "biggest," "most dangerous," "amazing," "spectacular," and similar expressions are common. I started by giving her a list of descriptions I knew the Córdobas would love. They hated her anyway. A girl stepping in to guide our show was an abomination to the men. The womenfolk loved her.

Phileap bellowed that I had better things to do than hang out with a freak and go to a dangerous Mexican city for spices. I went anyway, promising to return before dark because the wise never stayed in a border town after dark.

We chartered a van taxi, and eight of us squished inside, ready for a day of shopping at City Market in Ciudad Juarez. The driver promised to stay with us, following a barking command from the circus men, so we imagined we were safe. What they forgot to tell him was to drive safely. He barreled down the roads at sixty miles an hour, barely missing pedestrians and incessantly honking at other cars. We were all a bit carsick when he let us out at the large outdoor marketplace. Spanning at least three city blocks, the open stall market was a marvel. Everything you could want or desire was for sale, including salacious items.

Before entering the market, we noticed the vendors on the surrounding streets selling traditional pastries, *tlayudas* (sort of like a Mexican pizza), and *chapulines* (spicy grasshoppers). We took the time to stop and try a few things on the way in. Roughly organized into a grid, stalls were packed into every available space with a constant flow of people and goods. There was a massive range of products, including handicrafts; pottery; leather bags and belts; textiles and clothing; jewelry; flowers; baskets of every size, shape, and color; and piñatas. It was easy to spend a couple of hours wandering around and exploring the space.

There was a lot of food (fresh and prepared), including fruits and vegetables, mezcal, mole, cheese (queso fresco and quesillo), herbs and spices, quesadillas, tortas, *licuados* (smoothies), and more. Toward the back, we found a section for fresh meat and fish.

We huddled together as a group at first because only some of us spoke Spanish. Mine was passable and mainly consisted of directives and dirty words, so I kept my mouth shut. As we grew bolder, we splintered off, promising to meet at the van for lunch. I stayed with my sisters-in-law to avoid the wrath when I returned. The circus was the originator of the buddy system. We were never allowed to go anywhere alone for fear of the show forsaking us. Lose one trapeze artist, and the show goes on; lose two, and you have a problem. We walked with purpose, aware of our surroundings, and only sought out directions from matronly women with children or who worked in a shop.

Jody was an independent New Yorker with a bravado that eased her into any situation. She strode off in search of a fancy bottle of tequila. When we met for lunch, she was not there, but we had instructed the driver what time we were crossing the border, so we figured she would meet us there.

Our driver took us to eat outside the market—to a house, not a restaurant. The house was a ramshackle mess with a cardboard roof. I was shocked anything could look worse than the tin can trailer I lived in. It was 300 square feet and looked like ten people cohabitated there. Huge crosses with bleeding Jesuses adorned the walls; the curtains were rice sacks, and the floor was dirt.

The doors were pieces of fabric, and the makeshift table was a chunk of plywood on sawhorses. The stools were overturned paint buckets. They offered us Mexican Coca-Cola and cerveza. We took the Coke; it was so sweet, not anything like its American cousin. They brought out ceviche: a lime-marinated fish and shrimp dish with onions, tomatoes, and jalapeños, resting on a crunchy corn tortilla. They brought us birria tacos made with goat meat and topped with queso fresco, cilantro, and salsa. The third course was rice and beans served with chips and salsa. It was an exceptional meal we all loved. Juanita got recipes from the abuela, the true head of the family, and Abuela shared a pack of spices with us.

We called for the check, and when it came, it was $450. We knew we should have negotiated first, but politeness overtook common sense. Juanita reasoned and argued, but they were not moving on the price. Held hostage by the family and the driver, we had little ground to stand on. He loudly claimed the bill was $450 and included a ride back to the market. Juanita asked how much it was without the ride. His answer was $250. I understood his intent, if not his words.

We talked among ourselves, staying strong with words and body language. It was decided I would negotiate, as I clearly had handled the tough life with the Córdobas. I took out $40 and crossed the room, so I was face-to-face with him. I was terrified, but it only showed in the money quivering in my hand. I puffed up and handed him the money while looking him square in the eyes, knowing my blue eyes scared him.

He spit on my shoes.

"*Nos vamos a encontrar con un cura.*" My saying we were going to meet a priest, that this was a sin. These people were highly Catholic, but I believed this was our only way out. I turned to the ladies, who were all crossing themselves. I told him the father knew we were coming to this house. Knowing he had been outwitted, he snatched the twenties out of my hand, smiled, and opened the sheet flap that was their door, and we all hustled out.

We knew we were all in trouble if word of this got back to the show grounds. We agreed not to share this bit of adventure with our spouses. With more shopping to do and Jody to find, we had the driver take us back to the market.

The good thing about living in a nine-foot home is that there is no room for surplus items. I bought a lovely blanket, a hammock, and a marble chess set, along with spices and maize to make authentic meals for the family. We had split up to look for Jody, but she was nowhere to be found. A worried hysteria seized us. We circled the area, looking for her first, but we knew we had to get over the border or face the dire consequences as dusk approached. With the sun dipping dangerously toward the horizon, we headed home without Jody.

Back at the show grounds, the men mobilized to search and rescue Jody after the Juarez police told us to consider her dead. We sat around a barbecue and prayed for her safe return while making the men a meal for when they came back.

Around 3 a.m., they returned with a bloodied and battered Jody. She was not conscious, and we took her to the hospital. Her eyes were beaten and swollen shut, her jaw hung at a weird angle. Her clothes were ripped and tattered. She moaned and gulped like a fish underwater. The emergency room whisked her away on a gurney and told us they would send word to the circus owner after determining the extent of her injuries.

The next day we picked up stakes and moved to Fort Worth for another show. We never saw or heard from Jody again. The circus owner got a copy of the report but chose not to share it with us. A new male ringmaster was waiting for us in Fort Worth, and we were not allowed to speak of the incident ever again. I tried in the privacy of our dressing room with the other ladies but was shot down. Horrors of the road stayed secret, never spoken of or retold.

47

Winter, 1982, Seagoville, Texas, USA

Seagoville is a suburb of Dallas and a dusty hell. It's a collection of dirty roads, men in big hats driving trucks with rebel flags, and license plates reading "Texas Truck." The smell was of grime, the view drab, and the people extremely slow. Everyone was excited to be here, as the trapeze master owns this dirt.

We were staying on the compound of the flyer Anthony Rebra, the world's most famous trapeze artist. He was the only flyer to have completed a three-and-a-half somersault and offered to be a mentor to all of us. He was a man in his eighties with a quick wit, a twinkle in his eye, and unruly red curls crowning his head. We were instant friends. His compound was a twenty-acre lot with no running water or electricity, but it had three full trapezes, several single trapezes, silks, hoops, wire-walking practice equipment, and four trampolines. It was, for lack of a better term, a circus training camp.

Anthony demanded a strict regimen of workouts; practice; good eating; and sharing stories, wisdom, and guidance. He loved that I was a newbie and a Towner and could not wait to train me. We circled the trailers and settled in for a four-month stint. Phileap was training to up his ante to a quadruple somersault, for it was rumored that some young flyers had caught the three-and-a-half.

Anthony hadn't had a catcher since his Russian one was deported, but ours was able to do the job. Anthony and I walked to the trapeze together.

"I am so glad to have such strong catchers again."

"All the Córdobas are delighted you invited us. We are absorbing more tricks than ever. I'm glad to have an English-speaking coach."

"Who doesn't want you dead?"

"Ya, it's a bonus."

My friendship with Anthony made everyone mad.

"I still don't grasp why you stay with these people."

"It's a mystery. I feel stronger than ever."

I loved the daily routine of practice and the positive reinforcement I received from Anthony. Phileap's family only beat me into submission; Anthony encouraged me to succeed.

"You, my dear, are stronger than you know."

Since Bernice and I were the only English speakers, we were told to get jobs in town to support everyone because the last bit of cash we had was used for gas to get us here. Bernice got a job immediately at the Piggly Wiggly as a checker. They found her British accent exotic. I filled out applications all up and down Main Street, from fast food to bookstores.

We woke every morning at sunrise and started with the Anthony Rebra workout in the abandoned single-wide trailer on the property. The windows were blown out, so a nice breeze greeted us as we crunched, twisted, and thrust our pelvises into the air. Then it was off to trampoline training because

Anthony knew the tumbling needed to be mastered there before in the air. For upper body strength, we worked on the single trapeze and had a healthy lunch consisting only of green food. Anthony decided that green food was the secret to his success. I was glad to have some green proteins like olives, pepitas, pistachios, and lentils because rabbit food was never my favorite.

After lunch, we flew for at least four hours. It was grueling but so pleasurable. Papi was pissed that the coach role had been handed to someone else, but having never been a flyer, he sucked at it. At night, we ate a communal meal made by my sous-chefs (my pissed-off sisters-in-law) and me. I still had to adhere to the green food edict but was allowed to add succulent Texas beef. My culinary skills served me well, and it was refreshing to be recognized that I was good at something. The women did the Jane Fonda workout after dinner and a newfangled practice called yoga; we were taught by the tumbling troupe from India.

The only bad part of circus camp was that we still didn't have running water or a toilet in our camper. Because we were in an open field, late-night bathroom trips were still done in a sawed-off plastic milk gallon container and thrown out in the morning. Anything more substantial than pee had to be scheduled for when we were in town or at work. This Texas wasteland had nothing. I still had a plan to get a job in town, and my money would buy us a proper trailer.

There was an outdoor shower up against the hill. It was a hose cable tied to a pole, with our dressing room partitions around it. It was only cold water, but Texas was so hot, it was okay. Phileap invited me to join him for a shower.

"Where have you been?" he inquired as I stripped.

"I have been planting the herb garden all day. I'm covered in mud and sweat. But I'm grounded. Nothing fixes your soul more than touching the dirt and giving birth to food."

He came to me to kiss me, taste the salt on my lips.

"You're filthy!"

"Then clean me."

We went to the outside shower. I took the lavender soap and started to lather up. Phileap turned me to face him and lathered my hair.

"Nice."

He pulled my hair hard to let me know he was in charge.

"Lots of hair."

I turned to wash his hair. My strong hands rubbed his long hair down his back. With the soap, I cleaned his nooks and crannies. I turned him around and lathered his chest, moving down to his cock and massaging the soap on his balls and ass.

A quick rinse, and I went to my knees. I inhaled his cock like a starving girl as the cold water fell on my face and on his dick.

He mumbled, "Good girl."

I grabbed his ass and had him fuck my face. With my hair in his hand, he controlled the speed and depth of my devouring. He stopped me before he exploded and spun me so I was facing the showerhead.

"I have to make sure you're clean," he said, lathering up between my legs.

Soapy and slippery, he cleaned me deeply. I came as he played me like an instrument. After, we moved to the net, still dripping, and laid down to watch the expansive Texas sky while talking about our dreams. Mine was to write. His was to fly higher.

I applied for jobs at many different businesses, but my Nevada accent and lack of address (or admitting I lived on the circus compound) was a problem. No one wanted to hire an outsider. It struck me that, even with the Towners, I was an outsider now.

I landed a job at Dairy Queen; I had experience as a burger flipper and Frosty dipper at Wendy's when I was a teen. I faked a Texas accent during the interview, and I am sure the manager saw through it and hired me anyway with the promise I would take him to the elusive circus compound. People in Seagoville were equally horrified and curious about the traveling nomads that seemed to defy gravity and rarely came into town.

C>

I worked the night shift, which meant I needed to cut my trapeze lessons short and fix supper for everyone before I left. Phileap would drop me off and pick me up a block away. I never understood whether it was because he was embarrassed about being seen with me or he was ashamed for being a circus celebrity.

At Dairy Queen, I had a strange combination of dysfunction and freedom. My co-workers were all female, primarily teens with thick Texas accents, bad daddies, and worse boyfriends. During pauses in the fast-food rush hours, they told me stories of alcoholism, beatings, rapes, and worse. My recompense for working there was one circus or traveling story per day. None of them had ever been out of this dry county. Anecdotes of Las Vegas where liquor could be bought every day, seeing topless ladies on stage, and animal yarns were the most requested.

Being in one place, I could see pop culture again. When they showed me MTV with the Michael Jackson "Thriller" video, I was riveted. I returned to the circus complex with a tape of the new song, and from then on, it was the soundtrack to our warm-ups.

One girl I had taken a liking to was named Honey. She was sixteen and looked thirty years old. She had two children. One was fathered by an uncle who forced himself on her, and one was from a first cousin she desperately loved. Neither man talked to her or her children, so she supported her kids with this job. She took all the old burger patties home at night and turned them into a chili that she sold at the bars.

"Who buys this chili?" I tasted a bit, and it was as old and bland as I expected.

"Kind strangers after they have had eight beers."

"Isn't it kind of dangerous? You sitting in a car outside a bar at night with your toddlers."

"Not more perilous than hanging with elephants and weird clowns, I'd say!"

She was right. I had no right to judge as my life was always on the precipice of peril.

Anthony was a true teacher of all things trapeze and was full of wonderful stories about the old ways. He worked us like a drill sergeant but was pleasant in his manners and stories. I learned more than ever as words I recognized guided my body through the air as opposed to the hammering of wrong I had always received from the Córdobas.

The Jane Fonda and yoga workouts hardened our bodies in a way they have never been toned before. The addition of stretching, cooling down, and a bit of yoga made the women on the compound stronger than the men. We pointed it out and threw our tricks with more grace. They knew we were using the new disciplines learned from the cassette and begged to be let in to try them. We refused. It was a cold war of the sexes, led by Jane Fonda. Anthony approved of the workout and teased the men about being the weaker sex.

There was levity in the practice and living I had not experienced with the Córdobas before. With the power stripped from Papi, he became surlier and hid all day in the trailer. Mama openly flirted with Anthony to her sons' embarrassment and shame.

She was hanging her delicates out on the line when I heard her scream, *"Oya Phileap! ¿Cómo puedes elegir a esta puta sobre mí?"* (She still focused on me as a whore that he chose over her. Her lack of imagination thrilled me.)

"Pero Mama."

They got into a verbal scrap, and I walked away and got in the truck for my ride to work. It wasn't as bad since Phileap and I lived alone, and I got to leave the compound every day and talk with Towners. I was as ecstatic as a drunk gifted a barrel of whiskey.

There was a phone booth outside the Dairy Queen, so each week when I got paid, the first thing I did was call Nana and Becky. I hadn't had this much contact with them since I left, and it was helping me ground. They both claimed I'd picked up a Texas drawl. It was an easier way to talk, and I didn't stand out so much. I had become the consummate social chameleon.

Anthony and I had long conversations about the act of becoming a stronger flyer and how to be a better overall performer. He taught me ballet moves to make me look more authentic. His favorite conversation was how I ended up in the circus, which I repeated often.

I was on the outside trapeze bar mounted to the barn eves, going through the position as he tapped to Vivaldi playing on cassette.

"You were going to go to school, and college was all paid for?" he asked as I hung from one leg.

"Yes."

"How could you leave? Do you know how many people would kill for that opportunity?"

"Yes, but it wasn't for me."

Confused, he ordered me into another position, hanging by my knees.

"What wasn't?"

"That life."

"This life is better?"

He dramatically swept his arms to the dusty trailers, broken net, and scratched-up trucks. As if the universe was conspiring to make his point, Mama stuck her head out of the trailer and howled some expletives in Spanish at me. I ignored them.

"And that crazy lady hates you."

"But her son loves me. Or I am delusional."

I moved into an arch with my back nearly bent in half as I let go with one hand and styled.

"Nice. But couldn't you find a boy to love you outside the circus without the cracked family?"

"Honestly, I have no idea what love is. I believe I am in it. I have no example except my grandparents. They have never left their backyard. I wanted to see the world."

"Seagoville is part of the exotic world you wanted to visit?"

He laughed at his own joke and moved me to the next position of sitting on the bar and starting to swing.

"Honestly, I assumed it would be way more France and a little less Texas."

He laughed and spat his chaw into the dirt. We finished the lesson in silence, only broken by Mama opening the door again to tell me I was not welcome on this earth.

I received a telegram telling me that my sister, Sunrise, was dying. She had two young kids and seemed so healthy. While breastfeeding her boy, the nipple bled, and she got the diagnosis. I called her to console her and figure out a plan. I was sobbing in a phone booth on a dusty Texas corner.

"What did the oncologist say?"

"I need chemo and more. I will lose my hair."

"I'm sorry, but it will save you."

"No, it won't. I can tell this is a battle I won't win. We are all going to die someday."

"I get it, but you have little kids. What about them?"

"I was never in this for the long haul. They'll be fine."

It all seemed so weird. I called and talked to her husband the next day.

"She seems to have given up already. What's going on?"

"She is sure there is no reason to fight this. I am trying to convince her otherwise."

"Can a doctor talk to her? Give her some hope?"

"I'm going to try to make her fight, but she is adamant. She kinda gave up after you left."

"Are you kidding me? You are pinning this on me?"

"Not you, the situation."

"I feel bad. Should I come home?"

"That's the last thing she wants you to do."

"I will call her tomorrow."

The guilt of Sunrise being sick and alone was almost more than I could bear. I wanted to jump on a bus and go home, but I didn't have enough money for a ticket. This sense of fruitlessness seemed familiar and was breaking my heart. I saw that my sense of adventure could truly hurt someone I loved. But like most of my untethered life and immaturity, I ignored it for right now, with no sense of the future.

I meant to call Sunrise every day, but sometimes I went an entire week without doing so because I was so overwhelmed by what was happening to her. Our conversations were about her treatments, doctor appointments, fears, and pains. It broke my heart; I couldn't help at all.

I went back to the trailer and fell into bed with Phileap. When I was that sad and lonely, sex was the only thing that sustained me. Phileap was an attentive sexual partner. He was entirely in the moment. During lovemaking, he was aware of where I was emotionally. We seemed to move past the sweating, touching, stimulating, thrusting cliché of fucking and transcending into the coupling. This was part of my confusion. We were like the confluence of two rivers—one body of water continuously blending with the other until the two become one. I was not ready for emotional involvement. My learned skills and instinctual talents failed me as I tried to make sense of this new feeling. I couldn't make order of this emotionally chaotic event. Sunrise was sick, and I was flailing.

Looking back, I couldn't remember not floundering my entire life. I ran from disaster to disaster, expecting different outcomes. I felt if I could not control my life, how could I help Sunrise? The only thing I had controlled was my reaction to the shit show I found myself in right now. Which included my sister dying, which I could do nothing to prevent or stop. Even if I was at her side every day. Cancer was a freight train running over my sister. I was powerless. I also realized that Phileap was not something I could control; I was his to love or abuse. What I could control was my attitude and who I spent my time with until I could get back to my sister's side.

❦

Dove arrived with her elephants, and I was rapturous. This was one bright spot in my sinking world. After my workout, I would sprawl out on the net and talk to Zita. She helicoptered and bellowed, seeming to comprehend my words. Everyone teased me about this daily conversation that started with me bringing a big bag of wilted lettuce from Dairy Queen and feeding her one delicate leaf at a time while petting her magnificent head.

When Dove went to town, I stayed with the elephants. We developed a circle of trust with her elephants, if not her. I sat on the ground, and pachyderms circled me while I read to them. I insisted that they understood. I read them *Moby Dick*, a book pinched from the Phoenix library that I swore I would return the next time we passed that way. It was a funny sight: me sitting on the dusty Texas dirt, reading to six Indian elephants that could easily squash me with one foot.

There was a bunch of feral cats in the barn, and the elephants were fascinated by them. They were so gentle and curious with the tiny beings. I marveled at their vast bodies and their trunks, which were sensitive and a source of all their senses. They would lightly pet the kittens with their trunks and mimic their purrs. When they blew off the dust by huffing it out, the kittens became little arched, scary Halloween cats and ran away into the hay. Zita sent her trunk over to where they scurried, purring and encouraging them to come and play again. I wished I had a camera to capture those remarkable moments.

I worked at Dairy Queen for three months, and we saved every cent and were able to buy a proper twenty-four-foot trailer with a working bathroom and fridge. Life was looking up.

Dove came stomping into my new tin can castle, baring one of the small kittens. An all-black boy who was feisty and adorable.

"Wow, this is nice!"

"Thanks. I'm trying to make it mine. Why are you carrying a kitten?"

"He's for you. You need a friend by your side all the time."

"Phileap will never allow this."

"Who the fuck cares what Phileap thinks? You need this."

She shoved the kitten into my hands, and he crawled up my chest and nestled into my neck, falling to sleep.

"So, that's settled. I like the silk on the walls and the feather beds. This is a soft trailer."

"Ha! They have always considered me soft, so it fits."

"How are you doing emotionally?"

"I'm good. As good as any dysfunctional idiot who insists on residing with a family who doesn't want her."

"I heard about your sister. Gossip was you're leaving."

"Nope. Can't afford it. I have nothing there."

"The girl wedged between two realms. I'm glad you're here to help me with the elephants. They missed you."

"You missed me too."

"Not a chance, Blue Eyes. I'm only devoted to four-legged creatures. Never humans. Enjoy the pussy."

She left, and I followed her to watch the practice, still holding the kitten. When Phileap was done, he approached.

"What is that?"

"That is my cat."

"Where is this cat to live?"

"With us. His name is Kilgore Trout."

"I can't even say that! We are not cat people."

"I am. He is staying with us. You won't even know he's there."

"I said no."

"I don't care. I need someone to cuddle."

"Better him than me."

I went back to the trailer and got the kitten settled into a makeshift bed of old cape scraps and opened a can of tuna. While he napped, I commenced working on our new costumes. Every act needed its own unique wardrobe, and we had to make them. In Las Vegas, we had found a "show supply" store with a warehouse filled with shining sequins and things that glittered. It was difficult to imagine a circus without the glamorous costumes worn by performers. The vibrant colors, feathers, and luscious fabrics all help tell a story. Much effort went into new tights and capes.

Our circus costumes required specialized adaptions for each performer as the girls needed to seem almost naked but covered as a cocoon, and the catcher needed padding in his thighs. We needed the tights on the soles of our feet reinforced, as the net would tear them up. The sewing and sequins became my zen activity.

On a foggy morning, we loaded up and said goodbye. The night before, Dairy Queen had a Peanut Buster Parfait party for me to say farewell. Honey cried like she was losing a child. I felt bad for leaving her, but I promised to write. I gathered all their addresses, then stopped at the post office to get stamps. At least I could have pen pals as friends. My moving life enriched their extremely stuck one, and vice versa. There was a big part of me that wanted to set down roots at the Seagoville Dairy Queen.

Anthony was sad to see us go too. I made lasagna and garlic bread as our final meal. He presented me with custom-made leather bendts that he had inscribed with the words "always fly high." As we pulled away in our Texas truck from the dusty compound, I knew that the state had burned a special place in my heart, like love letters carved into a tree.

48

Spring, 1983, Denver, Colorado, USA

While a circus is a company of performers who put on diverse entertainment shows—including clowns, acrobats, trained animals, trapeze acts, musicians, dancers, hoopers, tightrope walkers, jugglers, magicians, unicyclists, and other stunt-oriented artists—the word also describes the performance, which has followed various formats through its 250-year modern history. The traditional format, in which a ringmaster introduces various choreographed acts set to music, developed in the latter part of the nineteenth century and remained the dominant format until the 1970s. Then the American circus became mostly mud and arena shows.

We worked mostly in the open with only a tent top. In the big cities, it was in a gym or concert venue. Each quarter, we joined another circus. This new one was an arena show.

The Tarzan Circus was unique with the owner and boss, a lion tamer, who had rebranded himself as Tarzan. He was a fifty-year-old man, barely covered in a leather loincloth. His muscles were well hidden under his beer belly. His wife did a single trapeze act over the open lion cage. Using no net or safety wires, she was truly the first aerialist daredevil. She hung by her fingers, swung to impossible heights, and bent in contortionist poses as she dangled from a tiny trapeze bar. Her finale was hanging by her heels as the trapeze swung. It was almost like she had a death wish. The loose cats paced in circles, looking up while she performed, expecting this shiny meal to fall down for them to feast upon.

Tarzan was high on self-esteem and low on people management abilities. He bellowed and loved to dock acts for missing a trick. He kept a black moleskin tucked into his loincloth for taking notes on reasons not to pay people. He was as surly as his black panther.

We signed up to do four acts: the trapeze, The Super Locos, the web, and a clown act. When an act was contracted, they also agreed to help with ancillary jobs like selling cotton candy, assisting jugglers or magicians, and office work. I signed up again to be the children's teacher.

The first show was at a convention center in Denver. I was still taken by the transformation of a big, ugly hall into a magical three-ring wonder, so I watched the set-up. A cockfight-like mentality took over the men constructing their particular acts. It was an atmosphere of rude testosterone and who could out-macho the rest instead of friendly greetings. Hammers were swung with abandon, men crawled on the catwalks without a safety line, and they all yelled nonstop. Sickened by the sound of men cursing in twelve languages, I headed to the dressing rooms to get our costumes and establish our green room.

Billy greeted me; his loathing look told me he was not going to be my friend today. His features were delicate and his skin translucent from hiding under pancake makeup his entire adult life. He was rail thin and not in a healthy way—more like a grey-toned skeleton.

He pointed, barely talking to me, as to which corner was ours and which costume to wear for spec and the web.

"Aren't you still a bit beefy for the trapeze?" His bitchy eyes scanned me in my pink sweatsuit.

"I'm fit! And I'm doing the web too."

He snarled, "Pity the man who has to catch and hold your stumpy body."

A beautiful French girl came to my rescue.

"Knock it off, Billy. She's going to be exotic with the tendrils of red hair."

Billy slithered away, mad at the world. I stuck out my hand to my new friend.

"I'm Gail, with the Flying Córdobas. Thanks for the assist."

Claudia was a classic beauty, born with perfect cheekbones and a mane of hair resembling a mermaid with shining colors swimming about. Her body was encased in a pink leotard that showed provocative muscles. She walked as if surfing on a cloud.

"I'm Claudia Bambini, the aerialist. Don't mind Billy. He's a fag and hates all the new girls until he figures out what he can get from them. Meanwhile, he's harmless."

"I worked with him before, when I first joined up."

"Good, so you know. It is the prop guys and other clowns you need to avoid at all costs. Thieves and rapists hiding on the road so the authorities can't find them. No better place to hide than as a clown in the circus."

"I'll take a wide berth. What is your act?"

"I am with my cousin's wire-walking act, and I help my dad with the cat act, my sister with the elephants, and a bit of everything else. What I want to do is trapeze. Can you teach me to fly?"

I nearly choked on laughter. "Me? Ha! I am new to the trapeze too, but I bet Marco would love to teach you. We are practicing at noon. Come join us, and I'll introduce you to everyone."

She floated out of the dressing room, a vision of grace and elegance. I was envious of her natural poise but excited to potentially have made a friend.

After the dressing room was secured, I went into the ring for my first round of practice. The web act happened in the air while they set up the ring for the cats. It was meant to distract the audience by having twelve beautiful women pirouetting on a rope thirty feet above the circus ring. The spotlights were on us, and the floor was dark while the prop guys erected the round cage and escorted the lions and tigers from their train of small cages into the ring. The web was a rope three inches in diameter that hung from the ceiling to the floor. About three feet from the top was a loop to put your hand in to twirl about on the rope. You also put your foot on the rope, so it was like standing sideways in the air as the web holder spun you slowly from below. We were synchronized, and the aerial dance was set to music. Claudia was on her web as we gathered at the bottom. She took us through the moves, even though most of us had done the web a hundred times.

"First, we climb. I want one foot out straight as the other wraps around the web, place your left hand in the loop, the right one on the web, body straight out as the web holders spin counterclockwise four times. Next, grab the loop and arch your back away from the web, left foot on the web, and style out with your right leg and arm elongating."

Someone shouted something in French, another queried a question in Spanish, the Russian girl mumbled, and Claudia continued, ignoring all.

"Next, climb up and place your left foot in the loop, release your hands and straighten into a stretched-out position as the web continues to spin clockwise, foot on the web, stretch out and arch for the ceiling. Climb back up and replace your foot with your left hand in the loop, body tight as the web holder spins faster and faster. You will know when to make the changes with the music crescendo. For the finale, slide down swiftly, but not too quickly, or you'll get rope burns."

She gracefully slid down with one leg erect in front of her and hit the ground on point, skipped like a gazelle to the center ring, bowed with arms spread, and curtsied into a resting position.

"I will never be able to move like you," I mumbled to no one and everyone. This brought snickers from all the ladies to whom this movement was second nature. They immediately sensed there was an interloper among them. I was surveyed from top to bottom, and a whisper went up amidst the web performers.

I ran to get Phileap because it was my time to climb the web, and I needed him as my web holder to be part of my act. I remained terrified; I possessed the skills and strength to do the aerial part, but not the grace. Phileap was testing the trapeze.

"Phileap, I need you to hold for the web for me."

"Take Payaso. He's doing nothing. I am too busy to hold a rope for you!"

"Phileap! I need you!"

"No, you do not. You need strong arms; Payaso can do it."

Pissed and a bit heartbroken, but without options, I found Payaso sitting on the ring curb, whittling. I had to be sure he was lucid. Any act done at thirty feet in the air with no net could be dangerous. I could fall if the web holder didn't pay attention.

"Phileap said you would help me with the web."

He mumbled, "Phileap, not boss."

My imploring eyes convinced him. He shuffled behind me, not saying a word, and grabbed the web. The other aerialists were already up to their ropes, so I climbed quickly but not elegantly, like a monkey scrambling for a banana. This garnered disapproval from Claudia.

"Gail! Leg out, wrap the other, and pull with your arms!"

I was a mixture of anger and shame. I went through each position and tried to look stylish. Payaso was passable as the web holder. We were both strong and awkward, but he didn't put me in danger. On the third time through the routine, my arms were fatigued, and I couldn't get my arm out of the loop. I was stuck thirty feet in the air. Panic overtook reason, and I fought instead of working with the rope. Again, the combination of internal opinions was affecting my performance. I knew there was no rescue; I had to get myself out of this situation. I couldn't hang there much longer without dislocating my shoulder.

Someone ran to get Phileap. He slowly came into the ring, embarrassed at the crowd gawking at me. He calmly told me each move I had to do to get out.

"Take a deep inhalation."

"I'm scared."

"You're fine."

"I don't have the strength to get out of this."

"You're going to have to find the strength. Relax."

"Okay." I stopped crying and slowed my pant.

"Wrap your legs around the web. Put your left over your right. This will hold you. Relax your wrist. Slip it out while you hold on below it."

I did what he told me, and I got free of the loop. I slowly worked my way down as Phileap gave me words of encouragement and helped me relax.

When I hit the sawdust, I was exhausted. I was also livid and embarrassed. A small round of applause erupted as I hugged Phileap. I retreated to the trailer, where I was met with sneers and snickers from Phileap's father, who had heard of my debacle. I changed into sweats and ran to the dressing room, breaking into tears on the way.

Inside was Claudia's sister Zoe who ran the elephant act. She was a tough-looking woman, thick and sure like me. She was physically the opposite of her sister, stocky and sturdy. Her dishwater brown hair was plated in a tight braid, and she wore not one touch of makeup. She had heard what had happened, as the circus telegraph is efficient and fast when someone makes a scene.

"Hey, I'm Zoe. You are Gail, correct?"

Sobs held back, I shook my tear-streaked face.

"Don't let the skinny bitches get you down. You will have the hang of it soon. Ha-ha! Hang! Get what I did there? I crack myself up!"

I snorted, which made her laugh harder.

"Want to help me with the elephant act? You won't look so big on the back of Mighty Mary!"

"Yes, thank you!"

We walked together to the ring where Tarzan was sporting his loincloth and a whip while practicing with the cats.

"Oh, my!" I gasped at the sight of the nearly naked man putting his head into a tiger's mouth.

"You consider your family bad? Look at my dad!"

"Ha!"

"Yo! Tarzan, put on some tights. Your balls are showing!" she bellowed at her father.

I snorted again, and we ran for the elephant truck, giggling like schoolgirls.

We never knew where our next destination would be. It was a temporary framework of big cities and states, with the lead clowns leaving after each show to go to the closest town and see if they could find a pasture or mud lot to fill in the dates. Usually, they found a small place and would get word back with the longitude and latitude of the show the next day. They also placed pink papers with tailless arrows on phone polls to guide us. Everyone left at different times, depending on how long it took to tear props down and load up. We were always last, so the "telephone" game of where we going to next had gotten jumbled. There were no cell phones and no way to reach the circus management, so we used CB radio with the truckers who would fill in the blanks of where we were to go. We rolled into a new area and looked for the edge of the town, by the soccer fields or at the high schools, and almost always see the entire show tucked into the parking lot with an octopus of extension cords leading into the building. My job was to level the trailer, hook up power and water if we had it, and then find the locker rooms to set up costumes and props. I spent every night stumbling over rocks or parking wheel stops with my arms full of sequins and heavy velvet capes, trying to find an unlocked door to an ancient gymnasium. It was a schedule that was constant yet never the same, a dichotomy of traveling with the circus in the middle of America.

49

Spring, 1983, Cheyenne, Wyoming, USA

Temperatures were still freezing in the spring in the northwest, and our tin homes, which were made for a weekend getaway in the summer, had no insulation. Only recycled beer cans sat between the roaring wind and our skin. Inside the trailers, we could see our breath. I warmed our trailer with the stove and oven while cooking, but we would lose the warmth the minute the flames flickered out. We slept in coats because the only external heat was a propane heater, which needed ventilation to be safe. Opening a window with the heat on was futile.

It was always cold inside the gyms too since they were made from concrete with no heating. The showers were on a 30-second timer—punch a button and after fifteen seconds get warm water, only to have it shut off soon after. I didn't think I would ever be warm again. It was only comfortable temperature-wise when the audience filled the arena with their body heat and excitement.

I loved watching the new acts; they were all a phenomenon to me. One of my favorites was a single trapeze act starring a husband and wife team. Their apparatus was a Lyra hoop. It is a form of aerial sport where the device is round, like a metal hula-hoop, and suspended from the ceiling with a single point of contact.

A single-point connection with your Lyra hoop allows you to spin using the hoop, whereas a double-point connection (like the single trapeze, which doesn't spin and is attached at each end) allows you to perform static, graceful poses. Eddy, the husband, hung upside down in a steel hoop. He held on to his wife, Edie, using props like a single trapeze, head web, and other hoops. Watching them was like magic, each knowing what the next would do and answering every move fifty feet in the air.

Both were ex–animal people, and their bodies reflected that. Where the acrobats were small and lithe, the animal trainers were thickset and heavy-duty. Eddy was Italian by descent and American by choice. He wore branded exercise wear and Nike shoes, a tribute to capitalism. Edie was a stunning Grecian beauty with black hair cropped short, which was sensible since she spent most of her time hanging upside down. They moved like shadow twins.

The single trapeze consisted of a horizontal steel bar that was suspended from Eddy's hands with the help of two ropes. With static trapeze, the apparatus is motionless, allowing for delicate, slow movements with ultimate precision and grace. It is one of the most physically demanding forms of aerial exercise.

They swung and dove and pretended to lose connection as the audience gasped in anticipation. Eddy's strong hands never let his wife slip.

He stood on his head on a small stand on the lowest point of the circle while swinging, holding his wife on the single trapeze below. All this was done without a net, but during practice, they used a safety belt suspended from the ceiling that kept them from the hard concrete below.

The final culmination of the act was a big swing, almost touching the ceiling on each side of the arc. Edie leapt off the bar, arms swung wide, and plummeted toward the center ring. A foot before her head connected with the ground, the bungee cord attached to her arms recoiled, and she shot back up to the ceiling. It was exhilarating. No one had worked with a bungee yet, and it was a surprise in every town.

On the ground, Eddy and Edie were thick as thieves and never left each other's side. They had escaped from animal families, a peculiarity not heard of before, and their "outside the lines" life was appreciated and welcomed by this town girl.

Edie approached me as I sat in awe of their performance.

"Hey, you're the new flyer, correct? I'm Edie!"

"Nice to meet you. That was inspiring. Wow!"

"It's nice to have someone see the act with new eyes. I hear you're a Towner who joined up with the Córdobas. How does that happen?"

"Yes, I'm Gail, the destroyer of circus traditions and flying families."

She laughed out loud. "Ha! I anticipated we were the only rebels. Welcome, Gail. I also hear you are a proficient cook, looks that way from your waist. Do you want to share talents?"

"I would love to. Your appearance is graceful. You make it look easy."

"That is the trick. I'll go scrub up and be at your trailer in about forty minutes."

"Sure, I will whip up lunch!"

She ran off to the dressing room as Eddy secured the rigging. I was thrilled to maybe have an acquaintance and loped back to my trailer. I made some cucumber sandwiches, a bright crudité, and a cheese platter. Phileap showed up as I was plating the feast and started to dig in. I slapped his hand away and told him we had guests coming. He was surprised.

I welcomed Eddy and Edie into our tiny abode. The boys shared workout tips, and Edie and I pooled cooking strategies. It was a new experience to break bread with a couple so like us. They were ostracized like Phileap and me and still managed to build their own life and identity. I saw hope for my relationship.

50

The show is a whirlwind of costume changes and nerves. We opened with a spec where I was mounted atop Mary, the elephant, with a four-foot-high hat of feathers and chicken wire holding the feathers inside. I did the web almost perfectly. Although clunky is how the girls described my styling. Next, I was a magician's assistant where being sawed in half was my most stylish hoax. I excelled at my timid bar-holding on the trapeze. Then the elephant act where I dance beside and on top of the beasts and, finally, the finale. Six acts, six costume changes in a two-hour period. We did this three times a day. Shows were 10 a.m., 3 p.m., and 7 p.m. every day. To say I was tired after the first week was an understatement. We also had to practice every night to make sure our tricks stuck or else we'd get docked in pay by Tarzan with his black book.

Friday came, and I was excited to finally be paid for my acts. I figured the elephant and magician assisting landed me at least $50 a week. I planned on using this money for groceries, as the flying diet was not my favorite. Phileap came into the trailer and told me we had made enough money for the gas we needed to get to the next stop and nothing more. I protested.

"But I'm doing the web and the other acts! I know we are getting paid more."

"Yes, but Papi says you are worth nothing."

"Are you fucking kidding me?"

"No, I am not. Seems I am now being punished for having you join us. Feel free to leave at any time."

I crawled into the bunk and cried myself to sleep. There was no way to leave. I hadn't a cent to my name. I was a hostage of my own making.

51

Spring, 1983, Pierre, South Dakota, USA

In the dressing room, I roused the women for makeup tips. I had a background in makeup for theater but not for an aerialist. Edie helped me, but I needed more. They shared cosmetic and false-eyelash tips and how to keep the makeup fresh all day long. We could not wash it off between shows, so maintenance of the face mask was required. With Zoe as the owner's daughter and elephant trainer on my side, the old-school circus people tolerated me.

"How do you get these spiderwebs to stay on your eyelids?"

"Superglue," a horsewoman shouted from the corner.

Zoe crossed over to me with a cowboy strut. She was the least girly girl on the planet. She was more comfortable scooping elephant dung than dressing up.

"Don't listen to that bitch. Here, try my glue."

"Thank you."

"Didn't your sister-in-law show you this stuff?"

"Na, they barely tolerate me."

"Why?"

"Because I exist. The whole troupe feels this way."

"Even your husband?"

"Especially him."

"Then what the fuck are you doing here?"

I open my arms wide and gesture to the men's locker room turned dressing room. "I am here for the glamour."

The flying and performing were glorious. I worshiped every act I performed in and excelled at riding a pachyderm and performing on the web. I started the new Scullery Maids with all the other older women who were sequestered in their trailers. We traded recipes, shared secrets, and made communal lunches for the whole show. A commissary was set up in the middle ring, and everyone loved the variety of food and choices. Tarzan softened a bit when he saw his mother so happy, finally having some interactions with the outside world. He gave us a weekly budget to prepare the meals, which we were thrilled about. What he did not tell us was that he was docking each act for the lunches, thus making a profit on our meals.

We set up a schedule using my chalkboard from school. It was still challenging because none of us spoke the same language. We would put the lady's first name on her day, and then she would write what she would make. We would call in the kids to translate to English for the grocery list.

Standing at the chalkboard, I wrote out the days of the week. These meant nothing to them as there were not weekends, days off, or Sundays in the circus. I erased those and put numerical versions on the board. Tomorrow was 1, day after tomorrow was 2, etc.

"Okay, let's start with meat. Carne. Anyone have a good recipe for the barbecue?"

That was a term they all knew. The Russian babushka held up her hand. Her granddaughter, who had been hiding under her apron, translated.

"She will make pirozhki."

"What are those?" I inquired.

"Little baked puff pastries packed full of potatoes, meat, cabbage, or cheese."

"Sounds great!"

The Argentinian abu who spoke pretty good English because she watched American soap operas, sprung up. "That sounds like empanadas!"

There was a general argument in six different languages that I did not want to be a part of.

"We need meat for the barbecue, so why don't you do that?"

"Argentinian meat is the best!" She puffed up her chest.

The Russian granddaughter quietly said, "No liver, please."

We all nodded in agreement.

The abu went on to pitch her food and tell me what to buy.

"We need four kinds of meat for the barbecue. I'll make a green salsa made of finely chopped parsley, oregano, onion, garlic, chili pepper flakes, olive oil, and a touch of vinegar. It is called chimichurri and is my country's go-to condiment."

With one day planned, we moved on to the next six.

Brazilian baianos, dulce de leche, empanadas, coq au vin, and cochinita pibil were slated. Everyone was thrilled with their new food options, and the Scullery Maids were teaching each dish they made with pride.

52

Spring, 1983, Des Moines, Iowa, USA

I practiced every night to get better at the tricks. I treasured the pace of the show and life because I did not have time to be lonely or homesick anymore. I was at home in the circus world for the first time. I was even making friends.

Jaquez was a French girl working the sway poles with her parents and uncles. The poles were attached to the ground and extended eighty feet in the air—the troupe would scale up them. The act consisted of daring stunts on the skyscraper of poles, free of stabilizing wires or safety nets. They bent their sway poles to a perilous forty-degree angle, doing tricks and posing. They also featured an unbelievable and risky midair sway pole exchange, where all members of the troupe exchanged poles with a leap in between the poles. In addition, they were the only performers anywhere to perform a grueling hand-over-hand climb up the poles. The act had a fantastic finale with an upside-down human free-fall plunge to the ground below.

Jaquez hailed from Martinique, an island in the Caribbean still subjugated by the French. Her skin was ebony and smooth like marble. Her night-sky hair was straight and fell past the small of her back, resting on a magnificent rump. She hated the constant practice required to keep the act in the air.

It was Sunday, a rare day off from performing, but we still had practice.

"I wanna piss off and drink champagne," she lamented as we donned our practice wear.

"You have champagne?" Excited for the chance to turn loose and have bubbly, I prayed she had some stowed in her trailer.

"No! We've been in a dry county for what feels like years. This is everything that is wrong with this place—no liquor sales."

I had to agree with her. Being raised in Nevada, where everything was legal and available twenty-four hours a day, the dry county concept boggled my mind. No liquor for sale anywhere, and if there was some, it was never on a Sunday.

"I have some rum left over; we can make weak Mai Tais."

"Sounds heavenly. I will be over after practice. Are we making a barbecue?"

I snorted laughing because we had both come to accept that "barbecue" was the universal term for having a party around a Weber grill using mostly liver.

"Yes, but we've got ribs. I'm making a few side dishes. Bring something French."

"Oysters and champagne it is."

"Oh, don't tease me!"

She pirouetted out of the dressing room and into the ring. For the next few hours, she was called an idiot in French on one side of the ring; on the other side, I was an awkward imbecile in Spanish.

At the barbecue, we both spoke of home and the people we missed. She was a Towner but from the Caribbean, so she was not made fun of like I was. She was also a dancer, so poise was her middle name. She helped me make my own G-strings and taught me how to style with more grace. What we shared most in common was the anguish with the circus; it was a magical place until you were a part of it.

53

Spring, 1983, Jefferson City, Missouri, USA

I made a deal with the circus parents to pay me directly for teaching their kids: twenty dollars per week for the family. It was a stretch at first, but everyone signed up after a week with positive reviews from the kids. Most children were from a two-language home. Dad spoke one, Mom spoke another, and only the kids spoke English.

These multi-generation circus kids were smart and unruly. They knew book learning would never help their lives; they were destined to be what each generation was before them. Rarely did an animal act become an aerialist. Never had a performer become a Towner. I had to make it interesting to get them to want to learn.

Math became the geometry of the trapeze; English, the lyrics to songs in the performance; and history aligned with their mother country's fables. I also taught them to cook, which we did as a combination of math and science.

In a dirt lot in Jefferson City, there was a public school across the street. I arranged for them to do a field trip on the little campus. None of them had ever stepped inside a real classroom—ours was held in the monkey wagon. They were amazed. They walked through the classrooms, seeing the kids sitting at desks in a row, marching in line to the same meal, and jesting on a playground of dirt and steel. We had chimpanzees mocking us as we learned and laughed. The circus kids felt sorry for the Towners; the thought of remaining every day in the same place seemed an unnecessary torture.

Most children of the circus start off in the act as soon as they can walk. This is a requirement of safety more than exploitation. When you move from town to town every day, there is no one to watch the baby because the whole family performs. Plus, the audience loves little kids who are proficient at something deemed extraordinary. Most babies, on the other hand, were locked in trunks during the performances to keep them from being stolen.

I had a toddler in my class who had already been performing with his parents' rhesus monkey and Afghan dog act since he was eighteen months old. He was a bright and kind boy with an incessant curiosity beyond grooming dogs for hours each night and somersaulting with small monkeys. It was clear to him and everyone else, that his parents loved the animals more than him. He was but a prop and a work hand. My class was a needed escape from the reality of his life. He was three.

"Miss Gail, can we learn about the amoebas?" Antonio had a science mind even at a young age, so I bought him a secondhand microscope. His parents hated it because it was one more thing they had to stow before traveling, so I kept it for him in my trailer.

"Yes, there is a pond behind the tiger trailer. Go get a scoop of water, and we will see what is in it."

All the kids ran off on the scientific exploration. The parents were not a fan of any learning besides English as a second language and math. They believed their children learned all they needed by practicing and working their acts. There was no hope for these children to be anything but ring slaves. I got the parents to agree by making them believe that more learning would increase their kids' chances of becoming circus agents or act bookers in addition to their own acts.

My other favorite kids were the identical triplet girls whose Mexican mother and French father were using them as a tool to get better jobs and higher pay. The girls wore necklaces with the letters A, B, and C to tell them apart. They worked as a unit and had their own language (bringing the total to four). They groomed each other like they had seen the monkeys do through the glass, as they listened to stories. They were preordained to be acrobats on the teeterboard, knowing that leaving the family or getting married was never to be in the cards. They were five years old.

We had another performing group of triplets that had come off five years with Ringling. They were ageless, but at least fifty years old, with platinum hair piled high and all wearing gold lamé pantsuits. They had trained poodles that all looked like one another, too. The dogs' hair was colored the same as the triplets. They dressed alike in the ring and during downtime. They all lived together in one motor home, which pulled the trailer with the dogs and the props. They rarely talked to anyone else.

Other kids included the offspring of the mean wire-walkers (their dad beat them every day), the clown's brood who were morose and scared, the Globe of Death children for whom danger was welcome, and the various aerialist and animal act children, all of whom knew what their whole life would look like as young as two years old.

The Globe parents wanted to know just what I would be feeding their children's heads.

"What subjects are you teaching our kids?"

"The usual: writing, reading, and arithmetic. With a bit of history now and then."

"Whose history? Our history is very different from your American history."

"I will stick to what the books say."

"How do you find these books?"

"I go to the library."

"Isn't the American library sponsored by the government? So, it is the American version of history?"

They had a point, so I compromised.

"How about I just teach them to read, to do math, and to write a bit in English? They can help you with navigating North America."

"I don't need help navigating. I always just follow the pink arrows."

"What I meant to say was that they can help you outside the circus."

"We avoid that at all costs."

This was another valid point: besides the occasional trip to the grocery market and daily gas stations, circus folk were extremely successful at avoiding the trappings of modern life. I had to find a solid plan to keep their children coming to school.

"How about if I teach them the math of the trapeze, the reading to study your contracts, and the writing so you can communicate with others in your family?"

"Our family doesn't read. Why would I write to them?"

I was being cornered, so came out with a gentle, "The writing will help you keep a history of your act. That way you will have a history to preserve in words."

"Seems silly but harmless. If they have their chores done, they can come to school."

I was excited to pass that hurdle. I knew they would tell the other parents what I said, and that would keep all the kids in school. I prized teaching and being in the circus monkey trailer school. The children seemed to enjoy my class, and this softened everyone's harsh view of me. La Diabla was now pretty much accepted everywhere, except in my own trailer.

54

Spring, 1983, Topeka, Kansas, USA

The show did a long stint of moving every day, an average of 150 miles per day, to a new venue. Every day we set up, did three shows, tore it all down, and hit the road for ninety solid days without one day off. I drove at night because the boys had to get up at 6 a.m. to set up. We were always the last troupe off the lot because the trapeze took that long to tear down. I was so tired my stomach hurt; I was hallucinating aliens on the side of the road. To stay awake, I talked to strange truck drivers on the CB radio. They were also dead tired and trying to stay awake, so my circus stories became well-known. My handle was Blue-Eyed Devil, which I grew to embrace.

As we barreled through Texas, a task that took three days no matter how fast you drove, I got on the CB to chat with my fellow late-night drivers.

"Breaker 1/9, this is Blue-Eyed Devil looking for some road updates. We are moving east on the 10."

After a few crackles of the radio, I heard a distinct southern drawl.

"Hey, Blue-Eyed Devil, welcome back to Texas."

"I never left, just slowly bouncing through every mudhole town. Who is this?"

"Rambling Raptor at your service. I'm hauling cattle."

"I'm hauling glamor and magic."

"That so? You the pharmaceutical truck?"

"Nope, the trapeze troupe."

"No kiddin'! They be talkin' 'bout you in the truck stop in Amarillo. Are you hauling pachyderms?"

"Nope, just tiny flyers."

"Well, watch out for the smokies up around Lubbock."

"Thanks, Raptor. We ran into a border check outside Waco."

"Thanks, my beef is all USDA. How'd that go for your brown horde?"

"We have all the paperwork in order, so just a five-minute cavity search."

"Hahaha! Bet the boys liked that. Catch y'all later. I'm gonna take a power nap."

"Stay clear of lot lizards."

"Always do. My missus is mean as a snake."

"That's good for you."

"Yes, she saves me every time I get home."

"Thanks for chatting, good buddy. Stay safe."

"Will do. Over and out."

55

Canada was unique in its passion for hockey, even more intense than the United States' thirst for football. Every town, no matter how small, had a skating rink. The boys threw pucks and sticks at each other while the girls twirled in short skirts. The stands behind the hockey glass were metal and only went up about five rows. The hockey glass kept the pucks from decapitating small children and separated the sound between the ice and the bleachers.

We put down quarter-inch plywood over the ice and tied off the trapeze to the bottom of the bleachers. We could barely see the audience through the scratched hockey glass and couldn't hear them at all. The silence and lack of happy faces witnessing my performance was a cold blast to my soul.

The circus here was a fundraiser for the Royal Canadian Mounted Police, so there were Dudley Do-Rights at every venue on horses guarding the entrance to the rink. It never ceased to amuse me.

Canadians were welcoming and usually showed up with their gleaned vegetables and fruit from the farms just as the elephants' rig rolled into town. The meat for the cats included ancient horses, cows, and non-laying chickens that their owners happily gave to us instead of the tallow truck. In the death of their animals, there was now a story that would be passed down for generations. The women were curious instead of scandalized by our makeup and costumes. The kids were captivated that the ordinary ice rink was now a place of magic, feats of daring, and dazzling delights.

We went from skating rink to skating rink in small towns. We crossed and traversed Victoria to Mississauga on the only highway in Canada at the time. The plywood on the ice prevented it from melting, but it was still freezing when you wore only fishnets and a bikini. The elephants hated it and would demand foot rubs after each performance.

From Medicine Hat to Lethbridge to Moose Jaw to Kamloops to Letterkenny, we visited Canada's hot spots. I fell in love with Coffee Crisp candy bars and Mackintosh toffee. The vast landscape and long stretches with nothing to look at were mind-numbing while moving every day. Even in the spring, it was cold as a snow cone. There was a gentleness to this country that I embraced.

Most of the people on the show were kind, so the abuse hurled at me inside the trailer didn't sting so bad. Phileap and I had figured out that we had nothing in common but our love for sex, so we would read from *Forum* while driving and often stop to scratch those sexual itches.

"I'm hungry, and I don't want to cook. Let's go to the next diner we see."

Phileap hated eating out because of his English and limited knowledge of food. I had learned so new many flavors from the Scullery Maids, I was dying to try new eateries.

We pulled into a small diner called Poutine Palace.

"What is poutine?" Phileap mumbled as we headed inside.

"I have no idea, but we are about to find out."

We sat at a plastic-covered booth with red-checkered paper tablecloths. The menu had six items, all a version of poutine. All they had to drink was water and hard cider.

The waitress came over to take our order.

"We are new to Canada. Can you tell me what poutine is?"

"Honey, welcome! Poutine is our national dish, and we have the finest anywhere! Poutine is a Québécois dish made of fresh-cut French fries topped with cheese curds and gravy."

"I have never heard of it. We will take two, and what's hard cider?"

"Good for you! Hard cider is apples made into an alcoholic beverage. We Canadians have always drunk it because when the Québec Liquor Commission was established in 1921, hard cider was overlooked on the bill that covered the sale and production of alcoholic beverages, making all other juice illegal to produce and sell for nearly 50 years. Cider saved us, eh."

"I am excited to try both new things."

"You are going to love this! Poutine first appeared in the 1950s in rural Quebec snack bars. It has become an iconic symbol of Canadian cuisine and refinement."

She left the table happy as the cultural ambassador.

Phileap looked wary. "I'm not eating that."

"Try the hard cider first, then everything will taste better."

He grumbled, but we ended up drinking three ciders and devouring the poutine. Too inebriated to drive, we did the horizontal tango to work off the cider. We napped for an hour and then returned to the fairgrounds.

I was in a state of near wakefulness. The sun cresting over the coliseum to the east reflected orange on the parking lot, and the sheer curtains hanging over the open window fluttered with the morning breeze. I could hear the animals waking and begging to be fed. Phileap slept peacefully on his back. His tanned body contrasted starkly with the crisp white sheets that were pushed off his muscled chest and were almost strategically wrinkled over his midsection. He looked like he had been staged for a commercial photo shoot. I viewed him with one eye barely cracked open. I didn't want to wake him. I enjoyed this early morning *alone* time for my private introspection and to replay some of the hot sex scenes we had experienced over the past few days. Remembering some of our passion moistened between my legs. I slowly pushed the sheets off and gently rolled to my stomach, placing my arms under my head. The open windows cooled the sweat from my naked back, bottom, and legs. The evaporating sweat caused a slight chill and raised goosebumps on my skin. I was sure that we would now enjoy some slow lovemaking.

The nasty loudspeaker echoed through the complex.

"Thirty minutes to showtime!"

Phileap shot up and pulled on his sweats. The thirty-minute countdown was a serious call, and we had gotten fined for not being in the ring for a previous call. He left without so much as a kiss, and I started the new circus day as the loudspeaker repeated the call in six languages.

"Trente minutos hasta el espectáculo."

"Tridtsat' minut, chtoby pokazat' vremya."

"Trinta minutos para a hora do show."

"Trente minutes pour afficher l'heure."

"Dreißig minuten, um die zeit anzuzeigen."

"Trenta minuti per mostrare il tempo."

And on it went, every five minutes until it was two minutes until show-time, and the demand was paired with a solid, rapid knock on all the trailers. Every show. Every day. All performers were required to be at all the shows. You can't call in sick in the circus.

56

Summer, 1983, Edmonton, Alberta, Canada

Halfway across the country, we landed in Alberta, where the world's largest mall was located. This was exciting for us because town highlights usually featured a local hardware store. We went to the mall for a publicity visit, and Phileap was instantly surrounded by a group of girls hugging and kissing him. I stepped back and questioned Marco about what was up. Marco explained that Phileap made *friends* with those girls last year and that Towners were going to take Phileap and him to dinner. I probed to see whether I was invited and was told to ride back with Bernice. Pissed and hurt, I slunk back to the trailer with my sister-in-law. She barely tolerated me because she was sure I wanted her husband, Nicolás. After all, he could throw the triple. A man in the circus is assessed for the tricks he can do—which dictate the income he can consistently produce—not on his strength of character or loving ways. I reminded Bernice I was not circus-born but was a Towner in love with Phileap. She shook her head like I was an idiot.

Back in the dressing room, I cried, lamenting that Phileap would cheat on me, right in front of me. The women petted me like I was a hurt dog. They explained in six languages that all men were pigs, but especially circus men.

"These men consider they have penises of gold," spat Jaquez.

"My horses have better manners than the men of this show," proclaimed Didra of the dressage Arabian horse act. They were an interesting family. They hailed from Romania and looked like triplets in their stature and appearance. In a tiny Airstream trailer lived Didra, her husband Phillip, his twin brother, Willet, and a small 12-year-old youngster who no one claimed as a son. They called him Boy. His job was to muck and feed the horses and get them ready to perform. He slept between the horses' legs at night on a straw layer, with no blanket, on the ground outside.

I never heard him utter a word, but we could hear the beatings when he did something wrong. I tried to get him into my school, but he gazed despondently when I approached him. The adults slept in one bed in the back of the trailer, shared a bar of soap (for the belief shampoo was an extravagant undertaking), and bathed once a week under duress. They smelled so bad that each week we would flip a coin to decide who would tell them it was time to shower. In the shower, I offered Didra a gift.

"I got these soap samples for free; you can have them."

"I will take them and put them in the trailer in case of an emergency."

"Why not use them now?"

"They need to simmer."

Confused, I pressed on. "Simmer?"

"We don't just use things. They must sit and grow into being with us."

"But soap is a daily necessity, right?"

"That is crazy talk. Your skin will peel off if you wash every day."

"I shower every day, and look, my skin is fine." I waved my forearm in front of her face.

"Look at those blisters. If you did not bathe every day, you wouldn't have those."

"I suppose you suggest having a child pee on them?"

"No, that is gross."

I spilled a dab of shampoo on my hand and reached out to her.

"Here, use my shampoo."

"Don't be silly. My hair has at least three more weeks before it needs to be washed."

Didra had bought a video recorder. They videoed every TV show that aired. Piles of tapes lined the walls but were never watched because they were continuously taping. They only ate leftovers; every troupe gave them what they couldn't eat. I found Didra sweeping up sequins that had fallen off the costumes in the dressing room to sew on hers. I probed Bernice about why they were so poor. She exclaimed, "They are the richest people here. They never buy anything but gas. The money is spent on the winter compound in Sarasota, Florida. They have a palace."

"Have you been in their trailer?"

"No! Why have you? You just can't help being nosy, can you?"

"I take them food every day."

"That is your excuse for getting in everyone's life. It would be better if you stayed with your own."

"Like you?"

"God, no!"

57

Summer, 1983, Calgary, Alberta, Canada

From the dressing room, I heard the gaggle of girls in the hall, fawning over Phileap. He had met them on our parade through town and talked them into coming back and being showgirls for spec. This happened in every town, but Billy was usually the recruiter. The clown gave them sequined gowns and told them to get dressed with us and report back at the entrance to learn where and how to walk during spec. They were giddy and excited. I remembered my first time doing spec with Becky, but since I was one of the circus folks now, I gave them evil eyes while they changed.

One of them asked, "What is it like to be with the circus?"

All the women ignored them, not glancing up from their mirrors. I felt for them. A few months ago, I was them.

"It's not as glamorous as it looks," I said. "The circus requires dedication and complete devotion."

"It must be so fun traveling and meeting new people."

"Only the men meet new people. We stay in our trailers when not performing."

"So . . . you're like slaves?"

Several of the women spat at this comment.

"Yes, we are flying slaves."

The girls shuffled out, not liking the information and wanting to access the magic that led them to our dressing room.

58

Summer, 1983, Lethbridge, Alberta, Canada

I loved the elephants, and along with riding them in each performance, I groomed their feet because they needed the whitewash paint on their toes every day. I petted and washed them, and they purred like kittens while I fussed over them. The elephants were controlled by voice commands. Zoe carried a bull hook but never used it. She was their master, and they gladly accepted the role if their meals came four times a day. I became second in command, and if one would pull on her chains while she tried to eat the tree at the coliseum, a sharp, "No!" stopped her in her tracks.

We had seven girls, from fifty-year-old Mary to ten-year-old Izabell. They all had distinct personalities, needs, and vocalizations. Mary was the alpha, while poor Izabell was barely allowed to have any food. I snuck her extra hay and vegetables when the others were asleep. The chains that held them were merely suggestions; they could break them easily with one tug. All had been born in the circus except for Mary, who was a zoo animal first.

They loved to perform, and it never troubled them to get into their costumes. Before each routine, we had to "crap them out," which was done because nobody wanted to see an elephant shit in the ring. We did it for all the animals by getting them to stand on their hind legs and letting gravity push down the poop, then the prop guys shoveled it up into a pile. We had convinced the farmers that elephant feces made the best compost, so we did not have to dispose of it.

The elephants could never be left alone, so prop guys slept with them and fed them in the middle of the night. They ate every four hours or else they got grumpy, and there is nothing more dangerous than a six-ton curmudgeon. I played the radio for them and sang them to sleep. They sleep standing up and purring. One stayed awake as a sentry because the tigers roared and panted at night two trailers away.

The elephants were intelligent and never forgot anything. They remembered venues from previous years where apples had been donated. Billy would arrive at each venue a day before we were due and arranged to receive vegetables and hay for the elephants and horses, fruit for the monkeys, and meat for the cats. He would also plaster posters around town, arrange for parades, and find out if any palms needed to be greased for a successful turnout.

As we pulled into a town, excited farmers were ready to give us a year's worth of crops to be able to pet an elephant, growl at a tiger, or wink at a monkey.

59

Summer, 1983, Medicine Hat, Alberta, Canada

We toured every town in Canada—exotic places like Ucluelet and Jasper. Doing three shows and moving every night was wearing thin on everyone. Zoe had to move the eighteen-wheeler full of seven elephants that swayed through the whole trip, making the chauffeur look like a drunk driver. Through the windiest roads, it took a skilled handler to keep the truck from tumbling down the steep ravines, plus you needed a particular driver's license. Zoe's house was also an eighteen-wheeler: a custom-made container transformed into a posh apartment.

Her husband, Tony, usually drove the home, and she drove the elephants. However, he was held behind in Prince George with a visa issue, leaving us looking for someone to drive the elephant trailer to the next town, which was eighty miles away. One prop guy had the proper license, and he seemed intelligent enough, so he was granted the responsibility.

I loaded the girls into the trailer and made sure the guy knew to drive carefully with the cargo. Although skittish with Zoe, Izabell would do anything I asked, so Zoe let me help. She had gone ahead, leaving the driver with instructions to unload them and feed them when they arrived. I left them loaded, and all that the prop guy had to do was attach the trailer and drive them to Kamloops. He didn't hear the important part of the instructions and drove the cab to Kamloops, parked it, and went to sleep.

60

Summer, 1983, Red Deer, Alberta, Canada

The following day, when Zoe went to feed and check on the girls, the trailer was not there. The front of the rig was there, but not the trailer nor the elephants. She ran to my tin home.

"Where the fuck are the elephants!" she screamed, banging on my door.

"Wherever the prop guy parked them! I loaded them up last night. They're in the trailer!"

"There is no trailer, only the cab!"

Panic set in as we grasped that the elephants were in their trailer and had been left in Medicine Hat.

She beat the prop guy about his head, screaming, "Fuck! How does someone lose seven elephants!" He mumbled that he thought they had been still during the drive. He never looked back and noticed that the trailer hadn't been attached. He assumed that I had hooked it up.

We drove like crazy women back to Medicine Hat with the unnerving thought of the seven girls still locked in a trailer and having missed two meals. They would be petrified, hungry, and livid. Nothing, not even a tiger, is so dangerous as an infuriated elephant. I worried for Izabell, knowing that anything high-stress would send her into a panic.

We arrived to what looked like the entire town surrounding the trailer. Like a Frankenstein movie, they had pitchforks, rifles, and axes. The elephants were unhinged and screaming, tearing the trailer apart from the inside. I jumped out first and hollered at everyone to get hay and vegetables. If the elephants saw food when they first got out, it would calm them.

Zoe approached the trailer and called them all by name, then commanded them to sit. This gave them a moment to pause, and the destruction stopped. We opened the back slowly, not wanting them to charge. The townsfolk had loaded rifles pointed at us. Izabell darted out first, shivering. She wrapped her trunk around me. I cooed and petted her. The other girls sensed the danger of the crowd, and it was harder to get them out. When a fresh bale of hay showed up, their hunger got the best of them, and they came out to eat. We chained and calmed them as they ate. The crowd put away the weapons.

We still had to be at the 10 a.m. show and drive 150 miles back to the circus. After we boarded up most of the holes using old vegetable boxes, we had to convince the elephants to get back into the trailer. It took a ten-pound bag of sweet apples to get Mary in. Then the others followed. There was still one hole on the passenger side, and they enjoyed sticking their trunks out as they were transported to Red Deer.

We made it before the start of the show, but I was in trouble for disappearing before I made everyone breakfast. My tale of losing seven elephants was not met with giggles until I told the girls in the dressing room. From then on, the ringmaster announced them as the great disappearing elephants.

61

Summer, 1983, Cherry Point, Alberta, Canada

One of the newest and most daring acts was the Globe of Death. It consisted of a giant seventeen-foot steel globe. It was wheeled out, the door opened, and one to three motorcycle stunt riders rode into it before the door closed. They raced at high speeds, narrowly missing each other, criss-crossing, and even racing upside down. It was a noisy and spectacular daredevil show. Marco was recruited for this, and he was thrilled to be in an act that was on the ground and so loud he couldn't hear his father critiquing him. Plus, it was extra cash for him. Watching this partnership, I learned to get paid directly for the acts and extra work I did so that I had money of my own.

Using this family of daredevils as a marketing ploy, Tarzan would make them do stunts with the small bikes throughout the town where we set up. The marketing scheme backfired as they were often arrested and their bikes impounded until Tarzan could get them out. While Ringling Brothers still paraded elephants through the municipality to the joy of the townspeople, we sent noisy, smoky dirt bikes.

Another testament to Tarzan's lack of judgment was how he made the

Canadian people feel bad by insisting that the American national anthem be played after "O Canada" at the start of every show. He was an early analogy for entitled Americans who believed they led and controlled the entire world.

Phileap and his family took advantage of these Globe of Death guys, requiring them to do net repair and lug the rigging to and from the truck. The Globe of Death guys felt less than the other acts, but because Marco worked with them, they always wanted to practice with us and learn the trapeze tricks, but they weren't welcome. I loved their mom and spent time in their cozy Airstream trailer, learning how to make bratwurst and huge pretzels. They were new to North America and marveled at how different it was from their small European tours where they moved through different countries and languages every day.

"My boys like these McDonald's and root beer food. I think it is bad," their grandma, the most talented of the Scullery Maids, told me.

Canada had just discovered McDonald's, and it was a hit, starting in Richmond, B.C. A&W had started cozy diners in small towns.

"It's bad. You are not wrong."

"Why they like this fast food?"

"I'm not sure. Maybe the sugar or salt added?"

"I don't think it's good for their bodies."

She was rolling an enormous sourdough pretzel and adding a ton of salt, so I wasn't sure whether the salt part was true. "I think it is because they see it on TV. It makes it unusual and popular."

I turned to her with a look of surprise at her astuteness. "You mean marketing?"

"Yes, this American thing of telling people what they want. Too bad Tarzan doesn't get this witchery. He only thinks about his pocket. Not the good of the show."

She was worried about her boys' criminal records and whether those records would follow them back to the U.S. or even Germany. I suggested, "Maybe tell Tarzan no more of the boys on the streets with their bikes. Tell him it's bad for the act."

She smiled as she punched the dough. "You are a smart girl. Why are you here?"

"That's a question I ask myself every day."

We worked for the next hour in silence, each contemplating our place in this show and in this country.

When Tarzan heard it was my idea that the boys not ride their motorcycles through town, I was paid back for my suggestions. His new plan was to send the lead clowns to the local car dealer to borrow five luxury vehicles for a daily impromptu parade. All the web women and clowns were required to suit up in full costumes and makeup. Shiny convertible Cadillacs were filled with clowns and beauties as our mini parade snaked through town. We sat up top, throwing our princess waves for virtually no one on the streets. We all had to spend a good portion of the morning doing this marketing ploy. Even the clowns were pissed at me now.

62

Summer, 1983, Indian Cabins, Alberta, Canada

The teeterboard act was made up of ten males from the same Salvadorian family. They came in all shapes and sizes, so the bigger one played the catcher. The well-trained flyer performs various aerial somersaults, landing on padded mats, a human pyramid, a specialized landing chair, stilts, or even a Russian bar.

The Russian bar is a circus act that combines the gymnastic skills of the balance beam, the rebound tempo skills of the trampoline, and the swing handstand skills of the uneven and parallel bars. The bar itself is a flexible vaulting pole around thirteen to fifteen feet long, typically made of fiberglass. The act involves two porters, or bases, balancing the bar on their shoulders and one flyer bouncing and performing aerial tricks and landing on the bar.

The flyer prepares for the bar's catapult when the bases give a ready signal (listo), and the base guides the flyer into tempo swings and transitional aerial moves.

Russian artist Alexander Moiseev created the act and brought it to the International Circus Festival of Monte Carlo. Once it was an award winner, many acrobatic families adopted it as their main act, mostly because the apparatus was easy to set up and move.

There was much machismo competition between the Salvadorian troupe and ours with them. They practiced more than we did, but they had so much more free time because setup was a breeze. They made a barbecue every Sunday. Attendance was mandatory, and after a couple of hours, the boys started hurling insults and challenging each other to do stupid feats of daring. Their females were required to stay put during the entire barbecue and serve the male family members' wishes. Their women were not allowed in the act, so they had to sell popcorn, cotton candy, and the cheap light-up toys available at every circus. The women were unhappy, rightly so. I stayed away. I only made friends with the matriarch, one of the Scullery Maids.

"I am making pupusas for Sunday."

"What is that?"

"It's Salvadorian street food. It is made with masa, beans, and cheese made into a tortilla shape. I stuff mine with *loroco*."

"I've never heard of *loroco*."

"It is a flower with a delicate taste. When you eat the pupusas, you spread vinegared shredded cabbage carrots on it and then slather it with a tomato sauce."

"Can I come watch you make them?"

"Yes, as long as you tell me why men are so stupid while I cook."

"Ha! That would take a year."

"You're going to have to explain it in a week, because then we leave."

"What makes you think I'm an expert on men?"

"Because you chose to be with one. We get placed in marriage. Any woman who chooses a man must know something I don't."

I hated to disappoint her, so I agreed and told stupid men stories as she taught me the delicious art of making pupusas.

63

We weaved and bobbed all over the country until crossing into Vancouver for a whole week, which was a welcome reprieve from moving every day. To be in one large city for seven days was a blissful holiday. When we arrived, not only was it a whole week of not moving, but it was also April Fools' Day.

After the constant moving and no actual contact with the real world, we begin to gel as a team of hostages for Tarzan. He was a tyrant with his cats and everyone else. He exuded superiority over us that was palpable. He loved when we missed or messed up a trick so he could dock us. He also sensed I was the weakest member of the team, so he teased and harassed me like a big fat lunchtime bully. I was friends with both of his daughters, so they taught me how to survive and thrive under his totalitarian outlook.

Tarzan encouraged practical jokes because he said they took brains. I set out to trick the master in his element. The cats were housed in a semitruck in small cages. When we did not have three shows a day, Tarzan would place them in the ring and let them be cats. They played with string (in this case, rope), batted around balls, laid in the sun, and spent hours grooming each other and themselves.

We had gotten a laser pointer to help measure the new venues when we set up the trapeze. I borrowed it without asking and took it to the center ring where the cats were lazing about in the afternoon sun. The male lion saw the red dot first as I swept it across the cage. He tilted his head from side to side, looking at this new intruder into his space. He leapt down and pounced on the dot as I moved it away. Not amused, he ran and slid into one of the female cats and was rewarded with a swat to the head by her firm paw. I had her attention. Laughing like a crazed woman, I teased and led the cats around, causing them to bump into each other and growl in disapproval. When Tarzan entered the ring to see what all the growling was about, he saw I was the source. Fascinated at how I controlled them, and pissed that I was messing with his animals, he was conflicted. He slapped the laser out of my hand and screamed at me to go back to my trailer. He later incorporated the laser into the act, and the audience found it as amusing as I did.

I have always been a prankster. I get it from my favorite uncle, who used to visit and terrorize my mother by nailing cookies to the ceiling. The "Jerry" was done by leaving hundreds of pictures of his face on top of all her pictures, in her drawers, under her pillow, at the end of toilet paper rolls, and taped on calendars for months to come. He lived to prank her, and with his help, April Fools' Day became my favorite holiday. Once, in the middle of March, I started to deliberate whether the Jerry would work with my circus counterparts. I wondered if April Fools' Day was a uniquely American concept or if other countries celebrated the day of the prankster. Asking would only tip my hand, so I proceeded with my agenda, hoping they would all enjoy a day of laughter.

I managed to develop a trick for every act and for each person I was close to. The day started with telling Didra that I thought I saw smoke coming from the trailer where her horse act was housed. She panicked and ran, touched the door to see if it was hot, and darted inside. I laughed hard from my spot in the load-in area. Remembering the early pranks Ramon and I did, I tied the silk kimono robes all performers wore to the chairs they were laid on. We all had clogs to slip into after we finished an act, so I nailed the shoes to the floor. I safety-pinned a double D bra to the catcher's back. He could not see it, but the audience could, and they howled with laughter. And for my own troupe, I made a meal of dog food meatloaf, mashed cauliflower, and chocolate-covered cotton balls. I filled artichokes with shampoo, so an endless cascade of foam came out when they were set to boil. Zoe was angry when I sullied her artichokes because they were the superlative French vegetable and not available anywhere in the east.

"Have you lost your mind?"

I was laughing like a hyena on crack, barely able to breathe with my fits of laughter. "You can rinse them out."

"It is past noon."

"What does that have to do with anything?"

"In Europe, the pranks stop at noon."

"I plan on going until midnight."

"You are sick in the brain."

"We already knew that. This is the most fun I have had in a year."

"The whole show is going to hate you."

"They already do. At least I had one good day."

Very few of my shenanigans were well received, and I was uniformly punished by having to repair everyone's costumes for a month. The "prankster fiend" was added to my already demonized profile.

64

Summer, 1983, Portland, Oregon, USA

As opening day in Portland approached, Billy began hiring local show-girls to perform in spec, during the finale, and in a few floor acts. He scoured the downtown area for the prettiest women and brought them back to fit them in sequined gowns and headpieces. He had around twelve of the most beautiful women I had ever seen.

On opening day, he finished practicing with them, showing them where to walk and how to style (which they all seemed to pick up quicker than I had), and he told them to report to me in the main women's dressing room where I was to hand out their assigned gowns. They were all gathered in a room, and I explained where they would dress and fix makeup (they had all come with extravagant makeup already done). When the first one requested another stool, the timbre of his voice told me he was a drag queen; they were all drag queens. The deep monotone of their voices was the only thing that gave their maleness away. I faltered and stuttered, then found another dressing room for them because they would not be welcome in the circus women's domain. I rolled in their rack of gowns and handed out costumes. They were kind and funny, and I took to them instantly. The loneliness of the road begged for someone new to talk to, and they knew makeup better than I ever would. They freely shared tips and ideas.

When dressed, they came out looking gorgeous, and the circus women were green with envy and hanging tight to their men. I shared the secret with them, and we all decided to let the boys discover the reality one embarrassing moment at a time. Even the married men were terrible flirts with Townies, much to their wives' dismay, but no woman dared complain. The hurt of the flirting was a deep-seated secret we all shared and, together, we looked forward to a bit of revenge.

Phileap was the first to approach the Amazon beauty in green. At five foot three, he came to her chest.

"Hello, beautiful! I am Phileap, the most famous flyer in the world."

She put out her hand for him to kiss.

"Can I take you for a stroll after the show?"

She batted her long false eyelashes and nodded her head.

This scenario swept over and over through the males, with the clowns and the girls waiting to see how far it would go. Grinning from ear to ear, we strolled out for the opening sequence.

"What has you so happy?" snapped Tarzan.

"I like the new girls."

"Watch it, or they will replace you in Phileap's bed and act."

"That I would like to see."

We were working with Tabernacle Circus, and they were notorious fez-wearing letches that loved to pat our butts as we entered the ring.

This Portland group was particularly bad. I was doubly thrilled when the fez heads gravitated to the drag queens. They flirted and groped until one of the ladies answered a question, and even the timbre of his voice didn't sway the would-be lothario.

The circus women were ablaze with giggles at the passive-aggressive amusement we had at the hands of the Tabernacle volunteers and our significant others. We poked and encouraged them to talk to them, all the while watching a moment of shame when the men figured out that they were hitting on boys.

My favorite of the showgirls was named Dora Jar. She was full of mirth and loved hearing my stories of the circus folk. As another outsider, we became simpatico, and she invited us to her drag show on Sunday night at a downtown nightclub. The men were pissed after being tricked, but curiosity overtook the shame, and they agreed to join us.

Not having to take off show makeup to go out was a bonus, and a night out of the trailer was a miracle. We never ventured out of the trailers to explore towns. It was frowned upon by the circus because they worried we would disrupt the small towns and destroy the illusion. Portland was a big enough city, and there was a group of ten going out together; thus, we were granted permission to go out.

Scrunched up in the truck, we ventured out in one unit. The club was in a seedy part of town, dripping with neon lights. A well-dressed woman huddled out front smoking. Billy was all decked out in black leather pants with no shirt—only his nipple rings and chains adorned his chest. He was in his element and flitted off to make new friends.

Dora greeted us and escorted us to a booth in front of a small stage with a runway jutting out. Behind us was a ledge about four feet wide that separated the booths. The club was dark except for a disco ball and stage lights. It smelled of warm whiskey and tears. The stage seemed to be made from mirrors with red satin drapes on the sides. It was tacky elegance.

I ordered ten beers because I was the only authentic English-speaking and drinking-experienced one of the group. The men were wide-eyed and looking like they might get their virginity stolen. The girls traded fashion and makeup tips as Dora brought over her friends to meet us.

"These are the world-famous flying act I told you about. They are incredible. The things they can do in midair are mind-boggling."

The men shook hands and nodded with heads down. They sucked on their beers, sneaking peeks.

"How do you get your lashes that long?" I began my litany of "how do you" questions. These ladies were pros at theatrical makeup, and I wanted to learn more and look like them.

As the music and lights came up, Dora Jar rushed backstage to get ready. First up was Cher, or the male facsimile of her. She had on six-inch platforms with heels, which made her seven feet tall. The skintight, sequined gown hugged her figure, and her large breasts jutted out. The performer sang, danced, told jokes, swept back her lengthy hair, and was highly entertaining. The next was a group in leotards doing an impression of Vegas showgirls with large feathers coming out of the back of their heads. They danced in unison to a disco tune in shiny, leopard-print suits that hugged their bodies tight. There was no evidence of their manhood. They moved off the stage and into the audience. Two climbed onto the small ledge behind us and danced over our heads like giant flamingos. Phileap was staring up at them in disbelief. One lady joined us at the booth and started stroking Marco's head while crooning love lyrics to him. He tried to pull away but was pinned. He was in a complete panic; I was internally laughing until my belly hurt.

Musical numbers by Barbra Streisand and Liza Minnelli thrilled us. With another round of beers, the boys started to relax, laugh, and applaud. When Dora joined us at intermission, the questions flew.

"How do you walk in those shoes?"

"It takes a bit of practice. We have them specially made and flown in from Vegas, as a size eleven stiletto is impossible to find."

"Where did you learn to do this?"

"Right here. We have a class every Wednesday for new boys who want to be girls."

Phileap finally spoke up. "In those leotards, where do you put your dicks? It was smooth like a lady when she was dancing over me."

Dora giggled. "This is the best secret of them all! We bend our cocks down and push them up between our asses."

Phileap was shocked and whispered he was going to try this when he got home.

I got up to use the ladies' room, which turned into a puzzle because both restrooms were used by the drag queens. I opted for the ladies' room and again queried for makeup tips from the lovely girls fixing their makeup. The boys would not leave the booth for fear of being taken hostage by these beautiful but tremendously robust women. To say I enjoyed how uncomfortable they were is an understatement. At the end of the night, I was pleasantly buzzed and loved the fact that three different performers came to hit on Phileap and Marco. We could not find Billy; he was left to his own twisted devices for the night. On the ride home, the women were fascinated, the men repulsed. I tried to compare the drag queens to the circus performer's life but was told to shut up and never talk about it again.

That night, Phileap fucked me hard and long as if he were trying to prove he was a man.

He tossed me onto our small bed and slammed his pelvis into me like he was a robot. He held himself up with his hands and knees, his body held off from mine in a push-up position, only our groins in contact. He was jackhammering into me, his eyes glazed. There was no emotional connection, only physical. It broke my happy mood and frightened me a little. It was almost like rape. We had made love, and we had had sex, as the occasion dictated, but this was different—I sensed I'd been used as a concubine. He finished with a shudder and a moan, then rolled off me. He swung his legs over the side of the bed and headed wordlessly to the bathroom.

I was in shock. I understood there was a little distance, some remoteness, in our lovemaking recently, but I dismissed it as me overanalyzing the situation. I heard the door slam and got out of bed to get a drink of water, a wet reminder of him trailing down the inside of my leg.

I found that the boys who played at girls were more of what a "man" should be because they chose and lived their own passions, not ones forced on them by family. I dared not repeat that aloud, or I would have been thrown out to sleep with the elephants.

65

Summer, 1983, Spokane, Washington, USA

Hot pans bubbled over, and meat sizzled. The sound of chopping was the rhythm of the afternoon in this small Airstream trailer. The Scullery Maids in the kitchen were dying to know every detail. I spun it significantly, and a bit pervertedly, as we made mole and blintzes together. Most of these slaves to the kitchen never even got to go to the market in town. They had to give lists of items for their husbands or sons to find. When I questioned why they were not let out into the world, they all shook their heads.

"It is a dangerous world here in America. People take ladies as sex slaves and beat them."

"Who told you?"

"It is common knowledge."

No news or communication with the outside world made these women dependent on the men. They invented the dangers. I knew most of the children had never been in a restaurant or department store. Their lives were the trailers, the venue, the lot, and the three rings. I also understood the utter helplessness of moving every day. No one knew where I was; there was no way to reach me. I had no way to contact anyone unless they were home when I had a quarter or my grandparents would accept a collect call. The Scullery Maids had no one to call collect. I was their first link to the outside world.

From then on, I only told happy and promising stories about the Towner worlds.

66

Summer, 1983, Boise, Idaho, USA

I found a handful of kittens in the barn where we kept the elephants. Everyone was fascinated with the tiny felines. The elephants hummed to them, gently stroking their fur. The big cats purred at the sight of them with no intent to eat their wobbly legs because they were used to their meat being frozen and without feathers or fur. My cat in the trailer was growing stronger and bolder. For the first few months, he never tried to leave the trailer. It was a world big enough for him. At four months, he started leaping toward the door when it opened. Sometimes I caught him mid-leap, and sometimes he got to explore for the day. This was not safe because we moved every day. As it got dark, I would open cans of cat food while begging him to come inside. Phileap had made it clear that we would not wait for the cat. If it was time to pull out and travel to the next city and Kilgore Trout was not in the trailer, he would be left.

We were in a suburb of Boise when Kilgore Trout would not come in the camper. I was hanging on the wire fence crying and pleading, "Here, kitty, kitty! Please come back. I can't leave you here. Please be smart, come back, kitty, kitty!"

Phileap did try to get him, as did I, but he ran behind a chain-link fence where we could not get over or around to reach Kilgore. We were going to Medford next and Olympia and then Reno. I cried as we drove away, inconsolable at the loss of my friend.

67

Summer, 1983, Concord, California, USA

Because of or despite my broken heart at losing my cat, Phileap agreed to take a week off and take me to see my nana. We were on the West Coast, so it was possible. Phileap had dislocated his shoulder during an attempt at the triple somersault. Despite the excruciating pain and weird angle of his arm, Papi decided it was best to put the shoulder back in himself. He laid Phileap on a wide wooden plank and used his knee to force the shoulder back in. I threw up watching it and promised Phileap a real doctor in Concord. My nana's neighbor was the doctor who had delivered her children and even grandchildren. He agreed to help Phileap if we came there. We traveled all night, and I was too excited to sleep with the impending three-day visit.

My grandparents' house was neatly tucked into a Bay Area suburb that was built in 1944. The G.I. Bill had earned them the house, which was tiny and tidy. The lawn was immaculate, and Papa swept the gutters in front of the house daily. Pyracantha bushes lined the front sidewalk. Inside, the furniture had been made for them by real quality artisans, so it stood the test of time. Not a knickknack had changed since I was a child, and that gave my nomadic heart great comfort.

Papa was permanently dressed in a baby blue one-piece polyester jump suit, and he hugged me tight.

"Toksy! You are here!" We hugged again, and then I introduced Phileap.

"Papa, this is Phileap."

"Hello, young man. If Toksy loves you, we love you!"

Phileap looked confused. He turned to me and asked, "Who is this Toksy?"

Papa and I laughed and embraced again.

"That is my name for your girl. I have always called her that."

"It is my nickname."

"What does it mean?"

"I have no idea, just felt like it fit her more than Gail, so that's what I call her."

Nana did not come to the door when we arrived, and Papa explained she wasn't feeling well and was napping. I was delighted to see my papa. Phileap jumped into the pool, having never seen a personal one in someone's back-yard. We went to see the doctor, who did an x-ray and gave us some physical therapy exercises for Phileap's shoulder.

Nana slept all day. When she did emerge, I was unnerved by the state of her. All my life, she had her hair in an up-do, a tightly wound beehive of red resting on top of her head with never a hair out of place. She slept with it wrapped in toilet paper and went to the hairdresser once a week. Now, it was a tangled, frizzy mess hanging in her face and down her back. She was not present and looked at me with accusing eyes. Papa said it was the medicine and that she would be better soon. I wasn't so sure. He assured me, pressed two $100 bills into my hand, and sent us back to the circus.

"Be safe, Toksy."

"I will, Papa. I want to stay and help you."

"Nana said no. We were not to interrupt your adventure."

"But what if she doesn't get better? My adventure means nothing if you aren't here."

"Toksy, Nana and I will always be right here." He took my hand and placed it on my heart as he kissed me on the cheek.

68

Summer, 1983, Salt Lake City, Utah, USA

We were in Salt Lake City two weeks after Kilgore Trout had run away. We stopped to spend the night on our way to hook up with the troupe in

Eugene. We worked at this fairground before and had made arrangements with the groundskeepers to sleep for free in the rodeo yard. It was something we always looked for if our drive to the next stop was an overnight one. There were not many campgrounds around. We mostly slept in truck-stop parking lots, which were extremely noisy, with big rigs coming and going all night. A quiet stable was preferred, even without permission. If we liked the grounds and knew where the gates were, we spent the night there.

After dinner, I went to empty the garbage—something you did three times a day when living in a small trailer. I was taking my sweet time getting back and talking to the stalled horses when I heard a meow coming from a hay bale. I investigated and called, "Kitty, kitty, kitty!"

And like a camouflage dart, this cat ran right past me and jumped into my trailer. When I climbed the stairs to see what was inside, I was shocked to see Kilgore Trout. He was thinner and two weeks, and 580 miles, from where I last saw him. Phileap took his paws and checked to see if he walked the whole way. Besides being hungry, he was okay. I was elated and felt my nana had sent him back to me.

69

Summer, 1983, Eugene, Oregon, USA

Talk got out that my cat was back. Everyone came to see if I had lost my mind, but there purring next to me was my pretty boy. We puzzled together that he must have gotten on the elephant truck after we left and had gotten out again when they had stopped in Salt Lake City overnight. He waited for me to arrive, and that I did.

The Scullery Maids came to inspect the newly found miracle and to find out what happened on my pilgrimage to my nana. As we talked, that wonderful cat never left my side.

"Why are you so sad?" asked sweet, portly Valerie.

"My nana is dying. I wasn't there for her."

"You can't be on the road and *there* for people. You must know that by now." Zoe's brashness was sometimes welcome, but not today. "Why didn't you stay?"

"And give up all this?" I swept my hand around the sawdust and decaying hay that was my front yard for the day. She dropped the line of questioning and moved on to theories about the cat.

I thought about it as we drove from Utah to Oregon. I already had concrete knowledge that the circus was not the travel and adventure fest that I thought it was going to be. I no longer belonged in the Towner world. Nana was so advanced in her illness that she didn't know who I was. The morphine they gave her to dull her excruciating pain made her mean. She complained about the nurses helping her and even claimed my papa dropped her in the bathtub. She was nothing like the angelic saint who had saved me. My tender self-esteem could not adjust to her end-of-life persona, so I did like I had been doing and followed Phileap blindly back into the circus grind.

"You need a baby." This proclamation had become persistent with the mothers of the show.

"I am married to a baby and his infant parents."

"You need a squishy, not a furry, brat," Zoe huffed into her stew pot.

"I'm trying."

"Ya, we know. We hear you and see the trailer rocking."

They tittered in their intimate knowledge of our love life.

70

Fall, 1983, Victoria, British Columbia, Canada

We ventured back into Canada again. The border crossing was tricky because most of the performers were in the U.S. on a visa. We also had to have a vet do a health check on the animals. Getting sixty people and over a hundred animals through border bureaucracy was a feat. I helped because I knew how to fill out forms, get the officers to laugh, and distract them with wild circus stories. It usually took forty-eight hours to get everyone across. We passed over in British Columbia, and our first venue was on the island of Victoria.

After the paperwork hell that was the border, we needed everyone on a ferry. The guards and people in charge always started strong with "NO WAY," but after a whiff of a pretty aerialist and getting to pet an elephant—or, for the more difficult ones, a tiger—they would sigh and let us on board, eager to go home and tell their spouses about the exciting passengers.

Victoria was beautiful and wild. I loved being on an island. Phileap and I walked to the shore in the morning, dug up clams, and foraged for mussels on the rocks to bring them back to the Scullery Maids to turn into delicious soups and fried offerings. We spent all morning at the shore, and when it heated up, we headed back to the trailer. I had started talking to Phileap about trying to have a baby and what that would look like for us on the road. I had a naive vision that we would miraculously leave his family and settle down once we had a child.

"That's crazy, Apple Pie!"

"What is?"

"I could never leave my family or Mama. Nicolás is getting old. I will have to throw the triple soon. I can't go anywhere."

"But you can!" I had heard this line of reasoning from the children and was now getting it from my husband. They were so wedged into circus life.

"No one has ever left the circus in my family for seven generations. Only way out is death."

"But more and more acts are working at the big shows or Circus Circus. Can't you do the same?"

"Only if everyone agrees. And it is not as much money as traveling."

"That is flawed logic. You may make more money, but you pay more in gas and other traveling expenses. If you stay in one place, you make more NET money."

"Our net is fine. We do not need money for it."

I laughed at his misunderstanding but left it there.

"Let's talk about this naked."

He stripped down, and so did I.

The nudity, the heat, the outdoors, and the sweating were all too much for our active libidos. It usually started with touching hands. The light touches turned into hand squeezes—him touching my nipples, me touching his stomach and slowly moving down south. We had both shaved our pubic hair and were baby-smooth. I leaned over and took him in my mouth. I loved his hard, brown cock. I loved it even more in my mouth. The hardness of the shaft and the velvety softness of the head stroked breathtakingly.

I loved the taste of him—the salty taste of his pre-cum and the fruity taste of his cum. He drank a lot of pineapple juice, and his semen tasted like it. I also loved to hold his balls in my hand as I sucked him. Usually, I would suck him until he was about to cum, then stop and allow him to recover again. I was adept at this edging process and could sustain him for hours. The bonus for both of us was when he finally came, he blew a massive load. For me, he began by slowly dragging his fingertips over my labia and along the creases where it joined my thigh. He would move slowly up the outside and around back toward my perineum, the sensitive area between my vagina and anus. I always produced copious amounts of moisture, and he used it freely to lubricate his fingers, allowing them to slide sensually over my sex. He always waited before touching my clit. He knew once he went there, the countdown toward my climax would be irreversible. I stood up and he slammed me, driving his hard cock deep inside.

The baby talk swirled in my head postcoital, and I wondered if this time his seed took.

71

all, 1983, Prince George, British Columbia, Canada

I had many jobs. Since the money we made with the trapeze act was distributed by Phileap's dad, with no rhyme or reason, there were weeks we didn't receive a cent. My extra jobs were the only way we could eat. My favorite part-time job was helping the Carlock family, who had a magic act, a rhesus monkey, and an Afghan animal act. The senior Carlock was seventh-generation animal circus and had a wicked sense of humor. Their *home* was a converted eighteen-wheeler specially made to house eight dogs, ten small monkeys, and a grooming facility in the middle. The upper deck was their living quarters. They were never away from the animals. That was a trait all animal circus people thrived on, living consistently with and for their animals.

The Afghan hounds had long, silky hair that required daily complete brush-outs. They were gorgeous as they ran around the ring with their hair flowing. Their act was led by Senior Carlock's three-year-old son, Antonio. Dressed in a little red tuxedo, he commanded the hounds to run, jump, twirl, and sit on stools. Senior Carlock was watching and doing clown elements in the background, but it was the boy and the dogs that were the show. The crowds loved the act because the tiny Antonio did tumbles and pratfalls, and the dogs would respond.

The act with the rhesus monkeys was serious business. They are the best-known species of macaque and measure about nineteen to twenty-five inches long, excluding the furry tail. They are small but mighty, with substantial canine teeth that are dangerous. They are stronger than a man, and if one bites you, it can cut into your bone.

For the act, they were dressed in tiny band uniforms and sat on a bleacher-like bench, wearing a collar connected to a stainless-steel leash attached to the bench. When they were up to perform, Senior Carlock unhooked the leash and brought them to the center. They were the cutest deadly thing in the ring—pint-sized, but more deadly than the tigers. Senior Carlock's secondary act was magic. He always hired an assistant from the other showgirls, and I was chosen one season.

I loved being the girl he sawed in half but hated that all magic was permanently ruined for me because I knew how each act was accomplished.

Between shows, I taught Antonio his ABCs and how to do math. I believed the boy was a thousand times wiser than I would ever be. The Carlock family was kind and generous to me, a rare trait that I cherished.

72

Fall, 1983, Chetwynd, British Columbia, Canada

With only one highway, moving across Canada was easy, but we often had to veer onto a country road to get to the next small town. Back on the ice rinks as each town had one, the elephants now needed industrial-sized leg warmers. The Scullery Maids were given a case of wool yarn and told to knit them for our pachyderms. I learned to knit, as a dropped stitch never bothered an elephant. Mine were rainbow-colored, which infuriated Zoe but made Billy so happy.

As we knitted, we planned the next week's meals.

The German oma had some grand ideas for making a barbecue dinner.

"I'm going to make a German feast. Lots of brat for meat and then *brot*, a crusty roll that must be served with every meal."

"That sounds wonderful. I think we have plenty of flour. What else?"

"I'm famous for my Käsespätzle."

"What is that?"

"It is a dish from my home in the southwestern regions of Germany. Käsespätzle is made from layering small spätzle pasta with grated cheese and topping with fried onion. I serve with applesauce."

A small American perked up. "That sounds like mac and cheese?"

"It is not from a box with neon dust sauce. This is real food."

Deflecting the culinary argument that came at every one of these meetings, I led her out of her anger. "What else?"

"A schnitzel. I use veal (if you can find it) and tenderize and then cover it in egg, flour, and breadcrumbs. Then I fry it up."

"One of the teens grumbled, "That sounds like the chicken fried steak they have at all these diners."

I stepped in and led the conversation to our many other night's menus.

Fall in Canada is no joke, and I ran from the ring to my trailer, drinking hot tea compulsively. To say I was cold for three months is an understatement. Imagine being in a tiny bikini and prancing around with only one inch of wood between you and the ice. We were still doing three shows a day and moving at least fifty miles every day. My cat kept me warm between shows, purring in my lap and kneading me.

It was grueling, with scarcely enough time to eat between shows. The Scullery Maids met to beef up our communal meals. The schedule was hard on every family, but a daily meal would keep everyone healthy and well-fed. The problem was that there were no big grocery markets, just small neighborhood stores that only had quick food. We needed a big source of meat that we could turn into a meal. In this part of Canada, the only meat we could find was black bear. They were getting it for the cats, but I wondered if humans could eat it.

"Is it safe for humans?"

The Russian babushka spoke up. "We eat bear all winter long. Black bear is better than grizzly because they only eat bugs and plants."

"How do we cook it?"

"Stew is the best. A lengthy cook makes the fat melt and flavor the meat. You cook it long enough, and it falls apart."

The French grand-mère spoke up. "Does it taste wild?"

"Not with the right seasoning. The problem is that the meat tastes like the last thing the bear ate, so hopefully it wasn't dead fish."

It was sounding less like a treat and more like an emergency meal. I was worried, but the Argentinian abu spoke up. "Chimichurri can make shoe leather taste good."

We all chuckled and agreed with that, and I set off to buy bear meat.

First, we made steaks, but not even the delicious Argentinian sauce helped it. Too tough to finish, it mostly got thrown to the cats. The next day, we did a stew that cooked on low heat all day. It was tasty and went a long way with a solid combination of spices and potatoes. Our French grand-mère made the liver into a pâté terrine that was so good, no one recognized it was liver. From then on, we made a pâté terrine every week, and the icky liver problem was solved. It was made with a mixture of ground meat and fat cooked in a vessel called a terrine. For a pâté, scraps and organ meats are ground up with muscle meat to create a beautiful little meatloaf—for that is ultimately what pâté is. We served it with crusty bread, tiny pickles (cornichons), and a jam. Now everyone loved the liver, and my cat got the leftovers.

73

Fall, 1983, Dawson Creek, British Columbia, Canada

We still worked out to our fitness movement, the Jane Fonda Workout. This cassette tape was the first of its kind to offer a fitness class, and we loved it. We shared it with all the other female performers. We did it every night and most mornings. "Feel the Burn" and "No Pain, No Gain" became our mantras. Fonda's accomplishment for women establishing the celebrity-as-fitness-instructor model was refreshing and inspiring. It was, for us, a new way to gain strength and self-esteem. The soothing music of the soundtrack was salve to my soul. Boz Scaggs, The Jacksons, REO Speedwagon, Billy Ocean, and Jimmy Buffett filled me daily with happiness. The idea that women could succeed in this male-dominated world started a nugget of hope for me.

One of the most significant issues with traveling was no music besides country, ranchera, or gospel on the radio in rural places. When we wandered into big cities, I found top-ten stations and kept them dialed in until they became a fuzzy mess of static.

We had live music from the band that traveled with us. The ensemble had five musicians and their wives. To me, they were magical but as scary as the prop guys. They were a close-knit crowd that played jazz music after the show only for their own entertainment, but never talked to the other performers. One of the players' wives had just given birth to a little girl they named Lyric. I had my in with their group after offering to watch the baby. I'd look after her when her mom had to sit in for a performance as an operatic voice and percussionist. We used the five-member band in small towns. In the big cities, their wives joined in, singing melodramatic, operatic arias as we performed. I found the full chorus poignant and lovely. Rocking little Lyric, I questioned her mom, Sonnet.

"Have you always sung like that? Your voice is hauntingly beautiful."

"I was trained with the Venice opera."

"No way, how did you end up with the circus?"

"Same way you did. I fell in love with a man who only knew one thing and wanted to travel. He joined up with this band and promised to show me the whole world."

"Wow" was all I could say as I drank in the smell of Lyric's baby head.

"And now, I have this baby. She's happy for now, but I'm not sure what to do once she starts crawling. Our trailer is too small, the arenas are too dirty, and the dressing rooms are disgusting."

I hadn't thought of that. My desire for a baby was not founded on logic—only my need to procreate. Did I really want a baby that would have to learn how to crawl on the net? Or worse?

74

F all, 1983, Grand Prairie, Alberta, Canada

One night we decided to be *normal* and go out for dinner, the whole performing circus. The problem was someone always had to be with the tigers and elephants. We choose two prop guys to watch them for the three hours we would be gone. They were instructed and reinstructed, and the twenty-five of us jumped into a caravan of trucks, ready to go out and be regular people out on a collective date. The dinner and the staff of Mee Hung Low were exceptional, and we tarried longer, enjoying sake and Sapporo. When we arrived back at the ice rink, we felt a horrible sense of déjà vu—the elephants were missing.

Panicked and loaded up with heads of lettuce, we circled the stadium, calling their names. Mary trumpeted, and we followed the sound. They were all in a thicket, tearing small saplings from their roots and eating the trees. They purred when they saw us and came eagerly because they were lost and afraid. As we walked back, we saw that our motley group had eaten or destroyed every tree around the rink. They had picked up and destroyed wheelbarrows, wooden boxes, even hockey sticks. It looked like a hurricane had sat down and swirled around the rink. We brought them back to their trailer and rewarded them with boxes of iceberg lettuce.

Sake hangovers were a new experience for us, so the following day was tough. The shrieking and discord from the rink owners added to our discomfort. They were unsure what had happened to wreak damage to their building but were sure it was the show's fault. The circus owner calmed them with the promise to come back next month and do three shows at no charge. He never meant to keep the promise and had us all out of the lot and on to the next town by 10 a.m. The prop guys that were supposed to be watching the elephants were left by the side of the road as punishment. They were as replaceable as the hay, with a new slew of derelicts to be picked up outside the jail as we left the township.

75

Fall, 1983, Saskatoon, Saskatchewan, Canada

Although I knew more people on the show, I was worried for my sister and nana. My days went from six in the morning until after midnight.

My living space was small and sad, so I escaped to Valerie's trailer to cook or to the arena when I woke up. I was actively living with all these people, but instead of intimacy, I felt alone. Phileap was my sleeping and fucking partner, but we never talked. I didn't trust him, and without trust, it was just dinners and porn. The icy abyss of traveling was wearing on me. When I found a payphone, I called Becky and lamented.

"Get your ass home," she screamed through the lion roars.

"I would have to go back and live with my parents. I can't!"

"You can crash on my couch, and we'll get you a job and a place to live. I miss you. I'm working at the bingo parlor at Harrah's now. I can get you a job there in no time. Please come home."

"I want to. I hate this. But I can't leave Phileap."

"Yes, you can. Sounds like he won't even notice you're gone."

"He'll miss the sex."

"Why aren't you on the pill?"

"They won't let you drink alcohol here; you think I can get the pill on the road?"

"This traveling sounds like it sucks."

"It does. I am stuck in the suck."

"Please come home."

"I'll think about it. Tell me about your job."

Becky spilled the hilarity of working with ninety-year-old ladies who took their bingo extremely seriously and the bartenders and card shufflers who made up the casino cast in Reno. The sound of her voice made me more homesick. The phone disconnected us mid-sentence. I had no more quarters, no way to call her or anyone back. I only had eight to begin with, and the first minute had taken six of them.

How could she so easily talk of escape when I had no way to do it? A bus ticket—hell, even getting to a bus station—would take a miracle. I cried into my cat's fur. I had experienced this seclusion before when my parents went on drinking binges. It was familiar, but painful.

I was still struggling with money with no access to banks or credit cards. Every cent I got paid for my extra jobs went toward eating and making new costumes. I had no means of contacting my family or friends except by letter or rare phone calls, and they could never find me. The letters they did send didn't reach me until the end of the season.

The Scullery Maids I cooked with and the children I taught could make me giggle, but it was temporary and not reciprocal. The lonely pit in my stomach, the place where love once lived for the first time, was now forlorn. I had made some circus friends but found that making friends only added to the despair. Our time together was usually a few months, and when we left to jump to the next show, I never saw or heard from them again. I had said too many goodbyes. I started this journey with the need for adventure, but now I was most proficient at farewells.

After talking to Becky, I threw up all day. I accredited it to a bad truck stop burger I got from a revolving oven. I still had to perform, and they made me puke in a bucket before the show. My father-in-law held the same bucket, still full, for me after the act as I flipped off the net.

76

Fall, 1983, Letterkenny, Ontario, Canada

We were in Letterkenny, and I spotted a women's clinic next to the grocery store. They let me do the shopping because Valerie and I prepared daily meals. It was a respite to be among Towners. I went into the clinic with my bags of groceries and asked to see a doctor about my symptoms. I was throwing up and tired and my boobs hurt. The receptionist whispered to the nurse, loud enough for me to hear, that a whore walked in and to make sure she put on gloves when dealing with me.

I sat on the cold bench, a paper blanket on my lap, with my socks the only part of my clothing left. The nurse was gloved and staring at my ridiculous makeup, asking my symptoms, taking my vitals. She seemed startled by my budding arm muscles and ripped stomach. The doctor walked in with a stogie in his mouth, its long ash threatening to spill and burn me. He tapped my knee with a rubber hammer; poked my stomach with gloved hands; and told me to scoot down, relax, and let my knees fall apart. His large digits invaded me, and when he stuck a finger up my ass, I screamed. With a creepy smile, he told me it was routine. He told me to get dressed and tossed the gloves into the silver trashcan.

He came back once I was dressed and told me that I had a kidney infection. He gave me a vial of pills and explained I must take every one. He also talked about hepatitis and the dangers of needle use. When I told him that I did not use drugs, he petted my thigh and said, "Bless your heart."

I left and made it back to do a double backflip on the second show. In the following three towns, I still threw up. I had no strength, and the pills seemed to make it worse.

One night, I slipped and fell outside the tiger cage. My stomach started the familiar cramps, and I cried out, only to be mocked by the loudness of the roars. The big cats paced and snarled in their cages as my womb emptied through my leotard and onto the straw. I told no one and returned to my bed around 2 a.m.

77

Fall, 1983, Mississauga, Ontario, Canada

While in Mississauga, Ontario for two days, I decided to see another doctor. I waited for an appointment in a sizable, sweaty emergency room with 100 of Canada's finest citizens. I missed the three o'clock show, but I had to figure out what made me sick and then miscarry. I gave the nurse my full history of pregnancies gone bad.

When the doctor finally examined me, he bellowed, "You lost another baby! This is not an emergency, and it never will be!"

He slammed the door, indicating that it was time for me to leave.

I walked destitute into the lot and let my fellow Scullery Maids know I lost another one. They were not surprised; they all claimed to have known. No one had cared to let me know that fact.

"You got so ugly; I knew it was a girl. I didn't say anything because no one wants a girl," Valerie proclaimed. I was devastated and decided not to respond. The other Scullery Maids chimed in.

"With all that spicy food you eat, I know the baby didn't stand a chance."

"And you daily stepped over rope."

"You rubbed it too much."

"I know you wished this baby away, that is all it takes."

Having heard enough, I said, "These are all old wives' tales!"

"Well, we are old wives. So, they are our truths."

"It was going to look like an elephant anyway, so you should be happy."

"Why would my child look like an elephant?"

"It is common knowledge that if a pregnant woman looks at an ugly animal, the baby will look like it."

"That is so stupid!"

Valerie jumped in, "I think my girls are beautiful, so shut up."

"This is all myths. None of it is real. I don't understand why I keep miscarrying."

"We all think your mother-in-law put a curse on you. You don't stand a chance."

Having heard enough of their complete nonsense, I waddled away to sit and read Tom Robbins in the elephant pen. The girls were nice to me there and petted my empty womb with their trunks.

78

F all, 1983, Sudbury, Ontario, Canada

We made love like an old married couple that was still passionately in love. Soft touches; caresses; light kisses; and long, slow copulation. No rush, no acrobatics, slow and easy, both climaxing at the same time and falling asleep with him slowly softening inside me.

"Apple Pie, we must stop trying to have a baby. Your tears are ruining our comforter."

I wasn't at all consoled by his devotion to a 300-thread-count blanket rather than my empty womb.

"That's harsh. It's not my fault."

"How do you know that? Maybe you are evil like Mama says."

"Fuck you." I sat up and shoved him, threw on a robe, and stomped out of the trailer.

I got to Valerie's trailer, ready to take my rage out by kneading bread. "Hey. Valerie. Need help with dinner?" I yelled through her door.

She flung the door open, smiling at my tear-streaked cheeks. "Mija, come in. I'll make you better with my magic stove."

I laughed and squeezed around her large constitution into the small kitchen. She had no storage space in the cupboards or the tiny fridge. Each day, she would crawl under the trailer to her plastic tubs and haul up her rice, flour, sugar, and dried herbs. They would rest on a table outside the front door like a makeshift pantry. I had purchased exotic spices like MSG, Calabrian chilis, and lemon pepper—things that would add umami when there was no meat to make the meal taste better. We introduced jalapeños and cheddar cheese to our bread recipes, and every family sought them.

After, we stowed the larder back underneath the trailer, and I walked from door to door, passing out bread and empanadas—little pastries full of ground meat, nutmeg, and raisins.

They all loved the gift of meat pies. I mused as I continued in the same pattern. The show parked the trailers the same way no matter where we stopped, which always fascinated me. They pulled the trailers into a horse-shoe with the opening facing the building. Animal people parked closest to the entrance to access the most power coming from the jump box placed outside the loading dock tunnel. We were usually the four trailers that completed the arch of the horseshoe. All the RVs looked shabby and dented, with duct tape decorating every exterior. They were not meant for long-haul and constant travel. Our water came teed off outdoor spigots and always tasted like hose. The flow was but a trickle. Paint buckets were used to bring water from the arena back to the trailer to wash dishes. The wealthy performers had Airstreams, which were sturdier but felt smaller with their curved roofs. The men spent hours pontificating about how they would make a perfect travel trailer, not these redone beer cans.

Back in our trailer, Phileap was still not talking to me as we loaded up for the next stop. When we left each town, we had to find an RV dump station for the grey water and sewage. If we couldn't find one of the obscure stations, we pulled over on the side of a freeway, opened the valves, and let the shit fly.

79

Fall, 1983, Moosonee, Ontario, Canada

Two of the pregnant girls took me with them to a women's clinic. Zoe, who was tough as nails, seemed to like me, and I would follow her anywhere. The ringmaster's wife, Lil, was pregnant too. She was shy to a fault, and I don't think I ever heard her speak. The doctor was a robust matriarchal type who was fascinated with us. Zoe spoke French, Lil didn't speak at all, so the questions were shot at me.

"What is it like moving every day?" the doctor asked as I did the scoot down and "let your knees fall to the sides" routine.

"It's hard for a lot of reasons, but every morning starts with the priority of finding a bathroom and place to shower."

"Where do you shower?"

"In the locker rooms wherever we perform."

"Do you have freaks on the show?"

Zoe barked, "That is the carnival. We are circus!"

The doctor gave her a fierce look, and I cringed and explained. "Circus is mostly the acrobats and wild animal acts. P. T. Barnum started with the carnival and circus mixed. Most families on this show come from Europe or South America and are generational with their acts. My husband is the seventh generation. Zoe is a tenth-generation animal trainer. Nowadays, the circus is feats of daring with three rings and animal acts, and the carnival is rides and freak shows."

"Except the midget and her kangaroo," Zoe grumbled.

The doctor peeked up from between my legs. "Tell me about the midget and the kangaroo!"

"Her name is Beverly, and her act is a boxing match between her and the kangaroo. The serious acts don't like it because it makes the line blurrier between freak and performance. You might meet her today; she swore she would come here between shows."

Zoe mumbled something in French about Beverly being a whore. We had all heard her fucking the prop guys in the dressing rooms late at night. The sounds that midget made while fucking were strange and disturbing, like a wounded goat. I spilled all that while I let her vacuum my womb.

The doctor finished and took my hand to help me sit up.

"I would love to help any of you," she said. "Let all the ladies know that they are welcome in my clinic at no charge. I want six tickets to the show tonight. I want to see you perform."

She turned back to me.

"By the way, you have negative blood. I am assuming your husband is positive, which is why you keep losing babies. It will always be a high-risk pregnancy. To keep you from bleeding out, I'm going to give you the Rh immunoglobulin (RhIg) shot. It's made from donated blood and is given to an Rh-negative woman who has not yet made antibodies against the Rh factor. It can prevent fetal hemolytic anemia."

I took the shot, and my butt ached for days.

Now I had my answer. Even my blood did not want a circus child. I ask the doctor for the pill, and she gave me an almost amused look.

"Those are not available in this conservative province, sorry. You can't get those in this part of the country. Maybe Nevada, the sin capitol of the planet, but not in Canada."

The pregnant girls were all told to go on bed rest, a hysterical and impossible suggestion for circus women.

Eight girls on the show had now found out they were pregnant, but I was the only one who seemed incapable of carrying a baby and doing her job. They let me in their tribe anyway because of my culinary skills. I loved how they shared tips and complaints, even as they held each other's hair and vomited.

In the waiting room, I chatted with the wire-walker. One thing I never understood is that all the women nursed their babies until they were five or six years old. It was not unusual to see a small child do an act and then run to their mom, flat hand pounding on her chest bone, demanding, "Tita!"

"Why does every circus mom nurse for so long?"

"How long is long?"

"We typically nurse our children for less than two years."

"That is crazy."

"That is all I know."

"We nurse so long because we often don't have money for food. If the child is nursing, it survives the food insecurity." She unintentionally brought her hand to her breast.

"So, all circus performers have periods without food?"

"Yes, that can't be helped."

"But it can. We have systems in place to help poor people."

"We are not a part of any system. We survive our way."

80

Fall, 1983, Kenora, Ontario, Canada

The fight came after the last performance. There were many reasons behind it, but it was the family versus me. United in their hatred for me, they sat on the same side of an issue for the first time. We had no new gig lined up, and a very heated argument shrouded the tiny dinner table concerning what the next step would be. The Flying Córdobas had been invited to Monaco for the Circus Olympics. The flight over would eat up the wages paid, leaving no profit. However, the accolade would pay off in future years because we could demand a higher price for the acts—if they won, if Nicolás could stick his triple, if Phileap could stick his blindfolded double layout.

It was risky. The other option was to return to Las Vegas and work in a casino show for a small payout, but there was no traveling. I was all for the no-traveling option as the road was eating at my soul.

I chimed in when not invited and enraged everyone. "You don't seem to understand that staying in one place—let's say, Circus Circus—is a holy grail. Getting a regular paycheck and having to only pay rent and a tiny bit of gas, you would ultimately make more money."

"You don't know anything, Towner. Shut your mouth," Nicolás said.

Phileap shot me a look that said the same thing with his eyes. I appealed to the women.

"Bernice, aren't you tired of buying a new trailer every year because they literally come apart on the road?" There was no way she would speak up against Nicolás or any of them, so she rolled her eyes at me and walked to the back of the trailer to check on her baby.

"Santiago, wouldn't you like to find a wife? Staying in one place has more options."

Santiago was the eldest and wisest of the family. He was kind and hard-working. I had a sense that he had been trapped his whole life. He never had a girlfriend, but I figured it was because he did not want to perpetuate his circus lineage.

Nicolás stepped forward and put his hand on my mouth in a rough way. He growled at me, and I took the moment to bite his pinkie. He yelped in pain, and I ran out the door.

Phileap was still pissed a week later. We argued in between shows and during practice. There was no break in anger or stopping for our roadside romances. The tension was palpable everywhere we went. Like a Mexican novella, every player had an angle and an agenda. The verdict was made that they would go to Monaco, but I was to stay behind. I was to be sent home, like a wounded dog. It was decided in Spanish without my input or approval.

Phileap told me about the news after lunch, and I was enraged. I begged and pleaded, but it fell on deaf, immoral ears. He found my resistance to the inevitable startling and surprising. Everyone in the family had learned to go along with the status quo, no matter what.

That night, I tried to change his mind with sex. We touched the divine, shared a moment of bliss, but after those moments, he reverted. I begged him to let me stay as we lay, his body still intertwined with mine. I whispered my secrets with our foreheads touching on the pillow. Our separation was not slow. He ruined my faith with his casual lies.

A week later, I said goodbye to the Scullery Maids as I gave them my larder. They understood I was being thrown away and were horrified for me because no one in the circus ever went anywhere alone. The thought that I was to cross the entire country by myself was unconscionable to them. They filled my bag with totems of good luck and love. It was the first time I had seen any of them cry.

"What are we going to do without you?" cried the abuelita.

"What are you going to do with that cat?" worried the oma.

"I'm taking him with me."

"We are going to miss you so much."

Though I loved the sentiment, they had all survived a long time on the road, and I knew I was but a dalliance in their predetermined lives.

"I love you for saying that, but you guys are good without me."

"We may be good, but we won't laugh as much. No one has ever pulled us together like you have. It has been fun."

"Ya, and life on the road is never fun."

"Please keep laughing and cooking together. Everyone is better because we all came together. I'm going to miss you all."

"You're going to miss the sex."

"Ha, but mostly you. I can get sex anywhere."

"The men have proved that."

"I will send you spices and recipes."

"We won't get them until we return to winter quarters."

"But you will have them there and for the next tour."

We all hugged in a communal circle. I was sobbing, they sniffled.

"I am going to miss you all so much," I said.

"Not after you sleep in a real bed, cook on a huge stove, and have a ginormous fridge and freezer."

They all looked at me with envy. They were truly envious that I had somewhere to go because they had nowhere. If their men ever cast them out, they would be truly alone. I wanted them to know that I would always be there for them.

"You are all always welcome in my home. Here is my parents' phone number. If you ever need anything, just call and I will get you on a bus to me."

That made them all start sobbing, and they wiped their tears on their aprons as I walked away with one suitcase and a cat in a pillowcase.

"Thank you all for including me. I promise to honor you by creating your recipes forever."

81

Fall, 1983, Toronto, Ontario, Canada

He put me on a bus. As I boarded, he threw my luggage under the carriage with no hesitation or regret, no warm goodbye kiss. I was yesterday's trash.

On the bus, my cat on my lap, tucked into a blanket, I sat with my head pressed against the windowpane. As the empty Canadian moonscape passed by, I pieced together the epic mistake I made in loving this man.

When the fighting had become more frequent than the fucking, I saw the passion for me perish in his eyes. I had thought that flicker was love, but I am an idiot at adoration. I had never trusted him, and I knew the elemental building block of love is trust. Regardless, my heart befitted his; it was his to break.

On the bus, I pretended I was anywhere but there. That is what I did daily, live in a make-believe space in my head. I was sad but relieved. The loneliness enveloped and nearly swallowed me. Thank God I had my purring stowaway.

Phileap was not a friend or a champion that most lovers become. I knew that without me, he would have a new girl at every stop. It was easy to do when the tights fit that perfect body like a nimbus and he was the shining star of the show. His exotic accent and immense, coffee-colored, sad eyes captured girls who were unaware they could be apprehended—like me. After the devotion and passion I gave him, I was just an afterthought. Already a memory, as distant as a teen's summer surprise first kiss. Tantalizing and all-encompassing at first, but with time and the road, a silver jewel was left in a black felt box. Forgotten and tarnished. I believed that there was a time when he would do anything for the honor of me in his bed—risk security and the status quo to possibly touch ecstasy with my firm, loving hands.

As the bus rumbled on, I realized that I was not his holy grail. I was merely a distraction in his regimented, well-ordered world. Which, paradoxically, I found to be pure chaos.

He made me go quietly away so as not to disturb his way of life. I sought him out because I wanted adventure and needed escape. I was no more than a dot on the highway. I was wrong. I usually am.

The bus was a long haul making its way across all of America, filled with misfits and pilgrims. Some running away, some running toward, but all encased in a sweaty, diesel-spewing missile headed to the next adventure.

A nice grandma from Topeka sat with me after I cried for three hours. She was in a grey housecoat with her snow-white hair short around her ears. She carried a bowling bag that she always kept on her lap.

"It can't be that bad, girly, can it? Do you want to talk?" She handed me a Kleenex and I blew hard. My sobs began to dissipate as I decided to tell her everything. I told her the beginning of the great love story that I had deemed

Phileap and I had been. After listening patiently for an hour, she reached in her granny bag and handed me a flask filled with rum. I sipped as she spilled her wisdom. Her name was Nadine, and I swear she was an angel. She was on her way home from visiting her daughter and grandkids in Canada.

"Love is a fleeting madness; it erupts like a volcano and then dwindles. And when it wanes, you must decide. You must work out whether your roots have so entwined together that it is inconceivable that you should ever part.

"Love is not breathlessness, it is not excitement, and it is not the declaration of eternal passion. That is just being in love, which any fool can do.

"Love itself is what is left over when being in love has burned away, and this is both an art and a fortunate coincidence. Those that truly love have roots that grow towards each other underground, and when all the pretty blossoms have fallen from their branches, they find that they are one tree."

I stared at her blankly, and she continued. "If you two can't root, then it is doomed, and the best thing he ever did was put you on this bus. It was a kindness."

"How can we ever find roots if we are always moving?"

"Many a wanderer has found true love, but I don't think that is what you are looking for."

"What?"

"You are looking for adventure, passion, and a story to tell. Not love."

I chewed on Nadine's wisdom, and it calmed me. Since I was not given any money when I was thrown away, she bought me food and a paperback novel. *Still Life with Woodpecker* by Tom Robbins. It saved my weary soul as we bounced across America. Through the character Leigh-Cheri and the mad arsonist, my little red head survived an eleven-day bus ride. I hugged Nadine goodbye in Kansas and promised to write her. Before she left me, she bought a duffel bag and filled it with apples, cheese, and bread for the rest of my trip.

82

Winter, 1983, Reno, Nevada, USA

I was living at home with my parents, but Kilgore Trout had to go stay with Stuart. I was miserable. Being confined in the smallness of my family and hometown was unbearable. I recognized my dichotomy. I wrote Phileap letters every day, but I knew he was not getting them. Whenever the house phone rang, I leapt for it, praying to hear him begging me to come home with that bad English accent of his.

My faux beau, Stuart, had offered me a no-threat romantic life of dinner and a movie on my days off and to visit with my cats. He knew I was broken, and he never even tried to kiss me. I felt a sickening sense of failure when I saw he had rescued my cats but no one could rescue me. He tried anyway with his quick wit and hospitality. He was the kindest human I knew.

Eternally curious about the trapeze, he grilled me. "Were you afraid up there?"

"Yes, always. Fear keeps you safe."

"Were you afraid that the catcher wouldn't catch you?"

"Yes, sometimes. If I listened to his calls, left the platform when called off, came out of my trick when he said 'Hup,' I knew he would catch me. But, if any of my overthinking took over my pea brain, he could and would drop me. It was always my fault."

"When you missed, did the net hurt?"

"If I landed wrong, yes."

"Are the performers only making it look easy?"

"That is the magic. My favorite performers were the ones who deliberately missed the tricks for dramatic effect. It takes more skill to miss and recover than to do the trick correctly."

"Okay, one last question for tonight. Do you miss it?"

That was a loaded question, one I wasn't sure I could answer. I seemed to miss moving every day because the sameness of home made me twitchy. The knowing where everything was located was boring. The not being challenged and fought with was too quiet. And, of course, I missed the sex, but wasn't telling him that.

Stuart got me into his gym with a spouse pass, and I worked out like a madwoman. I was ridiculously strong and in shape and didn't want to lose that. I saw Stuart and the cats every day, and he felt like a cashmere blanket after a rainstorm. He was safe and warm, but I felt no passion to fuck him. I could tell he wanted to because his pupils dilated every time I walked into the gym. He also reveled in my stories and was forever asking for more circus details. I felt like I was being debriefed.

Becky tried to get me to move on, but my soul wasn't in it. I said I was over it all, but she wouldn't be happy until I was doing the horizontal tango with someone, anyone.

"You have to get back in the saddle."

"No, I don't. I am riding single and bareback from now on."

"You don't want a fuck buddy? Stuart would volunteer."

"Nope, he's my friend. That's all."

"Are you waiting for the red-tighted dickhead to come back?"

"Not really. I haven't heard from him and don't expect to."

Becky got me drunk on shots of tequila that a man at her bar bought us because he was convinced that I was the actress who played the eldest sister on the TV show *Little House on the Prairie*. I told him over and over that I was NOT Mary Engels. When he snuck in for a hug, he felt how muscled I was and was even more sure that I was a famous actress. Becky brought me to Stuart's door and poured me into his bed. When I woke up the next morning, I turned to him and he said, "We've got to stop meeting like this."

I went to urgent care because I had a flu I could not beat. The doctor did all kinds of blood tests and pronounced me pregnant.

Fuck.

He gave me an RH shot even though I told him I would probably abort the baby. He sent me to a female OB who I told my story to, and all she did was gawk at me with her mouth open.

"Not one bit of that is true!"

I defended my story. "It is. I have proof."

"Oh yeah? What?"

I barely had pictures because photography was a luxury. The few circus programs I kept were at home already in the basement. "Feel these calluses." I reached out my scratchy and scarred hand.

"That proves nothing! You are pregnant, liar or not."

"That I know. I want to know my options?"

"You should abort. Either you are a pathological liar or a lunatic. Either way, you should not be a mother."

She stomped out of the office and I sat there, stunned. Maybe she had a point.

On Saturday afternoon, I got a collect call from Tijuana. My father started to refuse the charges, and I grabbed the phone out of his hand.

"Phileap?"

"Hello, Apple Pie! Como estas?"

"I am okay. Missing you. Where are you?"

"We are stuck in Mexico. Apple Pie, we need your help!"

My heart melted at the sound of his pathetic and scared voice, and all my resolve and anger disappeared immediately. So did my desire to terminate the pregnancy.

"Of course, I will help! I love you. What do you need?"

He explained how the visas were wrong once again when they went to Monaco, and they were sent out to Tijuana to get new ones. Now in Mexico, they couldn't get back into the U.S. I spent the next three weeks helping Stuart use every connection he had to untangle the paperwork problem. We succeeded, and I borrowed his truck to drive to Tijuana to pick them all up. I hadn't seen Phileap since he put me on the bus. I was nervous he was using me for my help and didn't really want to be with me. I had a secret I was not ready to share. He claimed that he loved me, and his calling was not simply because he needed help. For my desperate-to-be-loved constitution, the lie was enough.

83

Winter, 1983, Tijuana, Mexico

I crossed the border easily, the advantage of being the blue-eyed devil. On the phone, Phileap had told me about the seedy hotel where they were all shoved into one room—their home away from the trailer. In the hovel that is Tijuana, I had a hard time finding it. It was hot, and the smells of animals and home hearths filled the air. Trash lined the streets, cars up on blocks, twisted fences, and broken windows. This was not the tourist part of town.

Surrounded by cracked sidewalks and prostitutes, I spied El Cerrito. There was no front desk, simply rickety stairs and a mattress in the corner with a dog emitting a low growl while eating the fleas off his back. I went out into the street and yelled for Phileap. He couldn't hear me over the mariachi music and novellas blasting. I wondered if I was even at the right hotel. I bought a street taco and a Mexican Coke on the corner and sat, hoping he would come out of the hotel. A couple of hours went by. My butt was numb from sitting on the metal chair, and the taco stand owner was giving me the stink eye. At dusk, I saw Phileap come out of the hotel, and I jumped up, screaming his name. He was startled and surprised to see me.

"Apple Pie?"

"Yes! I am here to bring you home."

He embraced me with what felt like a mixture of relief and fear. The rescue would give me the upper hand, a shift in our old relationship. I would bring him to my home. My rules. My secret.

"I can't wait to leave this dirty place," he said. "Can everyone come? Did you get visas for everyone?"

I resisted the temptation to lie—I would have loved to leave them all there, but I knew he would spend all his time trying to save them.

"Everyone has a visa. Please, let's get out of here."

"But I am hungry. Can we eat first?"

I bought him a taco and Coke, which he scarfed down. I didn't figure they were out of money, but it made sense. I bought twelve tacos that he took to the room. I decided to stay at the stand, where the owner was more pleased with me now that I had been his biggest customer of the day.

Phileap took two hours to reappear. I guessed there was much negotiating and complaining that I was the one who had rescued them. I was glad not to witness it. I was conflicted; I didn't want to live with the entire family again, but I missed Phileap. I loved performing and the physical training of the trapeze. I loathed living with my parents again. I was stuck between a rock and a hard place. It never occurred to me there might be another choice.

They all appeared and snarled at me like I was a street dog. I did not care. We crossed the border with no problem. My paperwork was perfect and all in order. The family had one more year in the U.S. and then would need to apply again to stay in the country. The trailers had been left in Las Vegas; we were headed there.

I called Stuart to tell him of our success in crossing the border and to ask if he could keep Kilgore Trout a while longer.

"Are you really going back to him?"

"I have to."

"You have free will, Gail, you don't have to do anything."

"There are things you don't understand. I'm sorry. I must stay with him for now. There are things to work out. Will you keep the cat?"

"Of course. I will keep your real life while you tumble about the country." He sounded mad for the first time.

"Thank you for helping and keeping my kittens."

"Your kittens are safe with me, as is your heart, but you can't seem to see that."

Feeling sad that he still carried a torch for me, I figured I was doing him a favor by taking my dysfunctional soul far way.

84

Winter, 1983, Las Vegas, Nevada, USA

We landed back in Las Vegas, but in a new compound. Singer Gladys Knight was one of the first divas, and her home reflected that. Constructed in Italian marble, it was as shiny as the Pips' suits and timely as Rome. It was a vast sprawling compound with security, dazzlingly opulent with manicured gardens and spouting fountains. The ten-acre parcel had a high concrete wall all around it, keeping interlopers out. Gladys loved the trapeze and let us park in the back of the property.

This was a gift from Cupcake and Izic who were opening her show with the cat act. Phileap and I had purchased a camper, so we were back to being alone but with no bathroom. The groundskeeper took pity on us and gave us a key to the pool house. I felt a bit better about being in our own tin can home. We practiced eight hours a day, getting ready for the next tour starting in a month.

We would need money to go on the road, so I got a job working as a dresser for *Folies Bergère*.

Back at home among the circus folk, I was ignored by the Córdobas. Phileap settled with our routine. He was both angry at and grateful for me. While the passion had dissipated, I welcomed the idea that we were now going to be family, though I hadn't told anyone yet. I tried for one more romantic romp. That afternoon, alone in our trailer, I undressed him wantonly. I was on top of him and started with a deep, slow kiss. He knew he owned me like a song owned its notes. He also knew he was here because of me, yet I was his to do with what he willed. I knew he could sense my racing heartbeat against his. The kiss deepened as I rubbed against him, my nipples hardened. A knock at the trailer door interrupted us as Mama let herself in and started babbling in Spanish. I walked out the door and went to practice.

85

Spring, 1984, Flagstaff, Arizona, USA

We left Las Vegas for a new mud show, meaning the promoters had their own tent set up in muddy fields on the outskirts of town. There were no dressing rooms or places to escape. We were all sequestered inside the trailers when not performing. A new set of Scullery Maids needed to be established. I went from door to door to find them.

I gravitated to the elephant troupe. The big lugs showed me that I was trusted by six tons of pachyderms. I could get them to do anything with voice commands. It only took two feedings for them to decide I was a human to be trusted and listened to. I spent time between shows with them and their pregnant trainer, Kim. I also found us prenatal doctors when we rolled into town.

That skill set got me further than cooking because it seemed every week a new girl with the show was pregnant. We joked that it must be in the water, but our water source changed every day. Two of my sisters-in-law, the high-wire-walker, the chimpanzee trainer, and a teeterboard flyer were all harboring the next generation of circus performers. Having children in the circus is the easiest way to increase the act. I still hadn't told anyone, but my helping endeared me to those who would otherwise shun me because I was not born into the circus.

I started teaching the kids again and created a curriculum using circus examples for reading, writing, and arithmetic lessons.

"If a family of five flyers is paid $500 per week, how much does each member make in a month?"

86

S pring, 1984, Santa Fe, New Mexico, USA

I drove all the expectant mothers to an obstetrician, filled out their paperwork, and negotiated a lower fee in exchange for circus tickets. I made an appointment for myself and finally shared my secret. Everyone was kind but leery, as if they knew I was temporary but a baby would not be. With a baby, I would be tied to the Córdobas forever. This time, I was not sure the roots would take.

Phileap took the news lukewarm and was convinced that I would lose this baby like the other ones.

Living in the small camper was not an ideal place to start a life.

"Why are you doing this again?" Phileap badgered me as we got back to the trailer.

"Hey, it takes two to make a baby. You certainly did your part."

"That is the only reason I like you. The sex. And now you can't do that anymore."

"What? Of course, I can."

"No. My penis will kill the baby. It will break its head."

I laughed at the thought. There were so many old wives' tales spread in the circus. They believed them as gospel. When Phileap was little, he had a weak liver. His parents' answer was to buy a cow's liver, take a small chunk, make it into a mush to feed him, and then bury the rest in the dirt behind the trailer. Each day for a week, they walked around it four times, asking to cure their son. It worked; he got better. I'm sure it was from the eating and not the circle dance.

"You can't hurt the baby with your penis."

"I don't care what you say, I'm not doing the sexy anymore."

This was not exactly the response I was looking for, but my world had turned. It was no longer about Phileap. Life and priorities now revolved around my growing fetus.

87

Spring, 1984, Muskogee, Oklahoma, USA

We did three shows a day in small towns. The school kids came for the 10 a.m. show. The teens and families came for the 3 p.m. show, and curious adults showed up at 7 p.m. We folded it all up, packed it into our trucks, drove for three hours to the next town, and repeated it all in the morning.

It was a newfangled sight when we'd roll into a small town at night with a circle of Winnebagos and Airstreams. By 9 a.m., a magical tent appeared, surrounded by corrals featuring fancy horses, elephants, tigers, lions, chimpanzees, and more. The chatter of the animals, the blows of the sledge-hammers, and the pulling and ratcheting drifting on the breeze had these tiny towns mesmerized by us.

Towners flocked to and filled the tent at every show, hungry for live and exotic displays. Afterward, they hung around, wanting to ask questions, meet the animals, and form a memory. Most of the performers ignored them, but I spent time after every show, answering questions. I had learned not to spill secrets, so my shtick was on-the-road stories. They devoured those. The thought of all the miles and little towns we frequented was mind-blowing to them. I enjoyed the audience and the act of storytelling so much, the weary miles faded away.

88

Spring, 1984, Little Rock, Arkansas, USA

There were ten pregnant ladies on the show. They were excited and helped soothe my mind. We were bonded in our life-giving opportunities. As our bellies grew and the babies were born, we all helped with childcare and substituted for each other in our acts.

Lupe, the high-wire-walker, came to an obstetrician appointment with us because she had terrible cramps and wanted to have her IUD removed. She had three children and planned to leave her cruel French husband as soon as all the kids could be part of the act. She came out of the office with a look of terror on her face.

"What's the matter?"

"The doctor says I am pregnant. I could die!"

"What are you going to do?"

"In the next town, I will have them remove the IUD, and that should terminate the problem. Please do not tell your husbands. I do not want Jean Pierre to know."

We had all heard the weekly fights and whippings. Keeping mum was easy to do.

89

Spring, 1984, Memphis, Tennessee, USA

The obstetrician had gotten a new medical device called an ultrasound. He was excited to experiment with us. We all signed up for a free one with each examination. I saw my baby for the first time and was told with an air of smug assurance I was having a girl. I knew this was an undesirable gender for Phileap, so I kept my mouth shut. A baby girl would be scorned. I prayed for unforeseen charity for his daughter after she was born.

We all walked out with blurry black-and-white Polaroids, giddy and scared. Lupe was the last one out because she had her IUD removed, which they were sure would abort the baby. She walked out, shell-shocked, holding a familiar picture—only hers had three hearts! The triplets were robust even after the IUD removal.

The doctor placed her on strict bed rest, which made us all giggle. There would be no rest for her, much less bed rest. Her only hope of not getting kicked out of her own trailer was for her husband to see the value of having three more wire-walkers added to the act.

At this point, there were thirteen pregnant women on tour. It was a roly-poly show. As each baby was born, the horror stories of the births circulated the small kitchens. I was terrified. Everyone went into labor in a small town, and if they weren't ready to leave the hospital in twenty-four hours, they would be left there until it was convenient to circle back and get them. We were crisscrossing the country at this point; some were left for weeks with nowhere to stay and no money to help them. I taught them all about social services and how to get temporary shelter for the babies and themselves. They were shocked that a government could be used to help people. Nomadic people rarely interacted with the government. If they did, it was usually for trouble. The thought of agencies helping them was a bafflement.

90

Spring, 1984, Birmingham, Alabama, USA

My pregnancy was complicated. I had no regular doctor, so most obstetricians gave me the RhIg shot to be careful. They were painful. The spot would ache for a week, and I vomited violently after each one. Almost every doctor told me I should be on bed rest. I was still flying in every show, teaching school, and doing the web. Lupe had three babies inside her, and she never sat down. My in-laws saw me as weak and stupid, and they were terrified that I might have a blue-eyed Córdoba. There were many priest visits and exorcisms.

Lupe came to my trailer to eat my crudités, the only thing she could keep down. Kim was pregnant too and sick. She joined in. I made big pots of stew for them to take back to their husbands, because cooking was the last thing a nauseated pregnant girl wanted to do.

Lupe opened the big pot and inhaled the scent.

"I believe you are saving my life. Mine and my children. Thank you!"

"No problem. Aren't you supposed to be on bed rest?"

"Ha!" Her thunderous laughter shook our little trailer. "Jean Pierre would beat me if I stayed in bed."

"You are bigger than him," Kim interjected.

"I could sit on him and crush him like a bug. But it is not the marriage I signed up for. He beat me after our first date. I liked it. It felt sexy. Now he is cruel, but I learned to tolerate his thrashings."

"Why do you stay?"

"Like I have other options. This nomad life is the only one I know. No one has a home to go back to like you do."

The women here did not have options. I believed I didn't either. It was frightening and a bit comforting. I was stuck, but at least I had known a house without wheels before life on the road. This was all they knew.

Lupe was quiet as she munched on a carrot. Kim threw her a look.

"This unicorn right here got out of the monkey business, a first for the descendant of animal people." Kim was trying to be funny, but it fell flat on Lupe.

"I fell in love. Sue me."

"Now, you might fall on your head three times a day."

"Better than a life of having feces thrown at you. And I escaped my parents."

"True. These triplets will be with me until I die. They are circus gold."

It was weird to hear women talk about their unborn children as wage earners. But everything in my circus life was bizarre. I wondered how my minuscule embryo would like the nomadic and death-defying life.

91

Summer, 1984, Chattanooga, Tennessee, USA

I flew in the act until I was six months pregnant. My muscles held the baby bump in. On my last performance, I experienced the baby hit my rib cage as I hit the net. It reverberated against it, and I was terrified. I grounded myself, much to the family's protests. I became the magician's assistant and ran the elephant act while babysitting the newborns when their mothers had to perform. No trunk babies with me around.

Being pregnant on the road came with a whole new set of obstacles. I could not walk into any place that had a fryer in the kitchen. The rancid grease made me projectile vomit. I would go to the store with $100 and come home with a bag of green apples. It was the only thing that looked appealing.

Phileap and his brothers were back on a diet of liver and onions at least twice a week. I could not cook it. Mama took over Phileap's nightly meals, and I was deemed worthless. With my new belly, we could not fit in the camper. If we had to pass each other, I either had to get on the bed or get out of the camper.

The baby and I were having trouble getting along also, and the irony was not lost on me. I didn't want to have a baby while in the circus, and it seemed it didn't want to be born into the chaos. I believed it was a girl because of the ultrasounds; Phileap insisted it was a boy. He had positive blood, I had negative; his blood treated mine like poison. I needed RhoGAM shots at each appointment to help protect my baby. RhoGAM prevents the Rh-negative mother from making antibodies during her pregnancy.

Essentially, the shots helped make our blood get along. In addition to the pain, they made me listless. I found solace and rest in reading. I stayed in when not working, hallucinating while staring at reprocessed trees.

I finally learned to get books each time we were in a big town with a library. I would mail them back when done. Those novels saved my life. Tom Robbins and Kurt Vonnegut became my faithful companions. Once I had the novels, I was not as lonely.

92

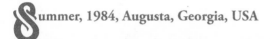

ummer, 1984, Augusta, Georgia, USA

I spent most days with the elephants and babies now, and that was fine with me. I found out one of the circus moms was parking her newborn in front of a TV with Disney films playing for hours at a time with only a bottle placed before him. I was horrified and went to rescue the baby. My own little daycare took place over by the elephants with a giant quilt I had sewn together from castaway trapeze capes. The elephants loved the cooing and gurgling of each baby. For the most part, it was easy to watch so many because none were crawling yet. My own belly tripled in size once I stopped flying, and that made it challenging to pick up the babies. I trained the eldest pachyderm to tuck them into her trunk and gently place them in my arms. The beasts were surprisingly gentle and loved the new skill they had learned. It was a *Wild Kingdom* nursery, including chimps vocalizing on one side in their glass enclosure while watching the babies with delight. I taught school using babies and formula as math, science, and history. The kids loved the time away, and again my storytelling was a springboard for my creativity and the kids' learning.

We had a special visitor to our school. He was an agent for many of the acts, and he wanted to talk to the kids about this career path and how the schooling they were receiving would help. Rudolfo was an ex-wire-walker, now residing in a wheelchair because of a fall ten years ago. He explained to the children what an agent was—that it was what you did when you were too injured to perform. The kids were more fascinated with his chair than his career advice.

"So did you fall during a performance?" the son of a wire-walker inquired.

"I did. I broke my hip, pelvis, and spine."

"How long were you in the hospital?" Now all the kids gathered around and paid attention.

"I was there for a year. Then I got my chair and learned to get around in it."

"How do you get in your trailer?"

"I don't live in a trailer. I have a home and a special van for my chair."

"If I hurt myself, I can have a home and a van?" This direct questioning was making everyone uncomfortable.

"It is much better to walk and be able to work."

"But I don't want to walk the wire. I was told I have no choice. Can I just start being an agent now and get the home and van?"

"I'm sorry, it doesn't work like that. Your family needs you in the act."

"So, I must fall and then I can be an agent?"

I didn't like where this was going, so I stepped in.

"Let's get back to the math of being an agent. Rudolfo, can you tell us how you make your money?"

The fact that Rudolfo made money without working, traveling, and risking his body intrigued the little minds.

Rudolfo gave the little kids a spin on his lap with the chair, and then the thirty-minute alarm sounded for the next show. The kids all ran to get into costume for their acts.

"Thank you for saving me. I will go talk to his parents and warn them that they must make him understand that being paralyzed is not a perk."

"I am curious. It seems all circus agents are disabled performers. Is that true?"

"Yes, as you may have already figured out, there is no way out of the circus life. Even broken, you must still find a way to work."

He left the barn, and I was struck with a strong sense of doom. I came here for the freedom the traveling life offered. I had not witnessed one ounce of freedom—only a people stuck forever.

93

Summer, 1984, Columbia, South Carolina, USA

The closing act, one that always left me gasping, was the Daring Spacewheel: a large, rotating apparatus with hooped tracks at either end that stood sixty feet in the air. The family-run and fast-paced act kept the audience on the edge of their seats. The revolving aerial pendulum had open cages at each end that rotated at high speeds while the family tumbled, moving up and down the Spacewheel. They performed leaps, somersaults, and handstands and walked the wheel blindfolded. The family was from Russia and, except for the friendship between the matriarch and me, they never talked with anyone outside their kin. The young daughter was fifteen and seemed lonely. I found her in the dressing room.

"Would you like to come to school? I teach all the kids at 8 a.m."

"I am too old to learn."

"Not true. Towner kids go to school until they are eighteen, and some continue with college."

"I know everything I need to know. I will die on this wheel."

"What about a husband? Do you want one?"

"I don't like boys. I will never marry; I will stay with my family. Forever."

She was a lesbian, a fate worse than leaving her family for the circus folks. My heart ached at the freedom that I had to love who I wanted and be who I was.

94

Summer, 1984, Raleigh, North Carolina, USA

I walked into the trailer with only a bag of apples.

"This is all you brought from the market?" Phileap looked at me with a low-level loathing.

"Everything else smelled rotten!"

"The entire store was rotten?"

"Smelled that way to me."

"What am I supposed to eat?"

"Apples?"

"Woman, I need protein!"

"So do I, but this is all I can do."

He stormed out of the trailer to forage for his supper.

Being pregnant on the road had its own set of challenges. The constant jostling of the truck as we moved each day hurt my belly. From that constant motion, I was forced to use pillows to support my tummy as we drove. I also hated the smell of every restaurant and had to go pee every thirty minutes. When the circus women told me stories of their pregnancies and births, it frightened me. I was scared. All these things were happening to my body, but I had no regular doctor. For the first time, I longed for my mother. As horrible as the idea of returning home had been, it became my solitary focus.

Stuart had reassured me that the police were no longer looking for me. The moving company folded, and the charges were dropped because my drug-dealing compatriots were now distributed around the world. Most of them were now employed as DJs and accountants.

95

Summer, 1984, Columbus, Ohio, USA

A group from the People's Republic of China joined us in Columbus. They were from an ancient civilization with a long history and a rich, brilliant culture. The ringmaster announced to the audience, "Over several millennia, China's peoples have created many forms of performing arts, each of them characterized by a host of schools and styles. They have followed, for centuries, a linear evolution aimed toward the extreme refinement of the skills involved in a particular art form."

There were twenty-two of them and no one spoke English, or was over the age of twenty-five, but they were curious and friendly. Their act consisted of contortion, foot juggling, and magic. Done in authentic Chinese style, the act began with them sitting with legs crossed and hands on their laps, their hats producing fans that magically rose and flew away.

The performers were tossed to each other with the top ones doing contortion and balancing. They used a small bounding board along with their bodies as catchers, bridges, and flyers. Then the top acrobats would fold themselves in half with their feet circling over the back of their heads to touch their noses. After that, they leapt into a double somersault and landed on another stack of people. It was a fast-moving and exceptional act that no one could figure out how to duplicate. We brought them on the trapeze, and they almost instantly took to it because they were so cross-trained and smart at knowing where they were in the air and how to control their bodies.

Their act became so popular, American agents were clamoring to get them signed permanently to stay in the U.S. and Canada. The Chinese government said a big "No," and their last meal was of the elusive and much-desired McDonald's. I was sad to see their smiling faces go.

96

Summer, 1984, London, Canada

Next stop: London (but in Canada, not England). I was convinced I would never get on a plane with the Córdobas. I was too pregnant to fly commercial or on the trapeze, so I waddled around and sold cotton candy. It was not lost on me that I was pregnant, stuck on the road, and in Canada.

My new favorite act was a version of the high-wire with three sisters. The act was called Koch Semaphore. Their grandmothers had invented the act in Russia in the 1950s. Their apparatus was a large moving wheel set on a high wire. They rode bicycles, crossed en point, and stacked each other three high to cross and move the wheel across the wire. It was unnecessarily dangerous. Two of their remaining grandmothers traveled with them and taught me to make Russian dumplings, borscht, and honey cake. They traveled with three hulky but mute prop guys who set up the impossible rigging. The grandmothers told me that the prop guys were also castrated, and their tongues were cut out, so as not to pose a threat to the girls' virginity. They were proud of the fact that their government had taken such great care of them. I was horrified but also knew that there was a secret romance going on with at least two of the girls with their prop guys. Even cruel governments can't stop love.

97

Summer, 1984, Toronto, Ontario, Canada

The circus was in Toronto and planning to cross back into the United States. We had been paid in half Canadian money and half U.S. dollars, but the exchange rate was low. It was not worth taking the colorful money with us. I bought all the baby's stuff—crib, layette, and stroller—and filled the back of the trailer with enough items for four babies. I was ready to start the journey home back to the West Coast. We had gigs planned in Niagara Falls (the Canadian side), New York, Baltimore, Kansas City, Denver, and Salt Lake City, and we planned to travel to Reno where I would give birth. The show dates were four days each and paid well. Performing more days in the same town meant the money went into our pockets and not gas stations. It would give us enough to survive the winter in Reno while the rest of the troupe went to Las Vegas.

98

Summer, 1984, Niagara Falls, Ontario, Canada

We performed for four days and took one day off to enjoy the Falls and do the border crossing. I helped get the veterinarian paperwork for the animals so that the crossing would go smoothly. The morning after we were supposed to leave and cross the border, I went to the circus manager's office to get our visas and passports.

I knocked staccato on his Airstream door. He answered in his usual state of aggravation, took one look at me, and told me to fuck off. "I can't help you," he said and turned to go back into the trailer.

"What does that mean?"

"Are you stupid?"

I was red-hot mad. This colossal asshole of a boss and manager was the worst. Docking our pay every week, changing the way we got paid and how much—I was at the end of my rope with the man.

"We need our passports and visas to pass the border today. You have them, we need them."

"Fuck you, Towner girl. I don't have them."

At that point, his daughter walked from the back of the trailer and elbowed her dad out of the way. He was fuming but quickly moved to avoid another conflict.

"What's going on?" I asked.

"I'm sorry, Gail. He screwed things up, and it looks like he never got visas approved for you guys to pass into Canada."

I gasped. "We're here illegally?"

"You aren't. You are American and can freely pass between countries. The Córdobas are the ones in trouble." She sighed at the heaviness of it all. "Their visas were from Chile and England. They were only issued to perform in America. Passing into Canada without those visas being renewed and updated is an INS violation."

"What?"

"It's your problem now."

"What should I do?"

"I am a circus performer, not a lawyer. I do not know. But he's right, you guys are fucked."

"What will happen to them?" The weight of the news made me fall back off the iron steps.

I talked to the family while Phileap translated. The Córdobas were citizens of Chile, Bernice of England, and I was the only American. I was the only one who hadn't broken international law. Moreover, we could not leave Canada without a working visa in the U.S., which the circus had not arranged for either. The manager drove off in the middle of the night. We were in purgatory. We had no money and no upcoming jobs in the States.

My pregnant belly was rumbling when the verbal thrashing from his family finally stopped. They were sure it was my fault. Phileap and I went back to our camper, and I prepared a lunch of shredded carrots and lemon juice. He usually required more food than my strange pregnancy palate allowed me to ingest, but he was happy with my simple fare this time.

"What are we going to do, Apple Pie?"

"I am going to call my lawyer friend and get some advice. We won't be able to cross the border today, or you will be deported. We must find a trailer park to stay in until I unravel this fiasco."

He came over and nuzzled my neck and patted my belly. An act of affection I had not received in a while and was instantly melted by. I grabbed my roll of quarters and headed off to the payphones on the fairground property.

My first stop was to the maintenance shop where the groundskeeper took pity on us and told me that we could stay parked there for a week while I tried to disentangle the visa mess. I had learned early on to make friends with the keepers of the keys—hot showers, good electricity, and a couple of free nights of parking were at their discretion. I had baked one of my famous apple pies (yes, it was a cliché, but it worked), and the fruits of the pie paid off with a two-week occupation.

My second task was to say goodbye to my circus acquaintances. I usually had a few weeks to prepare for the farewells, which was still hard. The instant departure of the babies, with me left behind in an uncertain future, wrecked me.

I explained over and over to each trailer why we were not joining the show for the last four dates, much to the anger of everyone, who didn't seem to understand why we were in this situation to begin with. This shitty manager was self-absorbed and made for a horrible leader, and his family was mortified that he had known about our visas and kept it to himself.

He had had three months to fix the situation, but his silence cost us dearly. We had no money and no idea when the next paycheck would come or how we would leave Canada. The other acts were generous, especially all the Scullery Maids. They brought over bags of groceries so we would not starve, and each gave me INS tips on how they had dealt with visa problems.

We cried in our ciders during our heartbreaking goodbyes at a colossal barbecue at a trailer park in Niagara Falls. Most everyone was going to Florida to winter, but I wanted my home, my doctor, and a shingled roof over my head. The plan was to drive to Reno, park the trailers in my parents' pasture, and set up the trapeze so they could practice every day. First, we had to make it out of Canada without getting arrested.

❦

After two weeks, we moved to a KOA campground in Niagara Falls and paid for a week. The first fight was over whether to let me handle the visa problem. As I could legally cross over each border, it made sense to me. I also spoke the language, and maybe they would take pity on the pregnant girl. All the men were against the idea but could not come up with another plan. Papi went to the Canadian Embassy one day and came back shaking his head. After two weeks of sitting and waiting, they agreed to let me try.

I went to the Embassy in Niagara Falls, Canada and got all the proper forms, filled them out with the help of friendly people, and headed back over to the American Embassy. They were closed. The U.S. Embassy was only open from 7 a.m. to noon on Tuesdays through Fridays. The Canadian Embassy was only open from noon to 4 p.m. on Mondays through Thursdays. With these challenging hours, I could only visit one embassy per day. I made twenty-two trips in six weeks to the embassy and consulate. We ran out of money and were starting to run out of food. We couldn't pay daily for the trailer park. We used a sharpie to change the departure date on the cards we placed in the truck window.

On the last day, everyone in both embassies knew who I was, what I was trying to do, and the impossibility of the act. The head of the American Embassy came over to me and put her hand on my shoulder and told me, once and for all, that I could not get the Córdobas into the States. I burst into tears, sobbing with snot running out of my nose. She tried to console me, but I cried harder. After an hour of watching me crumble, she marched into her office and reappeared with a stamped paper that gave us twenty-four hours to get over the border. We were out of Canada but not legally in the States.

99

There were volumes of fighting and yelling ricocheting off the tin walls. Phileap, Marco, and I were going to Reno. I could no longer drive, so Marco decided to help and possibly land a job in a casino in Reno. I was not looking forward to the marathon cross-county trip. The jarring of riding in the front of the truck still hurt my insides. I took all our pillows and braced them under my belly to cushion my body from the road. Phileap practiced saying "Good evening" without an accent. We knew we would have to pass through many border checks, having already traversed this path three times. Michigan, Texas, California, and New Mexico had random stops where papers were required. Both Marco and Phileap had American driver's licenses, and we had American visas that had been made unusable because we had passed into Canada. All we had to do was convince the officer who stopped us that we were tourists heading to Reno. Both Marco and Phileap practiced the greeting until there was no trace of an accent. They drove in shifts and crossed into Nevada on the third day, successfully making it through five border stops. My favorite border check was in Idaho, where the officer asked to see the back of the camper. It was filled with baby items, plus we had the entire trapeze on top. I told him that we were on vacation and that the steel poles and wires on top were an elaborate tent for camping. His flashlight rested on a picture on the wall of the three of us in a finale holding a banner that read "Circus." We all held in our breaths. He let us go.

100

We stopped for gas in Winnemucca and filled up for the last leg of the trip. Five miles after the unbranded and only choice for a gas station, the truck sputtered to a stop. Phileap got out and opened the hood. I was in the front seat, surrounded by nine pillows. It had taken me a while to get packed in there, so I stayed inside. Marco kept turning over the engine, and it sputtered and died. The gasoline had water in it. This had happened before in small towns where we were forced to buy from local owners. The fix was to pour pure gasoline into the carburetor. We had a container of good gas. Phileap poured it from a paper cup into the carburetor as Marco turned over the truck. It sparked and started but also caught the cup and the front of the truck on fire. Out of reflex, Marco threw the cup away from the engine, which caught the roadside ablaze. I screamed as I tried to get out from the trap of pillows. After what seemed like an eternity, I escaped from the pillow prison. I jumped out, landing on the side of the road that was on fire, which burned my hands and knees.

I wallowed on the road, screeching in pain and trying to roll away from the fiery pillows and weeds. Phileap stood on the side of the road, shocked. The lack of chivalry training on his part deemed him immobile. Instead, Marco came to help me up and off the burning field.

I had a fury in my heart that matched the burning on my palms. Once I was safe, the only thing to do was laugh until I cried and peed my pants a bit. Reno had never looked so good as we crested the mountains and saw the Biggest Little City's horizon.

101

Summer, 1984, Reno, Nevada, USA

The silence of hearing only English spoken was deafening. The luxury of cooking over a full-size gas stove with enough room to turn around to get a plate, sublime. The need to take eight whole steps to get something from the fridge was like a beautiful ballet. I was home. This time around, my parents and their house were a comfort and not a sodden scotch prison. It is incredible what eight months on the road can do for perspective. My belly was swollen with the impending Córdoba, the trapeze was set up in the pasture, and our trailers circled like wagons in a spaghetti western, giving the neighbors oodles to gossip about. Phileap and Marco practiced for hours every day, getting ready for the TV show *That's Incredible* that they were due to perform on the next month. They hoped to stick a couple of new tricks that no one else had ever done.

I spent most of the time in my mother's house, reading and recovering. She could tell that I was a bit broken; she was gentle with me. My stepfather stayed away from me, which was appreciated and unprecedented.

We had no money and weren't sure how we would get to Los Angeles for the TV taping, but as always, they remained delusional, convinced that it would work out.

It was on my shoulders to get a job, but it was not a possibility in my tremendously round state. I had applied for and gotten food stamps. At least we had nourishment. I was a self-imposed Scullery Maid, going from one meal to the next. With all the practice and free food, Phileap and Marco were eating huge meals three times a day. I was happy to cook for them in my mother's colossal tract home. I loved the kitchen's view of the silhouette of Mount Rose through the window.

My mom saw me staring at the snow-covered mountains.

"You look better today. Feeling a bit stronger?"

"Yes, thanks for asking. The pain from the constant movement has subsided."

She rubbed my shoulders. "Is the baby moving around less?"

"Yes, it's scary."

"Don't worry, it means it is almost time for him to come."

"That's what the doctor said, which is even scarier. Is it too late to change my mind?"

"About what?"

"About having a baby."

She snorted and shook her head at me. I waddled out to the pasture with a pitcher of greens and lemon juice for everyone.

Phileap saw me and smiled as he readied to leap off the platform, forcing the trapeze to swing higher than the rigging. Pumping high, the rigging came a bit out of the ground when the pinnacle of the arc was stretched; it reminded me of children swinging. On the second swing, he let go at the top of the arc and propelled himself, back arched, perfect body position, and did a triple layout—spinning three complete turns with his body extended. This trick was believed to be impossible, but Phileap had figured out how to do it into the net. The next step would be to complete it to the catcher.

Everyone insisted it couldn't be done, but he took great pleasure in ignoring them. I believed he could do it. Being away from his father had bolstered his confidence. Plus, he was under the impression that he had produced a miracle in making me pregnant. It was whispered loudly that I was too mean to be a mother. That even God saw how horrible I was. But there I was, in all my pregnant glory, about to give him a son. A girl would be unacceptable. I prayed that the one doctor who said it was a boy was right when six doctors proclaimed it would be a girl.

Phileap bounced three times on the net, grabbed the side, and flipped down into his clogs. He was nearly floating with pride in himself that he pulled off the triple layout, made even better by the audience of his tubby wife and a few neighbors.

"Apple Pie! Did you see it? I did it!"

He embraced me and canoodled my belly into his muscle-ripped stomach.

"It was spectacular," I whispered in his ear.

Over time, I learned to praise him as quietly as possible because if his brothers heard, they would mock him. But as his partner, it was my duty to bolster his self-esteem and praise him for a job well done.

"Thank you! Is that juice for me?"

"Yes, greens and lemon. Are you hungry for lunch?"

"I want to try a few more throws before I eat. Will you stay and watch? I would like your input."

"Yes, of course!" He pecked me on the cheek, downed the tart juice, and ran to climb the ladder again.

This was a new Phileap. I wasn't sure if it was the time away from his family or the pregnancy or the fact that I had found us a free place to live filled with government-supplied food, but I was grateful he was kind again. Twenty-one years on earth, and his hard, hateful exterior was softening. I guessed it was my swollen belly that turned all my monsters into the kinder fare. I really didn't care why. I was happy not being besieged by hate. In that respect, I loved being pregnant even though I was terrified to give birth. There wasn't any turning back.

102

Fall, 1984, Reno, Nevada, USA

As my belly grew and my roots sank deeper into my parents' pasture, I considered it was time Phileap and I got married. Using the tainted ring from Japan, I felt less than enthusiastic. He loved the idea of the green card that would result from the joining. I was under the illusion it would make us more tangible, that the certificate would give me power over him that being a "baby mama" would not. It was easy to do in Reno, one trip to the county clerk and a skip out front to the Chapel of the Bells—a $30 price tag to give your life away.

We decided to have the wedding the day after Thanksgiving, and I called my nana and papa.

"Nana, I am getting married on Friday!"

"This is wonderful news, Gail. Let me get Papa on the phone."

I heard the other line pick up, and my papa inhaled his Parliament cigarettes.

"Hey, my little circus traveler. What is up?"

"Phileap and I are getting married. I want you to be here!"

"When? That is a surprise."

"I know, Papa. I want you here. I am sorry. I miss you guys much. It is the day after Thanksgiving."

"Is he good to you? Do you love him?"

The answer was complicated. I was carrying his child and had made the decision to be his second best. I was not sure either of those things meant love. I knew he was recently nice to me, but not overall. Not to worry my grandparents about my complications, I simply answered, "Yes."

"I am sorry, Toksy, we can't come."

"You can come here for the holidays and be at my wedding. That's why I chose that date."

I was near hysteria. The idea that my grandparents who had always loved and supported me would miss my wedding was more than I could bear.

"Nana is sick, Toksy. She can't travel. I'm sorry."

Fear hit me with full velocity.

"What? I thought she was getting better?"

"She's sick. We will talk about it later. Be happy. Love you, Toksy."

He hung up, and I stared at the phone. Nana was still on the line, but I was too stunned to speak.

"Gail, I will be okay. I am getting good treatments, and I have wonderful medicine that takes all the pain away. Don't you get upset, dear; the baby doesn't like a distraught mama."

"Why didn't I know about this? I am coming to you tonight."

"No, you have a wedding to plan. I will be fine. Send me lots of pictures, and call me after your honeymoon."

"We're not having a honeymoon. Nana, I want to see you."

"I love you, Toksy," she sobbed and hung up.

I turned on my mother, yelling while crying.

"What is wrong with Nana?"

"She is worse. She didn't want you to know."

"Why?!"

I was yelling and crying, but no one could calm me. I stomped and slammed back to our camper. Phileap joined me an hour later.

"How are you doing? Is dinner ready?"

"Is that all you care about?"

I stomped and slammed again, this time out to the net. I climbed like a hippo and lay there, sobbing. I knew it was terrible for Nana if no one would tell me anything. I also knew I couldn't do anything about it.

103

Fall, 1984, Reno, Nevada, USA

The next day, we planned the wedding. Family and a few neighbors would be there. My former Girl Scout leader would be there, and her four-year-old daughter would be our flower girl. I upcycled an old Rainbow Girl dress to make a simple long, white gown that covered my enormous belly. Phileap bought a new white shirt. The reception would be back at my parents' house in the family room that now resembled an old western bar. Ancient barn wood adorned the walls and the top of the bar. Rusted farm elements and dusty animal heads embellished the partitions.

We had a subdued Thanksgiving now that the cat was out of the bag about my sick nana. The tradition of burnt turkey and rubbery potatoes continued. I was too distraught to prepare the meal, so my mom did all the cooking. Phileap was confused about the fuss for this American holiday because the food was terrible. After dinner, we performed for the neighbors, who were excited to have a flying family squatting in my parents' pasture.

On the morning of the wedding, I woke with sheer terror in my heart and went to my horse to console me. My subconscious was now so blind, it wanted advice from my horse. He looked at me with his giant honey eyes and swished his tail in a circle, placing his forehead on mine. I swore that meant he did not want me not to marry Phileap. Ignoring my faithful steed (and my own intuition), I curled my hair, put on my blue mascara, and was ready for the best day of a girl's life. The Chapel of the Bells stunk of stale beer and wet carpet. The minister was a failed Elvis impersonator. It was a brief and tacky ceremony, everything you could imagine in a twenty-four-hour chapel in the middle of the drug district. Becoming a bride for thirty dollars in this well-traveled place seemed all I deserved at this point. I recognized that the wedding matched all I had experienced with Phileap. My dream never quite fit into the reality I had captured myself in.

After, we went back to my parents' house, where my sister had hung white balloons, and went to Scolari's grocery store to purchase a stock wedding cake. The appetizers were American cheese in a can on Ritz crackers, and cream cheese rolled up in deli ham slices.

That day was another special wedding. Luke and Laura were getting married on the American daytime soap opera *General Hospital*, and we all had to all watch. My wedding reception included all the women sitting on my mother's bed, watching TV. Though Luke and Laura Spencer were fictional characters, they were like part of the family. Thirty million viewers joined us, and it was the best part of my wedding.

104

Winter, 1984, Reno, Nevada, USA

I waddled up the winding grand staircase of the walnut-laden building. Plush carpet and silk walls drove home the point that very expensive attorneys worked here. I was there to work on getting Phileap a visa or a green card. He was still illegal in the U.S. because of the circus mix-up. I sought out my faux beau, Stuart, who was now a Nevada State Legislator and still the keeper of my cats. He was shocked to see me in a round and bouncy condition, and even more surprised to hear I had married the circus performer. Everyone but me had had high hopes for my future, assuming I would go into law and politics.

Stuart crossed to me in his stately office and hugged me awkwardly. "Well, you're always one for taking great risks. I'm not surprised. It's such a novelty. You happy?"

I blushed. I didn't like to lie to this man who had helped me much.

"I am stuck. I will find happiness after the baby is born," was my soft reply.

"Babies don't cause happiness; they cause sleeplessness and terror. You better come up with a more solid plan."

I knew he was right and thanked him for helping me with the green card status. We talked about my cats, and he had pictures and stories to tell about this now-bonded pair. I knew I had made the right decision leaving them with Stuart. They were happy and secure. I could never offer another being that kind of stability. That thought terrified me as I lumbered over to the INS office with my paperwork and attorney advice. I was resolute I would leave there well on the path to getting my husband a green card.

105

Winter, 1984, Reno, Nevada, USA

The misery bounced off the walls, a cacophony of different languages whispered as they tried to find the right English words to say to the bored clerks. The beige walls and dirty carpet made the place look like a prison waiting room. The cracked brown plastic chairs bit my butt as I stood up when my number was called. A bespectacled clerk with his hair greased back grabbed my paperwork. I started to tell him my story, but he shushed me with a whistle through the gap in his teeth and a stern look. I went silent. He read over every paper and statement, then pulled out a stamp from the drawer, greased it with red ink, and stamped it hard. REJECTED across all my pages. He didn't say a word, just slid the paper back to me.

"But I am about to have his baby! I need a visa or green card for him!"

He shot me a look of disgust, then turned and left the window, grunting, "Go away, circus girl."

Shocked, I sat in the chair and begin crying. Even though the office was full, no one came to comfort me. Everyone else was in their own private hell and did not wish to get any of my misery on their shoes. I composed myself and drove home. I had made copies of all the paperwork. My plan was to make fifteen more copies and come back every day until someone in the office would help me.

Phileap had caught the triple layout back at the pasture and was throwing it over and over to lock in the muscle memory. I pulled in to see half the neighbors watching and cheering each time he landed it. Running on pure adrenaline, he seemed to float up the rope ladder, making it look as easy as walking. He would jump and come off the bar. Back arched, hands out straight, and toes perfectly pointed, he rotated three full times in midair, landing with expert precision into Marco's open hands. Marco would toss him high on the return, and Phileap did a full in-air pirouette and grabbed the bar, swinging back to the platform. It was beauty personified. I was proud.

Phileap not only caught it, but he improved it with the pirouette. The neighbors were cheering and loving being a part of this magical moment. I waddled over as they were planning a barbecue to celebrate this fantastic moment. I chose not to tell Phileap about the INS meeting. I would not put anything in his head except making this trick stick because we could sell it as part of our act.

I met with Stuart again the next day, and we tweaked the paperwork a bit. When I told him about *That's Incredible*, he offered to sponsor the trip. The act of kindness overwhelmed me. It was a light turned back on. This man made me believe in a happily ever after. If only I had chosen him.

I became a fixture at the INS office. It is hard not to miss a severely pregnant redhead trying to get her flying husband a green card. Some of the clerks were impenetrable and found something wrong with every approach. There was no black and white in this process. It was about a few forms, but the INS clerk had to rubber-stamp it to get to the next round of the application. A couple of clerks even threatened to send the police to arrest Phileap and Marco. I told them that we were living in a pasture and good luck finding it. I finally wore down a middle-aged woman, whose middle was as thick as mine. She told me to get them to Tijuana with a green stamped visa form and to find Hector at the American consulate, and they would be in the country legally, allowing me to start the green card process.

They would have to stay in Tijuana for three weeks, but we were closer to legality than we had ever been. Phileap thought I had been going to the doctor every day; this was the first time I mentioned INS and the status. He was not thrilled to spend three weeks in Tijuana, but when faced with the possibility that he would be a father of an American child without being able to legally stay in the United States, he acquiesced. A plan was hatched for him to go after his *That's Incredible* performance.

106

Winter, 1984, Burbank, California USA

We had packed up the trapeze and driven to ABC studios for the taping of the show. Checking into the studios was surreal and exciting. Our name was on the list, and they seemed excited to have a trapeze troupe on the lot. It had been agreed that we would spend three days teaching the host, Cathy Lee Crosby, to fly with us and have her be a part of the act. We drove on to the expansive lot, excited for the time in Hollywood. They had cleared out a parking lot for us to set up the trapeze. Professional prop guys helped us drive stakes into the concrete for anchors. The setup would take all day and, clearly, I could not help.

One of the prop guys offered to take me on a tour of the studios. I was thrilled and ambled to his golf cart. The ABC shows were shot at the studio. Housed in giant metal buildings were the sets and make-believe living rooms of *Laverne & Shirley*, *Dynasty*, and *Three's Company*. At that time, daytime soap operas reigned supreme; they outshone primetime watching. The biggest was *General Hospital*. It filmed twenty-four hours a day with a rotating cast and crew to give the ravenous public the best and most outrageous situations. It had been my show since I was six years old. I had started watching it with my nana.

I walked into a darkened building from the blinding Los Angeles sunshine, and when my eyes adjusted, I was standing across from the Quartermaines' dining room—the central family on *General Hospital*. I recognized it and more as I was led down the middle of the warehouse with ten-by-ten-foot sets with three walls and an open side where the camera and crew shot from. There were thirty of them—the Port Charles Hospital nurses' station, Luke's house, and all of Port Charles. Hyperventilating, I stood there in my fairy-tale TV realm, now made real. We turned a corner and ended up in a break room.

It was filled with actors dressed as characters that I had lived with for years. The actors were in curlers and makeup collars. They turned and rushed to me. I was surprised to find that I was the novelty. They had driven on to the lot that morning to see a trapeze being built, and all wanted to know what it was like to fly, to be in the circus. They gave me a glass bottle of water with the *General Hospital* logo on it as I spilled circus stories to an excited, interested, and impressed audience. I was in heaven.

My prop guide took me to watch as a scene was shot. I sat across in the Quartermaines' entryway as they rehearsed a scene with Robert Scorpio and Luke Spencer. The director was sitting in a room off of the set, watching the different angles and setting the blocking. Her British accent came booming through the set, saying, "Gustavo, darling, move here. Try it with more power. Gustavo, darling, that is perfect."

I had never heard the name Gustavo, and I vowed that it would be my son's name.

I was on set for two hours, and the cast signed a poster for me. I offered to let them all come to try the trapeze. Many wanted to try, but the insurance guy gave a big "No" because the actors were the money train for ABC. But over the next three days, they all came to see us and hang out. I got to spend time with Laura, and we laughed about our shared wedding dates. Mine was as unrealistic as hers. I got a human. She got an Emmy.

We began practicing with Cathy Lee Crosby. I had spent a couple of hours peppering her with advice from someone who didn't come out of the womb flying. She was excited to be a part of the event, and I traded secrets of the trapeze for some about her famous father, Bing Crosby, who was one of my heroes. Not a typical celebrity, she spent the next two days in a grilling crash course of trapeze. We had her on the mechanic and planned to shoot that way. She wanted to fly on her own without the mechanic safety belt.

The performance was flawless and impressive. Cathy did pull off her trick without a mechanic. It was a simple legs-across, but she did it with flair, much to the chagrin of the stunt coordinator and insurance guy on set. The boys were fabulous in their skin-tight red tights, and Phileap won over the crowd with his blindfolded double layout. The blindfold was a hoax. From far away, it appeared as if his head was completely covered. He wore a black sack that rested under his arms and around his waist. He did the "blind man" routine of reaching for the bar, almost missing it, and then flying elegantly to and from the catcher. With the "Hup" calls and all the practice, I was sure he could do this with his eyes closed. The illusion was that the blindfold sack was made of a fine mesh that he could see through. The wardrobe department wanted to iron the mask, but I refused them, stating that the fabric was too sensitive for the irons. I had learned at this point that the most critical part of the act was the illusions that should never be shattered.

Cathy Lee and Marco had a tempestuous affair, the tights doing to her what they had done to many before. The four of us went to Musso & Frank for dinner. The atmosphere of old Hollywood and the giddiness of the performance made for an exceptional evening for me.

107

Winter, 1984, Sparks, Nevada, USA

I was laying on the cold, hard bed. Draped only partially in a paper gown, I was cold and terrified. The appointment took too long. The technicians whispered and called for backups. They pointed at the screen as the cold gel and hard wand pushed on my belly. I could sense something was wrong but was too scared to ask. My bladder felt like it would explode. The doctor was green; my son was to be his fifth birth. He was young and kind, trying to set up a family practice with his wife as the nurse. His practice was so new there were no pictures on the walls, the magazines weren't dog-eared, and the fake plants were dust-free.

He was thrilled and terrified by me. It's always fun to begin a sentence with "My patient, who is a trapeze artist . . ."

My pregnancy was complicated. The baby and I had been fighting since conception. Now the baby was three weeks late and in a weird position. The doctor was appropriately worried about me because if any of the baby's blood leaked into mine, it would kill me. He had a conversation with Phileap about which patient would be the priority to save. Phileap said his son. I wasn't surprised.

Doubled in girth and size, three weeks overdue to give birth, I was miserable. I was also on my turf, so my mouth ran as wide as my middle. I only cared about getting this alien off my bladder. I took to jumping on the net, trying to coax my child out of me. I figured the bouncing would be comfortable to him as his bloodline of acrobats made up half of his DNA.

Going to the doctor every day was a burden on the gas budget, but I was overdue, uncomfortable, and at risk. On the day the doctor was to decide about doing a cesarean section, I couldn't wrap my head around it because I knew it would brand me as incompetent to Phileap's family since I couldn't even give birth like an ordinary woman. Phileap was impatient. "Can't you give her some castor oil to make the baby come?"

The doctor shook his head at the comment. "That would work if she was constipated, not pregnant."

"Can't you do something? This is inconvenient for me."

"You know I did my residency in Central America?"

Phileap sparred eyes with him. "Yes, I would prefer an American-trained doctor."

I slapped him with my eyes for the comment. "He was schooled here; he did his training in Mexico."

"He is so new, and you want him to deliver our son?"

"It was a personal choice to help the poor. I learned a great deal about natural births and how to make it the easiest on the mother."

"I want it easy for my child."

The doctor gave me a sympathetic smile, and I closed my eyes, wishing I could take back every decision I had made to end up here with Phileap.

"I am surprised you do not know this. In third-world countries, when it is time for the woman to give birth, the husband makes love to her. He also sucks on her nipples to stimulate the milk to come, which eases the birthing."

Phileap was startled.

"I can't make love to her like that!" He mimed a huge belly with his arms.

"There was not one baby I delivered that the mother did not have sperm in the canal. It works. Why don't you guys give it a try?"

Phileap mumbled something about cows on the drive home while I tried to work myself up for the deed ahead.

Phileap was not up for this activity, but he came around and did his fatherly duties; we made the tiny camper rock. Within two hours, I was in full labor. We went to the hospital at 11:30 p.m. When examined, the baby's head was in the wrong position. The doctor tried several times to move it, but the little one fought and forced itself back into a dangerous position. At 6:30 a.m., I had a C-section. My son, Gustavo, was born. I didn't get to see him for twenty-four hours. I felt I was a failure at motherhood from conception.

108

Winter, 1984, Reno, Nevada, USA

Gustavo did not take to nursing. My mother brought a parade of neighborhood women to give me tips on everything from how to get him to nurse, to how to clean his butt, and how to get some sleep. I was disheartened. I didn't have that moment everyone talked about when you look into your baby's eyes and fall immediately in love. With my brain hazy and my body in pain, I was recovering from surgery, and I had no instincts. I had given birth to another Córdoba who was eventually going to hate me.

At seven days old, the baby was cradled in my left arm while I drank a cup of coffee using my right hand when a bee landed on my arm. I dropped the baby, not the coffee, to brush it away. He rolled off my lap and onto the floor. He was uninjured, but I was devastated. Sobbing hysterically, I took him to my mother.

"I am not worthy. Please take this boy from me."

She took the baby and made tea for me.

"What is going on? Gail, you are usually strong, sure of yourself to a fault. What is this all about?"

"I'm not me anymore. I'm a thing to be hated, shamed, and beaten down."

Recognizing the horrible emotional state, I was in, she took action. She could see it wasn't postpartum. My life has been turned around to the point that I believed I was the villain in my own story. Every day for the next two months, my mom came and helped, offering me praise and love. She taught me how to love my son.

We had to buy a bigger trailer to house our little family, so we found a used one that fit a crib and bed in the back. We needed a fresh truck because ours had a lot of miles on it, but we couldn't afford a new one. I decorated the place using Mom's leftover blankets, curtains, and scarves. My neighbors donated all kinds of feather beds that we used to hang on the walls to insulate around the baby so he would not get cold. I long-term borrowed a ton of cooking items and spices galore from my parents' kitchen. When we were done, it felt homey and warm. I felt like the master of my domain and that I could keep us warm and fed on the road.

We had to leave to reach Texas for the next massive paying gig. I would have to fly in the act. Forty days after a cesarean, I climbed the ladder to practice. I was sure when the weight of my body hit as I jumped from the platform, my guts would fly open and my uterus would land on the net. It didn't; the female body is a fantastic thing. With big milk-filled breasts, I was to perform in Texas with a two-month-old baby.

As we packed up the trailer, I had a parade of goodbyes. I had a master's degree in farewells, but leaving my family, friends, and entire support group petrified me. Plus, Sunshine was extremely sick, and my nana was still not telling me the truth about her health. I could neither control nor help with either, so the road seemed an easier way to deal with them.

This is where the paradox of desiring to be on the road, believing I loved Phileap, took an abysmal view. I was now a mother, and this silly dream didn't seem so important anymore. But I had just married Phileap, convinced that this leap of faith required more time from me. I couldn't stay behind, but I did not want to go. At this point, I looked at every move as temporary, with the solitary purpose of ending up in one place with my husband and child. That delusional element that spurred my entire life was still there.

109

Spring, 1985, Amarillo, Texas, USA

I spoon-fed the brown spinach into my son's mouth as we hit a pothole in the road. The spinach went more on his forehead than in his mouth. He cried out hungrily and we tried again. Navigating life on the road as a mother was a merciless task. My poor son never got to see anything except for the trailer and the truck's front seat. I held him every minute he wasn't asleep. I had nothing but eternal love for him. I hadn't a home or a root system, but I loved him utterly. Everyone teased me because I never put him down. I wouldn't even use a stroller.

I watched as Lupe stuffed and shushed her three toddlers into a sizable wooden costume trunk set outside the ring.

"I can watch them for you! The act is only six minutes."

"My husband would be livid and beat me. They are fine."

She closed the lid amid whines of terror coming from her children. They thumped on the cover once they heard the lock.

"This isn't necessary. I am right here."

"But tomorrow, you may not be. They must get used to this or join the act. It is the only safe way."

This had been a tradition for hundreds of years, but now that I had a child of my own, I was having none of it. Phileap was pissed I would not do the same.

"Marco and I spent many fun times in Mama's trunk. The baby will be fine."

"I am not putting my baby in a trunk!" I stomped off, the bravest woman on the show because I did not fear my husband.

I made friends with another aerialist mom I trusted. She held the baby where I could see him in the audience while we performed. The funny thing was if he cried, my breast leaked. Picture me fifty feet in the air with nipple milk running down my torso while the catcher tries to dodge my slippery breast milk.

Phileap liked the baby, liked the idea of having a son. I was even more outspoken and even more of a mama bear with a child in tow. Phileap on the road was now distant and spent more time in the dressing rooms—meaning he was bringing town girls in there to give him pleasure.

He explained his belief to me. "Now that you are a mother, you can no longer be my sexual companion."

"Wait. What?" I yelled loud enough for the baby to pop off my nipple and look at me with a milk mustache.

"It is common in my country for the men to have a couple of girlfriends and the mother to raise babies."

"If you haven't noticed, we are not in your country anymore. You cannot tell me we are never going to have sex again!"

"I did you a favor to get him here." He pointed at the baby.

"That was not a favor, and damn it, you do not get to have a girlfriend!"

Gustavo was crying, and Phileap shook his head like I was an idiot and stepped out of the trailer.

110

Spring, 1985, Austin, Texas, USA

Gustavo learned to crawl in the straw of the elephant pen. Between the giant legs of the elephants, my tiny son navigated on his hands and knees. We also had five-month-old baby tigers who he would cuddle with and whose ears he would chew. It all seemed normal to me, but at the same time, I longed for a white picket fence with green grass and a swing set. Our reality was a travel trailer, a cold bathroom floor, the sawdust of the animal pens or, worse yet, out in the audience alongside strangers.

I spent time doing circus research for the book I hoped to write one day. I took my baby to the Austin library and let him crawl around the children's book area. The warmth and cleanliness of the library made me feel like a better mother. While he chewed the corners of baby board books, I researched. None of the performers with any of the shows I traveled with could offer me a real history of the American trapeze.

The Ringling Brothers and Barnum & Bailey, who were circus owners and promoters, traveled the globe and brought back acts and animals for the circuses, but I wanted to know about the flyers. The Imperial Flyers, who started their circus at the YMCA in Denver in 1920, fascinated me.

The two founders of what eventually became the Denver Imperial Flyers Trapeze club were both born in the 1800s. Mabel Rilling was born in 1883 and lived until 1972, and Granville Johnson was born in 1897 and lived until 1956.

The first circus shows included boxing and wrestling exhibitions. They also had gymnastics, acrobatics, and dance numbers. In 1921, there were "three rings" in the gymnasium. In that space was where the tumbling, flying rings, vaulting on the horse, and parallel and horizontal bars took place. But there were also pyramids or group balancing, tight-wires, revolving ladders, clowns, and even trampolines, which at that time were considered a vaudeville show gimmick. The balancing trapeze, single trapeze, double trapeze, and flying trapeze were also part of the program.

The Denver Imperial Flyers are the only flying group that has had a master's thesis written about them. It was written by Lisa Hofsess as part of the requirements for her degree in kinesiology at Iowa State University in 1981. It tested John Kenyon's vertigo theory about risk takers. This theory implied that people who sought high-risk behaviors were in it for the adrenaline. The question the research asked was whether trapeze flyers wanted to be out of control and experience vertigo when they were pursuing the activity.

The concept had previously been tested on skydivers. Lisa's population was the Denver Imperial Flyers. The control group was a YMCA aerobic exercise class. She gave each person in both groups a battery of tests and gave the flyers a set of items in an interview protocol. The two groups answered the test questions differently; flyers are different from non-flyers, it seems. The results demonstrated that being out of control or being dizzy and disoriented were undesirable feelings for flyers. They expressed that they wanted to be in control of their bodies and their perceptions during the activity. Although they wanted to be at the limits of what they were able to do, none of them felt that they were putting themselves in excessive danger. Both males and females reported mastery (a sense of accomplishment, achievement, or challenge) as the most enjoyable aspect of flying. They reported the thrill or excitement of flying as another enjoyable aspect and said that there was something aesthetically beautiful about trapeze that non-flyers were unable either to see or appreciate. One called it the "beauty of the moment."

Without a degree or even knowledge of what a thesis was, I knew she was correct.

111

Summer, 1985, Galveston, Texas, USA

Traveling with the circus was a blood sport when it came to parking. Each day when pulling into new fairgrounds, the race was to get closest to the jump box, the lifeline of electricity to our trailers. Our lead clown would plug the box into a 220-volt outlet at the venue, and we would plug into it, thus providing light, heat, water pumps, and more for rolling homes.

This jump box provided electricity for fifteen trailers. Thirty-three house trailers made up the entire show on the road. Those who had to piggyback got less voltage and more blackouts.

On one rare occasion, we got into the fairground first. In some stupid part of my brain, I thought having a new baby would make the circus consider me a priority, but the chimpanzees remained supreme.

Parked next to the chimpanzee truck was a dangerous but welcome new place for me. We had full air—which helped with the 99-degree, humidity-filled Galveston—but having my front window facing the primates made life intriguing.

The eight chimps in the show were ferocious. While dressed like little soldiers and queens in the ring, they appeared adorable as they went through their routine of pratfalls and funny situations.

My next-door neighbors were in a cage with an entire glass front to watch the world as they played in their twenty-eight-foot by seven-foot prison. They were understandably pissed off. The act's original two chimps had mated, and the act was now all in the family. Their trainers were from Germany: a cranky couple named the Gremlins who only interacted with the circus folk to receive their paychecks and tell us at the beginning of each season to "stay the fuck away from them and their chimps." They looked like twins, acted like enemies, and smelled like feces. I heeded their advice.

⁂

I existed in peace during the day with my baby in this premier spot. The circus arena was a hot, dusty, and dangerous place for a baby trying to crawl. Gustavo had taken to standing on the couch and looking out the window to see the colors and animals go by. Here, to his delight, he could see the primates. The Gremlins were pissed that we were their neighbors for the next three days because Gustavo made the chimps come unglued when he looked, waved, and giggled at them. He was obsessed with the hairy beasts that could swing from the artificial branch and throw their bodies at the glass in a threatening manner. It had to be the funniest spectacle he had witnessed in his ten months with the circus. Upon waking, he would crawl to the couch and climb up, dragging the curtains open for the show. All the while, the Gremlins complained and threatened.

The circus manager directed me to move the trailer back to my usual spot in the rearmost part of the lot with the watered-down electricity. I refused, and the constant war between the animal people and the acrobats intensified. Mysteriously, our trapeze guidelines were loosened, our net displayed cagey holes, and our capes were ripped. My family begged me to move to condense the conflict, but I was determined to have three days with air conditioning.

On the second day, a blast of 220-volt electricity blew through our trailer, frying every appliance. These plugs, the most powerful found in the United States, are meant for large ovens, dryers, and other high-powered appliances you can't power with a standard 110-volt outlet. The jump boxes converted the power to the lower 110 volts.

When the 220 volts ran through our tiny trailer, it destroyed everything plugged in. Some declared it an unfortunate accident, but I knew better. Before we moved, I spent an hour educating the swinging simian neighbors on giving an insulting salute. Using their dexterous hands, each learned to extend the middle finger. That night, the crowd was horrified and hysterical when the chimps used their new skill to tell everyone what went unspoken about how they felt about being circus animals.

112

Summer, 1985, Tombstone, Arizona, USA

Sitting in the bleachers and watching the show for the hundredth time, I was still in awe. The mastery it took to keep the act solid was something I now understood. I watched the bamboo act, which featured an aerial perch that blew everyone's mind and made the trapeze artists extremely jealous. Set incredibly high at around seventy-five feet in the air, a long pole with a perch at the top is attached to a wire. The perch is an equilibristic balancing act where one performer is poised atop a pole balanced by another performer. Each perch pole has a loop at the top into which the performer may insert either a hand or a foot to perform a variety of tricks while hanging from the loop. During the whole routine, the catcher or base at the bottom must balance the pole as the flier shifts their weight from one position to another, climbs up and down, and balances at the top.

In our show, Devin had one foot in a loop attached to the pole while his wife, Angelina, sat on the perch and was tossed around, doing aerobatic tricks. They used no net or mechanic. She did back-to-back layouts—caught by the hands and then the feet—then double somersaults and twists, returning to his hands as he stood perpendicular on the steel pole. For the finale, Angelina attached two loops to her ankles and Devin threw her down. When the ropes went taught, seeming to split her in two, the audience gasped. She held the split and was lowered to the ground. It never got old to watch and always made me gulp.

In person, Angelina was shy and never spoke. Devin was gorgeous and flirty. It always seemed to me that she was a prisoner of her talent and love for him. Being a circus veteran now, I invited her to join the Scullery Maids and "Let's Go to the Women's Clinic" gang. She only smiled her sly smile and faded back into her dressing room.

By the time I got to the dressing room, she was already dressed. She wore a crystal broach on her sweater. I crossed to ask her about it because I had never seen any circus people wear jewelry. Not even wedding rings because they could get caught on costumes, rigging, and more. She was startled when I came up to her.

"That is a beautiful broach! Where did you get that?"

She smiled, and I knew I had a subject she would talk about. She reached her hand up to touch the broach, and it moved.

"Did that jewelry move?"

She giggled and started to explain quietly as the broach did circles on her sweater.

"It is a makech. She is a beetle from Yucatan."

I was a bit freaked out. But this was the first that I had heard her speak, so I asked for more.

"Are you the only one who has one?"

"No, it is a tradition to wear a living pendant. For centuries, the Mayans have worn them."

I yelped as it moved.

"How does it stay on your sweater?"

She pulled it up and revealed that it was attached by the rhinestones on its back and a small gold chain pinned to the sweater.

"Vendors in Mexico sell the beetles covered in rhinestones, each one fixed with a gold chain and pin that serves as a leash so that the bedazzled bug can walk around on my shirt."

"I have to know why you would wear a bug?"

"It is for my one love. We have a Yucatan legend involving an ancient princess. She was Mayan nobility—and she had a lover. Their love was forbidden. The princess was heartbroken when she discovered that her lover was sentenced to death. A shaman changed the man into a shining beetle that could be decorated and worn over the princess's heart as a reminder of their eternal bond."

"That is the best story I have heard in a long time. Do you have more than one?"

"I do. I have six." She tittered a bit.

"You have six lovers?"

"No, I love my man six times over."

I was impressed and again invited her to come to the next Scullery Maid meeting, which she declined, but they were fascinated by the story and made me vow to get one.

The Arizona show had more than its fair share of balancing acts, which used various skills involving balance such as juggling, tightrope walking, or riding a unicycle. We had some original jugglers who did an aerial bamboo act with a clown and three artful jugglers; one was Tamy, my favorite person on that show. A woman in a predominately male act, she was scrappy and full of stories.

Tamy's act started with the clubs (think bowling pins, only lighter) tossed back and forth while juggling eight at a time. Tamy tried to teach me how to juggle just two clubs, and when I failed, she took me back to beanbags and then scarves. It was harder than learning how to fly.

They also used platforms and did tumbling with the clubs always flying and never hitting the ground. It was spectacular. Their finale was a daring combination of aerial tumbling and juggling. Their hands moved so fast and precise that you could barely see them. Tamy worked with me every day in between acts backstage, and I became quite proficient at the beanbags.

"Thanks for helping me learn this."

"Yeah, beanbags will get you fucking far in life."

"I'm enjoying learning something new." Balancing the baby on my hip while juggling was a challenge.

"Why aren't you spending more time learning trapeze tricks?"

"Because it means more time with THEM."

"You mean the family that you live with that hates your guts?"

"Yes."

"Why the fuck are you staying?"

"I ask myself that more and more."

"You could be a professor or some kind of teacher. I don't understand why you would choose this life when you have so many options. I think that is why most circus folks loathe you. You have choices, they don't."

"I don't believe that. Everyone has choices. It is just harder for the circus people because that is all they know. If they go work in Las Vegas and stay in one place, they can learn how to live in one spot."

"Like roots and shit?"

"Yes. I believe that Phileap and I will put down some roots and shit soon."

"Are you sure you like him enough to plant your ass with him?"

"That is a concrete question."

113

Fall, 1985, Wickenburg, Arizona, USA

Sitting on the picnic table, balancing my boy on my lap, and enjoying the high desert views outside, I tasted the most delectable pizza I had ever tried. As I ate with one of my favorite families from Italy, the family chattered on in lyrical Italian and laughed often. Their nonna was the most prolific and talented of my Scullery Maids on this show, and they performed a Risley juggling act. This is when the catcher, lying on their back on a slant board, uses their feet and hands to juggle other members of the troupe. They do layouts, back flips, and amazing balancing.

I loved everything about this happy Italian family. They were very close, but often brought me into their home and made me feel like I belonged. They loved on my son while sharing family circus stories that dated back to

1877. They told of performing for kings, beheadings if royalty wasn't pleased, and traveling in a traditional wooden circus wagon. Then they would argue for hours about who married whom and who was with which act. It was the longest circus historical family I had met, but I still was not sure whether I wanted a circus heritage and future for my son.

"Don't worry, your boy can join us if his family no longer wants him." Nonna was perceptive of my melancholy.

"Ha! I wish!"

"You could just go home?"

"I'm not sure I could. I made a promise to stick this year out. Before, I was selfish and self-absorbed, but now I care only for my son. I believe being with his father is the best thing for the baby."

"Phileap will never leave his family. He will choose them first."

"I've already experienced that and chose to stay. I just need to spend more time with you!"

"My little storyteller, you will always be welcome in our family."

114

Winter, 1985, Las Vegas, Nevada, USA

One of the advantages of working with the circus was the small side gigs up for grabs when it's winter weather in the rest of the country. Circus people tend to "winter" in Nevada or Florida. The old families and animal acts went to Florida because it was still an empty empire of swamps, and Towners stayed off their backs. The aerialists started going to Nevada because they could get gigs in the casino shows with small novelty acts. Hollywood was a short drive, and there were large sums of money if you could get a gig as a stunt guy or a performer at a star-studded party. Circus acts were still novel and quickly bought. The Hollywood elite would hire us to perform at their parties. The TV show *Circus of the Stars* was popular at this point, and you could fill a whole month training a B-star and then performing with them. This helped the resume and garnered more money when looking for our next show from March through October. Our agent was also a performer in Las Vegas. Sebastián got us jobs beginning in November because we always came off the road dead broke. We did The Super Loco's act at *Folies Bergère*, and because I was a new mommy, I stayed home and sewed costumes. Phileap only worked nights. We were once again parked in Gladys Knight's back lot. She was barely home, and the novelty of having a trapeze in her yard always won over her friends.

We were all back together and living in the Vegas dirt again. The baby kept me focused or cried enough so that I couldn't hear the blue-eyed devil references. We practiced and lived our separate lives, though only parked three meters from each other's tin cans. I wished the baby would bring everyone closer to me, an acceptance of some kind. But releasing a child from my womb was not the miracle I believed it was. To them, I was just another cow, keeping the next generation of flyers fed.

115

Winter, 1985, Malibu, California, USA

Driving up the Malibu highway, I rejoiced at the sight of the roaring ocean and epic mansions up on the hill. We were driving our trailers in a caravan, and it embarrassed me to be in viewing range of all this wealth while we were common gypsies. We were on our way to a gig in Hollywood for a wedding. They wanted the full trapeze and two performances—one before the ceremony and one during the reception. We did not know who was getting married or what the setup was until we arrived in Malibu on an empty ten-acre parcel and saw the sign "Spelling Wedding" on the property.

The famous TV producer was getting married. They had ten carnival rides set up next to us as well as a huge tent with a ring and food vendors around the edges. The white wedding tent had ten white baby grand pianos and more gardenias than grow in Honolulu. While the boys set up, I wandered around with Gustavo. He was eleven months old, adorable, and a good conversation starter. When the reception began, I mingled with the guests. People adored the baby.

"That is one cute kid," squealed Florence Henderson, who had played the mother on *The Brady Bunch*. "Can I hold him?"

"Of course!"

She coddled the baby, and he cooed back. I still have a picture of Florence holding Gustavo with Dick Clark, Ed McMahon, and Alan Alda. They fired circus questions at me.

Johnny Carson joined in and inquired if it was her grandkid. She stomped his foot. He laughed and wanted to know who I was. I told him I was with the trapeze troupe, and he was fascinated.

"You fly?"

"I do!"

"Were you born into it?"

"Nope, I ran away and joined the circus to avoid law school."

He threw his head back, laughing.

"I have never met anyone who ran away from real life. Do you have good stories?"

"I lived with elephants, monkeys, and tigers. I have great stories. In fact, the only reason I am sticking around now is for the stories."

Florence looked at me. "And the baby."

"Oh, yeah, him too."

I told them about being parked next to the chimp truck and what it was like, and as if on cue, Gustavo let out a chimpanzee call.

They all chuckled.

"That's going to be a problem. I'm going to need to fund a therapy endowment instead of college for this one."

They all howled with laughter and moved on to ride the scrambler. I went inside the wedding reception tent. It was right out of a movie. Faux circus wagons were laden with the most exotic of foods. It was a complete culinary circus. One wagon had Cristal champagne, hundreds of bottles. One had four pounds of caviar with three attendants spreading crème fraîche on a cracker and as much caviar as the guests wanted. The seafood cart was filled with steamed Alaskan crab legs and lobster still moving from Maine. The decorative net over the top held six huge crab claw legs that were about five pounds each. There were piles of fresh oysters with men in sailor suits shucking as fast as their hands could carry them. There was typical circus food like cotton candy (regular and truffle) and popcorn with six different spice mixtures to put on it. A Spanish Iberico station and countless delicious cheese and charcuterie platters made me wish I had brought a paper sack to take some back to the trailer. I sat with a bunch of performers. There were four long-haired and clearly not circus people sitting with me. Robert Gruenberg was the leader, and he told me they were opening. They were a juggling act that had been discovered on the Venice Beach boardwalk. They got up to do their act, and I was beyond impressed. They juggled chainsaws, flaming knives, and rakes, never missing a beat. They were funny and super talented. I saw them a month later on Johnny Carson's show and in the movie *Romancing the Stone*, starring Michael Douglas, who was also one of the guests at the wedding.

Right after the ceremony, as the newlyweds left the white tent and took the walkway that was under the trapeze, the crescendo came up. Phileap, Marco, and Nicolás threw trick after trick, and the crowd was mesmerized. It went on for twenty minutes until a pony pulling a twenty-layer cake ran into the reception tent, and everyone followed. There was a circus ring in the middle, and Ed McMahon was the emcee. He welcomed Aaron Spelling and his new bride while attendants in Venetian joker suits poured champagne into crystal goblets. Then out came the Golden Statues, a group we had worked with many times. Their skin was painted head to toe with gold paint, and they wore only gold Speedos while standing frozen in place on a spinning platform. Then they moved slowly into impossible positions using each other's bodies as props and ladders. It is hard to understand the amount of strength it took to do these postures, but to do them slowly and sustain them was herculean. It was always the most popular act anywhere we played, and tonight, even the uber-rich and jaded Hollywood elite were wooed. A Cuban (and illegal) cigar tent was outside after the cake was cut and distributed. The rare-scotch station was as popular as the port and single-sourced chocolates from Guatemala.

I had to put Gustavo down for the night. I strolled among the rides as the sequined stars spun and screamed with delight. When I was leaving, one of the jugglers asked if I liked crab. I had seen the food but was not sure it was okay to consume it because I was an employee, not a guest. He told me to go put the baby down and come back and share his. I sprinted to the trailer. Embarrassed to be living in such squalor in the light of all the decadence, I put the baby to bed. Phileap grunted at me as I told him I was going back. He was already on his post-show vigil of liver and onions and Telemundo.

When I returned, the juggler pulled a giant Alaskan king crab leg from his coat. I feasted on everything and had a ball talking with creative and brilliant individuals.

The party was over, and they were tearing everything down. The caterers were offering all the food to the performers. The guests had wiped out the caviar and truffles, but the crab legs were left along with a few lobster tails. I ate until I almost exploded as we shared performing stories, the tuxedoed crew fascinated by each tale. With the moon setting over the Malibu Beach mansion, I strolled about in my tracksuit. I had half a bottle of Cristal champagne I had liberated from a table and marveled that this was my show business.

116

The roar of the lion woke my dad up, and he grumbled that I didn't really need to bring the entire circus home with me, just his grandson. We moved back to Reno and my parents' pasture after the special events. I was thrilled at not being on the move again because I was having trouble adjusting to life on the road with Gustavo. My son only ate in the front of the truck because we were always going to the next show. On the road, the clowns set him up to be in spec, which Phileap found embarrassing.

The tiger act had come with us, so we had the cats in the pasture at home. I spent a great deal of time with them. I was trying to get back in shape. I flew every day. My muscle memory was good, so it did not take long to be in top performing shape.

My oldest friend, Kim, was still a neighbor of my parents. It was good to have her around. She was fascinated with the tigers and rode her horse, Chipper, daily to hang with the cats and watch me fly.

"That which does not kill us makes us stronger" was the motto most befitting Kim. She was the strongest, most *alive* person I knew. She lived every day as if it was her last, never shying away from any desire, fear, or obstacle. She was one of the reasons it was easy for me to join the circus.

She was now twenty-one and had decided it was time to get married to the sweet cowboy who worked on the farm. He was smitten with the woman who could wrestle the most energetic calf to the ground. Her family had long since given up trying to talk her out of anything.

We threw them a big western and circus wedding in her garden. It was a magical day with wild lilies strung about the hay bales and checkerboard tablecloths over the fences. Chipper was the best man and wore a bow tie. We danced, drank, and toasted the young couple. It was a sweet and straightforward romantic wedding. The couple waved goodbye and drove away in their decorated Chevy one-ton dually.

They were moving to Montana. Kim had five dogs at that point, all amazingly gifted animals that responded to her commands and knew her needs before she did. She had two horses: the stud, Chipper, and a Palomino mare. We waved goodbye as her husband drove the moving van and Kim drove the horse trailer with the dogs. They were off for a new life and a big adventure.

We got the call at midnight. Outside Salt Lake City, a big rig driving 85 miles per hour had stopped their dreams and silenced all their lives. It was a rainy night, and the driver had hydroplaned, hitting Kim and her animals head-on, killing everyone. Her short life was over, and her dogs and horses went to heaven with her. Her husband abandoned days after his wedding.

Kim's funeral was a heavily attended event with her jean-covered casket centerpiece. When they sang Willie Nelson's "Angel Flying Too Close to the Sun," we all sobbed for our lost friend. I was devastated. Her death and motherhood changed something in me. After all, it could all be lost in a blink of an eye.

Death is natural. Death is systematic. Death is preordained. Those left behind grieve and throw the unfairness card of a vibrant life struck down. In the end, Kim was newly in love, playful, and determined. She had unfinished business, and although I was livid at the loss of this incendiary soul, my job was to make sure she was remembered by parting off her belongings.

Her husband was but a ghost of a man, barely breathing and wearing his death mask. He was determined to follow her as soon as possible. I wouldn't have been surprised if they found him dead of his own hand. It wasn't a great love, but it was a sustainable one. Nothing seemed bearable without her. While the world was missing her, he was dying of a broken heart. I do not know which was harder to watch.

We handle death robotically in our culture; friends and family had already written her obituary. Her mom wanted me to take her things, but I had nowhere to put them. It felt like a theft. One she was watching and encouraging, but a heist all the same. Upon her mom's insistence, I chose an amethyst statue and a plaque that read "The shortest distance between us is laughter." I wished I could make her laugh again.

She fought like a warrior to do life on her own terms. When she was diagnosed with Type 1 diabetes, she was told she would only live until she was thirteen at the most. Happily, and greedily, she proved everyone wrong by living to adulthood because of her will and belief that living positively with the love from her community would sustain her. Everyone needs a Kim in their life. I was not surprised that it was a sudden summer rain on the day she died; the thunderclaps rattled and lightning scorched the sky as she took her last breath.

117

Spring, 1986, San Bernardino, California, USA

Phileap accepted an invitation to travel again with the mud show through the southern part of the United States without consulting me. After my fiery reaction calmed down, he convinced me there would be more money if we took the southern route, Highway 10, instead of crisscrossing all other the country with the Tabernacle circuses. I wanted to stay home, but we were out of money, and the traveling circus was our only option if we were going to keep eating. The I-10 stretches from the Pacific Ocean at State Route 1 (Pacific Coast Highway) in Santa Monica, California and goes to I-95 in Jacksonville, Florida. We started in Orange County at a state fairground and put in three months following the route.

The new group was a group of Syrians that juggled large curved knives and then each other. There were twenty of them, and every night after the show, they gathered around a hookah. Smoking fruit pulp and telling stories, they were an animated group full of laughter. I had never seen a hookah pipe and wanted to try it. Their jadda invited me in to make shawarma to share with everyone. She didn't speak English, but that did not stop us from creating together.

The show was a small one with each family required to provide at least six acts, three girls for the web, and three family members to take tickets or sell snacks and trinkets. We performed three shows a day; it was grueling with no downtime.

We provided the flying trapeze and a single trapeze act with me holding Phileap—a novelty in the circus world, but I was bigger than he was. We also did The Super Loco's, and Bernice and Nicolás did a dancing gaucho act. Payaso filled our clown requirements. The gaucho act was a new one to the U.S. but was popular all over South America. The highly energetic and diverse show was packed with drumming, dancing, boleadoras, malambo, audience interaction, and the right amount of comedy.

It was developed as a spectacular dance based on the boleadora, an Argentinean folk dance. Initially, the bola was a primitive hunting tool used by the Inuits and native South Americans. It is a projectile weapon made of a cord with wooden weights attached to either end, designed to capture animals by entangling in their legs or wings. The boleadora dance uses the bolas in a spectacular way, both as a percussion instrument and a juggling prop. They also used big drums for waking up the audience with fierce rhythms. Bernice was a natural, having come from a dancing background, but Nicolás struggled with being light—his assholeness ran bone-deep.

118

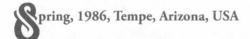

Spring, 1986, Tempe, Arizona, USA

The teeterboard troupe was a bizarre group of characters from one family all hailing from Jalisco, Mexico. They were rejects from the main family, brought together as primos (cousins). Derelicts, perverts, and weirdos were the main adjectives used to describe this group of men. There were thirteen in all, all distantly related, and the rest of us took a wide berth around them in and out of the ring. A circus is the best place to hide your less-than-moral bloodline because the law never caught up, and they were never in one place long enough to do too much damage.

I watched their act with fascination. Their big trick was the basket toss, an acrobatic act involving two base performers, the fat guys known as carriers, who use their interlaced hands or arms to catapult a flyer, the skinny ones, into the air. They perform acrobatic leaps and then either return to the starting point, the ground, or another team of carriers. The ground-to-air group act involves propelling a performer into the air to do single or multiple tricks. The flyer can go from the floor to the group or be pitched from group to group. The human pitching act also involved tumbling, acrobatics, and adagio. You could tell from their body language they all loathed each other, and the skinny guys often got pitched into the crowd.

They tried to talk to me because it was clear I was a Towner. At every new show we played with, the rumors and gossip started about me, the Towner. This was no different. Circus men believed that women Towners were of loose morals and willing to do anything to be with a man in tights. One of the teeterboard group tried to lure me into his trailer after my act, but I trumpeted like an elephant and went to hide. These repudiates traveled with no women, mamas, or Scullery Maids. Later, I agreed to help one of the skinny ones learn how to cook. He failed, and soon part of my income came from making a daily pot of stew for them to devour. I made Phileap deliver the containers of food.

119

Spring, 1986, El Paso, Texas, USA

Phileap and I had our own single trapeze act, an aerial apparatus with a small round bar suspended by ropes or metal straps from a roof point. Our act included static tricks, swinging tricks, and catch-and-release flying trapeze stunts.

It was unique with me as the catcher and him the flyer. My job was to hang upside down on the swinging bar and not let go of him. While I was plenty strong to hold his tiny frame, hanging upside down for five minutes was challenging at first. My head would throb, my nose would leak, and I would have to flip up. Phileap wanted me to speed up my adjustment period by sleeping with my head off the bed, which I refused. I was a new mother, performed in five acts, sold popcorn, taught the kids' school, and fed reprobates. I was too busy to be lonely, which was a blessing.

"Can you style with more style?" Phileap sneered at me as I progressed into our next move.

"This is the only style I have."

"After all these years, have you learned nothing but how to make my food too spicy from the circus women?"

We moved to the next position, and the audience applauded.

"I'm doing the best I can."

"That's my worry. You have never been enough."

Resisting the urge to drop him, I released my grip a bit to send adrenaline through his smug mind.

As we were lowered to the center ring and bowed to the crescendo of music, our names, and applause, he glared at me.

"You are an idiot. I won't be home tonight. I'm going into town to meet friends."

I smiled and thought, *He thinks that is punishment.*

120

Spring, 1986, Fort Stockton, Texas, USA

We had trouble with Payaso, who was getting creepier and bolder now that Papi and Mama were not on the road with us. We had sent them back to Las Vegas with Marta, a decision based on their inability (and refusal) to learn English or get along with any of the other circus folk. It was nice to have the parents gone. All the Córdobas were almost civil and getting along. One night, the tiger trainer banged on our door and accused Payaso of lurid behavior with two of his cats. I did not know the exact words screamed in Spanish, but I knew it was terrible. A few weeks later, I caught Payaso skulking around after the kids had left their school lessons. He tried to act like he was here to entertain them, but the kids ran home from the freak. I approached the subject with Phileap.

"We must do something with Payaso. He is getting too untethered and creepy."

"I don't understand either of the words, Apple Pie."

"He is acting weird around children. It is not okay."

"Payaso has always done that. He is not harmful, likes to show parts of himself to small kids."

"And how is that okay? Why don't you guys make him stop? He could be dangerous to the youngsters."

"I will talk to him. But he has been like this forever. When I was little, he was fascinated with me and offered to give me a bath every day."

"Whoa. That is not okay."

"We are what we are. There is no changing."

"That is the stupidest thing I have ever heard. He should be locked up."

The conversation upset me, and I decided to keep my son and every tyke away from the potential child molester.

We got a knock at the door around 1 a.m. The local police had caught Payaso holding two preadolescent girls hostages in his box trailer. The girls were taken to the hospital. Payaso was taken to jail. We had to travel the next day and left him there. The other Córdobas were only upset because we had to find a new clown. One of the teeterboard flyers joined us. Now we had an unknown pervert in the act—one more creepy clown.

121

§ummer, 1986, Montgomery, Alabama, USA

We had been invited to go on a European tour again, which interrupted the circuit we were on. The money was double, but we had to figure out a way to leave but not break the contract we were under. The decision was made behind my back. They planned to leave Payaso (who someone had bailed out and put on a bus to catch up with us), Bernice, Nicolás, and me behind. Bernice was pregnant but could still style and wear ruffles around her waist to hide the belly. They recruited a few of the primo flyers to help with our various acts. I was pissed, but by the time I had been told, the plan was cast in stone.

I had been doing a web-type act using a ladder in the air while Phileap did the traditional ladder underneath me on the ground. It was a breath-taking performance, though simple to perform. I would attach my hand to a web and be whisked up to the ceiling where I threaded my body through a six-rung bounded ladder. I was squarely in there; it was much easier than the web where I had to hold on to a rope to keep me aloft.

The ladder is an acrobatic/manipulation act where the performer climbs and balances on an unsupported, freestanding ladder using a rocking motion. It includes juggling and balancing objects on the performer's head while doing handstands. Phileap was again the star, while I was a sparkly accoutrement in the air. The new plan meant Phileap would be replaced by a big primo, who both frightened and sickened me since I was sure he hadn't bathed in ten years. I refused to practice with him, but that did not stop the abandonment machine from chugging forward.

"I can't believe you are leaving me with a bunch of perverts. What if they come after your son?"

"Don't overreact. The clowns and priests came after me in South America, and I am okay."

"You are condoning this act because it happened to you? That is some bullshit logic there."

"The circus people appreciate the sacrifice. That is mostly why you don't fit in. You think you are above us all."

"I am above you all. And I know a shit ton of people who agree with me."

"Then you should go live with them."

"Fuck you."

122

ummer, 1986, New Orleans, Louisiana, USA

The good part of the cyclone of fits I executed after hearing I would be left was that Phileap had found Ramon. He requested that he stay with me while they were in Europe. Ramon had been my first and oldest circus friend, and with his wicked sense of humor, I knew my son would be safe and I would be entertained. Plus, the Primo Perverts were terrified of him, a bonus contribution.

Ramon's act was a mixture of several different tumbling, balancing, and juggling disciplines. He was ever the entertainer, making the audience gasp and laugh throughout his performances. It was one of the most technical acts on the circuit, but he worked hard to make it look easy and as if he was a baboon.

He used a form of slapstick, honed by Buster Keaton, to keep the story of the act entertaining. Using a rolla bolla, an act involving the performer balancing on one or more cylinders while standing on a flat board, he would employ feats such as skipping, juggling, handstands, and balancing objects on his head. The physical humor he used included slapping, kicking, and use of comic timing. He would run into a door or fall off his apparatus, appear to get hurt, and use exaggeration to make the audience react. He moved on to the spinning bowls, which was a manipulation apparatus, originally from China, involving a length of rope with weights (or bowls) attached to either end. The performer spins and manipulates the rope quickly and throws the apparatus in the air. While it is airborne, the spinner does tricks, catching and flicking the rope using different body parts. The bowls are filled with water, and the centrifugal force pulls the rope taut, keeping the liquid inside. It was a difficult trick, requiring hand-eye coordination but made to look effortless.

Phileap and the others left on a Sunday without a goodbye. I made my own welcome barbecue for Ramon. He was great at playing the Phileap part to my acts and the compadre part to my son. I enjoyed the Córdobas being gone.

123

Summer, 1986, Macon, Georgia, USA

With Phileap and his family gone, I settled into a single mother/performer vibe. My friends watched Gustavo as I performed, saving him from the trunk tradition. I liked setting my own tricks and having my own money, though it was depleted without the trapeze paycheck. I managed by only buying food for myself. If anyone wanted me to cook, I made them pay for the groceries and my time. It was a new me on the road, not the wet rug I was in the past.

Ramon brought joy and laughter; he spent each jubilant night teaching my son to giggle and tumble. Gustavo was a natural, and the new clowns wanted him to be part of their act. Modern clowns are not as dangerous as the old ones. Ringling Brothers opened a Clown College where aspiring performers earned credentials and were not escaped perverts.

The clowns were two husband and wife teams that integrated music and small dogs into their act. Their pièce de résistance involved a broom handle, a roll of toilet paper, and a hairdryer. The hairdryer blows the toilet paper out with dips and dives. The course of the act was unraveling an entire roll of toilet paper in the air and virtually juggling it. It was both hysterical and mesmerizing. They wanted Gustavo to be part of the act where they pushed a baby carriage, threw junk in it and, at the end, produced a real baby. They showed me the sleight of hand of changing carriages for the grand reveal. Ramon and I believed it was magnificent. I let them have my boy as a part of the act. He started in show business as fake trash, just like his mother.

124

Summer, 1986, Charlotte, North Carolina, USA

I sat in the bleachers in Charlotte, watching the clowns parade my baby around, and a jolt of sadness sliced through me. I gasped for air, and tears fell. I closed my eyes and tried to slow my lament, and I saw my nana, her smile radiant, her head shimmering.

Deep in my soul, I heard her say, "Hey, Toksy. I am going to have to leave you now. I am sorry I didn't meet your baby or your husband. I know you are strong and loving. Please stay in your bliss."

My heart began to break.

Had I made all the wrong decisions by going on the road?

Leaving her?

Marrying a man I barely liked?

Adding to another generation of circus kids?

I went to bed devastated. Though no announcement had gotten to me,

I knew down to my bones that Nana had passed. It took three weeks for the telegram to reach me; she had died at the precise time I had seen her in my mind.

Nana wanted no funeral and was cremated. She didn't want to bother anyone or make a fuss. The Scullery Maids made a special dinner in her honor and let me indulge them with anecdotes. My friend, Nonna, reminded me that she lived on in my son's and my vibrant red hair.

125

Summer, 1986, Durham, North Carolina, USA

It was just Gustavo and me. I had started eating at truck stops while moving from place to place. Greasy spoon diners were the only available eateries on the long stretches of highway between the small towns we played in that had no restaurants at all.

Burgers, corned beef hash, towering cinnamon rolls, and fresh pies were the specialty at most of these twenty-four-hour eateries. It was decadent and fattening, and I loved every bite. The waitresses went gaga for the baby, and I didn't have to do dishes by carrying a bucket of water to my trailer.

The circus people frowned upon my corrupt culinary habit because they barely wandered outside their trailers for anything but a grocery store. The gossipmongers pontificated and made striking accusations about what else this Towner was doing in town with the truckers.

We pulled into a small truck stop in the Appalachian Mountains. Appalachia was comprised of a complex mix of ethnic groups. The one common trait that bound them all together was that they were used to working hard and being self-reliant. They had the intestinal fortitude it took to rough it out in the backcountry of the rugged Blue Ridge Mountains. They did not take kindly to strangers, even those gassing up for a minute.

The circus people believed the citizens in this region were cannibals. Reports from the 1930s indicated that residents of the Appalachian Mountains practiced a form of ritualistic cannibalism during which people ate parts of their dead relatives to honor them. We were told to never need gas in this area. I was hungry and did not believe in all the hullabaloo and went for the cherry pie with Ramon. I walked in with Gustavo tucked on my hip. We took a booth and waited for menus. None came.

I walked to the front and asked the waitress for menus. She glared at me. For a minute, I thought that I was in full makeup and looking like one of Beelzebub's girls. But I was a plain-faced redhead fitting in with their German heritage like a beer stein. I soon realized it was the Spanish chatter and dark skin of my dining companion that was the offense. I got Ramon's order and went to the counter to place it. The waitress stared at me like I was from another planet.

"You part of this group?"

"Yes, we are with the circus."

"Circus, like Gypsies?"

"Not like Gypsies, except we do move around a lot. We are performers. I do the trapeze, and he does a teeterboard act."

"Do he steal?"

"No! He is an international superstar."

"Why do he talk like that?"

"It's Spanish. He is from Mexico City."

"We don't serve foreigners here."

I didn't know what to say. Clearly, I was getting nowhere, and everyone in the diner stared at our booth like it was about to catch fire.

"Please, can we fuel up and take some food to go? We haven't seen any other options, and we are about to run out of gas."

"You can go now. Like I said, we don't serve foreigners here."

I was pissed and went back to the table to tell Ramon we couldn't eat here or even get gas. He wasn't surprised. With his dark skin and Mayan features, he was no stranger to the treatment. As we filed out the door, all eyes were on us. Ramon was the last out, and before he shut the door, he threw one of his performance smoke bombs into the diner. It cracked with a boom, startling everyone and filling the restaurant with smoke. We ran to our trucks, giggling and squealing tires out of there.

126

Fall, 1986, Philadelphia, Pennsylvania, USA

I had not heard from Phileap or any of the other Córdobas in over two months. I was more empowered than ever. I did the driving, setting up, and performing, all while being a single mom. Without someone telling me how "less than" I was, I started seeing my potential. I felt like Jane Fonda, blazing a new trail where only men had dared. I was sure Phileap had another lover on the show in Europe. While that embarrassed me, it did not break my heart.

I kept to myself around the circus folk, and only Ramon had permission to come into my trailer to keep tongues from wagging. I missed having a lover—the closeness of a human body, the heat of the passion.

As always, I hung out mostly with the elephants and parked next to the monkeys. Gustavo now spoke more monkey than English. The elephants loved to rock him in their giant trunks, and the infant tigers played with him. I took many unusual photos of my boy and the animals living the circus life. I was sure no one had ever seen pictures like this before. I sent several to the *National Enquirer*, hoping I would be rewarded the $500 they paid for published photos. I received a telegram stating that they wanted to come take more pictures and to tell how the animals were treated. This was at the time when PETA said that circus animals were abused. I knew it wasn't true. I had never seen an animal performer hurt or forced to do something they did not want to. Unlike the women, the animals were treated with respect. I went to talk to the trainers.

"This might be a good way to get ahead of the PETA accusations," I explained as we gathered by their trailers.

"I don't believe we can trust a news source like the *National Enquirer* to tell our story," said the tiger trainer who held a two-month-old tiger chewing on his hat. "They are looking for sensationalism."

The elephant man, who was sweeping up the precious compost we sold at every stop, said, "We are on the right side of the story, and maybe it will help. The protests are getting worse in the big towns. I am afraid for my animals."

I was still naively convinced I could control the press and the story. "We should give it a try."

They all shook their heads.

"Sorry, Gail, we know you mean well," the tiger trainer said. "It is too risky."

I sent the telegram back saying we were not interested in the story. Despite that, they showed up in San Antonio. The journalist was kicked off the lot, and the prop guys found the hidden camera. It was a scene of betrayal and fury that cemented the journalist's idea that the animal trainers were hiding something. They were only hiding the magic that had been handed down for generations: "Don't let the Towners see the back of the show."

The trouble was all my doing. By sending in the photos, I fueled the fire. To counter what had happened, I sent weekly slices of life to the *National Enquirer*, hoping to change the direction of the story. They started running them, and they were popular. I made some good money being a circus stringer for them. However, PETA was already on a trajectory to ban performing animals, and even my cute little articles couldn't stop this storm.

127

Fall, 1986, Staten Island, New York, USA

I was enjoying the solitude but was getting physically lonely. I daily had to quiet the demons in my head that echoed that I was not enough. The lasting effect of emotional abuse is that the victim plays the hurtful words in a continuous loop long after the voice of the abuser is silenced. I was busy with my many roles with the show but felt as if I was the lone survivor of a magnificent ship that had slipped under the waves, the sea silencing all.

The circus rolled into a town and set up in the field next to the baseball diamond. The rhythmic sound of the tent posts being hammered down, the smell of exotic animals, and the acrobats flying through the air as if they had wings drew the attention of the entire town. As it turned out, guys who slung balls for a living were attracted to the circus.

While the show was being set up, I went into town to get groceries for the making a barbecue celebration we had planned. I was dressed as a Towner: no heavy performance makeup, no G-string. My son was left with Ramon. I wore a short skirt and a strappy blouse, but this small town sensed a stranger from a mile away. People stared. They were less than friendly, but I was used to it.

In the produce section, I spied a man by the mangos, picking them up and setting them down. He seemed perplexed, but his friendly demeanor as he smiled at the fruit drew me to him.

"Can I help you pick out a good mango?" I asked as I approached him with a smile. "We did a tour of Mexico, and I know mangos."

He looked up, and a surge of electricity seemed to crackle between us.

"You know mangos?"

"I do." I recited the rules—"firm but pliable"—and squeezed and handed him some perfect fruity specimens. Our hands touched in the passing, and the current sparked. We both looked with surprise into each other's eyes. Although strangers, there was recognition. We smiled at one another.

"You're not from around here?"

"No. I'm with the circus. I'm Gail, and you are Malloy," I said, eyeing the name on his uniform.

We shook hands, and light beams shot across our bodies.

"What do you do with the circus besides choose mangos?"

I instantly loved his wit and those smiling green eyes.

"I'm a trapeze artist. But I work with the elephants, do the web, and teach the kids their schoolwork. We all have many hats. Oh, I am also the head chef for our celebrations."

"Are you prepping for dinner tonight?" he asked, glancing at my basket full of meat and vegetables.

"Yes!"

"I'm an aspiring chef too."

"How would you like to be my guest for the show tonight and my assistant chef?"

"Ma'am, it would be my greatest honor."

I shared the menu with him, and we finished shopping together. We quickly moved into a comfortable dance of talking, teasing, and laughing, as if we were old friends.

When we left the store, I gave him a ticket to the show, and he promised to bring his many sharp knives to help cook dinner after.

At the performance, he marveled over the grace and beauty of the single trapeze. It was dangerous, but we made it look easy. As part of the performance, I also came out on the back of an elephant and hung from a large rope, twirling and posing. After the show, he came to my trailer.

It was small but as clean and cozy as an apartment. No one he had ever known lived in these recreational vehicles. He was intrigued. It was clear that it was my home, my sanctuary with the original art and fine silks on the walls. I told him I wanted to write, and he teased me. "You are living in the middle of a novel. Why not write it all down?"

The next day, he returned to the trailer with a flower-studded journal and a German ink pen wrapped in pink paper. I opened it slowly, knowing that this was the beginning.

"Wow! And thank you! This is the most generous gift I have ever received."

"Write it all down. The smells, the people, the feelings, the loneliness. Do it for me if you won't do it for you."

I hugged him until my arms went numb. His heartbeat left a soundtrack for my mind to remember, his generosity of spirit reviving my broken one.

We decided to prepare the barbecue meal together, which in the small trailer was challenging with two chefs. We were using a newfangled French technique called sous vide, which involved cooking using a hot water bath. We seasoned the meat and then set it in a warm bath of 160 degrees. It made the meat delicious. We quickly fell into a choreographed dance with our bodies touching while discussing recipes. Soon, we were tasting off each other's fingers, ensuring the spice and flavor were right. It was as if we had been doing it for years.

He talked about his life and desire to go on the road with a band. He was a drummer as well as a baseball player. I shared road stories. We laughed, and I felt full, although we had not eaten besides the tasting bites.

The circus people went wild for our culinary offerings, and many tried to recruit him to join the show (they had a live band). Ramon asked if Gustavo could spend the night with him.

When everyone was gone, we sat by the makeshift fire pit. Before I knew what happened, we were holding hands. The silence felt comfortable.

"Well, I better go," he said, glancing at his watch.

"Why?"

Without a reply, he followed me into the trailer.

We fell upon each other like starving people. He took my head in his strong hands and slowed the passion down so we could explore. With my lips parted, he kissed me feather-light. I moaned with pleasure.

We explored with restless hands running over the curves of each other's bodies. He pulled back and looked into my eyes. His body had a visceral reaction to the smoldering look I gave him. I took him by the hand and led him to the sleeping area. Piled with silk and feather beds, we had sunk into a place of comfort and desire. Swimming in a sea of passion, we learned each other's bodies like reading braille. For hours, we gave and received pleasure, never once feeling sated, each wanting more. Although it wasn't spoken, we were both wildly aware this one night was a gift never to be repeated.

I loved the weight of him on top of me; the way he stroked my petals and found pleasure centers. The slow and mindful way he made love held emotion in every sensation. He went wild with lust and treated my body like water he hadn't tasted in years, as if I would perish if he did not deposit his love into me.

I rode on top of him, controlling the strokes and the depth of the joining. My hands on his magnificent chest, I rocked and circled my pelvis until he coated my insides with his flame.

We broke for a drink, and I took his cock into my mouth. I suckled like it was a lifeline, keeping him at the edge. When I finally released him, we crashed onto our sides, face to face, staring into each other's eyes as we orgasmed again. The sunrise peeked through the curtains as we spooned, still stroking and caressing each other.

"I have to go. I'm in a tournament today."

"Stay" was the only word I could express.

"I will be back for your last show. I promise."

I knew it was the last promise he would not be able to keep.

As we parted, both exhausted but happier than we had ever been, we promised to keep in touch. We knew it was a lie and an impossibility. We were from different worlds, and though our souls recognized each other, it was not meant to be. He left only his scent.

The next day, I heard the morning birds singing as I woke from a dream of him. The roar of the lion reminded me I was still with the circus and not in his bed. I knew he would occupy my dreams frequently. It was there we talked, made love, and had a life. Only there. He did not come to the last show.

In the short time we had together, he'd left a handprint on my heart. I did not give him an address because I had no idea where I would be located from week to week. I knew where he lived. At the next stop, I sent him a postcard.

"My conscience has taken a flip. My desire has not. I've always understood that the ones you walk with in life—those who soothe you, raise babies to adults with, and experience your growing pains—are not necessarily the ones who stoke your fire."

I wrote weekly, and with each postcard I included a line of a love story/novel. I didn't keep copies. I sent him the only gift a writer can give.

128

Fall, 1986, Baltimore, Maryland, USA

I finally knew I would become a writer and kept a journal of daily circus life, figuring that not many people had experienced the intimate view I had. The road was lonely survival, but with the memory and the retelling, it came alive.

My first journal entry did not tell of a happy life:

I'm pacing the cage. This tin can cage is my home. I'm forced to eat here. Shit here and fuck here, while they watch. The only time I am let out is when I perform. The audience decides whether I live or die. The applause decides. I loathe this cage. But I know I built it. It's of my own doing. I made choices that became iron bars. I made decisions that became cold meat. I made friends with the watchful eye of the audience. They became my drug, my reason to forgo living life to stay in this limbo of performance, solitude, and dysfunction. I chose this circus.

Life on the road seemed romantic when I longed for it. After twenty-two months, the only thing romantic was when the trailer broke down and I got to stay in a Motel 6. A crappy hotel in Baltimore became my paradise. It had a bathtub, dirty from the last guest's pond scum, but there was enough shampoo to use as a bubble bath. There were phones in the room, an immediate and constant connection to the outside world I hadn't had in a long time. Dial nine, and you can talk to anyone. Then there are Magic Fingers. A gyrating, vibrating joy that with a quarter shakes you into pleasure. I always have a roll of quarters with me for phone booths and Magic Fingers, two things that are my escape from the cage.

The family and Phileap returned from Monaco. I picked them up at the airport, missing two days of performances, and brought them back to the show. Prop guys had been moving and staying in their trailers, so they threw them out and dispassionately took over my life again.

They did receive a gold medal for the trapeze, which would help market the next circus we were booked to perform. The whole family seemed furious that I had not imploded on the road.

Full of themselves and the medals they had won, they were instantly miserable on the road. They did not want to travel with what they deemed an unimportant show. I mused that they all had finally tasted a bit of freedom, and now Phileap wanted more. He was happy to see his son, lukewarm to see me, and disgusted with the weather in the middle of the United States.

It was snowing, and road conditions were miserable. They longed for Monaco.

129

Fall, 1986, Wichita, Kansas, USA

We were stuck in Kansas as the roads were closed due to snow in September. Blizzard conditions shut down the freeways. Nicolás wanted to go anyway until the highway patrol left a leaflet on our windshields saying that they would confiscate everything on the freeway if people were caught driving. In our case, it was our house, our life.

We pulled into a truck stop, lucky again to have a Motel 6 next to it. We got a room with two beds. I was excited to sleep alone with Gustavo and not have Phileap's body pressed against me like in the single bed we shared in the trailer. He would breathe through his mouth at night, and I could smell the rancid liver and onions he had for lunch. More important than my own bed is the phone.

I could call Becky, my mom, and my sister—friendly people with stories to tell about regular life who are interested in where I am, who I am, and where I am going.

I was in a sea of loneliness with my baby and sure that I was ruining him. I got ready to move before I fed him because the performance and tear-down come first—not my child. We learned how to spoon pureed carrots while bouncing down the road. Potholes do not help digestion. His worldview is a bug-splatted windshield.

The animals were all stored in the big truck bays, and it seemed the entire town snowmobiled in to meet elephants, tigers, and chimpanzees, which all were pacing in their cages. They didn't get out except to perform, which was not possible here.

I visited them often with treats from the diner. Chicken fried steak for the tigers, blueberry muffins for the chimps, and fruit-based Popsicles for the elephants. I felt like we would be trapped there forever. I knew they did too. They were used to exercising and performing every day. The walls of snow obliterated the view, and it kept falling like the aftermath of a pillow fight.

The locals, who were used to being snowed in, saw us as a divine treat—a gift from God during the most mundane part of the year. They accepted the pacing of the white cage because they had meadows and streams in the spring. The circus has no seasons. We are always dying gracefully.

After five days of snow and eating every morsel of food at the truck stop, the road opened. We loaded everything up and said goodbye to our Kansas friends. We would be an anecdote that they told their grandchildren. We would not reminisce about them or their hospitality, but rather roll to the next town where I couldn't dial nine.

130

F all, 1986, Atlanta, Georgia, USA

We were set to be a part of the New Coke rollout. Coca-Cola was head-quartered in Atlanta; the company wanted a big fuss on the day of the new flavor coming out. We set up the trapeze in the town square, and the company had made us Coca-Cola tights for the performance. We also had the motor-cycle globe of death, the rocket launch, the elephants, and a wheel of death. It was all the jaw-dropping parts of the show, and I was glad to see some old friends again.

Zoe was there with her elephants and the rocket launch; I was excited to spend time with my elephant friends and their human cohorts. Zoe looked great, and I loved seeing her baby, who was now a walker.

"How are you? Did you travel alone with the baby the entire time?"

"I did!"

"Well, you are no longer a Towner anymore. Welcome to the tribe."

"Thanks, but I don't belong anywhere."

"You have always done life on the fringes. It suits you."

"Ha! Like I have a choice."

"There are always choices."

We performed three shows in the middle of the town and attended the fireworks that night when the city lit up under Coke-shaped sparklers in the sky.

Gustavo had a low-grade fever at lunch that quickly became a furnace. I did not know what to do, so I took him to the emergency room. Having never stepped into a big-city hospital, I was shocked to see over 150 people waiting to be seen. I took my number and waited with new-mommy dread soaking through my brain. Drug addicts twitched, limbs hung at precarious angles, blood oozed out of heads, and more. After four hours, an overworked nurse finally saw me.

"Where do you live?"

"I'm with the circus. We are here performing for the new Coke."

"That is a hippie plot to take over America. Are you a hippie?"

"No, I am a trapeze artist."

"Sounds like a hippie life to me." She took his temperature roughly, then handed me a baby Tylenol liquid cap. "He needs a tepid bath."

"I don't have a bathtub."

"Do you have a bucket?"

"Yes, I think the elephants do."

"That is the most hippie comment I have ever heard. Go back to where you came from."

She shoved me out of the door, and I was once again struck by the fact I had nowhere to go.

Gustavo's fever broke at 2:00 a.m., and I fell into an exhausted sleep. At 6:00 a.m., we had to move again; I drove blurry-eyed with a baby strapped to my chest.

131

Fall, 1986, Birmingham, Alabama, USA

We were about to leave for Las Vegas to meet up with Ramon and winter there. Just before our planned departure, a family meeting was called. The older brothers had decided they did not want to work or live with Nicolás, Phileap, and Marco. They had decided to go off on their own with the name The Famous Flying Córdobas, and we were to take the name The Family Córdobas. The younger brothers were angry that the pronouncement was unilaterally made without even consulting them. The argument went on for hours. I caught only half of the Spanish, but I did know I was the main problem. That is what I unequivocally understood, anyway.

We had two trapezes because of our splits in Canada, but the other problem was who got custody of Payaso. The decision was made to send Payaso to Las Vegas to live with his parents, Marta, and Sebastián.

We all pulled out of the lot simultaneously, heading in different directions, a broken circus troupe.

132

Winter, 1986, Reno, Nevada, USA

We went to Reno knowing we could all stay in my parents' pasture. We circled the wagons and put up the trapeze. Bernice and I got jobs at the casino, slinging cocktails to slot machine players. I was making good money but hated the holding pattern. The boys practiced. Even though they could brag about the best trapeze act in the world, they couldn't get jobs. We had no prospects of jobs in sight. The older brothers had decided our fate for years, Marco and Phileap's whole life.

Marco took over as the catcher, and Nicolás did simpler tricks because he was getting old. Phileap was the big trick producer. His triple, the double layout, and passing leap were easy staples for the act.

After a month, Nicolás and Phileap got into their traditional head-butting match at practice. It went from words to fists and stayed a screaming match for two hours. Nicolás and Bernice left that night while we slept. We had no idea where they went.

When I was young, I measured my time through weekends. What pleasure would the phone bring on Friday night? What trail would I ride on Saturday? What after-dark play would the neighborhood kids invent on Saturday night? What novel I would fall into on Sunday, knowing that church was the most sacred place to read?

Trash days (Wednesdays) were now my timekeepers and paydays, twice a month if I was lucky. Then there were surviving Mondays.

God must have a particular disdain for Mondays. They are universally shit shows. Mondays don't discriminate; they fuck with everyone. Even after a three-day weekend, where Tuesday becomes Monday, it's a paradox of horrible. Traffic, forgotten breakfast, lost lunches, bosses livid, angry customers, and grumpy children were bad enough, but don't forget broken promises, bad dinners, and lying husbands. Everything systemically goes to crap on Mondays, especially the one I was living that winter day.

The doctor's office left an answer on the machine, saying, "Sorry, you're pregnant again." Because the light wasn't blinking, I knew Phileap had heard the message.

Fuck.

I didn't want another circus kid to live a circus life.

Fuck.

I didn't want to ever see my husband again. A voice inside me whispered, "Why the hell did you fuck him?" I knew it was Kim.

133

Winter, 1986, Reno, Nevada, USA

Phileap got a call at my parents' house from Ramon, who was in Reno visiting. We were invited to make a barbecue. When we got to the house he was visiting, we discovered it was a permanent circus camp. There were twenty different riggings over the five-acre tumbleweed area.

The Novas, the family who owned the place, were a trapeze troupe working at Circus Circus. They invited us to watch them perform. I loved seeing permanent rigging. They showed up, put on tights and makeup, and performed four times a night, then went home to a brick-and-mortar domicile. It seemed like heaven to me.

"What is it like not traveling?" I asked the matriarch, Antoinette. Antoinette was a dainty French redhead with a Barbie-sized waist and huge breasts.

Her personality did not match her appearance; she would make a Moulin Rouge dancer blush with her language. She was profane in three languages, and it was impressive.

"It is heaven. I have three children that go to school each day. We have the trapeze here, so their homework is flying."

"I hated the traveling. Which is funny because that is why I signed up. Now, I ended up right where I started."

"You are from Reno?"

"I am, and I'm glad to be back, which I never thought I would say."

"You will love it at Circus Circus. People are more accepting."

"I could use a little of that."

"When are you due?"

"I'm halfway there. With my first, I flew until I was six months along."

"I will plan your baby shower and have it here!"

"That's so kind."

"Let's take your boy and show him the trampoline."

The men gathered around the barbecue, spilling lies and sauce. Antoinette's husband, Mateo, was the catcher: a jubilant, full-mustached man who loved his family as much as the spotlight. He filled his leotard with tank-like muscles and never dropped a member of his troupe. He was as quick to laugh as he was to swat a smart mouth. He ruled in the air while Antoinette led him to believe he also ruled the home.

Ramon talked them into letting Phileap fly after the promenade closed at Circus Circus. They loved him and hired him immediately. Marco got jealous and left my parents' pasture before we even got home. We were in one spot without his parents or his brothers, and I was in heaven. All was clear on the Córdoba front, except for my loathsome husband who now blamed me for the family's demise.

I was glad to be home with my family and friends, although Becky lived in Las Vegas. Phileap, Gustavo, and I settled into a rhythm, and I was so happy my child wasn't being raised in the front of a truck and on sawdust-covered floors. I was also glad I was near my little sister. Sunshine had been dying for two years. It was a roller coaster ride, not for the faint of heart.

She beat cancer once, filling her veins with poison and losing her hair, only to not be able to afford the medicine that would have kept the disease from coming back. This time it was her other breast, and she got skin cancer from the radiation. Her fight was over, and it was only a matter of when she would pass from a wife and mother to a headstone.

Sunrise had to go to the hospital at least once a week for complications, blood transfusions, and other unpleasant cancer-related treatments. Cancer had spread to her bones and brain. Pain medications were tricky and seldom worked without colossal complications for more than a week.

My mind was becoming overwhelmed between my baby coming and my sister going.

I tried to swim each day at the local pool that had a naturally fed hot spring. I liked to go into the big pool and sit at the bottom, meditating on the quiet of the water. I could talk to Sunrise's soul, not the sick person. I could listen to my heart. Every day, I said the mantra "Happy, healthy, wealthy, wise, and loved" repeatedly to calm my mind.

Her sickness was a nightmare of emotional kidnapping, blaming, and prescription drugs. Twice we had been rushed to her bedside with minutes to spare. Twice we had to make life-and-death decisions for her and her kids. After the first time, we were told there was no hope for a cure. We all knew she would die, but not when and not where and certainly not how to make the end of her life any better than the short amount of time she had spent on the earth.

Everyone joined a support group. Sunrise, one for dying people; Mom, one for the mothers of dying people, and so on. I sent a postcard to the cancer society, asking for a family support group. They wrote back and told me of a group in my area, when the meeting was, and where it was held. I was relieved. I finally had someone to talk to who could grasp my situation and not see me as a huge whiner.

The next postcard announced that the entire group consisted of one person, me. The following postcard congratulated me and elected me president of the group and told me to report back to them. I told my family, and they said I should keep trying because the groups had helped them.

I talked Phileap into being a member by promising him that we met at the local all-you-can-eat crab restaurant. The support group remained just the two of us, but I didn't register him or report our meetings because it was the two of us out for a night of sea spiders and crying.

The next time I heard from the cancer society, I was fired as the group leader for not turning in my meeting/itineraries. Not only was I by myself, but I was canned by an unsigned postcard.

134

Winter, 1986, Reno, Nevada, USA

I was sick for about a week, unable to do anything but watch the dreaded TV. At least I did not have to travel anywhere. My bald sister brought me soup while I recovered. We watched *Oprah* and *Court TV. Judge Judy* was her favorite.

I had never watched Oprah and didn't understand her hold on the female mind. Oprah said to read a book, and millions of people did. Oprah said this diet is good for you, and people starved themselves in her honor. She made stars out of nobodies who claimed to be doctors and gave the illusion of giving loads of presents away to people for no reason at all. Meanwhile, she was a billionaire, had never been married nor had a child. Yet, trillions of coupon-cutting housewives hung on her every word and did what she told them to do. It was like getting marriage advice from a priest. I didn't get it.

The giveaways were given to her by companies to promote their products. She didn't give one cent out of pocket to gift 100 people a car, but the recipients did. They had to pay taxes on the gifts. On the show, she appeared bored out of her mind and possibly thinking about where her next hamburger was coming from. She was of average weight and size for a woman her age, but she was always trying to "lose" weight, giving the masses no hope—if a billionaire with every resource at her beck and call cannot lose weight, no one can. It baffled me. I would only have that much interest in someone who had discovered electricity or found a cure for cancer or painted comparable to Leonardo da Vinci.

135

Spring, 1987, Reno, Nevada, USA

Circus Circus Reno became our new exploiter. We had four shows per day, each twenty minutes long. Between shows, the boredom of the casino crept into our souls. The windowless, smoke-filled facade was our prison. We could not leave the property (their rules) nor could we mingle with the newlywed, overfed, and nearly dead on the promenade. Neither of us gambled nor had an extra nickel to do so. One of the job's perks was that we could eat at the buffet at no charge, but the food was terrible, even dangerous when left sitting out on buffet stands all day. We rarely strolled down the aisles of piles of shrimp and crab legs.

In between shows, we sat in the dressing rooms, shared gossip about those still on the road, and I read. The circus world had one magazine that was copied and stapled monthly and mailed to our winter quarters. It was filled with news about various acts and clown celebrities, tips on highway closures, new ways to sew sequins, baby additions, engagements, mergers, and ads for prop makers. It was written and produced by an ancient, retired clown who collected information via letters. Most of the information was six weeks old and had already traveled the sawdust telegraph, but it was the highlight of the month. We would pour over the details and debate the sanity and profitableness of each new addition and story.

⬱

I enjoyed being friends with the Novas. They had three children, all who flew, and one female flyer friend. It was a wholesome environment for my little family because there was no internal drama, just regular family living with a steady job. They owned a home and the kids went to school, and I thought I had found the middle ground of a nontoxic life to share while keeping the trapeze tradition going.

I was introduced to life on the midway with Gustavo in a stroller and another flyer visibly in my tummy. While the Mardi Gras carpet welcomed the gamblers to the Midway, Antoinette hurled insults to slot players from above in the black abyss that was the top of the concrete Circus Circus tent. Her scratchy voice stopped the children in their tracks. She was the ruler of this land.

The oldest daughter, Lela, had been flying since she was three years old. At the wise old age of fourteen, she looked and acted like she was thirty-eight. Possessing both attributes of her parents, cinderblock muscles and wanton femininity, she was a beauty in the air and on the ground. She was suited for the air, tumbling and posing, but on the ground, she was a shrew.

Charise was ten, and her body was stick-like, her stature demure. She struggled, unsure and gangly, whereas her sister was quick to learn and master tricks. Everyone believed she would grow out of the stage and blossom like her sibling, but she remained a twig. She was sweet, the only personality not assigned to anyone in the Novas' household.

The youngest suffered from being the only boy and never really found his identity. He was named Junior, and from birth, it was his sole responsibility to be like his dad. At four, he was still a toddler in mind but flew daily, using the most sought-after commodity of circus parents, cute innocence. If you had a well-functioning child in your act, the price you contracted was twice as much as an established act.

They were the band of characters with whom we spent our days within the windowless promenade, the sound of slot machines vomiting coins wafting from down below. It was smaller and more concentrated, but I loved not moving every day. They had added a Russian swing to the act, which was the job we did. It's a metal apparatus that is attached to the bottom of the platform. Instead of swinging on the bar, the flyer is "swung" (like a children's swing) and must jump at the catcher. There were two people on the swing with the flyer whose job it was to make it go back and forth—that was mine and Cherise's job. We pumped like a pair of strange bookends until Phileap was called off by the catcher. The swing was where they placed the misfits. Pregnancy had changed my body, and my larger-than-life breasts were too heavy and movable to ever appear graceful.

Phileap had entered radiology school at this point. He had bought into my nagging about staying in one place to raise the kids, and he had started a new path. This threw his family into fits. No one for generations had been anything but a circus performer. There was never a need for school. This cemented the fact, in their minds, that I was pure evil.

The problem was keeping Phileap's dick in his pants when every community college dropout wanted to disrobe and fuck him. The last time we had fucked was when we conceived our daughter, and he still hadn't forgiven me for creating a girl. She wasn't even born yet, and he already decided he didn't want her.

136

Summer, 1987, Reno, Nevada, USA

We worked with several acts each day and rotated so we could all have two days a week off. This softened Phileap, considering we had barely had even an hour off for the last few years. We had to find other ways to distract our traveling minds. Seeing the same road every day was a kind of madness. Knowing where to buy a bag of diapers and where your next meal was going to come from was blissful insanity. Traveling people do not hold still well.

Travelers move or die. While my soul and heart were recuperating, his was unraveling.

Angel was on the show and one of my favorite people. He was a catcher in a teeterboard troupe and married to a Russian ballerina, Susan, who worked as a dancer at Flamingo Hilton. He was from Columbia and trying to learn English better to be able to communicate in one language. Susan did not want to learn English or Spanish or be married. She simply wanted out of the USSR, and Angel was her ticket. He loved her deeply; she deeply loathed him. Angel and I became cooking buddies, my male Scullery Maid. He came to my house twice a week to learn to cook. I loved having him around, especially since Phileap was always practicing.

"Why did we both marry poorly?"

I commiserated while shredding cauliflower. "That is a good question. Maybe we don't believe we are worthy of real love?"

"I love her."

"I know you do. I chose to be the second choice; I get everything I deserve. Doesn't make it sting worse, though."

We chopped and simmered and enjoyed our time together. My son loved having him around because he was full of belly laughs and twirling arms. Angel made everything sparkle.

We worked on the top floor of a casino called The Promenade. It had a swirly carpet and no windows or clocks, which were all meant to hold the visitor in place for the maximum amount of time. They employed the same technique for keeping kids there as they did on the slot floor below: the sounds of winning—the sounds of coins dropping and the sounds of fun and hope. With each bell ringing in the distance, it gave a burst of "It could be me" to anyone within earshot. For the lady with a roll of quarters, it could be hope, optimism for her future, her retirement plan.

The Midway had a ring of carnival games of chance around the walls. Each with a perceived value proposition; it cost a quarter but yielded a six-foot-tall stuffed dragon. The plushy behemoths hung from above the games, with wide plastic eyes and cuddly, soft, outstretched arms inviting the child to win. These toys would stave off all closet and under-the-bed monsters. As with all carnival activity, the odds were stacked against the children, and $100 in quarters rarely produced more than a six-inch Chinese knock-off cartoon character.

Circus Circus was the first casino to market to children. The stuffy Nevada Gaming Authority should have stopped the wicked scheme, but soon it became its most bankable model in Las Vegas. The Circus Circus casino floor was three stories with a giant hole in the middle. Guests could play the slots and watch the trapeze act with an extreme upward extension of their neck—or, from the top floor, they could watch their parents squander the rest of the rent money.

The Midway had unsupervised children, local teens acting as carnies, and stupefied circus performers. It was a well-yield soup of drama.

137

Fall, 1987, Reno, Nevada, USA

My daughter was born on a Tuesday under a full moon, and I loved her profoundly. Motherhood is a unique condition wrapped with joy and fury, pride and disappointment, love and fear. I feared for my girl and protected her as if she were a torn doll.

Our children's hearts beat loudly in our chests long after they have left our bodies. We feel every note the child expresses and worry they will lose their song. It's a pure-hearted state, passed from woman to woman. I'm proud of the mothers I'd known and influenced. For they were all my friends, and that is an army of joy that can never be defeated. I am stronger for knowing and loving them all.

"She is beautiful!" Angel held his goddaughter delicately. I loved that we were now officially family. He was my compadre. Traditionally among

Latin Americans, the godfather relationship formalizes an existing friendship, which results in a strong lifelong bond between compadres. In its original form, the compadre relationship is among the strongest types of family love after one's nuclear family. I couldn't ask for better family than Angel.

"She holds my heart even firmer than her brother. Does that make me a bad mom?"

"You are a great mom in a difficult situation."

"But aren't moms supposed to have their shit together before they start breeding?"

"You seem to be a prolific breeder. You love unconditionally. That can never be wrong."

"I am so blessed to have you in our life."

"I feel the same way. She needs to be changed; that is your department."

He handed me the baby as he kissed her head. True love radiated off him. I knew she would always be safe with Angel by her side.

138

Fall, 1987, Lemon Valley, Nevada, USA

Beverly, the midget who boxed and danced with a kangaroo as part of her act, was back with our show. She was a welcome comedy relief. The Tigger-inspired dance made the children gasp and hoot. Being invited for the first time to openly gaze at an "imperfect" body and join in the joke and laugh with the performer was cathartic and popular. Beverly and the Roo-Bop loved not having to travel as much as they loved an actual brick-and-mortar home.

Beverly and Bop took the stage inside animal carts with black drapes covering their forms. The two large cages, with pictures of big cats on the sides, were wheeled onto the stage as the swirl of "Waltzing Matilda" blared. As the ring master's voice (a recording) blared about danger and the need to stand back, the audience moved in for a closer look. Beverly would then tumble out of the cage dressed in a leopard print leotard. Expecting a dangerous feline and getting a scantily clad midget made them all exhale.

Beverly also did a small teeterboard act. Her tumbling was good, but her shape made it funny. Again, the audience was not sure whether to laugh or look away. At a perfectly timed moment of audience retention and fineness, she released the kangaroo, eliciting a burst of uncomfortable laughter from the audience. The kangaroo stood eight feet tall. It seemed there was no way this small human could control the giant rat. The amazing part of it was that they boxed like drunken fighters. Beverly put boxing mitts on Bop, and they went at it. The strong kangaroo's punch would send her flying into the air after an uppercut to the chin. He would rest his leather-covered paws on her shoulder, sit on his tail, and kick her across the ring. She took a solid beating three times a day, five days a week. She was the biggest draw at the casino, and her off-stage demeanor was like that of a Hollywood starlet.

Beverly drank like a sailor in a rumrunner's boat. She was nearly always drunk. Finding her passed out in the dressing room, drooling and dry-mouthed, was not unusual.

Our weekly "make a BBQ" was at the Novas' house and was the only place Bop got out of the cage that was not on a stage. They had an acre of fenced land. Bop happily hopped around the fence, kicking at the dogs nipping at Beverly, and punching the gate. Beverly would drink until she passed out, and Mateo would put her in his daughter's bed.

I was surprised one day when Beverly asked to talk to me privately. We walked into the main restrooms on the mezzanine to have a private conversation among the bingo players sneaking a cigarette.

"I am worried." She wrung her hands as she paced the floors.

"What's up?"

"I went to the doctor for the stomach flu I keep getting."

"We call that a hangover. Maybe a little less gin?"

"No, you idiot! I am pregnant!"

Beverly had no boyfriend or even a suitor I knew of. "Wait, what? How?"

"You've had two kids, and you are asking ME how?"

I was trying to apprehend these physics, but she clearly had no time for my thought process. "By whom?" I knew this was a rude question, but there was no protocol for discussing life options with a midget in a casino bathroom.

"None of your business. It's my secret to keep!"

"Okay, but when the baby is born, won't we know who the father is?"

She scrunched up her nose at me. "That is my question. Won't the baby look like me if I am not married?"

I was always amazed at how little circus folks knew about life. They could defy gravity but didn't know how to vacuum a carpet or where babies came from.

"The baby is part of both the male and the female genes," I fumbled.

"So, there is a chance it won't be a midget?"

"Yes, it's all a matter of genes."

"Like Levi's?"

I withheld a giggle because she was earnest and honestly baffled.

"Genes with a 'g.' It means the child has attributes from each the father and the mother. It is a gamble as to which one each child gets, but some are dominant, and some are recessive. I have blue eyes, recessive, and Phileap has brown eyes, dominant, and our kids have brown."

"I am a strong midget; the baby will be strong!"

"That is all that matters."

My mind returned to who the father was, and she saw she had lost my attention. She waddled out onto the mezzanine. I followed and watched as people never once looked her in the eye. They looked down as she passed and then whispered behind her back. No wonder she drank like a sailor.

The rumor mill and her budding tummy did their swiftest work, and soon everyone was whispering about the father of the unborn boxer. The casino bookies even had a spread on who it was. I was terrified for all the men yet disgusted with each because no one came forward to claim the baby. We all knew Beverly was promiscuous, and that the males were curious, but someone would be revealed as a cad.

After six months, Beverly's baby bump made it so she could not do her act because the casino was afraid Bop would kick her one day and the baby would come squirting out onto the center ring. She was welcomed into Antoinette's house as a tenant until the baby came. Bop was thrilled to hop around all day, never entering a box cage again. We were visiting for the weekly BBQ when she went into labor. The women joined around to count the times between contractions and ask curiosity-driven questions about midget physiology. The men were nowhere to be found.

Antoinette loaded Beverly into the car to go to the hospital, and I went to find Phileap. The kids were busy bouncing on the trampoline and terrorizing the kangaroo through the fence, but Phileap was nowhere to be found. Several travel trailers were parked in the back acres, and after three sweeps of the house and yard, I ventured out there.

In a horrifying but accurate moment, I saw the trailer rocking. Someone was fucking, and I was going to knock. My thunderous paws on the tin sounded like Bop was trying to get in. The rocking stopped, and no answer came. I struck again and threatened that I was entering. As I opened the door, Phileap emerged with his shirt on inside out and disheveled hair.

"What the fuck?" I raged, trying to push my way into the trailer. He fully blocked my attempt.

"Go back to the house, Apple Pie. This is for me."

"What the fuck does that mean?"

"This is no concern of yours. You are to be my children's mother, and that is all now."

These words were no surprise to me but burrowed a hole into my soul. I was determined to see who the hell he was fucking. I took all the strength of my betrayal and pushed him aside. There, lying on the bed, was a smug girl from the Midway. Her pink mohawk made her a creature of intrigue, and the men loved to talk with her. I raged at her and lunged for her hair. I gripped it with my hands and drug her out of the trailer and down the metal steps. She thumped into the dry tumbleweeds, screaming as a crowd began to gather. I threw punches, and Bop shadowed me behind me, throwing like punches. Phileap grabbed me and bound my arms with his. He yelled at her to get lost. She looked at me with hate in her eyes as she scrambled away. Philip's soothing yet threatening words were lost on me as I raged. I recognized the residuum of my life if I didn't do something. I was trying to make a tiger lose his stripes. Giving up was my only hope.

139

Winter, 1987, Reno, Nevada, USA

Later that night, he walked into the room carefully, knowing his wife could be murderous—or worse.

"Hey, Apple Pie. How was your night?"

"The babies are asleep."

He sat lightly next to me and secured my left hand; it could have been an act of aggression or maybe self-preservation. He pretended to cuddle.

"Do you want to go to bed with me?" I meant it to be sarcastic, but he missed it.

"I'd rather watch *Circus of the Stars*. They might play MY episode again. Plus, your breasts leak, and it's gross."

Embarrassed, my hands flew to my dry breasts.

"It's not gross! It's your daughter's food."

Staring at the TV, wishing for his likeness to appear, he muttered, "I don't like it. You don't need sex anymore. You're a mom!"

"But I'm still human," I said, feeling defeated.

Still looking for an out, he said, "You say you're tired."

"Of course, I'm tired, but I still love you."

Without missing a beat, he blurted, "Then make me a sandwich."

He switched the channel on the TV, and I went to the kitchen, which had always been my fail-safe when I was uncomfortable and not sure what to do with my life. I wish I had a Scullery Maid to work this through with the dough I was prepping for empanadas.

140

Winter, 1987, Sparks, Nevada, USA

We were distracted by Beverly's baby's paternity. She had a boy, but no one had seen him yet. The delivery was tricky, and the baby suffered. They were both in ICU. Speculation swirled the Midway as everyone with a penis was suspect, even the clowns who were openly gay.

Antoinette recruited me to come with her to pick up mama and baby because I knew the new art of car seats and swaddling. When we walked into Beverly's room, she was holding the baby on her bed and sobbing. Antoinette ran to her side to hug and comfort what she thought was postpartum blues. As she cooed in French to her friend and new baby, the child looked up. In the beautiful blue knitted blanket was a face that looked like Mateo, Antoinette's husband. No mistaking; the exact likeness of him. The baby smiled as Antoinette shrieked.

141

Winter, 1987, Reno, Nevada, USA

"I'm done. I've had enough. He has humiliated me for the last time."

Becky arrived in Reno at my request. She watched with a pang of deep sadness as I tossed his clothes into an ancient trunk. "He told me that this is the trunk his parents used as a babysitter when they were young." I sighed as I tossed his tights.

Becky said, "He has had a fucked-up life, you know that. Maybe you should forgive him and teach him it's not okay to lie and cheat."

Becky was practical, and she knew that being a single mom would be difficult, plus she liked Phileap. Phileap had made it clear that things had changed now that I was a mother. He had told me I wasn't his lover anymore. He was finding another. That was the way of his family.

He had alleged all the men in his family took lovers after their wives bore children. In my American sensibility, I found his way to be outrageous.

As I packed him and planned his clearance out of my life, Becky watched and rocked the baby.

"Are you sure you want to be alone? I thought you adored him?"

"Things have changed since we moved here. Since I became a mother. The kids are my whole life now. And even though he is their father, I feel I need to protect them from him. From what his value system is, the price of loving him."

"Wow! That is a change for you. You are not madly in love with him anymore?"

"I was smitten by the idea of him and the road. Both were overrated and not worth the hassle."

Becky wanted the best for me; she thought staying was it. She begged me to give him one more try, just one more day.

Becky left for her flight back to Las Vegas. I stopped packing and opened a bottle of wine, turned on the TV, and waited for him to come home. When he did, I looked at him and felt nothing other than a pang of sadness for what would happen to my children, but I felt it was the best alternative to them being dragged around the world by a broken dream. Phileap would never be the big star he had intended for himself. Every time he made progress, the weight of his family threw his axis off. He allowed it all; there was no hope for this mama's boy. As if reading my thoughts, he came to me and asked, "Did my mama call? I missed her yesterday."

"She did. Insulted me a few times and then hung up."

He said, wistfully and quietly, "I wish there was a way I could talk to her without involving you."

142

pring, 1988, Sparks, Nevada, USA

Since I could not fly anymore, as the second birth and not practicing had taken a toll on my body, I worked as a bartender at a casino from 6 p.m. to 2 a.m. five nights a week. I would get home at 2:30 in the morning, nurse the baby, who we named Amore, and fall asleep by 3:00 a.m. Gustavo was up at 6 a.m., and Phileap slept in until 10 a.m. He would leave for Circus Circus at noon and come home at 5:00 p.m. in time for me to go to my job.

It was impossible to find time to talk or be intimate. We didn't fight anymore; we were ships passing in the night. My passion for Phileap had dissipated with motherhood. He was still my friend, but his extramarital activities were not as bothering to me as they had been.

He watched the kids at night or let them run amok at the casino where, more than once, our daughter was found curled up asleep in a casino cabaret lounge because when he wasn't working, he was practicing.

One night, I got off early and came home to find an empty house. I called the backstage phone at Circus Circus to see if they were all there. I was told that they weren't and hadn't been in that night. I called Antionette, who said she hadn't seen any of them but promised to call if she did.

I waited, trying not to worry. He did have other performer friends here, but I didn't know their phone numbers. I watched the latest *Circus of the Stars*, and it was good to see my old friends, if only on the small screen. That is the heartbreaking part of circus life. When I finally did make friends, there was a good chance I would never see them again. There was no way to stay connected. We had even lost touch with Ramon, which broke my heart. I wanted Gustavo to know his compadre, and I missed my friend.

At about 10:00 that night, Phileap walked in, and both kids were still wide-awake. I was instantly pissed because it meant my schedule would be all messed up the next day. Who keeps babies out that late?

I nursed Amore, put the kids to bed, and joined Phileap on the couch.

"Where were you guys tonight?"

"Out."

"Out where?"

"Get out. Leave me alone. I'm watching *Circus of the Stars*."

I was irritated now; my fear had dissipated. I got up and turned off the TV.

"Why did you do that? I told you I was watching!"

"I asked you where you were tonight!"

He patted the empty couch beside him and motioned for me to sit. "Come, you need your fire put out."

"What?"

"I am going to make love to you. Mateo says it helps."

"Helps what?"

"Calm hysterical women,"

"I am not hysterical, and I do not believe you should be getting marriage advice from Mateo. He is a full-on charlatan and misogynist."

"You are using big words I don't understand to make me stupid. I will have no more of this, woman!"

He crossed the floor and fervently grabbed and kissed me. It had been so long that I welcomed the passion. We kissed, but something was not right. He tasted different. He moved his head down to my breasts, and I smelled the top of his head. I stopped dead when I recognized the smell—pussy. His hair smelled like pussy. I immediately imagined a scene where he was eating out the pink-haired carny as my children watched.

I pushed him off me. Calmly, I said to him, "I am done."

Not the whirlwind of pain and angst he had anticipated. I just knew in my bones. I was done with him. I had no more emotion to waste on him. I crossed to the phone and dialed Angel.

"Hey, can Phileap come spend the rest of his life at your house?"

Angel replied, "That bad? Yes, I will be right there. He can sleep with Patroleo."

Patroleo was Angel's dog and best friend. He had brought him back from Bolivia. The dog was an overweight wiener dog that was black as the night and slippery. He escaped every day. Thus, he was Patroleo (tar in Spanish).

I hung up and began to pack his bag.

"Apple Pie, you are wrong. I did nothing."

"I can smell her on you. And with my children watching?"

"They weren't watching. I put them in her den."

The minute he said it, he knew he was fucked. This calmness, this certainty, told him it was the finish line.

He did not come back the next day or ever again. I was struck with relief. My friends rallied with me; we smoked cigarettes, drank cheap wine, and talked shit about him. I was glad he was staying with Angel. I had been holding on to the bucking bronco that was our marriage for so long, I did not notice that the horse had died.

He was born on the road, and the sedentary life was a big adjustment for him. I figured it was a phase. I was wrong. He loved the best he knew how. He had gotten trapped with me time and again because my English skills and lawyer friend helped the family.

I went to bed, expecting to sob my pillow wet, but I just turned on the TV while the sound of the circus shows filled the air.

I had assumed stability would save us. There was not an "us" to save. We were a fling that went too far. Life had ripped at us like a fat lady in a leotard. I was not surprised. Playing at love and making children is a sin when it is not true love.

143

Sunrise died, and our family was determined to put the *fun* back in *funeral*. Dysfunction loves tragedy. We created a multimedia tribute to Sunrise using her favorite music and hundreds of pictures of her. Her children were in the front row, sobbing. I was a blubbering mess.

Her father, who had been paralyzed with grief the night before, announced he had invited Sunrise's favorite Tabernacle Circus clown to the funeral. He thought it would be a tribute to both Sunrise and his circus stepdaughter. We ignored him, sure it was the grief talking.

With the mortuary hall full of family and friends, in walked a circus clown in full makeup, funny shoes, and all. I was shocked. Everyone was sure it was my doing. Sunrise's husband was pissed that someone had made a mockery of Sunrise's life.

We sent Sunrise's godmother after the clown. When she came back, she reported that he promised to stay in the back and that no one would notice him. Everyone did.

With hundreds of people there, some we had not seen since childhood, we started our tribute to Sunrise. We gave praise, prayed, listened to beautiful songs sung by talented singers, and cried.

After the formal comments, people were invited to stand up and say a memory or tribute to Sunrise. Many did, and many were funny. In the end, we asked all the Rainbow Girls to gather in a circle at the front and sing "Rainbow Dreams," the song performed at the end of every Rainbow meeting. We held hands and sang love to our lost Rainbow Girl.

The service was over, and then my stepdad stood up. He walked to the front of the hall and thanked people for coming, and then he pointed out the clown in the back corner. Even worse, he invited him up to the front.

A circus clown we recognized as a pervert named Frank lumbered up the funeral aisle in full makeup, huge shoes, and a red nose. Dad informed everyone that he was Sunrise's favorite clown. I knew this was not accurate because we all saw Frank as a pervert. No one seemed to know how to act at the inappropriateness of it all. We all awkwardly laughed, except Sunrise's husband. The funeral director later said that in thirty years of being in the business, they had never had a clown at a service, not even at a child's funeral.

144

§ummer, 1988, Reno, Nevada, USA

Too many deaths. My nana, Kim, and now Sunrise were dead. My marriage had ended, but it just felt like a new chapter, with Phileap and I successful co-parents. I was in my hometown, but I felt invisible.

I was a beached whale with leaking breasts and a brand-new daughter. No one came to visit except Angel, who helped me make up the nursery. He appreciated my seclusion. His wife left him in the middle of the night—a decade of romance lost with no reason why. No one was surprised, except that she had not gone sooner.

"I have to escape," I told him as we pieced together a new playpen.

"Where would you go?"

"I don't know. I have nowhere."

"I found twenty acres in Lemon Valley. I bought it. You could move there."

"Move back into a trailer? No way."

"There are no trailers allowed there. We must get approval from the H.O.A. for all buildings. I thought we could create a retired circus animal sanctuary."

"This is a fantastic idea."

"Contribute a new life to old friends and start a new life for you. Give it some contemplation."

"I will. Thank you for loving my children and me. I do think you are the first male I have ever been successful friends with."

He gave me a slide glance. "What about Ramon? What about Stuart?"

"Yes, I guess you are right. They both have always been there for me. No matter how wretched I get."

Angel left, and I got out my yellow pad. I wrote two columns: "Be a bartender" and "Save Animals with Angel." Not one comment except "daily cash" went into the bartender column. The other column was filled with a passion I had not felt since my days of learning to fly. I contacted Stuart and asked how I would put this circus animal refuge together. The wheels moved through my brain like a train building up steam.

Later, on our faux beau date, Stuart treated me to a French restaurant and a luscious bottle of wine. I felt so happy with the great food and drink and a friend this dear. I gave him more details about the animal sanctuary, and he loved the idea. We talked for hours about it, my future, and the kids. I was so thankful that from the beginning he was on my side.

After dinner, we walked along the Truckee River, enjoying the sound of the rumbling cold water clearing our heads from the whole bottle of wine we consumed. I laughed when he grabbed my hand and spun me. I looked at him with surprise, and he blurted out, "I love you!"

"What are you talking about? Of course, you do! We're friends."

He pulled me in closer. "I don't want to be only your friend. I want to be your lover, the bonus father to your children, your support group, your housemate. I want your cats and you under the same roof. I want to be there when you are happy and when you are raging. I want us to be the forever couple. I love you."

He kissed me deeply. Sparks flew. He looked me in the eyes and then led me back to his car. I was in shock, and drunk. I jumped out as soon as he pulled into my driveway.

Stuart saying that he loved me surprised only me. For years, he had been at my side, helping when no one else would. He had shown he would do anything for me, including wait. I was not completely ready but found the quietness he gave my soul a solid idea for my future. I had to learn to fall in love with a good guy.

The next day, he opened a bank account for the sanctuary and deposited a sizable amount for the nonprofit to save animals. The newly hatched dream was now a reality. I could have my circus, stay in one place, and help the animals.

145

Fall, 1988, Pyramid Lake, Nevada, USA

Stuart and Angel got along famously as we built and planned. I was still working nights; Angel was my night nanny. He loved the kids more than anyone, and his light personality began to coax laughter out of my all-too-serious children. Having happy children makes all the hard work worth it. We had three trailers on the lot with the hope of building real brick homes that no wind could blow down. The cats were now working as a pair of mousers and greeters and were so happy to be with all of us together.

I was not in touch with any circus people anymore because they all saw my act of leaving Phileap as a betrayal. They did not care that my little family was much happier on our own path and not tagging along on the Córdoba trail. The eight generations of circus performers ended with my children. I vowed that they would only know stories and not the harsh reality of traveling with the circus. I was still confused by the fact that I had fallen in love with a man like Phileap and stayed with him. After much therapy, I chalked it up to my sense of abandonment and being a stupid 20-year-old who wanted an adventure.

❧

Stuart would come over on my nights off from the bar, and we discussed the issue.

"I have a question. Can a man love a woman and not be aroused by her?"

He looked at me quizzically at the loaded question. "Yes, the mind may not match the body."

"That must be why those little blue pills exist."

"Yes! And to piss off seventy-year-old women who thought they were done with sex shit."

I laughed and reached out to touch his hand.

"Who wants to be done with sex? Why would anyone not want the fantastic way sex makes you alive?"

"Men and arousal, does it work that way for women?"

"Yes, I believe so. Our arousal isn't obvious."

"Do I arouse you?"

"Ha, yes! Whatever this is we have, it has had me in a constant state of arousal. But I'm trying to be careful. To change my patterns."

"That's good, right?"

"I believe it's pure magic. And frightening. My love record is impossible."

"Impossible is nothing."

He took my face into his hands and kissed me. After which, my heart was thumping, and my mind went dirty. I was damned scared and wholly aroused. He left, and I threw myself into bed and had steaming dreams of him.

The soon-to-be-named Animal Circus Refuge had picked up steam like a locomotive going down a mountain, and we had many donations, help, and good press. We were a success from the first day when I got my first animal, an old friend.

Zita was retiring, and it was time for her to leave the road. As they unloaded her from the eighteen-wheeler, I stood with a watermelon in my hand and Amore in the stroller next to me. Zita saw me and sprinted in my direction, scaring the prop guys trying to wrangle her. Her trunk went first to my face. Her rough skin circled my cheek, and a sweet kissing noise escaped from her. She lowered her massive head and placed her forehead on mine. That's when she saw the baby, her pink hat askew and sticking out of the blankets as she napped, exhausted from learning to crawl on the office floor. Zita extended her trunk in the baby bundle and fixed Amore's hat, and I watched my daughter wake and gurgle with delight. Zita answered back with her own purr. We had found our tribe. We were home.

146

Winter, 1988, Washoe Valley, Nevada, USA

Stuart and I had moved in together in his rustic house overlooking the ancient lake. The kids loved their new rooms and the huge pasture filled with farm animals. The cats came home with us, as our little farm and family needed them. The kids were in preschool and thriving. Stuart worked from home, and I had taken the day off from the sanctuary.

I had learned to love a nice guy. To find my steady and stable life sexy.

We were happy. I walked over to his writing table; he was immersed in his work. Scribbling for hours, never even looking up.

I stood by the edge, waiting for him to sense my presence. When he looked up, I heard the sharp intake of his breath. I was wearing the black corset; my breasts pushed up from the tight boning, perched on edge, my hard nipples were exposed and at attention. And I had on those long pearls. Those pearls made him hard because he knew I meant to wrap them around his dick as I sucked him.

He shook his head as if to erase me from his mind. I smiled and straddled him. Now he saw I had no panties and was clean-shaven. With the last paragraph he was writing still swirling in his head, his body responded.

I kissed his neck and slid down his trunk like a python while unzipping his pants and freeing his hard cock. His brain was beginning to slow down and catch up to what I was doing to his body as I swallowed him.

The sight of my red hair bobbing between his legs brought him to the present. I wrapped the pearls around the base of his manhood—the cold, intricate beads conflicting with my hot breath and soft tongue.

He threw his head back and abandoned himself to me. I worked him for a long time—taking him to the edge and backing down so he could ride the high of the pleasure. I was never in a hurry to finish, constantly discerning ways to keep him in this place of erotic desire.

147

Spring, 1989, Pyramid Lake, Nevada, USA

The sounds of the chainsaws were now for building and not killing. We worked for months to get the sanctuary ready for our next permanent resident, my dear Alex: the full-of-personality male lion that I used to live with in Las Vegas. Cupcake and Izic had divorced, and she got Alex in the divorce. She wanted to retire in Florida and not have to feed a whole chicken three times a day to a silver-haired lion. Brigit was off in Argentina as an aerialist and author (I took partial credit for the writing part). I purchased her books, and they were a fascinating look at what it was to be the real child of animal people. It was sad and true, but few people believed the recounting because they had no frame of reference.

Zita loved her retirement. She thrived on interaction with people, so a zoo would not have been the right place for her. She was born into the circus and performing, and frankly loved to act for a group of people. Dove decided that we were the right fit because Zita knew me (an elephant never forgets) and because I knew how to engage her with make-believe play. I had tea each day with Zita and then had her do her mini performances with just the staff clapping and encouraging her. If I missed a day, she performed all by herself, the tumbleweed as her only audience.

Our animal sanctuary had five areas. They consisted of free spaces filled with ponds and trees for the elephants. The six-acre enclosed cat area was planted with bamboo grown high so the cats could hide in it. They had a cement pond if they wanted to dip and large evergreens to scratch their claws on. The three other areas were for domestic birds, monkeys and apes, large animals, reptiles, and tortoises. We hired animal trainers and zoologists to make sure our areas were safe and stimulating for the animals.

In the middle, we installed a trapeze with an in-ground trampoline and many single aerialist apparatuses. It was a circus haven for newcomers to use for learning. That revenue helped support the feeding of the animals. I made a deal with all the local casinos to donate their fruits and vegetables from the buffet to our sanctuary. They also donated expired frozen meats for the cats. We only paid the veterinarian, and the rest of us were all volunteers. I had to figure out how to make a living because I wanted to ensure nothing was taken away from the animals. We built a restaurant on site and called it The Scullery Maid. It was a combination of all the foods I learned to cook on the road. It also had ten tiny cabins behind it where we housed the retired Scullery Maids. There is no retirement home for the circus elderly, so they usually died early on the road. Here, they had a place, a purpose, and a home. I was most proud of this and welcomed my old friends and some new ones. Because we are a nonprofit, we charged nothing.

I earned a teaching credential and started teaching English as a second language based on my time in the circus. I worked with 5-to-7-year-olds and prided myself on instilling in them the love of reading and the idea that anyone can write a novel, script, research paper, or news article.

Angel was the manager on site at the sanctuary. We visited every day. He took videos of me working with Zita. Pretending that we were in a show, she would twirl and bowl and lift me onto her back. Then I would feed her a watermelon, her current favorite food. She had three barn cats that lived with her, and we had many pictures of the kittens curled up with Zita. She loved those cats. The purring they all did together was so soothing, we recorded it and sold it as a relaxation tool.

Alex loved never seeing a cage again. He was king of his pasture, and we provided him with a few old female cats, and he easily became their beau.

148

Summer, 1989, Pyramid Lake, Nevada, USA

We see the circus everywhere. And it is broken into single compartments. Performances in the big Cirque shows and all-inclusive resorts all over the world. Their work includes vibrant costumes, lighting, choreography, and scenes with a message. The acts are the same. Stunning feats of physical impossibility exist in a theater setting versus a dirt floor. We see them on TV and in movies, where the popcorn is less dusty.

The mud shows of the past still exist—if you look hard. The sight of a cow pasture now laid out with a large purple canopy, rising to become the big top, causes my heart to jump. When I visit these shows, the smell hits me first, the fake smoke, the lights, the greasepaint. The illusion is still there, and it makes my heart happy. I hope none of my children will ever became performers and will find a life of predictability, accountants' jobs, and daily commutes and won't have to exist in the traveling dysfunction that the old circuses offered.

We still had dinner once a week—Stuart, Angel, and the kids and I at The Scullery Maid. I would cook for hours with my friends to make a gourmet meal. The kids said the meals were gross and usually left the table to watch old *Circus of the Stars* videos. Angel shared gossip about the circus world because acquiring animals for the sanctuary kept him in contact with circus folks.

Stuart was always fascinated with these stories and egged Angel on for more details about every act. Phileap had moved to Brazil and the kids never saw him, so Stuart and Angel took over as the father figures in their lives.

They both encouraged me to write about my time when I ran away and joined the circus. I was still too much in the muck of it to write it down. I was grateful to them. They had saved me. I intended to save them every day with the greatest of ease.

AFTERWORD

You can find these real animal sanctuaries and donate your time or funds to help the animals and the dear people who chose to help them every day.

ANIMAL ARK

Animal Ark started as a dream, held by its founders Aaron and Diana Hiibel. They began a small wildlife rescue operation, originating from their lifelong fondness of animals. Animal Ark is a 38-acre wildlife sanctuary located in the Northern Nevada foothills with a history as intriguing and exciting as its animal residents.

https://animalark.org/the-animals/

TWO TAILS RANCH

Two Tails Ranch was founded in 1984 by Theodore H. Svertesky (1954-1994) and Patricia L. Zerbini. The ranch is the only privately owned elephant facility of its kind. The natural coast of Florida is a prime location for elephants. The climate is almost identical to their native countries. The location of the ranch is surrounded by green grass, live oaks, and natural wildlife. It is a very peaceful environment that both animals and guests can enjoy. The ranch was built to board both Asian and African elephants needing temporary or permanent housing, regardless of health or dispositions. Over 250 elephants have passed through the gates of the ranch for a variety of reasons. Some stayed temporarily while their own exhibits were being remodeled or built. Others stayed for retirement, medical needs, behavior problems, or even in emergencies after hurricanes destroyed their zoos.

https://allaboutelephants.com/

TURTLE AND TORTOISE RESCUE AND ANIMAL SANCTUARY

For over 30 years, the Turtle and Tortoise Rescue of Arroyo Grande, California has been fulfilling its mission to rescue, protect, and house turtles, tortoises, and other animals in its ecologically friendly five-acre sanctuary. It was built from the ground up by Bob Thomas, a lifelong keeper of chelonians and reptiles, with a passion and knowledge that led him to become a caretaker for a number of unwanted pets and abandoned animals in need.

https://www.turtleandtortoiserescueofarroyogrande.org

PACIFIC WILDLIFE CARE

We treat nearly 3,000 wild animal patients every year, from over 200 different species. Our goal? To return healthy animals to the wild! We also provide educational presentations for local organizations and schools Pacific Wildlife Care (PWC) was founded in 1987 in reaction to the Apex Houston oil spill that brought several oiled pelicans to the beaches of San Luis Obispo County. Since that time, we have grown from a small group of dedicated home rehabilitators into a successful non-profit organization with a well-equipped rehabilitation center, a full-time wildlife veterinarian, a small paid staff, and over 200 volunteers. In addition to the Rehabilitation Center, which is open every day of the year, we maintain a hotline that the public can call to report distressed wildlife (injured, sick, orphaned) and to receive information about our local wildlife.

https://www.pacificwildlifecare.org

LIONS TIGERS & BEARS SANCTUARY

An exotic animal sanctuary and educational facility in Alpine, California

Lions Tigers & Bears is an animal sanctuary for rescued big cats, bears, and other exotic animals in beautiful San Diego County. Nestled in a scenic landscape of majestic oak trees, meadows, and rolling hills, our sanctuary offers an idyllic, natural habitat for more than 60 animals who have been neglected and abused in captivity across the country. The ranch provides a peaceful refuge for the animals to live with dignity in a safe, nurturing environment, where they can run, play, swim and enjoy fresh air.

https://www.lionstigersandbears.org/gift-experiences

Trapeze Dictionary of Terms

- Hup: Signal to leave the board and/or the fly bar. Sometimes used by the catcher to tell the flyer to let go after a catch when landing in the net.
- Catch Bar: The trapeze that the catcher swings on
- Fly Bar: The bar the flyer uses
- Apron: The net in front of the catch bar. (The back apron is the net behind the board.)
- Rise/Riser: A narrow board placed on the rungs of the ladder to allow the flyer to take off from a higher point
- Mount: When the flyer mounts the board after a return.
- Return: When the flyer, after a successful catch, manages to return to the fly bar, and often all the way back to the board. In professional shows, the flyers rarely come down from the board.
- Grips: Can be gymnastics grips or ones made of tape. They are used to protect the flyer's hands.
- Chalk: Used by the flyer and catcher to absorb wetness and to reduce sticking to things such as the fly bar.
- Force Out: Kicking the legs out at the peak of the flyer's swing to gain height.
- Hollow: Comes right after the force-out. It is basically a neutral position.
- Sweep: Comes after hollow. Signifies kicking the legs back.
- Seven: The last part of a force-out swing. Flyer brings legs in front of them so they will not hit the board.

- Cutaway Bar: The bar that the catcher holds when the flyer executes tricks to the catcher such as normal Cutaways and Reverse Knee-Hangs.
- Cut (as in Cut Catch): The flyer is caught in legs catch and swings out into the apron. On the next swing into the apron, the flyer thrusts their body up, and the catcher lets go of the flyer's legs and grabs their hands.
- Strike: To take down the circus rigging.

FLYING TRAPEZE TRICKS THAT CAN BE THROWN TO A CATCHER

- Feet Across (a.k.a. "Legs")
- Heels Off
- Hocks Off
- Splits (Front End/Back End)
- Straddle Whip (Front End/Back End)
- Whip (Front End/Back End)
- Bird's Nest/Birdie (Front End/Back End)
- Shooting Star
- Half Turn
- Straight Jump
- Cut Catch
- Uprise Shoot
- Forward Over
- Forward Under
- Double Over
- Passing Leap
- Piggyback
- Pullover Shoot
- Reverse Knee Hang
- One Knee Hang
- Flexus
- Somersault
- Hocks Salto

- Front Hip Circle/Back Hip Circle
- Seat Roll/Penny Roll (Full Time/Half Time)
- Planche (Front End/Back End)
- Pirouette (540)
- Layout
- One and a half Somersault
- Cutaway
- Cutaway Half
- Cutaway Full
- Double Somersault
- Double Cutaway
- Double Cutaway and a half twist
- Double Layout
- Full Twisting Double
- Double-Double
- Triple Somersault
- Triple Twisting Double
- Full Twisting Triple
- Triple Twisting Double
- Triple Layout
- Quadruple Somersault

A Daring Young Man On The Flying Trapeze

Lyrics by George Leybourne

Once I was happy but now I'm forlorn
Like an old coat that is tattered and torn
Left on this wide world to fret and to mourn,
Betrayed by a maid in her teens
The girl that I loved she was handsome
I tried all I knew her to please
But I could not please her one quarter so well
Like that man up on the trapeze

CHORUS:
He'd fly through the air with the greatest of ease
A daring young man on the flying trapeze
His movements were graceful, all girls he could please
And my love he purloined away.

This young man by name was Signor Bona Slang
Tall, big, and handsome as well made as Chang
Where'er he appeared the hall loudly rang
With ovation from all people there
He'd smile from the bar on the people below
And one night he smiled on my love
She winked back at him and she shouted, "Bravo!"
As he hung by his nose up above!

CHORUS

Her father and mother were both on my side
And hard tried to make her my own bride
Her father he sighed and her mother she cried
To see her throw herself away
'Twas all no avail she went there ev'ry night
And would throw him bouquets on the stage
Which caused him to meet her, how he ran me down
To tell you would take a whole page

CHORUS

One night I as usual went to her dear home,
Found there her father and mother alone
I asked for my love and soon they made known
To my horror that she'd run away!
She'd packed up her box and eloped in the night
With him with the greatest of ease
From two stories high, he had lowered her down
To the ground on his flying trapeze!
Some months after this I went to a hall
Was greatly surprised to see on the wall
A bill in red letters which did my heart gall,
That she was appearing with him
He taught her gymnastics and dressed her in tights
To help him to live at his ease
And made her assume a masculine name
And now she goes on the trapeze!
She floats through the air with the greatest of ease
You'd think her a man on the flying trapeze
She does all the work while he takes his ease
And that's what's become of my love.

ACKNOWLEDGMENTS

As with any vast accomplishment, it did not happen in a void. In fact, it almost didn't materialize. Many people helped to get this tome out of my head and into the world. Gratitude is a strong emotion, and I have so much adoration for my family and friends. Thank you for giving me the support to achieve this dream.

First, my husband, best friend, and partner in crime, Gary Bayus. Thank you for giving me the time and encouragement as I pounded the keyboards for years. My love for you is eternal and boundless.

To my literary strategist, Zoe Quinton, the wisdom and love you presented to me, and this story are unprecedented. I'm sorry I was a whiny baby at first. As I pulled up my big girl panties and turned this into a book with your wise advice, the gift of encouragement will always be the most genuine act of love. You are my shining star.

My copy editor, Theresa Maria Wilson. You've been the auto-correct in my head for over 20 years, and I love you for that. Because of your knowledge and professionalism, I can freely vomit my stories on a page.

To my final editor, Kate Hofmeister. Thank you for sweeping up the sawdust and making this book spotless.

To Karen Richardson of Indie Pub Solutions who bravely took on the publication and distribution of the book, your patience and professionalism got me to my finish line. It would still be in a drawer if not for you.

To Jay Stringer, your cover art captured the essence of this book. Thank you for the gorgeous artwork.

To my life coach and dear friend, Lori Barrow, you gave me the courage to finish this. As the pandemic raged, our front porch session gave me the strength to write every day without listening to those evil voices in my head.

To my Author Runaway Hosts, Caryn Young of Avila Hideaway, Pattea Torrence of the Bees Knees Farm Stay, and Avila Bay Athletic Club thank you for giving me the time and place to collect my thoughts and tap my fingers to get this novel done.

To Jim Lemon and Valerie Vicroy, you were my first cheerleaders and encouraged me to keep writing and telling stories. Love you both so much.

To my parents, I love you for all that you are and all that you taught me. Thank you for everything!

To my CCWC family (Scribe Tribe), thank you for encouraging and indulging me. Sharing your brilliance, time, and love for the written word strengthened me. Your friendships over the years turned me into a brave writer.

To my children, Michelle, Tristan, and Chere. Thank you for humoring my love of stories and letting me tell the beginning of yours.

To my grands, Julian, Izic, and Izabell, for letting Nana spin yarns and sparking my creativity. You taught me how to love again. To see the wonder in the world and let my creative soul take over. You are my greatest joy and love.

To my beta readers, Garret Matsuura, Bruce Huston, and Dove Daniel. Thank you for your kindness and gift of your time. I am forever grateful.

My OG writing group that got this ball rolling told me to "go on from there," bless you. Kathy, Dove, Janice, Jenny, Steve, T, & Tia, thank you for sharing my story and charcuterie.

ABOUT THE AUTHOR

Teri Bayus is a writer of words and a builder of worlds.

She has self-published two novels and optioned three screenplays and two teleplays. Her current novel, The Greatest Of Ease, (www.TheGreatesOfEase.com) is about her time as a trapeze artist in a traveling circus. Her previous novel, *Consumed* (http://www.amzn.to/1jFEeQH) is the genre of culinary erotica. She has a nonfiction book, *The Universal Conspiracy* (www.theuniversalconspiracy.com) about how the universe collaborates to make everyone's dreams a reality.

Before the plague, she hosted and produced the TV show *Taste Buds* (www.tastebuds.tv), highlighting the chefs' talents and restaurants worldwide. She was a food and film critic for twenty years and the executive director of the Central Coast Writers Conference for six years. She has taught many writing and marketing classes at colleges and adult education forums.

Her love for inspiring others has brought her to the path of a professional speaker. She adores sharing her journeys with others by facilitating many workshops, classes, and marketing seminars. She is a serial entrepreneur having owned 28 businesses in the last 30 years.

She lives with her husband, who is a wild entrepreneur, two terrible dogs, and a wonderful cat in Pismo Beach, California.

Find more information and contact at www.teribayus.com.

Teri Bayus is available to talk to your book club, writing club or any group that would like to know more about circus and writing life. If you'd like to contact the author:

Teri Bayus
791 Price Street #103
Pismo Beach, CA 93449

thegreatestofease21@gmail.com
www.thegreatestofease.com

Social Media sites for *The Greatest of Ease* and Teri Bayus:

- www.facebook.com/MeetTeriBayus

- @thegreatestofease

- @the_greatest_of_ease

- www.youtube.com/channel/UC055LN81ztL3bzLOEh_KivA

- www.linkedin.com/company/teri-bayus-siafu-marketing/

CPSIA information can be obtained
at www.ICGtesting.com
Printed in the USA
BVHW040337131222
654042BV00012B/25